At Variance

5 two-hour books
adapted from screenplays

David R. Beshears

Greybeard Publishing
Washington State

Greybeard Publishing
P.O. Box 480
McCleary, WA 98557-0480

ISBN 978-0-9773646-4-0

At Variance

Introduction

Movie Novella Series
Two-hour books adapted directly from screenplays.

The five novellas included in At Variance are based on screenplays written over several years. Each has previously been published as an individual novella.

The narratives follow as closely as possible the original screenplays. The result of this very painstaking balancing act are five films flickering before the eyes of the reader.

And these five stories couldn't be more different from one another: family sci-fi adventure, dark satire fantasy, science fiction, holiday family fantasy, and post-apocalyptic scifi/horror.

Welcome to the multiplex...
Choose your screen and enjoy the movie...

Table of Contents

Ravenhill Court

Prolog

Present Day

Ben Foster drove the fifties era Mercury slowly across the Edgewood Street intersection and into Ravenhill Court. He turned into the driveway of the second house on the right and stopped. Turning off the engine, he took a few moments to look out at the old neighborhood.

There were nine houses on the dead-end cul-de-sac, nestled into the grassy California foothills. They had once been comfortable, middleclass homes. They were now fifty years old and long abandoned. Lawns were overgrown and yellowed. Some of the doors stood open; a curtain fluttered through an open window; a rain gutter had pulled away from an eave; a screen door, bent and torn, slapped against its jamb in the slight breeze.

He opened the door and climbed out of the car. The quiet felt heavy. There was the sound of the breeze brushing past his ears, and the sound of the screen door across the street, and nothing else. No other sounds at all; not from the other houses, not from the surrounding hills, and no sound reached into Ravenhill Court from the outside. It was as if this street and its collection of houses were all that existed. There was no outside world.

Ben Foster, middle-aged, hair slightly graying, a job in the city, hadn't been in Ravenhill in forty years or more. He wasn't sure why, but for some strange reason he wasn't able to pin down exactly when he had left. And it hadn't just been him... everyone had left.

He turned his attention back to the trunk of the car. Reaching in, he brought out a large, leather-bound book. With the journal in hand, he walked down to the sidewalk and stood at the curb. Another strange sensation, as if the past was reaching out across the years and touching him on the shoulder. He looked at the house across the street; at Peter's house.

Mrs. Murray called out to him; a distant, far-away voice. "Ben? Ben... where's Peter?"

Ben Foster sat down on the curb and rested the journal in his lap. He rubbed his hand across the leather cover. He heard a child's voice then. His voice.

"Hey, Mrs. Murray. He had to stay after."

Peter had to stay after. Ben's skin felt as though he had walked into a spider's web. He fought the urge to wipe his face. He looked down at the journal, stirred up the courage and finally opened it. The pages were yellowed. On the first page was written *The Ravenhill Journals*. The words had been carefully written, as if the young author had been very serious about what he was starting. There was something fateful about those three words.

But then, that had been Peter.

Ben turned the page. There was a drawing of Ravenhill Court, an overhead view showing the nine homes, each home labeled with the name of the family living there. Surrounding the neighborhood, locations had been precisely labeled: Blue Clay Ravine, Ravenhill Ridge, Nike Base, Pirate's Cove, and others.

On the next page were hand-drawn images of young people, their names written beneath them. Ben laid a hand gently on the drawings: Peter, Julie, Louis, and Ben. He had been about thirteen at the time. He hadn't realized how good an artist Peter had been.

The next few pages held drawings of others from the neighborhood: Professor LaMothe, Mrs. Murray, Ben's mom and dad, Danny Bigalow, the Margolis brothers, Tony and Mike; Charlene. Each drawing was painstakingly labeled.

There were drawings then of some of the places where it had all taken place... images that brought the memories flooding back, memories of events that he hadn't so much forgotten, but that no longer seemed real. They were of a very different place and time. He saw the gnarled tree; a creek disappearing beneath overhanging brush; a cliff with a narrow ledge two-thirds of the way up; and there were the great, metal doors set into a hillside...

Ben Foster turned the page again...

Chapter One

June 1964

Ben Foster made the tight corner off Edgewood and into Ravenhill Court, the metal wheels of his red skateboard just touching the edge of the curb as he leaned heavily into it and swung back to the middle of the sidewalk. He rushed past the first house and turned down the driveway and onto the street. The sound of the wheels changed from a smooth roar to a low rumble as they rolled from concrete to asphalt. He lifted one foot off the board and shifted easily from rider to walker. Moving his schoolbook from one hand to the other, he reached down and picked up the skateboard. He continued across the street toward his house.

"Ben?" Mrs. Murray was standing at her front door. The Murray house was behind him, directly across the street from the Foster house. "Ben... where's Peter?"

"Hey, Mrs. Murray," Ben called out over his shoulder. "He had to stay after."

"Not again..."

Ben shrugged his shoulders and kept walking. He reached the short, steep driveway and started up, walked into the open garage of the Foster house. It was a roomy, two-car garage, with a 1960 Chevy Impala taking up the right half. A lawn mower was parked against one wall, with an assortment of lawn and garden tools hanging on the wall above it. Two Schwinn Sting-Ray bicycles were parked in front of a workbench; one a boy's bike, the other a girl's.

Ben set his skateboard down on the bench and continued on into the house, taking the two steps up and through the door to the kitchen. He dropped his book onto the table and went straight to the cupboard.

"I'm home," he called out dutifully. He took a glass down from the cupboard and filled it at the faucet.

His mother called back from somewhere at the back of the house. "How was your day?"

"Peter got in trouble again." Ben set the glass in the sink and walked out of the kitchen, started down the hall. Mrs. Foster came out of Julie's room with a bundle of clothes in her arms.

"I don't know why your sister insists on living like a pig," she said.

"Hey, when you adopt, you never know what you're gonna get."

Mrs. Foster gave Ben a pointed look as they passed each other in the hall. "That's not nice. And Julie is not adopted. I wish you would quit saying that."

Ben reached the open back door. He pushed the screen door open and jumped past the step, landing on the back lawn. As the screen door slapped shut, he heard his mother cry out, "Get your schoolbook off my kitchen table!"

Ben was already approaching the back fence. He pushed the gate open and hurried through. It closed behind him with a banging clatter. He followed the well-traveled trail that ran along the back fences of the Ravenhill Court neighborhood. Tall, thick brush lined the right side of the trail.

He passed the Bigalow's back yard. The trail turned to the right. Before cutting back to follow along the Addison's fence, Ben left the trail and squeezed through the brush, trying as best he could to not leave any sign. Six steps in, he pushed some branches aside, revealing the weathered wood of a small door, about three and a half feet high and two feet wide. A shiny combination lock with a black dial hung on a latch. Ben reached in and began turning the knob on the lock.

Once inside the fort, he closed the door behind him and slid the inside latch to lock it.

The main room of the fort was a good eight feet wide by ten feet long. In the center of the room sat a wooden table and three chairs. A bench along one wall was made of two wooden boxes and a heavy plank. There were crude shelves on most of the walls with books and a number of odds and ends. Ben lit several thick candles that rested on their own short, narrow shelves.

A window, six inches high and eighteen inches wide, was set into the wall above the bench. Thick glass was set into the window opening and was held in place by an old picture frame. A wooden ladder was nailed to the wall in the far corner of the room, leading up to a small opening in the ceiling and a small square room on the second floor. The small room was large enough for a chair and little else.

Ben heard rustling outside, then the secret knock at the door. He reached over and pulled the latch aside. As Ben stepped back and sat on the bench, Peter came in and latched the door behind him.

"What are you doing here?"

Peter sat at the table with a loud grunt. "Hey, what can they do to me?"

Ben raised his gaze to look directly at Peter. They were both thirteen, but Peter was smaller and looked younger.

"You didn't go home?"

"No."

"Your mom was asking about you."

There was more rustling outside, and the secret knock. Instead of going to the door, Peter went to the ladder and climbed up into the tower. Ben went to the door and slid aside the latch, pulled the door open.

"Hey, Julie," he said.

"Hey." Julie went to the table. As she sat down, she peered up toward to the tower.

"Yeah," said Ben. He locked the door and returned to the bench. "He's here."

"Some real boss moves, Peter," Julie called out.

"Whatever," groaned Peter.

Ben smiled and leaned back, rested his head against the wall. "Don't be mean."

"Come on, Ben." Julie was a year older than Ben, but they could have passed for twins. "He stood up in class, during a test no less, and said *they're coming.*"

"It wasn't like that," said Ben. He had been there. After a few moments, "Okay... it was like that, but--"

Peter called down from the tower, "Don't make it sound so weird."

"It was weird," said Julie. "The whole school thinks you're peculiar."

Ben suddenly held a hand up for quiet. Julie turned her head to listen. There was only quiet. Ben shook his hand at her and listened more intently.

Up in the tower, Peter was looking through narrow slits set into the wall at eye level. The tower itself was hidden by the thick brush growing up around the fort. Peter wasn't able to see anyone yet, but he could hear a voice. It was coming from the direction of the trail. Then, as they came around the bend in the trail, Peter saw them. He clinched his teeth and held his breath.

It was Tony Margolis and his pet worm Danny Bigalow. Danny was in the same class as Peter and Ben.

"...and Miss Harris sent him to the principal," said Danny. He had a huge, rat grin on his face. "And Walker sent him to the nurse. And he was supposed to see the dean after school, but guess what? He didn't show up."

Tony Margolis was two years older than Danny. He listened quietly to the kid's unbounded glee.

"Man, oh man," said Danny. "It was so boss."

They reached the point in the trail where the hidden path forked off and led to the fort. They continued past along the main trail.

"What did he mean?" asked Tony, his eyes on the trail.

"Don't know. Maybe he told Walker." Danny bubbled with joy. "He is so weird."

Tony spoke as if to himself, "He is a strange little creep, all right."

They disappeared around the curve of the trail. Peter watched until he was sure they were gone, then climbed the ladder down into the main room.

Ben watched him, noting his expressionless face. He knew that look. He had known Peter all his life. Peter was working hard to keep it all down. He didn't want anyone to know that he was hurting.

"They're gone," said Peter. "Tony and his toady."

Ben nodded. "We heard."

Julie moved to another chair so Peter could sit down. "How can he let that weasel pant after him like that?"

"We are witness to hero worship at its most disgusting," said Peter. "Tony Margolis eats it up. It's what he lives for."

"Tony's nothing like his brother," said Ben.

"Mike's all right, I guess," said Peter. "Hard to believe they're related."

"Tony was adopted," said Ben.

"Ben!" Julie said sharply. She was getting really, really tired of this adoption stuff.

Peter grinned, leaned over the table. "You know, Julie, you and Tony do bear a striking resemblance. Perhaps--"

"Funny. Did that come to you in another of your visions?"

The three of them grew suddenly very quiet. Ben gave Julie a stern look. In the silence, he could hear the sounds of the candle wicks sizzling in their pools of liquid wax. The tiny flames flickered and sent shadows dancing across their faces. Ben let out a breath he hadn't known he was holding.

"Tell us what you saw, Peter."

Peter looked at Ben, then Julie. He wanted to tell them. He always told them. There was something about this one, though. It was different; different, and yet not different. They were always different, sort of. This one... this one was... *bad.*

"It was like a doorway," he said. "It was a... gateway..."

"What kind of gateway?" Julie slid nearer. "To where?"

"Like a door. Like an open door. It glowed. Blue. I saw shadows on the other side. Shadows of..." Peter tried to see what lay just beyond, but he couldn't seem to reach it.

"What... like monsters?" asked Ben.

Peter shook his head, discouraged.

"Go on," said Julie. "What were the shadows doing?"

"I think they were trying to come through, but something was stopping them."

"Do you know why they wanted to come through?"

"No," said Peter. He looked directly at Julie then, and spoke certainly. "No. But it didn't feel right."

Ben let out another heavy breath. "His visions may not always be right, but the feelings that he gets about 'em usually are."

Julie looked back at Peter, "What made you, ya' know... jump up like that... in class?"

"Yeah," said Ben. "We try to keep your weirdness just between us. Ya' know?"

"No sense in letting the whole world know how peculiar you are," said Julie.

Peter shifted about nervously. This was the different part. This was what made this vision so very different from the others.

"This time... this one... this one was... *different.*"

"Different how?"

"One of the shadows reached out..." He looked quickly from Ben to Julie, then back to Ben. They squirmed impatiently.

"Yeah?" Ben urged.

"You know... from the other side. It reached out... It touched me; on the shoulder."

Chapter Two

The next morning was like most Saturday mornings in the Foster house. When Ben came into the kitchen, he found his dad at the breakfast table reading a newspaper, a cup of coffee sitting on the table in front of him, dressed as if planning the spend the day kickin' around the house. His mom was standing at the counter buttering slices of toast.

"Good morning, Ben." She placed the dish of toast onto the table.

"'morning." He watched as she returned to the counter, poured a glass of orange juice and set it in front of him. He continued to watch as she went to the cupboard and brought back the box of Cheerios, then a cereal bowl, a spoon, and finally the milk from the refrigerator.

"Eat your breakfast," she said absently.

"Thanks, Mom."

"Good morning," said Julie, coming into the kitchen.

Ben continued to watch silently as Saturday morning methodically played itself out.

"Good morning, Julie," said Mom. She poured a glass of juice and set it in front of Julie.

"Good morning, sweetie," said Dad from behind his newspaper.

Mom took a cereal bowl down from the cupboard, a spoon from the drawer, and set them in front of Julie. "Eat your breakfast."

"Thanks, Mom."

Ben and Julie filled their bowls with Cheerios and milk and began eating. Mrs. Foster fussed about cleaning up the counter before sitting down herself to coffee and toast. Mr. Foster continued reading the newspaper, occasionally reaching around for his coffee cup or another slice of toast.

"So," said Mrs. Foster, watching her children spoon cereal into their mouths and Mr. Foster as he absently searched for his coffee cup. "How does everyone plan to spend their day?"

Ben shrugged. "Hang out."

"Me, too," said Julie.

"Mmm," said Dad.

Mom gave the newspaper a sharp look. "Honey?"

"How's Peter?" he asked, without lowering the paper.

"Okay," said Ben.

"Weird," said Julie.

Mom shook her head sadly, sipped her coffee.

"He's not weird," said Ben. He leaned forward and grabbed a slice of toast from the stack. "Okay, so he's weird."

"That poor boy," said Mom, smiling sympathetically. She gave the newspaper another sharp look. "He hasn't had a father to help him, the way you two have."

Mr. Foster ignored the subtle jab, and apparently also the conversation that was going on beyond the newspaper. "They're dropping off the Mercury this morning."

"Hmm," said Mrs. Foster, not particularly pleased.

"You kids make sure the garage is clear," said Dad.

"No problem," said Ben.

"The game is on the radio this afternoon," said Mr. Foster.

"I don't know why you bought that old thing," said Mrs. Foster.

Mr. Foster gave a pleasant sigh, lowered the paper and gave his wife a gentle look. "What better way to spend an afternoon? Tinkering under the hood of a grand old automobile... listening to the ballgame..."

"What happened to Peter's father?" Julie asked suddenly. Mom and Dad gave each other a quick glance and there was an uncomfortable, if brief, moment of silence.

Ben's mouth was full of Cheerios. "He just up and disappeared," he mumbled.

"No one knows what happened, dear," said Mom.

"Peter never talks about it," said Julie. "All we know is that he disappeared."

Ben watched curiously as Mom gave Dad another very quick glance before picking up her coffee cup and taking another sip. She held the cup in front of her face as she spoke. "Peter was just a baby at the time," she said. "John left for work one morning and never came home."

"Did ya know him?"

"Very well."

"What was he like?"

"Peculiar?" asked Ben, smiling. "Like Peter?"

"John Murray was a good man," said Dad. He gave the newspaper a stern shake and turned the page, was once again hidden from view. "A good man."

"He was a very gentle man," said Mom.

Julie looked thoughtfully at her half-empty bowl of Cheerios, stirred the floating cereal with her spoon. "Some of the kids are thinking, you know, with Peter being... like he is... that maybe his father just..."

"Not at all," said Mom.

"Claptrap," said Dad from behind the newspaper. "Nonsense."

Ben watched the shifting newspaper for some further comment, but none came. He looked then at Mom, who was just looking away from Dad. She gave Ben a slight smile and carefully set the cup down in front of her. Ben smiled back, then stood and took his cereal bowl and juice glass to the sink.

"Gotta go," he said.

Mrs. Murray had finished her breakfast of eggs and toast, was staring absently across the table at Peter. She cradled her lukewarm coffee in one hand and held a cigarette in the other. Peter ignored her, busily wiped the egg yolk from his plate with a half-slice of toast.

There was a heavy knock at the kitchen door. Mrs. Murray gave the door only a casual glance before Peter called out. "Come in."

"Hey, Peter," said Ben. He left the door open, but let the screen door slap shut behind him. "Good Morning, Mrs. Murray."

"Hey," said Peter.

"Good morning, Ben," said Mrs. Murray. She was wearing a long white robe and fluffy slippers, had her hair brushed back and pulled into a pony tail.

Ben plopped himself down in the nearest chair. The tiny kitchen smelled of fried eggs, toast and butter, cigarette smoke, and the ever-present half-filled ashtray sitting within easy reach beside Mrs. Murray's breakfast plate.

Peter stood up quickly and stuffed the last of his toast into his mouth. "I'm done," he said. He carried his plate to the sink while washing the toast down with the last of his juice.

Mrs. Murray gave Peter a motherly look. "Don't rush, sweetie. You'll make yourself sick."

"Gotta go, Mom." Peter was at the screen door and out.

Ben hurried after him, calling back, "Bye, Mrs. Murray."

Mrs. Murray stared at the closing door. The kitchen was quiet again; a slight breeze coming in from outside pushed the cigarette smoke away from her face. She tapped the ash into the ashtray and took another sip of her coffee.

Ben caught up with Peter out on the sidewalk. The morning was clear and sunny. Across the street, the garage door to the Foster house was open and Ben could see his dad moving about inside. Over at the Margolis house, Mike Margolis was climbing into his 58 Chevy. Further down the street, Mr. Addison was bringing out his lawnmower. At the Bigalow house, Mr. Bigalow was standing out on his lawn, wrapped in an old robe, giving his newspaper the once-over.

Saturday was getting started in Ravenhill Court.

Julie came out of the Foster house through the garage, walked down the driveway and crossed the street.

"Hey," she said.

"Hey," said Peter.

Julie looked up the street. Mike had started his car and was letting it warm up. Mr. Addison was trying to get his lawnmower started. Mr. Bigalow was scratching at his backside as he headed in the general direction of his front door.

"You guys ready?" she asked.

" 'course not," said Peter.

Ben frowned. "If anyone knows what's going on, it'll be the Professor."

"I suppose," said Peter.

"Yeah," said Julie.

"The Professor is a good guy."

"I never said different."

They all turned at the sound of a door closing. Donna Osborne had come out of her house next door and was staring at the three of them from her porch. She gave Peter a big, jeering grin. "Hey, Peter, seen any Martians?"

"Just the big one I'm lookin' at."

"Shut up, Donna," said Ben.

Donna continued eyeing Peter. "Are these your Martian comrades?"

"You're such an ignoramus," said Julie.

"Why do you hang out with these losers, Julie? Ya' can't get any real friends?"

Mike Margolis had backed his car out of his driveway. He drove it past the group on his way out of Ravenhill Court. Donna smiled broadly and waved as he passed. Mike ignored all of them.

"Let's go," said Ben. He started up the street toward Professor LaMothe's house. Peter and Julie followed after him.

Once Donna was certain that Mike had gone, she turned her attention back to Peter and his moron friends.

"Hey, Peter! You let me know if you see any aliens, eh?"

Up in the heart of the Court, Mr. Addison had begun mowing his yard. Mr. Bigalow had gone back into his house. At Mrs. Weatherby's house, a twirling sprinkler spun slowly, watering a small circle of lawn.

Everything was normal.

Everything was 1964, small-town America.

Chapter Three

Mrs. LaMothe was small in stature, and a rather demure woman, but she carried herself with a sophisticated presence that insisted her station in society was above whatever her surroundings might imply. She had done what she could with the simple, middle-class home that she found herself living in, and there was a definite contrast between the neighborhood outside and the home inside. There was a calm elegance within, with lace and crystal, fine woods and thick, tasteful carpet.

She walked across the front room as if someone might be watching and opened the door. She looked down, as best her height would allow, at the three young people standing on her large, covered porch.

"Hello, Mrs. LaMothe," said Ben.

"Good morning, Benjamin," said Mrs. LaMothe warily. She gave each of the children a studied look. "How can I help you?"

"We would like to see the Professor, please," said Julie.

"A bit early for callers, young lady."

"It's kind of important, ma'am," said Peter.

Mrs. LaMothe gave Peter another studied look and a raised brow. She turned her gaze again to Ben, knowing that whatever they were about, Benjamin Foster was the likely instigator.

"Professor LaMothe is in his den," she said. She made no effort to move aside, leaving them to stand uncertainly on the porch, waiting for some sign to enter. She finally turned about in one sweeping motion and started away from the door. "This way. Close the door behind you."

She led them from the front hall and across the main living area. All was prim and proper, and far too refined to be touched. They held their arms close at their sides. A clock on a shelf loudly ticked off the passing seconds.

She opened the door to the professor's den. The room was as different from the rest of the house as the house was from the neighborhood. It was a world unto itself, large and filled with deep shadows and the smells of old paper and book leather. Scattered haphazardly about the room were old lamps of various designs, assorted side tables and high-back wooden chairs, and the professor's large roll-top desk with its cubbyholes crammed with papers and odds-and-ends. The walls were floor-to-ceiling shelves filled with books, and on the tables were dozens of old leather-bound volumes, brought down from the shelves in times past and never returned.

Mrs. LaMothe spoke officiously, "Professor LaMothe, you have guests."

The professor looked up from a large, dusty book and twisted about in his chair. There was a loud squeaking sound as he leaned forward. He answered with a bit of mocking officiousness.

"Thank you... Mrs. LaMothe."

Mrs. LaMothe raised a brow, backed out of the room and closed the door. The professor smiled.

"Welcome, welcome." He gave Peter a sparkling sharp eye. "I hear you've been spreading fear and unrest, young Master Murray."

"No, sir."

"Hmm." The professor leaned back. His chair let out more painful squeals. He waved his hands about for the three to come nearer and find places to sit. He watched each of them closely as they struggled to clear chairs of piles of books. Once they were settled in, he looked directly at Ben. Ben looked first at the others, then spoke forcefully.

"He sees things, Professor."

"So I understand."

"And he can sense things. He feels things."

The professor's stare made Ben uncomfortable, but he didn't turn away. He had known Professor LaMothe all his life, and he had been in this room many times. He liked the professor. And he knew that the professor liked him. The professor was a brilliant man, and he knew things that no normal person knew.

Ben also understood that when the professor looked at you, he was seeing things that no normal person saw. It was just the way he was. All Ben could do was look right back.

Professor LaMothe turned his gaze on Peter. "And what did you see yesterday, Peter?"

"I..." Peter looked to Ben for support. Ben only nodded encouragingly. Peter turned back to the professor. "I saw a doorway."

Professor LaMothe shifted imperceptibly, and the chair let out a short squeak. "No ordinary doorway, I wager."

"No, sir."

"A gateway, perhaps."

The children all perked up. Julie eyed the professor suspiciously, but said nothing. Professor LaMothe gave her a quick glance and slight nod, but kept his attention on Peter.

"A portal to... someplace else," he said, his tone flat.

"Yessir."

"How could you know that, Professor?" asked Julie.

The professor leaned back heavily, taking in the chair's answering cry. He continued to watch Peter.

"We hoped you could tell us what it means," said Ben.

Professor LaMothe looked as if he was sorting through a library of thoughts, finally gave Ben a reassuring smile. "I will tell you what I can, of course."

"Then you do know what's going on."

"I should be able to give you a good start on finding the answers that you are seeking."

"What does that mean?" asked Julie. There was something really, *really* fishy about this.

Professor LaMothe let his gaze wander over the book-lined walls of his den. He would have to handle this very carefully.

How much to tell the children?

"It has been a very long time... but the reappearance of the gateway is not unexpected."

"It's been here before?" asked Ben.

"Oh, yes. It has most definitely been here before."

"Is it bad?"

"In and of themselves, the gateways are not bad. They do, however, portend *interesting* times ahead."

"And what does that mean?" Julie's question was more of a frustrating demand. "You're not telling us anything, Professor."

Ben shot Julie an angry look, but the professor only smiled kindly. Peter sat silent and unmoving, not taking his eyes off the professor. The professor gave Peter another reassuring nod and turned to Julie.

"I am sorry. I suppose I do sound a bit cryptic."

"She's just like that, Professor," said Ben.

"No, no," said the professor. "Your sister is quite right, and I do apologize. I said I would tell you what I can, and I certainly will."

What I can, Julie thought. *He said 'what I can'. What does he know that he can't tell us?*

"There just seems to be a lot of strange stuff going on these days, Professor," said Ben. "And Peter usually sees it coming."

"Did you see anything inside the gateway, son?" The professor asked Peter.

"Just shadows."

"Did you sense anything from these shadows?"

"One reached out," said Ben. "It touched him."

"Yes?" asked the professor, not really surprised.

Peter only nodded.

"Please, Professor," said Julie.

For several long moments, he kept his gaze on Peter, probing, seeking, looking for something. Then, as if he had found what he wanted, he leaned back and calmly turned so that he was looking in the general direction of the window across the room, though he was looking at nothing in particular.

"Ravenhill Court is a very special place, Miss Foster. I have no doubt that you already know that. We who live here are a part of what makes this place special. Young Peter, of all of us, is most special indeed."

"How, why, what? I'm sorry, Professor, but you're still not telling us anything."

"I tell you what I can."

"But not necessarily what you know."

"Julie!" Ben hissed.

"Quite all right, Ben," said the professor. "Your sister is very perceptive."

"Sir?"

The professor spoke directly to Julie. "I don't have all the answers, Julie. I in fact have many questions of my own. I am hoping that you can help me answer some of them. And, perhaps, with these answers, will come those that you yourself are seeking."

Peter cleared his throat, as if trying to catch someone's attention. "What do you want us to do, Professor?"

"I need for you find that gateway, son."

"It isn't open," said Peter. "Not now. I can't see it."

"It will open again."

"How do we find it?" asked Ben. He hadn't thought that it actually existed, not as a real thing that you could walk up to and touch.

"Peter will find it for you. It won't be far away." The professor began rummaging through the drawers and cubby holes of his desk.

"Why won't you tell us more?" Julie pleaded.

"What do we do when we find it?" asked Ben. "Are we supposed to go through it?"

"No." Professor LaMothe said quickly, then returned to his hunt. "Do not go through the gateway."

"Professor LaMothe!" Julie demanded.

The professor found what he was looking for. It was a small, black cloth bag with a tie string. He turned back to the children and held it out in the palm of one hand.

"You must take this to the gateway."

"Why?" Julie asked sharply. "What is it?"

The professor tossed the bag to Julie. She opened it and pulled out a crystal the size of a large walnut. She studied it carefully, and held it out for the others to see.

"That crystal must get to the other side of the gateway," said the professor.

"But you can't tell us why."

"I'm sorry, Miss Foster. Please be patient. The answers will come."

Ben had the crystal now. "We'll do it, Professor." He handed it back to Julie, who dropped it back into the bag.

Professor LaMothe set a hand palm down onto the top of his desk and looked across at Peter. "Now... Julie, hand Peter the crystal."

"Oh-kay..." Julie handed the bag over to Peter with a mocking delicacy.

"Peter, this is important. You must be the one to get the crystal to the other side... but you must wait until you know the time is right."

"I don't know..."

"You will. Do not give up the crystal until you know the time is right."

Peter stared anxiously at the professor, but Ben spoke up firmly.

"We'll take care of it, Professor," he said.

"I know you will." The professor's gaze glided slowly across the three of them. "One more thing,"

"Here it comes," said Julie.

"You will in all probability not be the only ones searching for the gateway."

"What?"

"Their goal and yours are not the same. At least, not exactly. You must get there first, and you must get the crystal through."

"Are these guys dangerous?"

The professor seemed to struggle for an answer. "They have no desire to harm you, but they are sincere in their efforts and will do whatever is necessary to stop you from getting the crystal across."

"Why?" asked Julie.

Again the professor struggled for an adequate answer. "Opinions differ as to how to resolve our problem."

"What problem?" Julie was growing more frustrated by the moment.

The professor's response was very long in coming.

"I'm sorry."

Chapter Four

Ben was the second one to the fort the next morning. Peter was already there and had to open the door for him. Once inside, he set the scout backpack on the table and Peter began loading it up with the supplies that he had gathered.

"Be careful. There's sandwiches in there," said Ben. "I don't want 'em all squished."

"Anything to drink?"

"We'll take a canteen."

"That'll work," said Peter. "We can fill it up at the creek."

"Is that where we're going?"

Peter stopped packing. "I think so," he said.

They heard the secret knock at the door, and Ben pulled back the latch to let Julie in.

"Hey," she said, latching the door behind her.

"Hey," said Peter.

"Man, it's really foggy out there."

"Did Mom say anything?" asked Ben.

"Nah. I think her and Dad had a fight about the new car."

Peter grinned. "That is one really butt-ugly piece of automobile."

"It's a classic," Julie said, mocking her father.

"I think it's kinda' boss," said Ben.

"Maybe Dad will leave it to you in his will."

Peter closed up the day pack, stared at it and took two deep breaths. "That's it. I'm as ready as I'll ever be."

"So let's split," said Julie.

Once back on the trail, they followed it past the Addison's backyard and on around to the Weatherby's, where the trail forked. Following the left fork would have taken them around behind the houses on the other side of Ravenhill Court. They took the right fork instead, which took them inland along Raven's Creek. In most places, the creek was narrow enough that a hop-skip-and-jump could take them from one side to the other with barely a splash. Low rolling hills rose up on either side.

The morning was gray and the air was damp. Mossy branches hung heavy over the stream and the winding trail that followed it, blocking out what little light there was and keeping Ben, Julie and Peter in shadows most of the time. For the first few hundred yards, the only sound was that of snapping twigs as they pushed aside the brush and low-hanging branches, and the occasional splash as they were forced off the trail and into the water. They wanted to put some distance between themselves and the neighborhood before they spoke. It was still pretty early on a quiet Sunday morning, and they were afraid that their voices would carry all the way out onto the street. They didn't want to draw attention to themselves.

Ben was leading the way, with Julie not far behind and Peter following clumsily along after them. He had first shift with the backpack.

"There's the clearing," said Ben. The brush was as thick as ever and closed in tight to the creek, but there was a bright opening up ahead. It was the first major clearing on Raven's Creek and a common location for those traveling the trail to stop and dry out, readjust their gear and get set for the next leg. For many, it was the final destination, being an out-of-the-way hangout not too far from the neighborhood.

For the last few yards before the clearing, the trail ran directly alongside the creek and was wet and slippery. Ben had to dance some careful maneuvers to not fall in and hopped the last steps out into the brightening gray morning. He stopped suddenly, and Julie and then Peter both jumped off-balance to one side in order not to run into him.

Ben was staring at Louis Bennett, who sat quietly on a small hillock at the far edge of the clearing.

"Hey," said Louis. He was in the eighth grade with Ben and Peter, but was a year younger. He lived on the corner next door to Ben. The Bennetts were the only black family in the neighborhood. In fact, they were the only black family that Ben knew personally.

"Hey," he said back. Over the surprise, he walked into the center of the clearing and called back to Peter, "How about that canteen? The water's clearest over there." He pointed to a wide spot in the creek where the water ran over some river-rock.

"Yeah, yeah... gimme a sec," said Peter. He was struggling to get the day pack off. Julie finally went over to help. Meanwhile, Ben was looking at Louis and Louis was looking up at Ben.

"Whatcha' doin' here, Louis?"

"Hangin'."

"Yeah?" Ben was doubtful.

"Yeah." The gray skies were continuing to brighten and Louis had to squint now to keep eye-to-eye with Ben. The fog was going to burn off early.

"How long ya' plan on *hangin'*?"

Louis shrugged. "Bit longer." He smiled.

Ben smiled back. "Give, Louis..."

Louis' smile broadened. He finally looked away and shrugged. "Prof thought I should come along."

"Along?"

"With you guys." Louis looked up at Julie's approach. She stood beside her brother. Peter was kneeling at the creek, filling the canteen.

"What do you know of it?" asked Julie.

"A bit."

"What did LaMothe tell you?"

"Just that you guys were doing something important; that you might need me."

"Need you for what?" asked Ben.

Louis shrugged, leaned forward and stood up. He was four inches shorter than Ben. He brushed his pants clean and took a step closer to Ben. "Listen, man, I'm just doing what the Prof asked me. You think I like coming out here on a cold, wet morning and spending my Sunday traipsing around the hills with you guys?"

"Then why do it?" asked Julie. Unlike Ben and Louis, she had yet to smile.

"Because the Prof asked me to."

"You always do what the professor asks?"

"Yeah," said Louis. "I do."

"Why?"

Louis gave her a cool steady look. "Cause he's the Prof," he said. He watched Peter come up to them, struggling to get the cap back on the canteen.

He turned his attention back to Julie. "I see that you're out here, on this wet, gray morning... just as the professor told you."

"Ouch," said Ben.

"I'm out here because Peter needs us," said Julie. "Whatever Professor LaMothe is after, I'm here to watch Peter's back."

The four of them stood silent. Peter began to look uncomfortable. Louis finally gave a short, curt nod.

"I dig that," he said quietly.

"Cool," said Ben, flatly. He turned then and started across the clearing. "Let's go."

His sudden departure took the others by surprise and they had to scramble to follow after him. Peter picked up the backpack and trailed after the others, holding the pack out in front of him.

"Hey! Hey, you guys! Somebody else's turn with this. Hey!"

The trail stayed close to the meandering creek, veering off only when it had to, when the brush grew too thick or large boulders pushed up from the ground, or the banks rose up too steeply. They followed the trail for several hours, spoke only occasionally, sometimes mumbling a warning of nearby poison oak or some other danger, but more often a comment on near-miss stumbles with near-miraculous recoveries that saved one and then another of them from making the big splash.

At each clearing along the way they would stop and look to Peter. At each clearing Peter would say only 'Not far... up ahead.' The small pack would change hands and they would go on. Ben continued to lead the way.

They stopped for lunch at a large clearing with several fallen logs and a number of circles of rocks where people had made campfires. It was only eleven o'clock, but this was as far as any of them had ever traveled Raven's Creek, and they didn't know if there would be another good spot further on to take a break. At the far end of the clearing, the stream disappeared once again into thick brush and low-hanging trees and shadows.

Julie sat with Peter on one log, some distance from Ben and Louis. This gave Ben an opportunity to share a sandwich and ask Louis more about how and why Professor LaMothe had asked him to join them.

Louis had shown up at the LaMothe house the previous afternoon to mow their yard. In addition to his own yard, Ben knew that Louis had the LaMothe house and Mrs. Weatherby's, as well as several others over on Edgewood.

He had finished the front lawn and was pushing the mower around to the back yard when the professor called him into his den. Ben could just imagine what Mrs. LaMothe thought of a neighborhood kid tracking freshly cut grass into the house, but Louis didn't say anything about it.

The professor had told Louis that Ben, Julie and Peter were going to be traveling up Raven's Creek the next morning, and that what they were doing was very important. He asked Louis if he would be available to go with them, to help them if he could. The professor told Louis that his help might be needed on this journey or the next. He warned that it might be dangerous, but that the future of Ravenhill Court was at stake.

Louis didn't know what Prof meant by *'this journey or the next'*, and when Ben asked how the professor knew that they would be traveling up Raven's Creek, Louis said that he thought that's where Prof had told them to go.

Hadn't he told them where to go?

Ben knew they hadn't talked about where the gateway was. He remembered specifically that the professor had told them that Peter would know how to find it.

Then he remembered... the professor hadn't actually said that he didn't know where the gateway was, only that Peter would be able to find it.

Then it was Ben's turn to fill Louis in on what little he knew. Louis had pretty much figured out that it had to have been something to do with the scene that Peter had made at school, but the gateway thing and the deal with the crystal was news to him. The professor hadn't told him anything about it. And while he had said that it might get dangerous, he hadn't told Louis that there might be others out here trying to stop what the professor had sent them out to do.

Once he had laid out the whole story to Louis, Ben asked if he still wanted come along. He felt Louis deserved the chance to back out. Ben didn't believe that he should have to face what they might be facing without at least having the few facts that he could give him, however few they might be.

Ben found that he was strangely relieved when Louis said that he would continue on with them. If anything, Louis was more determined than ever to go on. Ben realized then that, despite the fact that the kid was a year younger and smaller, with Louis along he was just a little less anxious about what might lay ahead.

For as long as he could remember, it had always been Ben and Julie and Peter. Having an outsider in their midst had at first been unsettling. They had all felt it. They liked Louis well enough, but no one could simply walk in and suddenly be one of them. Still, by the time they had stopped for lunch, and certainly by the time they had finished lunch, Ben was at least okay with having Louis around, whether he was one of them or not.

They started out again, Ben continuing to lead, with Peter guiding them ever forward. From here on out, the trail was used mostly by deer and smaller animals, only occasionally by people. Being less traveled, it was less well-defined, but still easy enough to follow. There were also fewer trees, but the brush was thicker and taller. There were fewer clearings, but the sky was more visible, with the openings overhead coming more frequently.

Twenty minutes from the lunch clearing, the trail turned down toward the brook and stopped at the water's edge. Ben saw several stones in the water and the trail continuing on the other side. He looked back at the others, then at Peter.

Peter confidently pointed upstream. Ben saw something in Peter's expression. There was something different. Something had changed. Peter was sensing something...

Ben leapt from the bank, hopped from one stone to the other and reached the other side, the others following quickly behind. Several yards on, the trail turned away from the bank, winding away until the brook was no longer visible. The brush on either side of the trail was twice as tall as Ben, and the last of the trees were left behind. The fog was gone and the sky overhead was light blue.

Ben stopped suddenly, frozen in midstride. The others stopped where they were, either because they had heard what he had heard or they could see that he had heard something.

Someone or something was out there.

It was too quiet to be in the brush. It was either up ahead on the same trail they were traveling, or maybe on another one nearby.

Ben indicated to the others that they should wait where they were. He moved off then, quickly and quietly down the trail. He rounded a bend and stopped at the next. He knelt behind a bush and carefully peeked around the corner.

A man was stepping down onto the trail from another steep path that wound down from the hillside. He was dressed in rugged outdoor garb and a military cap. Following after him were three men in military khakis. All wore sidearms.

Once on the trail, they headed away from Ben, quickly disappearing around the next bend.

"Who are they?" whispered Julie, close enough that Ben felt her breath on his ear. Ben almost jumped into the bushes.

"I told you to stay where you were."

"Yeah? Who died and made you boss?"

The others scrambled up behind Julie.

"What are they doing here?" asked Louis.

Ben looked irritated. "I imagine the same thing we are; looking for the gateway."

"I'll bet they're the ones the professor was talking about," said Peter.

"Ya' think?"

"LaMothe needs to spill it about what's going on," said Julie. She jabbed a finger in the direction the men had taken. "That was a government spook."

"A spy?" asked Louis. "Really?"

"Some kind of a special agent... and with a military escort, no less."

Peter stood up slowly. He looked half-dazed. The others stood then, knowing that something was up, half expecting him to go into another of his weird fits.

"Peter?" Ben finally asked.

"It's open," he said.

Ben looked up the trail, in the direction the government man and his escort had gone. He turned back to Peter. "Do you know where it is? Can you get us there?"

Peter nodded.

"Okay," said Ben. "We gotta get there first."

Chapter Five

They hoped to find a spot where they could get around the four men, and then once past them to hurry down the trail as fast as they could. The problem was, the trail offered not only the easiest travel, but also the most direct route down the valley. Getting around the men, who were traveling that trail, wasn't going to be easy.

They followed along at a safe distance, waiting for their chance. They had gone about a quarter of a mile when Peter tapped Ben on the shoulder. The trail twisted right, but Peter pointed straight ahead.

"Ya' sure?" Ben whispered.

Peter nodded and pointed. Straight ahead.

The brush wasn't too thick here, and it looked like the going wouldn't be too bad. The trail the government men were taking continued to follow along the creek bank.

"All right," said Ben, and led the way into the bushes.

Another few hundred yards and they came out of the brush near the opening to a narrow ravine that cut into the left slope of the valley. Ben gave Peter only a quick glance before going in.

The ravine was no more than eight or ten feet wide most of the way, occasionally widening out to form high-walled clearings filled with brush and large granite stones. The sun's rays reached down to the floor in narrow beams.

The floor of the ravine rose steadily as they continued forward, becoming steep in some places.

They heard voices behind them. The government man and his escort had found the ravine.

"Come on," said Ben and they picked up the pace. Behind them, the voices grew louder, grew nearer. They were gaining. It became clear to Ben that while they might get there first, there was no way they would be able to do anything before those coming up the ravine joined them.

There was a crevice in the wall up ahead. Ben ran to it and waved the others in, then hurriedly followed in after. He had just backed into the shadows of the fissure when the government man rounded the bend and approached, the three escort right behind him. They passed by the crevice without looking in and were gone.

Ben stepped out, and then the others.

"This isn't good," said Peter.

"Now what?" Julie whispered.

In answer, Ben started silently forward, hurrying after the four men but careful to stay out of sight.

They came up to a low wall that jutted out from one side of the ravine, crouched low and used it as cover.

The clearing beyond glowed a bright, clear blue. In the center stood the gateway, from which the glow emanated. It had the dimensions of a regular doorway, but looked completely transparent; Ben could see through the gateway to the rock walls of the clearing beyond.

The government man stood directly in front of the gateway, forming a dark silhouette before it, and the three military men stood at the edges of clearing, surrounding the shimmering object before them.

Peter looked entranced by the scene. After several moments huddled behind the wall, he stood and started around the others toward the heart of the clearing. Ben grabbed at him, just managing to hold onto him.

The government man sensed movement behind him and turned around. His face shimmered in the blue glow. He looked carefully at Peter. His appearance was calm and deliberate.

At the man's movement, the military men had turned to Peter as well, taking a defensive posture. At the slightest gesture of their leader, the men stopped and held their position.

The government man turned his attention back to the gateway. There were shadows moving about within it, movement as of someone walking across a room beyond the doorway. Everyone in the clearing stood very still. Over a period of several seconds, the shadows slowly took form, becoming finally the silhouette of a man. The government man looked calmly on, waiting patiently, the shimmering of light and shadow bringing the clearing to life.

The man beyond the gateway stepped through, but kept his back just within the flickering light. He had the same internal glow as the gateway, but to all appearances looked to be completely normal. Peter took a step closer, with Ben and the others right behind him.

"Hello, Ashton," said the man from the gateway.

"Hello, John," said the government man.

John looked around the clearing. He saw the military escort that Ashton had brought with him, and then the young people standing five yards behind Ashton.

"Interesting welcoming committee." he said.

"I'm here to help, John."

John laughed sharply. He shook his head and studied Ashton. "All I need is the crystal," he said.

"I don't have it."

Peter started to speak up, but Ben stopped him. He remembered what the professor had said. *Wait until the time is right.*

"Then they will be lost," said John.

"Giving you the crystal won't help that," said the government man.

"It's the only thing that will."

"And if it fails?"

John looked frustrated, as if he had been fighting this same fight, arguing this same argument, for a very long time. "You must get me the crystal."

"Sorry, John. It isn't going to happen."

"Ashton, I can save them."

"John Murray, savior?"

Peter stiffened at hearing the name.

John Murray...

"Your father!" Julie hissed in a harsh whisper. Peter said nothing, but took another step closer.

John Murray shook his head sadly. "You know better than that, Ashton."

"I certainly do," said Ashton. The tone was accusatory. "You've done enough. We'll take it from here. Hopefully, we can salvage something from this mess."

Ben calmly placed the small black bag into Peter's hand. Peter gripped it tightly, took two guarded steps forward. He was within arm's reach of Ashton, standing off to one side. Ashton turned his head enough to watch the boy while still keeping an eye on John Murray. When one of the military escort started forward, Ashton held up a halting hand.

"You're my dad?" Peter asked the gateway man.

John Murray looked uncertainly at the boy. When he turned back to Ashton, the government man nodded. Murray let out a long breath.

"How long?" he asked.

"Almost twelve years on this side."

"We knew that there would be... but it can't..."

"Think about what that does to the calculations," said Ashton. "Think about what it means for us, John."

John Murray looked to Ashton for some further clarification, but nothing came. He looked over at Peter, took a step from the gateway. Still shrouded in the aura of the gateway, he knelt on one knee. Peter approached, looking down into the face of the father that he had never known. John Murray held out a hand.

"I'm sorry, son."

Peter placed his hand in his father's. The blue glow surrounding John Murray radiated out to Peter's hand and part way up his arm. John Murray's eyes sparkled imperceptibly as he felt the bag containing the crystal in Peter's hand.

Still looking at Peter, he spoke to the government man.

"I'll not let the boy down, Ashton," he said. He stood then and let go of Peter's hand. He took a step back. The gateway shimmered and flickered at John Murray's presence.

"We can work together, John."

"Apparently not," he said. He looked at Peter. "Tell the professor I said hello."

Peter could only nod, numbed by the strange turn of events.

Ashton pleaded, "John, please."

John Murray gave Ashton only a cursory glance, looked again at his son. "Six, three, six," he said, and took the final step back into the gateway. His image shifted to silhouette, then slowly dissolved to a mix of swimming shadows. The gateway darkened, and the eerie glow in the clearing began to fade. The gateway vanished. The clearing grew gray, almost colorless, with only a thin band of light from the weak afternoon sun reaching down to the floor of the ravine.

The three military men still stood around the edge of the clearing, surrounding Ashton and Peter. The others remained at a safe distance.

For several long seconds, no one moved, no one spoke. Ashton finally looked down at Peter, turned slowly about and gave Ben a long, studied look. Ben managed to hide a sudden dread. He had no idea what Ashton might do now.

"Wow," said Ben. "Bummer."

Ashton's expression was almost sad. "Yeah," he said finally. The sadness in his face was reflected in the tone of his voice.

"Well," Ben tried to smile. "I guess we gotta split."

He took a step back, watching for some reaction from Ashton. Julie and Louis stepped back with him. Ben stiffly waved for Peter to follow. Peter had trouble moving his legs, but finally got the first foot out, then the other. Using only his eyes, Ashton let his men know to hold their positions and let the kids go. Once they were gone, Ashton turned back to where the gateway had been.

"Bummer," he mumbled to himself.

Chapter Six

Ben was sitting on the bench in the fort, his back against the wall. Peter sat at the table scribbling in his new journal. He had picked it up at the variety store right after school the day before and had hardly taken his nose out of it since.

He spoke up while still writing. "Maybe it's a combination," he said.

"Combination, maybe, but not to any ordinary lock," said Ben.

"I think the professor knows, no matter what he said."

Julie called out then from her place up in the tower. "Here comes Louis."

Ben slid down the bench toward the door. When he heard the secret knock, he opened it and let Louis in, latched it shut behind him.

"Hey, guys," said Louis. He looked admiringly around the room. "Cool."

"Welcome," said Peter, only briefly looking up from his journal.

Ben slid back to his place on the bench. "Well?"

Louis sat down beside him and shook his head. "No sign of Prof anywhere."

"Where's he gone off to?" Ben asked sullenly.

"Ya' think he's hiding?"

Julie climbed down from the tower. "*Hiding* is definitely the operative word," she said.

"Wherever he's hiding," said Ben, "or *whatever* he's hiding, he's still on our side. We don't want to lose sight of that."

"What's the good of having him on our side if he doesn't tell us anything?" Julie sat down opposite Peter and glanced curiously at the pictures he was drawing in the journal. One of them looked a lot like her.

Ben was having an increasingly difficult time defending the professor. "All right. I agree that he knows more than he's letting on, but we can still learn from him."

"So what do you think he's not telling?" asked Louis.

"Only everything," said Julie.

Peter hardly looked up from his journal. "Getting that crystal to my dad was sure important to him."

My dad... they all caught that.

"Sure," said Julie. "That was probably the only reason he told us anything at all."

"I don't think so," said Ben. "He wants to tell us more, but he can't."

"Geez, Ben." Julie grew more exasperated by the second. "We've run his little errand for him, he doesn't need us anymore, and now he's off to who-knows-where."

There was a long, uncomfortable silence. The only sound was that of Peter's pencil scratching across the thick, rough paper.

Over the last day, they had been thinking about the same thing, had been sorting and resorting what little they knew, and had been coming up with the same conclusion. No one had yet been willing to voice their thoughts aloud.

"Everyone knows about it," Louis finally said.

Peter stopped scribbling. The others looked at him. He looked up at Louis, then at the others.

"Everyone over thirty anyway," he mumbled.

Ben leaned forward, looked carefully at Peter and gave him a half nod. He turned to his sister.

"Remember when we asked Mom and Dad about Peter's father?"

"Sure. They didn't want to talk about it."

"I just figured they didn't want to talk about a messy marriage breakup."

"We know now that's not what happened." She perked up, began to show some interest in the direction that Ben was going. "Since they were hiding the reason behind John Murray's disappearance from us, and since we know that John Murray's disappearance has something to do with the gateway--"

Ben nodded sharply, "A plus B equals C, therefore A equals C and Mom and Dad know about the gateway."

"And if they know, and if the professor knows, then others in Ravenhill Court know."

"Like I said," Peter started scribbling in his journal again. "They all know. Everyone over thirty."

Julie sighed dejectedly. "But what is it they know—"

"—that we don't know," finished Louis.

Again there was only the scribbling of Peter's pencil as he drew in the journal. The others watched him as he worked, oblivious as to the attention being paid to him.

Julie looked up from Peter's journal. "You know what I think?" She pursed her lips and waited until she had everyone's attention; all but Peter's. "I think maybe Peter's father made that gate, and now he's stuck."

Peter had been paying attention after all. "Stuck where?"

"I'm not so sure that's it," said Louis. "I mean, that would make it important to Mr. Murray, but Ashton didn't look all that interested in bringing him back. There's something else going on."

"He's right," said Ben. "Ashton was real concerned about something, and it wasn't about bringing Peter's dad back from the other side."

"But he's still stuck," said Peter.

"But he was more concerned about some *others*. He said they would be lost if he didn't get the crystal."

"Now he has the crystal," said Peter.

Julie thought aloud, "And using it is dangerous."

"Looks like Ashton thinks so," said Ben. "I'll bet he's working for whoever controls the gate."

"That could be," agreed Julie. She leaned tiredly away from the table. "That still leaves the deep, dark secret of how this all came about to begin with."

"A deep, dark secret that this entire neighborhood is sittin' on."

Ben was sitting on the curb in front of his house, his feet resting on his red skateboard in front of him. The neighborhood was quiet on a warm afternoon. The last day of school. Summer was finally here.

Peter came out of his house and trudged slowly across the street. He dropped down beside Ben without a word.

For Peter, it had been a tough last couple of days at school. The incident the previous week had been only one more in a long line of incidents. A lot of people thought there might be something wrong with him.

"You all right?" asked Ben. He was staring down at his skateboard.

"Fine. I had to talk with some shrink for an hour."

"I heard."

"I think I have him convinced I'm a kid with abandonment issues."

Ben put on a fiendish grin. "You know..."

"I'm not adopted."

They sat quiet for a long time. The sun felt good. They knew that with school out of the way, they had all summer to devote to figuring out what was going on.

"I was thinking," Ben said finally.

"Let me know how that works for ya."

Ben let the skateboard roll back and forth under his feet. The metal wheels rumbled noisily across the asphalt.

"Twelve years," he said.

"What?"

"Ashton said twelve years. Your dad asked how long, and Ashton said *'twelve years on this side.'*"

"Yeah, that's right. My dad was real surprised... like maybe not that much time has gone by where he is."

Ben looked up from his skateboard at the neighborhood him. "So twelve years goes by here. Ashton, the professor, and who knows who else, are all waiting for the gateway to show up."

"The professor did say that he was expecting it."

"For a very long time..."

They fell silent again, and then Ben turned and gave Peter such a penetrating look that Peter began to squirm.

"Stop doing that."

"You, Peter... are connected somehow."

"Huh?"

"Your visions."

"What about 'em?" Peter asked defensively. "I've always had 'em."

"For about twelve years." Ben turned his attention back to his skateboard. "Kinda' weird."

Mike Margolis turned his car into Ravenhill Court and let it glide slowly up toward his house.

Up behind Ben and Peter, the garage door opened. Mr. Foster was going to spend what was left of the afternoon working on his old Mercury.

Adult Ben Foster was sitting on the curb in front of the old Foster house, the journal resting in his lap. He closed it and looked around at the abandoned neighborhood. The sky had grown gray with the oncoming dusk and shadows had started to finger their way amongst the empty houses.

He climbed to his feet and walked over to the old Mercury. His father's old Mercury. He brought a scruffy suitcase out of the trunk, slapped the trunk closed, and walked up the steep driveway to the house.

He put the suitcase down on the floor just inside the living room and set the journal on a side table. Dull light shone in from the large front window. He flipped the light switch on the wall and the lamp standing beside the couch turned on.

The house had power. That was good. The utility company had been there. *Weird.* He knew that he had contacted them, but he couldn't remember when. Things had been in a bit of turmoil lately.

He wandered down the hall and looked briefly in each of the rooms. Returning to the front of the house, Ben found himself standing in the kitchen, staring at the metal-legged table with a sense of melancholy.

He went back into the living room and picked up the journal. He sat down in his father's old easy chair and laid the book in his lap.

Chapter Seven

The Foster's garage door was open, as was usually the case on Saturdays. The old Mercury took up the right half of the garage. Mr. Foster was tinkering around under the hood, and young Ben was leaning on the fender, his back against the car.

"Dad..."

"Yeah, Ben." Mr. Foster reached an arm out and picked up a wrench without lifting himself from under the hood.

"What did Mr. Murray do?"

"Waddya mean, *'what did he do'*?"

"For a living. What kind of work did he do?"

There was a slight pause. Ben could tell that his dad had stopped whatever he was doing in there.

"Why?" Mr. Foster finally asked. The tinkering under hood started up again.

"Just curious."

Mr. Foster didn't answer right away. There was the dull clinking of metal against cast iron.

"Scientific research. Smart man, John Murray."

Ben turned about at that and leaned forward over the fender. There was the hint of rising excitement in his voice. "Research? Really? Like what?"

"Couldn't say." Mr. Foster glanced up briefly, looked directly at Ben, then returned to the shadows of the engine compartment. "Secretive lot, that bunch."

"Yeah?"

Mr. Foster glanced up again, and again only briefly.

"Very."

Ben, Julie and Louis were sitting about the table in the fort. Peter was out of sight, sitting up in the tower. They had gone nowhere in solving the mystery, lately only coming up with more questions. There was a growing sense of frustration.

Ben was impatient. "We're going to have to go back to the ravine."

"What good would that do?" groaned Julie.

Peter called down from the tower. "The gateway is closed."

"Yeah... it was closed before," said Ben. "But it opened."

"Doesn't mean it will again," said Julie.

"That's true." Louis straightened and nodded sharply.

"It wouldn't hurt to go back," said Ben.

"That's true, too," nodded Louis.

"What about the professor?" asked Peter. The others could hear him moving about. He was positioning himself to come down from the tower.

"What about him?" asked Ben.

Julie's face twisted and she almost growled. "You mean other than the fact that he's gone? That he took our number and split?"

Peter was halfway down the ladder. He stepped from the last rung. "Secret code..."

"That he tried to make out meant nothing."

Louis gave yet another sharp nod. "That is certainly true."

Julie turned a deadly eye to Louis. "Stop doing that."

Ben was staring down at the table in front of him. He had been listening to the banter back and forth, and it was the same conversation they always had. There wasn't enough new information coming in.

"We're talking in circles," he said softly, but the frustration was as evident as ever. "We've done good, we know a lot more than we did, but without more *intel*, we're not going any further with this." He lifted his gaze from the surface of the table and up to the faces of the others. "We have two sources to get more: the professor, and the ravine."

The room was painfully quiet for several moments before Julie spoke up.

"There's the government spook," she offered.

"Yeah..." Ben mumbled patiently. "Yeah, there's Ashton. But how would we find him?"

Julie started to answer, then stopped herself, scrunched up her face and nodded silently.

Louis, however, was willing to respond. "By way of the ravine and the gateway, or through the Prof."

"Like I said. Two sources."

"Well... I've said it all along," said Julie, folding her arms. "The professor needs to spill what he knows."

Louis stood on the sidewalk outside the Foster house. Sunday was looking like it would shape up to be a pleasant early summer day. The sun was out and already working to burn off the coastal fog. Up the street, Mr. Addison was dragging his garden hose out, holding a sprinkler with his free hand.

But not all was pleasant.

Across the street, Donna Osborne came around from her side yard and walked across her front lawn. She gave Louis a dark look before stepping up onto her porch.

Louis turned toward the intersection when he heard voices.

Tony Margolis and his toady Danny Bigalow were starting across the street, coming right toward Louis. As they came nearer, Danny's grin grew.

Tony's expression looked much more threatening.

"Who let you out, Bennett?" he sneered.

"No one." Louis knew there was no way to win this thing. For now, he wanted to wait to see which way the confrontation would go in order to decide which way to turn. Still, his response was way too weak and he knew it. He hadn't been on his toes; his mistake for letting the nice morning distract him.

Tony stepped up to within a few inches of Louis, glared down at him. Tony was big for his age, which was three years older than Louis, and Louis was small for his.

"Then you shouldn't be out, should ya', boy?"

Danny stood beside Tony, sneering and bubbling with pleasure.

Tony's smile sent a cold finger down Louis' spine. "You lookin' maybe to rob somebody?"

"No," said Louis flatly.

Tony glanced behind Louis, up at the Foster's open garage.

"I think maybe ya' are. I think maybe you're lookin' to rip off the Fosters."

"Yeah," Danny could hardly restrain himself. "That's what I think."

"Ben's my friend," said Louis.

"Friend?" Tony feigned shock and surprise. "Friend? You got friends?"

"I have lots of friends."

Tony moved up quickly, even before Louis could finish the statement. His body pushed against Louis. The words came colder now. "Not here, you don't, boy. Maybe you're thinking of someplace else."

"Yeah." Danny moved in closer.

"That right?" There was a sparkle in Tony's glare. "You thinkin' someplace else?"

"Yeah," Danny said eagerly. "Like Africa!"

Louis stood frozen in place.

A car turned off Edgewood and into Ravenhill Court. Louis kept his eyes fixed on Tony. They could hear the car come to an easy stop behind Tony and Danny.

Danny turned to see who it was, then quickly turned back and looked up at Tony. He spoke low and soft and somewhat urgently.

"It's Mike," he said.

Tony slowly eased back from Louis. He turned and looked behind him at his big brother. He still wore the dark, angry look, and it was clear that he wasn't happy at having his fun interrupted.

Mike Margolis gave Tony a long, very definitive stare from his position behind the steering wheel of his Chevy.

Tony finally backed down. He turned and gave Louis a hard shove.

"This ain't done," he said abruptly and stalked off. Danny Bigalow glared back at Louis as he quickly followed after Tony.

Mike Margolis gave Louis only a quick glance, revealing nothing, before letting his foot off the brake and coasting his car up into the court.

Ben came up behind Louis from the direction of his house.

"What was that about?"

"Nothing," Louis said sharply.

"Nothing my Aunt Bessie's behind."

Louis was still trying to get over the shakes. He shoved his hands into his pants pockets. "Same ol', same ol'."

Ben could still see the receding figures of Tony and Danny. He knew from personal experience what they could be like. He also had a pretty good idea how they would work on Louis.

"You say so," he said.

"I say so."

The sound of a screen door slapping shut broke through the Sunday morning silence. Across the street, Peter was coming across his yard. He started across the street toward them.

Julie came out of the Foster garage. She called down to the others long before reaching them.

"What's everybody standin' around for? Let's do this."

The four of them started up into the court. Ahead of them on the right, Mike Margolis was walking around to the front of his car. He lifted the hood to have a look at the idling engine.

Up on the left, almost opposite the Margolis', stood the LaMothe house. A covered deck ran the width of the house. They reached the wooden steps, climbed up onto the deck, and Julie reached out and knocked.

They waited in silence. When no one answered, Julie knocked again.

"Maybe she's not home," said Peter.

"Where would she go?" asked Julie. "I don't think she's left the house since she retired."

"What did she do?" asked Louis.

The others looked at him curiously.

"She was the principle at the school," said Julie.

"Our school?"

"Yeah, Louis... our school... big building with desks..."

"It was awful," grumbled Peter.

"She wasn't that bad," said Ben, grinning broadly.

Julie could only half agree. "Far as principles go."

The front door opened then and all four were immediately silent. Mrs. LaMothe stared haughtily down at them. It was several seconds before she said anything.

"I believe I advised you yesterday that the Professor was not available."

"Yes ma'am," said Ben. "But... we were hoping you could tell us where he went--"

"And when we might expect his return," finished Julie.

It didn't appear as though Mrs. LaMothe was going to respond to this. She said nothing for a long time, continued to look down the bridge of her long nose at them.

Louis and Peter grew nervous.

Ben waited expectantly.

Julie just waited.

"The Professor's date of return is not known," said Mrs. LaMothe at last. There was another very long pause. "Was there something else?"

Julie started to say something, but Ben cut her off.

"No ma'am," he jumped in. "Thank you for your time, Mrs. LaMothe."

Ben turned away, and Louis and Peter quickly stepped off the porch ahead of him.

Julie stared silently up into the steady gaze of Mrs. LaMothe. She wasn't about to let this old school principle psych her out.

Ben, still on the deck, looked back over his shoulder. "Julie?" he urged.

Julie smiled thinly at Mrs. LaMothe, but said nothing.

Mrs. LaMothe gave the girl a dismissive nod. "Miss Foster," she said officiously.

"Thank you, Mrs. LaMothe." Julie turned around and she and Ben stepped down from the deck together. "So much for that," she said to Ben. "I guess we take a hike."

Several hours later, they found themselves in the clearing in the ravine. The four of them were kneeling around a small fire pit they had put together in one corner. Ben was trying to get a fire going using the kindling they had gathered together into a small pile within the circle of stones.

There was no sign of the gateway and the clearing was thick with shadows.

"LaMothe is on no business trip," Julie grumbled loudly.

"Julie... obvious," said Ben.

"Where would he go?" asked Peter.

"Wherever those numbers we gave him sent him," said Julie.

"And just where would that be?"

"How would I know?"

"What do you do with a number?" asked Louis. "It isn't like it's a locker number in some bus terminal."

"How do you know that?" Julie asked sharply, sending Louis back into silence.

Ben sat back and watched the small fire come to life. "Because, Julie, it is very unlikely that Peter's father would reach out from some alternate universe and give us the number of a locker in a bus terminal."

The four of them were startled at the sound of Ashton's voice.

"It's not an alternate universe," he said calmly. He stood behind them, near the heart of the clearing. He had come alone. He was looking to where the gateway had made its last appearance. "John is in, shall we say... the universe."

They were all standing now, Julie's stance more defiant than the others. "If it's different than ours, doesn't that make it alternate?"

"I'm afraid not."

"That doesn't make any sense."

"Therein lies part of the problem."

"What problem?"

Ashton strolled toward the group until he was standing before the slowly growing campfire. The others eyed him suspiciously, following his movements.

Ben echoed Julie's question. "What problem?"

Ashton spoke without looking directly at anyone. "John was conducting some rather unique experiments for our organization."

"We get that," said Julie. "And something went wrong."

"You might say that," Ashton smiled thinly, gave a slight, sardonic chuckle.

"I would be more interested in hearing what <u>you</u> have to say."

"I suppose you would." Ashton looked at Julie for a few moments, glanced at the others, finally turned his back to them and indicated the clearing they were in. "Look around you. Look at the clearing we're in. The rock walls. The fire at your feet."

"Yeah..." Julie urged cautiously.

Ashton turned again, slowly about, and looked directly at the group of young people. "Nothing that I'm looking at is real. This place... doesn't exist. It's a figment. It's all illusion. Everything. Those that were caught up in John Murray's experiment... they were caught up in this fabrication."

They stared at Ashton in open confusion.

"I don't understand," mumbled Ben.

"I would be very surprised if you did, young man." Ashton grew thoughtful, turned introspective. "So... they bring in the cavalry. That's me." He looked upward as if taking in the world around them. "Look where I end up."

Everyone was very quiet for a long time. None of what Ashton had said made any kind of sense, so what was there to say? How could they respond? What was there to ask?

As for Ashton, he had apparently said all that he was going to say on the matter, whatever the matter was. He wasn't likely to give them answers, only more questions.

Peter finally broke the awkward silence.

"This is way too weird. You are way too weird."

This took Ben off guard, but he had to agree. "And that's saying something, coming from Peter."

Ashton smiled sadly at them both.

"More so than you realize." He turned and looked again at the heart of the clearing. "I can guarantee you that John will not be making an appearance here today."

"Is that right?" Julie was eager to get back into the conversation. "We don't really know what your guarantees are worth, though, do we, Mr. Ashton?"

Ashton didn't really care. He gave a half shrug as he turned to leave. There was a tiredness to his gesture and his tone of voice.

"As you wish, Miss Foster." He started toward the opening that would take him back down the ravine. "I would suggest that you leave in time to get home before nightfall. I know I wouldn't want to be traipsing in this brush in the dark."

§

Mr. and Mrs. Foster were sitting in the darkened living room watching television. The only sound was that of the television program coming through the small speakers. The flickering of the black and white screen created shadows and light that danced across the walls of the room.

Ben and Julie came in through the back door at the far end of the hall. Julie turned and went into her bedroom, and Ben continued on alone. He stopped just before coming into the living room and silently observed his parents.

The flickering of the television screen sent light and shadows across their faces, just as it did the walls of the room. They both seemed to be entranced by the show.

After a few moments, though, Dad turned his head and looked over at Ben. It was a perceptive gaze, as if he... *understood.*

He said nothing. His expression changed little. He turned his attention slowly back to the television.

Ben continued to stand there, just inside the darkened hall, silently observing his parents, as if seeing them for the first time. It was as though, if he watched them long enough, the secret might be revealed to him.

That he, too, would understand.

Chapter Eight

Peter sat writing single-mindedly in his journal, as he most always did now whenever they were in the fort. He pretty much ignored the somewhat heated conversation that Ben and Julie were having.

"I don't buy it," said Ben.

"It makes a kind of sense," said Julie.

"Sense? Sense? It doesn't make any sense. What does *'none of it is real'* mean? That's crazier than anything Peter's ever said."

Julie's expression grew a hint darker. "And yet you believe Peter..."

Ben was suddenly flustered, and it took him a moment to recover. When he spoke again, his words were soft and precise.

"Ashton is not Peter."

"Then you explain what's going on."

They both involuntarily sucked in a frantic breath at the sound of angry voices coming from outside. A second later, Julie rushed toward the ladder to the tower and Ben slid down the bench to the wall beside the front door. He peered through a narrow crack between the boards.

Peter looked calmly up from his journal, but said nothing. He didn't seem to be affected by the activity around him. He seemed almost apart from it.

Julie was already scrambling back down from the tower.

"They got Louis," she whispered harshly.

Ben could see Tony forcibly pushing Louis toward the fort, Danny trailing behind them along the very narrow trail running from the main trail up to the fort.

When they got to the fort, Tony reached around Louis and banged on the wall beside the door.

"Open up!"

When the door didn't immediately open, Tony leaned up close to the wall and his voice became a low, menacing whisper.

"How 'bout I hurt your boy?"

"Waddya want, Tony?"

"You deaf as well as dumb, Foster? I told ya' what I want."
Tony yelled out loud and harsh, "Open the door!"

Ben looked anxiously over at Julie. Ben didn't frighten easily,
but he also really didn't like not being in control of the situation.
This was one more in a long line of uncontrollable situations that
had come up the last few weeks.

Julie nodded curtly. Open the door. What else was there to
do?

Ben slid the latch aside. The door burst open as Tony shoved
Louis in ahead of him before pushing his own way in. He moved
around the table and slid in on the bench.

"So," he said. He looked content. "What do we have here?"

Danny stepped in and closed the door.

"Playing house, huh?" His words were almost giggles.

Tony liked the suggestion. He eyed Julie. "Now that has
possibilities."

"Dream on," said Julie.

Tony sighed tritely, looked at the others in the room. Louis
had moved over beside Julie, near the tower ladder. Peter stood in
one corner.

Tony looked sharply at Ben, who was sitting at the table
opposite him. He jabbed a thumb in Louis' direction.

"I wanted to warn you about that one there. He's been casing
out the neighborhood." Tony gave Julie another once-over. "Who
knows what else?"

"You're a pig," Julie said with a disgusted sneer.

Danny made snorting sounds.

Tony smiled thinly. "Gotta protect our own, Miss Julie."

Ben spoke softly, so that everyone was forced to stop and
listen more closely.

"On that we agree."

"Ohhhh," Tony's smile broadened. "Is that a threat, Foster?"

Ben didn't respond. The calm expression on his face remained
unchanged.

Tony decided to move on. He leaned back and studied the
room again.

"Not a bad setup," he said appreciatively. "A few changes, I do
believe I could feel right at home here."

"Yeah," Danny bubbled.

"I'd burn it down first," said Ben.

Tony finally lost his sense of humor. His tone turned
dangerous. He leaned forward.

"I don't think you appreciate the seriousness of your situation, Foster. This party has the potential of going any number of ways. Most of 'em are painful."

"You don't frighten me," said Ben.

Over in the corner, Peter had a blank stare. His skin had turned pasty.

Something wasn't quite right...

Tony leaned even closer to Ben, now halfway over the table.

"Really? I think I..." He sniffed at the air. "Yes... I smell *fear* in the air."

Ben leaned the rest of the way over the table until the two of them were almost nose to nose.

"I think it's crap you smell. Not surprising. Your mouth is right under your nose."

Tony started to rise up in anger. But halfway to his feet his expression changed. His movement unexpectedly slowed.

In the corner of the room, the blank expression on Peter's face had turned glassy.

Tony rose slowly up the rest of the way to his feet. He gazed at Ben with a look of confusion.

Something wasn't quite right...

Ben stared back at Tony, somewhat bewildered.

He looked over at Julie. *What the heck's going on?*

In response, Julie contorted her face. *I don't know.*

Ben turned back to Tony. "Uh... heh? Tony?"

Tony twisted his head mechanically to the left, then to the right. He frowned.

His facial muscles suddenly relaxed. He turned and started toward the door. Danny stepped aside to let him pass. He started to say something to Tony, but before he had a chance, his own expression turned to a dull emptiness.

Tony opened the door and stepped outside.

Danny looked at the group in the fort, but there wasn't anything behind the eyes. He turned and followed Tony out the door.

Julie immediately jumped up onto the wooden ladder and was up inside the tower in seconds. Looking through the slatted opening, she watched Tony and Danny as they stepped from the side trail and out onto the main trail.

The moment they were on the main trail, they began talking.

Something isn't right...

It took Julie a few moments before she realized...

Tony and Danny were repeating their conversation from days earlier... *word for word...*

Tony Margolis was walking confidently along the trail, with Danny Bigalow following along beside him.

"...and Miss Harris sent him to the principal," said Danny. He had a huge, rat grin on his face. "And Walker sent him to the nurse. And he was supposed to see the dean after school, but guess what... He didn't show up."

Tony Margolis listened quietly to the kid's unbounded glee.

"Man, oh man," said Danny. "It was so boss."

They reached the point in the trail where the hidden path forked off and led to the fort. They continued past along the main trail.

"What did he mean?" asked Tony.

"Don't know. Maybe he told Walker." Danny bubbled with joy. "He is so weird."

Tony spoke as if to himself, "He is a strange little creep, all right."

Julie climbed down out of the tower.

"You are not going to believe this--" She stopped when she saw the way Ben was silently watching Peter.

Peter had returned to the table. He had his journal out and was contentedly writing. He was either ignoring or was unaware of all that had just happened.

"What's going on?" she whispered, then looked around the room. Her head was swimming. "Where's Louis?"

There was only Ben and Julie... and Peter hunched over his journal.

Chapter Nine

The Foster family sat around the dinner table, which was the breakfast table with a table cloth thrown over it. There was an uncomfortable silence in the room.

Mrs. Foster set down her fork, took a drink of milk, then carefully set down the glass.

"I understand that Professor LaMothe has returned from his business trip," she said. She picked up her fork and took another bite of her dinner.

Mr. Foster responded without looking up from his meal. "Is that so?"

"So I understand."

The exchange was stilted and forced. Ben and Julie looked at each other with barely hidden skepticism.

"What kind of business?" asked Ben.

Both parents looked confused.

"Just... business." Mrs. Foster held her fork out over her plate. "What does it matter?"

Mr. Foster thought he had the answer. "The professor has involved himself in a number of business interests since retiring."

Ben nodded, as if he might half believe that if he would just give himself a chance; which he wouldn't.

Julie returned to eating, almost as mechanically as the conversation she was witnessing. She spoke up without looking up from her food.

"Do you know Mr. Ashton?" she asked.

Ben watched Dad.

Dad considered the question thoughtfully. "I... don't believe so. Why do you ask?"

"Just someone we ran into."

"At school?"

"He knows John Murray," said Ben, deflecting the question. He thought it was a reasonable answer, and hoped that his father's response might provide some insight.

Dad smiled confidently. "Ah... *that* crowd."

"Weird guy" said Julie. "Weirder ideas."

"Being a part of that bunch, I wouldn't doubt it."

"So, you've never heard of him, then?" asked Ben.

"Can't say as I have," Dad sighed. "But then, I didn't move in the same circles as John."

Ben was sitting at the table in the fort, Peter's journal lay opened in front of him. The light coming in through the small windows was enough to read by.

On the first page was an overhead sketch of Ravenhill Court, showing the nine homes, each one labeled with the family's name.

The next few pages had drawings of some of the locations around Ravenhill, these too carefully labeled. There was Blue Clay Ravine, Ravenhill Ridge, Pirate's Cove...

The next pages showed drawings of the people living in Ravenhill Court. Peter was very good, and even without the names that he had meticulously printed beneath each picture, Ben easily recognized everyone.

Ben turned the page again and began reading of Peter's recent experiences, or more precisely about their experiences as seen through Peter's eyes. He skimmed these quickly, feeling a bit guilty about sneaking a look at the journal without asking. But it was important that he find out what was going on in Peter's head.

He stopped at an odd passage and read more slowly, more carefully:

> The laboratory was a large room, the walls lined with counters and glass-faced cabinets. There was a shelf rack filled with metal boxes fronted with levers, dials and buttons.

Ben felt a cold, tingling sensation spread throughout his entire body. *What laboratory?*

> Cables ran from the machine rack to a tall, rectangular framework the size and shape of a large doorway.

There was a panicked banging on the door and Ben nearly fell back off the bench and onto the floor.

Julie called out loud and desperate. "Ben! Ben! Open up!"

Ben hurried to the door and slid the latch aside. Julie reached in and grabbed Ben's arm even before the door was fully open.

"You gotta come!" She pulled at him. "Now. There's a spy sedan outside Peter's house."

"A what?"

"A shiny black car. Come on!"

Ben had to struggle to turn and get the door closed and locked before Julie had him scrambling down the trail.

They stumbled out into the street, coming from between the Margolis and Addison houses.

Peter was being led across his front yard toward a black sedan that was parked in the street in front of his house. The uniformed figures on either side of Peter were the associates that had been with Ashton at the ravine.

Ashton was speaking with Mrs. Murray on the porch. They appeared to be in calm conversation. She had her arms wrapped around herself, a cigarette held between her fingers.

Once they finished their exchange, Ashton placed a comforting hand on Mrs. Murray's arm, stepped off the porch and walked toward the car, following Peter.

Peter stopped beside the waiting car and looked up into the court. He had to have seen Ben and Julie, but gave no sign. A moment later he climbed into the back seat of the vehicle.

Ashton, one hand now on the roof of the sedan, heard the pounding footsteps, looked up and saw Ben and Julie running down the street toward him. Without acknowledging them, he climbed into the back seat beside Peter, and the vehicle pulled away from the curb.

Ben and Julie, still rushing headlong in the direction of the black sedan that was slowly heading out of the cul-de-sac, came to a stumbling, faltering stop.

They tried to catch their breath.

"Great..." said Ben, sucking in air, "Just great... what now?"

Julie nudged Ben with her elbow. She was looking back behind them, in the direction of the LaMothe house.

"Maybe he can tell us," she said.

Professor LaMothe was standing in front of his house. He wasn't looking at the activity going on down the street at the Murray's. He was watching Ben and Julie.

He turned about and walked back to his house, took the front steps one at a time. By the time he reached the large chair at the far end of the deck, Ben was at the steps, and Julie was right behind him.

Ben sat in the small deck chair near the Professor, but Julie chose to stand near the railing, arms folded. Her gaze was sharp and accusatory, as was her stance.

She let Ben talk first.

"What are they doing with Peter, Professor?" he asked. "Where are they taking him?"

The professor put on his most thoughtful face.

"How long have you known Louis, Ben?"

Ben and Julie both looked taken aback.

"Wha-- uh... I don't know... a while."

"What does that have to do with Peter?" asked Julie.

"Please," the Professor said gently. "You've known Louis for... *a while,* you say."

"Yeah. He's in my class."

The professor nodded sagely."And... his family lives in a house just outside the Court."

"Yeah, that's right. On the corner, across the street."

"Do either of you happen to remember when they moved into the house?"

Ben looked over at Julie. The two appeared to be trying to draw an answer from one another; unsuccessfully. Julie looked away from Ben then and turned a piercing glare on the professor.

"What is this about, Professor?"

"We'll get there, Julie. I promise." The professor spoke again to them both. "Do you recall the Bennett family moving in?"

"I don't know," said Ben. "I think so. I guess it had to have been a long time ago."

"In point of fact," said the professor, "it was a few days ago."

"Professor—" Julie grumbled.

"That's crazy," said Ben. "He's been in my class for, geez... for as long as I can remember."

"Louis Bennett has never been in your class."

Ben and Julie squirmed uncomfortably.

Something is very, very wrong...

"But we've know Louis for," Julie struggled to remember. "For... *always.*"

There was a moment of heavy silence, and then the professor leaned forward and spoke into that silence.

"You saw Louis for the first time in the clearing while on your way to the ravine in which you found the gateway."

"But I know him," Ben said pleadingly.

"Ben... Ben, listen to me. Prior to that encounter... Louis did not exist."

The hint of fear washed across Ben's face. Julie wrapped her arms around herself and took hold, as if to keep herself from fading away. It felt as though their world was turning into mist around them.

"I created him," the professor continued. "I created a fellow traveler, with all the complex issues and problems arising from within this time and place in our history."

"Are you... what Ashton told us..." Ben wasn't sure he wanted to know the answer. "It's true?"

"That would depend entirely on what Mr. Ashton told you."

Julie spoke in a faint whisper. "None of this is real," she said.

The professor leaned back in his chair. He looked at the young people standing in front of him as if examining them for flaws. He turned his attention then out beyond his covered deck, took in the quiet scene of the neighborhood. When he finally responded, his voice was calm and the tone was cool and low.

"Not the school that you attend, not the jobs that your parents go to each morning. Not that hint of the ocean that I smell in the air."

"That's not possible," said Ben.

"The world, and all that is taking place in the world, is illusion."

"How?"

"What does it mean?" asked Julie.

The professor continued to focus his attention on the neighborhood. "Nothing outside the Court is happening beyond the minds and imaginations of the adults in Ravenhill Court. People and places and things exist only during the moments when someone in Ravenhill Court is thinking of them."

"That..." Julie struggled to wrap her mind around it. "That sounds a lot like a dream."

The professor looked up into Julie's face and smiled, albeit sadly. "That's right. That's exactly right, dear girl. We are living in a dream."

Ben stepped out into the street. Behind him, on the lawn in front of the professor's deck, stood Julie and the Professor. Neither of them spoke. They watched Ben in silence, motionless.

Ben studied the neighborhood that was spread out before him, seemingly looking for something, anything, that would tell him for sure that none of what the professor had said was true.

Throughout Ravenhill Court, all had returned to normalcy. It was a bright, clear day.

Mrs. Murray was going back inside.

The garage door to the Foster house was open and Ben saw his dad walk around behind the old Mercury before stepping back into the shadow of the garage.

At the Margolis house, Mike climbed into his fifties Chevy. He backed it out onto the street and drove slowly toward the intersection at the entrance of the Court.

Naturally, Donna was waiting on the curb in front of her house. She waved joyfully at Mike as he passed. He ignored her, as always. Naturally...

Mr. Addison was kneeling beside his lawn mower, giving it a good going over before starting in up. Mr. Addison always seemed to be mowing his yard.

Professor LaMothe stepped up beside Ben.

"It's true," said Ben, barely above a whisper.

"Yes."

"But it's more than that. It's more than what you've told us. Isn't it?"

The professor answered hesitantly.

"I'm afraid so."

Chapter Ten

Looking up from the journal, the middle-aged Ben Foster saw that the sun had set and the evening beyond the front window was a dull, faded gray.

He set the journal aside and stood up. His body was more than half a century old and he could feel every day of it in his bones. He carefully stretched as he walked across the living room and stood at the large window that looked out on the neighborhood of Ravenhill Court.

Two people were sitting on the curb in front of the Foster house, their backs to Ben Foster. From behind, even in the gloomy dusk, Ben could see that they were both about his age; one was a woman with long brown hair, the other a black man.

Ben stepped out the front door and walked down the lawn. He sat beside them on the curb.

"Hey, Julie."

"Hey, Ben," she answered. There was a tinge of sadness in her voice. "Long time, huh?"

"Looks that way." Ben leaned forward and looked across at Louis. "Louis. A bit surprised to see you."

"Can't keep a good man down," said Louis. "I don't get this."

"Yeah... that's right. Crazy if you did. You weren't around for the last of it." Ben nodded at his sister. "Julie gettin' you caught up?"

"Enough to confuse me," said Louis. "We were created? We were part of a dream?"

Julie smiled grimly. "Only the adults in Ravenhill Court were real."

"And Peter," Ben corrected.

"Yes," said Julie. "And Peter."

Louis had a bit of a revelation. "His visions..."

Julie gave another thin smile in answer, but said nothing. Ben nodded once, and then again, but said nothing.

Louis continued to struggle to process it all. After a few moments, he indicated the abandoned neighborhood that they found themselves in.

"But what about--"

"They went home," said Julie, cutting him off.

"Home?"

"To the waking world. And we... we came here."

"Okay..." Louis still didn't have a firm grasp on it all. "So... and just where is here?"

"A generated universe," said Ben. "The world of the dream bubble that we had been living in before... sort of... not quite. All the same bits and pieces, put together by John Murray, to give us, the children of Ravenhill Court, a place to live out our lives." Ben leaned forward and slowly stood up. "What say we go inside?"

Ben led them up to the house and inside. Once in the living room, Ben silently beckoned them in. Julie smiled nostalgically as she stepped into the center of the room.

"It's smaller than I remember."

"That's what they say about going home again," said Ben.

Louis moved over to the large picture window and looked out on the neighborhood. Ben stepped up beside him.

"You okay?" he asked.

It was several seconds before Louis could respond.

"I don't think so."

Young Ben and Julie followed the same trail they had travelled on their two previous trips to the ravine. They reached the fork in the trail where they had first seen Ashton. The left fork would eventually take them to the ravine; the right fork would take them to wherever Ashton had come from.

Ben started up the right fork without slowing his steady pace. Julie followed silently behind him. After a few dozen yards, they came to wooden steps set into a steep hillside. A rickety wooden rail ran along the left side of the staircase.

At the top of the steps, they came out onto a clearing of dirt and dry grass. A dirt road emptied into the clearing from the right, and there was a worn tire path running from the road up to steel double doors, twelve feet high and ten feet wide, that were set into the hillside on the other side of the landing.

One of the doors stood ajar. Ben and Julie approached and Ben peered into the dark cavern.

"See anything?" asked Julie.

"Dark," said Ben. After only a moment's hesitation, he slipped inside. Again, Julie was right behind him.

The empty hall was fourteen feet wide, eighteen feet high, and extended into the mountain as far as they could see. It wasn't completely dark. There were small light fixtures hanging on the walls on either side about twelve feet up and spaced out every dozen paces. These provided just enough illumination to create shadows.

The massive room was empty. If not for the faintly glowing lamps, the place would seem to be abandoned. The floor and walls were made of concrete, and as Ben and Julie walked down the great tunnel, their footsteps echoed hollowly out into the darkness.

They saw a pair of lights hanging on the left wall in the distance, set lower than the other fixtures. As they came nearer, they saw that the fixtures were set to either side of a standard sized door.

Standing directly before it, Ben looked questioningly at Julie.

Julie shrugged a shoulder despondently. "What do we have to lose?"

With that, Ben reached out and took hold of the knob. It turned easily and he opened the door.

The long, narrow hallway was lit with fluorescent lights. Doors were set every sixteen feet, each inset with frosted glass panels.

Ashton was standing at the third door down, looking in their direction. He didn't seem at all surprised to see them. He gave a beckoning wave before disappearing through the door.

What do we have to lose?

Ben and Julie started down the hall. Reaching the door, Ben paused long enough to take an extra breath, but not so long that he might change his mind, before stepping through.

The laboratory was a large room. The walls were lined with counters and glass-faced cabinets. Drafting tables and more counters were scattered haphazardly around the room. Lamps and fixtures were set in strategic locations, offering plenty of light at their target locations but creating moving shadows.

The men who had escorted Ashton to the ravine days before were standing amidst the tables and counters. They watched silently as the two young people came further into the room.

"This is what Peter wrote about," Ben said softly. He moved into an open area beyond the counters. An electric generator was visible through an open doorway in a far wall. Cables ran from the other room into the laboratory and up to a shelf rack of metal boxes fronted with levers, dials and buttons. More cables ran from the machine rack over to a tall, rectangular framework the size and shape of a large doorway.

Several floor fans labored to cool the room, but at best were only managing to keep the air circulated.

Ashton stood in the center of the open area. Peter was standing beside him.

Julie stepped up beside Ben.

"Holy cow," she said.

"You said it."

Ashton half turned and looked at Ben, then looked to the shadows beyond, in the direction of the main door. He spoke to someone behind Ben and Julie.

"Their presence here must be your doing," he said.

Ben and Julie turned and saw Professor LaMothe standing just inside the doorway. He started across the room.

"I thought it only fair they be here for this," he said.

"How much do they know?"

"Not much beyond what you told them." The professor reached the center of the open area. He studied the gateway apparatus, and after a long time nodded in a begrudging sign of approval.

"Not bad," he said. "Considering you scratched it together with nothing but sixties tech."

"It should do the job," said Ashton.

He looked over at one of his assistants and nodded. The assistant went into the other room and started the generator. The sound threatened to drown out all other sound in the room until he pulled the door closed. A corner of the door had been cut away in order to allow the cabling to come through. This, like everything else, had the appearance of being makeshift.

Julie leaned close to Ben and whispered harshly. "You see? The professor is with them. Ben, we've been had."

Ben looked sharply at the professor. "What's going on, Professor?"

"Everything is going to be all right, son."

Ashton watched the assistant walk over to the machine rack, then looked over at Ben.

"We're going to try it your way, young man," he said, then turned an intense eye to the professor. "But hang onto your hat, LaMothe. If it doesn't work, we're committed. The bubble will collapse."

"Of course." Professor LaMothe nodded his head in slow agreement.

With that, Ashton turned again to his assistant standing in front of the equipment rack.

"Do it," he said.

The man turned and reached for the first dial. He slowly turned it the number "6". One band encircling the opening in the gateway brightened as power began to surge through it. He reached then for the second dial, calmly turned it to the "3".

The second band encircling the opening in the gateway apparatus sparked and sputtered as power surged through.

"So," said Julie, "Now we know what the numbers mean."

Professor LaMothe spoke quietly to Ben and Julie as he calmly watched the assistant move over to the third and final dial.

"John Murray has been attempting to build a permanent bridge between the waking world and the dream world in which we find ourselves."

The man at the equipment rack turned the third dial to "6". The third band encircling the gateway apparatus brightened as power surged through it.

The professor struggled to maintain a sense of calm. "There are two critical components to accomplishing this bridge," he said. "The first is to synchronize the portal on the outside with this one inside the bubble."

"But Professor," Ben looked confused. "If none of this is real, then this gateway isn't real. How can he create a bridge between a real gateway and one that isn't real?"

The professor smiled approvingly and lifted a finger. "Ah... therein lies the second critical component."

"The crystal," said Julie.

"The crystal," said the professor.

"But that's not real, either," said Ben.

"The crystal was a virtual representation of the data that comprises this dream bubble."

"I don't get it."

"The bubble is a collection of thousands of trillions of bits of information, a copy of which was contained in the data crystal. When Peter handed it to his father, and John carried it back across the portal threshold, the virtual essence of the crystal was lost, but the data within it was ascertained by John's equipment."

Adult Ben Foster was sitting in his father's old easy chair, a thermos cup held in one hand. He leaned forward and handed the thermos bottle and a large ceramic cup to Julie. He slid back in the chair then, took a sip of coffee and looked over at Louis.

"Peter's father was conducting shared dream experiments when something unexpected happened," said Ben. "A fully realized dream bubble formed. That's what they called it. A 'dream bubble'."

"I'm with you," said Louis, "sort of."

"Very exciting at first, this virtual world. Those within it living lives and the world going along its very merry way. Then, somehow, I don't know the details, John Murray got pulled out of our happy little existence. This created a cascade effect of problems back in the real world, and those involved in the dream experiment were trapped here."

Julie set her coffee mug down on the arm of the couch. "Life continued on in Ravenhill Court."

"While back in the real world, John Murray frantically sought a solution."

"Remember," said Julie. "Time passes at a different speed here than in the waking world."

"Which compounded the problem." Ben shifted forward in his chair, made certain that Louis was paying attention. "For you see, the primary dreamer, the person through which the dream bubble was formed, was Peter."

"And back in the real world," said Julie, "Peter was only a baby."

Louis, who had begun to think he might be getting a handle on this, was visibly shaken. "How could a baby create a world like Ravenhill Court? And everything else?"

"Peter was the channel," said Ben. "The contents of the bubble were generated collectively by all the members of the dream experiment."

Julie waited until Louis had a few moments to let all this sink in, then she slid forward until she was sitting on the edge of the couch. She spoke to both Louis and her brother.

"You know the bizarre thing? We really don't know how true to life any of what we experienced was."

"Our entire universe was just a dream," Ben agreed.

"Our universe was an accident."

Ashton gave his assistant a silent signal. The man lifted a wide-handled lever.

A spiderweb of electricity materialized within the opening of the gateway apparatus. A moment later, the portal opened and the entire room glowed a bright, clear blue, the blue emanating from within the gateway.

The room on the other side of the portal was filled with very advanced equipment, all high tech, all highly polished.

John Murray stepped into view.

Ashton stepped directly in front of the gateway. "All right, John," he said. "Good luck to you."

"Appreciate it." John looked beyond Ashton at the others in the laboratory. "Good to see you, Professor."

"John," the professor gave a slight bow.

John smiled at Peter. "Hey, kiddo." With that, he stepped to one side and began working at a computer that was sitting on a counter.

"Initiating," he said. Everyone was silent, anxiously watching John work on the other side of the portal. "Engaging."

The room on the other side went very white, then glowed a bright blue.

"All right," said John. "Beginning synchronization."

The images within the gateway flickered, popped, exploded into and out of existence.

The image settled.

John Murray smiled.

"Okay..." he said. "You ready?"

Ashton looked tense. This was where John Murray would try to have his system take control of the portal on both sides. "Moment of truth, John. I do wish you luck."

"Thank you, Ashton..." John said matter-of-factly. "But you're ready in any case."

Ashton allowed a quick glance at Peter before responding.

"We're ready." Ashton hesitated, then signaled to his assistant, who was patiently standing at the lever he had raised to first engage the gateway.

The assistant lowered the lever.

Other than a slight flickering of electricity along the three bands encircling the portal, there was no change.

"You have 'em both," Ashton told John Murray.

John was carefully monitoring his boards and monitors. Everyone on both sides of the gateway appeared to be holding a collective breath.

John finally gave a cautious nod. "Bridge is holding."

Ashton waited a few more seconds before finally allowing himself a slight smile.

"Fantastic, John."

"Certainly is," said John.

One of the three bands encircling the portal flickered.

"John?" Ashton asked anxiously.

"I'm on it."

Everyone waited. The professor stood stoically in the background. Those gathered around him watched nervously, uncertain as to what was going on.

"John?" Ashton repeated. He placed a hand gently on Peter's shoulder.

"It's the time differential algorithm," said John. "Give me a second."

"You only have a second."

John continued to work frantically at his computer.

The image flickered again.

John Murray looked up at Ashton. He looked calm but crestfallen.

"The time flow on your side isn't static," he explained. "There's no way the algorithm can adapt." He glanced again at one of his monitors, then spoke coolly. "Collapse imminent."

"I understand," said Ashton. "I am really sorry, John."

Ben, standing directly beside Professor LaMothe, had an idea of what this meant. "Professor?"

The professor didn't respond, couldn't look down into the questioning face of the boy.

Ashton spoke evenly. "I'm sending Peter over."

John Murray wouldn't be able to stop the collapse of the bubble, but he wasn't quite finished.

"Not yet!"

"If we don't get him to the other side before the bubble collapses, we're all--"

"I know! I know!"

"Then what--"

"I can still save the children."

"How?"

John Murray was too busy to respond.

Julie moved nearer the professor.

"What does he mean?" she asked.

The professor, after a moment's hesitation, answered without looking away from the portal.

"Peter must be awakened. He must pass through the portal before it closes or those on the dream side will never reintegrate... and we will never wake."

"The children, Professor. What about the children?"

"When the bubble collapses..."

Ben spoke with a sense of finality. "Like the rest of the dream... we will cease to exist."

The professor did not acknowledge the comment. He said nothing further, focused his attention again fully on the gateway and on John Murray, who was hurrying frenziedly about in the laboratory in the real world.

Ashton took a hesitant step nearer the portal, bringing Peter with him.

"John?" he urged anxiously.

"I got it!" John blurted. "I got it! Send him!"

Ashton slid his hand from Peter's shoulder to the middle of his back and pushed him gently but firmly toward the gateway.

Peter looked lost. Stumbling nearer the portal, he turned his head and looked back at Ben and Julie. He became a dark silhouette in front of the bright blue of the gateway.

Ben lifted a hand to bid Peter goodbye, but Peter was already turning his head forward.

Ben lowered his hand back to his side.

Peter stepped through.

"Done!" Ashton called out.

At that moment, the gateway silently shut down.

A heartbeat later, Ashton vanished. There was no sound, no sudden flash. He just wasn't there anymore.

His assistants disappeared.

Professor LaMothe took a deep breath. Ben turned to look up at him, but he wasn't in time. The professor was gone.

The room grew deadly quiet. Not even the sound of the generator in the other room could be heard. Ben looked around them in quiet desperation, eventually faced Julie.

"What do you think is going to happen?" he asked.

There was a very faint whispering noise, as of a light breeze blowing through trees that were still clinging to dry leaves.

The sound grew steadily louder.

"Julie?"

Julie turned slowly about, but could see nothing that would cause the sound. She looked over at Ben and shook her head in answer.

The walls around them slowly faded, turning a misty gray. The mist was emptiness... a void.

The void crept in on them from all directions. As it did, objects dematerialized, faded into nothing.

Julie tried her best to give her brother a comforting smile.

"I guess I'll see ya' later, Ben."

The void enveloped everything.

Chapter Eleven

Adult Ben Foster leaned against the wall beside the front window. He looked calmly out at the neighborhood.

Julie and Louis were sitting on the other side of the living room. Louis was watching Ben, but Julie was looking down, her hands resting in her lap.

Ben let out a half-satisfied sigh. "John Murray had managed to create this... *world*... just in time. He got us out."

"S'pose so," said Julie.

"We're here."

"Yeah..." Julie brought her hands up and folded her arms.

Ben looked questioning at his grown sister. "Yeah..."

Louis didn't like the sound of this. "What's that supposed to mean?" he asked. He didn't direct his question to one or the other. He would accept an answer from either one.

Ben shrugged and turned back to the window.

Julie leaned back in her seat.

Louis was growing perturbed. "Hey. We <u>are</u> here... right?"

"We're here," said Ben.

"Well okay, then."

The three of them grew quiet again. The room, the house, the neighborhood, the world, all fell into a heavy silence. Julie and Louis settled back in the couch. Ben continued to study the scene outside.

When he spoke again, he didn't look back in the room. "I have the weirdest feeling," he said. His words sent barely a ripple through the quiet, and yet there was an ominous quality to the words.

"Yeah, well I was fine until a minute ago," said Louis.

Ben grinned, but continued to look outside. "Sorry," he said apologetically.

The silence closed in again, but Louis wasn't going to let it stay.

"You can't just say something like that and then drop it, Ben."

"It feels like... it's almost as though..." Ben let the sentence fade.

Julie picked up the thought. "As though one second you're in the laboratory, and the next you're here."

Ben stared curiously at Julie, deciphering her words. He struggled with the concept.

"Something like that."

Louis was growing increasingly unsettled, as he often did when around these two. "I don't like where this is going," he mumbled, almost to himself.

Ben was still leaning beside the window, but he was now looking at his companions in the room.

"I feel like I have the history of all these years, but no real memories of them passing."

"Like data," said Julie.

"Like data." Ben visibly struggled with his thoughts for a long time. He finally pushed himself from the wall and stepped directly in front of the window. He stuffed his hands into his pockets. "I know that Mike Margolis fought in some war and became a hero. His brother Tony was a state senator, but had to resign in disgrace. I don't remember why. Donna is working on her third marriage, has four kids, most of 'em grown; named the first one Mike."

Ben looked over his shoulder at Louis. "You're an associate professor," he said, then looked at Julie before turning back to the window. "You're a lawyer for an advocacy group."

"And you're a writer," said Julie. She tried to remember, but... "I have nothing about Peter... he's not here."

"You and I spend all our holidays together," said Ben. "The fact that we never see our parents never seems to come up in conversation."

Louis slid forward and sat on the edge of the couch. "If John Murray created this world for us, why not put our parents in it?"

"He duplicated the world of the dream bubble, including us," said Ben.

"But our parents weren't of the dream bubble," finished Julie. "They were real."

Louis let that settle in for a few seconds before bringing it back around to the larger question.

"Real or not, have we lived our lives all these years or not?"

"I don't think so," Julie said flatly.

"But..."

"John Murray didn't want to abandon the children," said Ben. "Born in the dream bubble or not. He could save us, but then what? A neighborhood of children, suddenly without parents? But what if he could add in an algorithm that could extrapolate out likely events running out from the moment of the bubble's collapse, and create an alternate world set decades later? Children all grown up?"

"He gave us lives lived," said Julie.

"I don't know, man," Louis said, still unsure. "That's way too weird."

"Maybe, but it answers this odd feeling I have," said Ben.

"I agree," said Julie. "But... then... we don't know what we're supposed to feel like. What's normal?"

At the sound of an engine, Ben turned around again to the window. He watched a fifty year old moving van come into Ravenhill Court. It stopped a house or two up from the Foster house.

Julie and Louis came up beside Ben. They watched a middle-aged woman step out of the passenger side. A moment later, a similarly aged man came around from the other side of the vehicle and studied the neighborhood.

"I think that's Mike," said Ben.

"Could be," said Louis.

Julie watched the activity in the street for a few moments, then frowned, crinkled her brows.

"I have a question for you..." she said.

Louis looked at her expectantly. Ben, however, continued to look out the window. He had a hardened expression on his face.

Julie let out a sigh, then another. "What are we doing here?" she finally asked.

"What do you mean?" asked Louis.

"What made you come here, Louis? Today?"

"I..." Louis had no answer.

"And what about Mike? He's moving back? On the same day that we just happen to show up?"

Ben spoke softly but with a calm certainty. "We're all coming back... we're coming home."

An early sixties era car pulled into the driveway of the Osborne home across the street. A grown Donna Osborne climbed out of the passenger, her husband from the driver's side.

Donna looked a bit bewildered.

Julie gently clasped her brother's arm.

Ben, Julie and Louis looked silently out on the neighborhood that would be their home for as long as this virtual world existed.

Julie sensed something in her brother and looked up at him. She saw a warm grin slowly appear on his face.

"What is it?"

Ben tried to dismiss the question, but Julie was intrigued by his growing change of emotion. She leaned in and raised a brow in one her 'come on, give...' expressions.

"It's nothing, really..." he said. "I was just wondering, you know... what they're doing out in the real world right now. I mean, think about it... what if only a few seconds have passed since they left?"

Unsettled looks spread across the faces of both Julie and Louis.

Ben watched side-glance as Julie slowly tilted her head slightly and glanced upward.

"Helloooo?" she called out softly.

Ben shook his head and grinned openly. "Geez, Julie..."

Louis managed to relax then, and put on a genuine smile of his own.

"Man, this is too weird," he said.

Ben continued to look out on the activity going on in street below them, but couldn't help but glance a bit anxiously up at the evening sky overhead...

end

KHDZ

Chapter 1

The station floor of KHDZ occupied a large, cavern-like room; wherever the walls were visible shown reddish-brown, rough-hewn rock. Several small program sets for the locally produced television shows lined one wall. There was a cooking show, a morning talk show, and others. Oddly, there were no cameras.

A walkway ran along the opposite wall, emptying into hallways at both corners.

There was a small cluster of desks in the center of the room, one occupied by a middle-aged, slightly balding man with a disheveled look.

Set in a third wall was the station manager's office, made evident by the words 'Mr. Henderson Station Manager' stenciled onto the smoked glass window set in the door.

There was a small waiting area with two chairs outside the manager's office.

John Smith sat in one of the chairs, a manila folder in his lap. John was in his early thirties. He looked out of place and more than a little uncomfortable.

Troy, a three and half foot tall, gnome-like man, was sitting in the other chair. He crossed his impossibly thin, spindly legs and smiled at John. It was a friendly smile.

This made John even more uncomfortable, but he managed an awkward smile in response.

Troy finally broke the silence. "Helluva day, eh?"

John attempted another smile. He was only half successful.

"It could have gone better," he said.

Troy nodded slowly, knowingly. He let out a long, drawn out sigh. "Ah... yep."

At that moment, the station manager's door opened. Mr. Henderson stuck his head through the opening. When he saw John, he stepped fully out of his office.

He was a large, middle-aged man with an air of administrative authority about him. He looked at John with some sense of puzzlement.

"Who are you?" he asked.

John stood. "John Smith."

Mr. Henderson looked suspiciously around the station. Satisfied that everything was as it should be, at least for the moment, he turned his attention back to the newcomer.

"That a fact," he managed. "Waddya want?"

John handed Mr. Henderson the folder that he had been holding. The station manager cautiously took it, opened it and glanced at several of the pages. After a few moments' study, he silently indicated that John should step into his office.

He spoke over his shoulder before disappearing through his door.

"Get to work, Troy."

Troy stood, grinned and gave a playful salute.

"Right away, sir."

The manager's office was sparsely furnished. There was a desk and chair, several file cabinets, and a guest chair. John waited as Mr. Henderson walked around his desk, continuing to look through the contents of the folder, positioning himself finally behind his desk.

"Hmm. Wow. Tough break, Mr. Smith." He sat down, indicated the guest chair. He spoke casually as he closed the folder and tossed it onto the desk, watched John Smith sit. "Sorry about Troy. Owner's cousin."

"No problem," said John, rather noncommittally.

"So tell me, what's an associate producer, and what have I done to deserve one?"

"I don't know."

"You do know where you are..." urged Mr. Henderson.

"I guess so," said John. "But it's a mistake."

"Yeah." Mr. Henderson pointed to the folder now sitting atop his desk. "In your case, that's actually true." He warily eyed John. "Odd, really. I've never heard of such a thing."

"My luck," said John.

"Screwed up your paperwork? That's gotta suck."

"It does."

Mr. Henderson was still not completely certain about this strange turn of events. He spoke hesitantly. "So they give you to me?"

"Just until they get it straightened out. Shouldn't be too long, you think?"

"Yeah, right." Mr. Henderson pursed his lips then, breathed noisily, as if trying to decide whether to accept this unprecedented situation for what it appeared to be. "It's better than waiting, you know, *down the hall.*"

John thought he understood what that meant, but he couldn't be sure. Still, he nodded in silent agreement.

Mr. Henderson studied John a moment longer. "Associate producer, eh? You ever done any associate producing, Mr. Smith?"

John shrugged in silent answer.

"Ya' ever been involved in television?" asked Mr. Henderson.

"Was in a studio audience once."

Mr. Henderson's expression slowly shifted to: *what the hell am I supposed to do with this guy?* It hung there for several seconds before he finally came to a management decision. He slid his chair back and stood up.

"That'll have to do then, won't it?" He held out a hand and they shook. "Welcome to Hell, John Smith."

Mr. Henderson came out of his office, John following two paces behind. The station manager spoke over his shoulder without looking back. The words sounded canned and oft-repeated.

"KHDZ. Serving Hades and outlying suburbs. Broadcasting local programming 24 hours a day. Over there are several of our sets." He turned and indicated one of the passageways. "The front lobby is down that hall. It's where you came in. It's the only way in." He indicated the other passageway. "The... *you know...* is down that way."

John glanced nervously at the threshold leading to '*you know*', and quickly turned back to the center of the station floor. They walked to middle of the room, toward the one occupied desk.

Hector stood and held out his hand. "Hey," he said, half nodding.

Mr. Henderson spoke as Hector and John shook hands. "This is John Smith. He'll be associate producing for a while."

Hector looked confused.

Mr. Henderson shook his head. "I have no idea."

John jumped in. "I'm just here until they get the paperwork sorted out."

Hector looked even more confused. He slowly sat back down. "Sure."

Mr. Henderson indicated the empty space beside Hector's desk. "We'll put you here," he said to John.

He saw Janice the Janitor coming from the hall leading to the lobby and continuing toward the hall that led to '*you know*'. She had a push broom in hand. She was carrying it, not using it.

Janice was in her early thirties, attractive, dressed in clean coveralls. Her long hair was pulled back into a ponytail; her makeup was enough to do the job without anything extra.

"Janice!" Mr. Henderson called out. "I need you to bring this man a desk."

"I clean the station," said Janice, not stopping. "I don't furnish it."

"Then find Troy," growled Mr. Henderson.

Janice continued across the way, and the others could just make out the words: *yes, sir. Certainly, sir.*

With that, Mr. Henderson looked around the room as if evaluating to ensure the situation was well in hand. Satisfied, he started back toward his office.

"Take him under your wing, Hector," he said, then to John: "Welcome aboard, John Smith."

John watched the station manager return to his office, then turned to look down at Hector.

Hector grinned at the new arrival. "Hey," he said.

John looked up from Hector and glanced around the room. He saw the big "KHDZ" sign that hung on one wall.

"A television station?"

"We develop all our own shows, right from here."

"But... that's crazy. Isn't it?"

"The owner would disagree." Hector indicated a large, heavy plank door directly below the 'KHDZ' sign. "Mr. Horn," he said.

John looked apprehensively toward the door. A small plaque read 'private'.

"KHDZ," said Hector, leaning back in his chair again. "Serving Hades and outlying suburbs. Broadcasting local programming 24 hours a day."

"So I heard," said John.

"Welcome to the organization. Make yourself comfy."

"I'm not going to be around long enough to get comfy. As soon as the paperwork gets straightened out, I'm gone." John pointed heavenward. "Ya know?"

"Sure." Hector turned his attention to Miss Constance, who was approaching from the direction of the program sets.

Miss Constance was a tall, attractive, middle-aged woman who used makeup and attire in an attempt to not look middle-aged.

"A new face," she said cheerily.

Hector remained sitting, but spoke formally. "Miss Constance. Meet John Smith, recently arrived from topside."

John reached out and shook hands with Miss Constance. "Just here temporarily," he stated quickly. "Until the paperwork gets straightened out."

"Of course, dear," she answered coolly.

"Miss Constance is the hostess of 'Up All Night with Miss Constance'," said Hector.

"Ah. I see," said John.

"And just what is it that you will be doing here, John Smith?" asked Miss Constance.

"Call me John."

"If you like," she said smoothly, raising a brow.

"I guess I'm going to be the associate producer."

"Is that so?" Miss Constance looked to Hector. "We don't have a producer, do we Hector?"

Hector shook his head calmly from side to side and Miss Constance turned her attention back to John.

"We don't have a producer, John," said Miss Constance. "We only have our station manager. In order for there to be an associate producer, I would think that we would first need a producer."

"I don't know. I suppose," said John. "I mean, that makes sense."

"Come to think of it, I should think my program would have its own producer. Yes?"

John looked as though he had been cornered. "I guess so."

Miss Constance smiled sweetly. "How would you like to be my producer, John?"

"I don't know."

"Come, come dear. A promotion. And this being your first day."

"Well, I—"

"Enough said." Miss Constance turned away dismissively and started toward Mr. Henderson's office.

"Yes," said Hector, a quiet calm. "That would be Miss Constance."

Chapter 2

John and Hector stood before a television monitor mounted on a wall in the station floor. Behind them, Mike Johansen stepped around the desk and came up beside them.

"Mr. Smith," he said with a nod. He was a well-groomed man in his early sixties, with a smooth, polished look. Mike was the host of "*Good Morning with Mike Johansen*".

"Mr. Johansen," said John. "I caught part of your show this morning. Interesting."

"Thank you." Mike's attention was focused on the television. "Did I miss it?"

"Jim just asked him the final question," said Hector without looking away from the monitor.

Jim, host of "*The Hot Seat*", had an excited, happy voice no matter what the circumstance. "Oh... I'm sorry, Bob. That's wrong," he said cheerily. "You know what that means... *that's right*... it's time for..."

The unseen audience joined in for Jim's finale: "... *the Hot Seat!*"

This was immediately followed by Bob's horrifying scream: "Ahhhhh!!!"

John, Hector and Mike Johansen all grimaced. For Hector and Mike it appeared more playful than genuine.

"That's all for today, folks," Jim said cheerily. "Join us next time, when Bob once again takes—"

The unseen audience again joined in with a roaring cheer: "... *the Hot Seat!!!*"

John, Hector and Mike turned away from the television monitor. John looked horrified.

"What kind of sadistic game show was that?"

"Hector spoke matter-of-factly. "The Hot Seat," he said. He stepped around behind his desk and sat down.

"What'd you expect, son?" asked Mike.

"I didn't expect any of this." John pointed accusingly at the monitor. "But that..."

"Yes." Mike grimaced and grinned at the same time. "Poor ole Bob."

"Every day?" asked John.

"Every day," said Mike.

"Until he wins," Hector sighed.

"Then what?"

Mike sat on the edge of Hector's desk and shrugged a shoulder. "Then they invite some other poor shmuck from down the hall."

John's gaze kept returning to the television monitor, now turned off. "How long as Bob been... *losing?*"

"Oh, must be what?" Mike looked thoughtfully over at Hector.

"About a year." Hector shrugged. "A little more."

"It'll be a sad day around here when Bob leaves," said Mike, standing. He made ready to get about his business. "He's been a ratings bonanza."

John watched in disbelief as Mike Johansen strolled away, heading in the direction of the wall of sets, finally disappearing around a corner.

"I can see why he's here," said John.

Hector smiled an understanding smile. "Mike's not so bad," he said. "And he puts on a heck of a good program."

"Yes. I saw." He said mocking, "I'm Mike Johansen, and you're watching '*Good Morning with Mike Johansen*'."

"That's pretty good," said Hector. "Don't let Mike catch you doing that. He's got a copyright on it and it's fully registered with the head office."

A desk suddenly appeared from the passageway. The tiny figure of Troy was hunched behind it, pushing it noisily across the floor. He maneuvered it around the other furniture and slid it into position beside Hector's desk.

He grinned a satisfied, gnome-like grin. "One desk, as requested."

John placed the fingertips of one hand hesitantly on the top of the desk, as if not ready to accept what this meant, not ready to acknowledge that he now had a place here.

He gave a silent thank you nod. Troy proudly strutted off.

Hector waited just long enough for Troy to disappear around the corner before commenting. He turned slowly about in his chair, spoke in a calm statement.

"That desk works better with a chair, John."

There was a golden glow to the tunnel that came from unseen lighting. John walked down the center of the hallway, occasionally glancing down at a small piece of paper with his room number scribbled on it.

He stopped at '63C' and stuffed the paper into his jacket pocket. He pulled out an ornate key and unlocked the door.

His cell was a small, high-ceilinged cave. A faded area rug covered the center of the floor. There was a bed, a desk and chair, and a dresser. Another door opened to an empty closet, and an open archway led to a small bathroom.

John was surprised to see a closed curtain on the far wall. Behind the curtain, however, he found only more rock. He let it fall back into position and wandered over to the bed. He sat down with a heavy plop.

"It could be worse," he mumbled. "Not much. But worse."

Mike Johansen sat in one of two comfortable easy chairs on the set of his program 'Good Morning with Mike Johansen'. The Mayor of Hades sat in the other chair, a large coffee cup in hand. He was an older, overstuffed gentleman. He had a pleasant appearance about him. He looked very comfortable on the set, very familiar with the surroundings.

Behind them was a red stone wall. Hanging on the wall was a sign that read 'Good Morning with Mike Johansen'. To one side of the set was the entrance to a dark tunnel leading to backstage.

As with all the KHDZ programming, there were no cameras visible.

"We're back," said Mike Johansen, "and we're talking with the Mayor about plans for the upcoming celebrations. Mr. Mayor, before the break you were hinting that your office has a few new events in the works. Care to elaborate?"

"And spoil the surprise?" The Mayor grinned playfully. "You know me better than that, Mike. Let me just say that we're doing our best to make this the finest Founder's Day ever."

"You're setting the bar awfully high, Mr. Mayor. I've been through a few real gems in my time."

"And I've been personally involved in the planning of two hundred and ninety six of them."

"Has it really been that long?" asked Mike. "I can hardly believe it."

"It's true. It's true. In four months, I'll have served this community as its mayor for two hundred and ninety six years."

There was the sound of light applause in the background.

"And you've served us so very well, Mr. Mayor," said Mike Johansen.

More light applause.

"I appreciate your kind words," said the Mayor.

"Well deserved, sir." Mike shifted position and put on an investigative look. "Can you tell us who we might expect to see standing at the speaker's podium this year?"

"I know what you're asking, Mike," said the Mayor, slowly shaking his head from side to side, "and I'm afraid I can't give you a definite 'yes' on that. I don't know whether or not he'll make it back in time. What I am certain of is that he will try."

"So, you haven't spoken with him, then?"

"I wouldn't know how to contact him. Would you?"

At that, there was more light, gentle laughter in the background.

Mike Johansen grinned slyly. "I'll get my staff right on it." Once the follow-up laughter had faded, Mike's smile also faded. "Seriously, though... he has been away quite a long time."

"To our loss, Mr. Horn has been unable to attend the last two of our Founder's Day celebrations."

"And we all know how much he enjoys them," said Mike, smiling genuinely.

"Perhaps this year, Mike. I certainly hope so."

John came into the station floor. He saw Hector sitting at his desk, watching the conclusion to Mike's *Good Morning* show on the monitor. He was calm and quiet, and seemed to be enjoying the program.

John heard Mike Johansen's voice coming over the speakers.

"You unquestionably speak for us all, Mr. Mayor," said Mike. "Well sir, it has been absolutely great talking with you, and I hope you'll come back to visit us again real soon."

"I certainly will, Mike," came the voice of the Mayor. "Thank you so much for having me."

Mike's tone changed as he turned his attention to the viewers. "Next up, we're going to taking a closer look at the *Bob* phenomenon. Bob is a favorite of KHDZ viewers, and of the staff here at the station. What is it about this exceptional individual that keeps us tuning in day after day? What makes Bob so hot? What makes Bob *sizzle*?"

There was pause for effect, then Mike spoke more formally. "We're back in sixty seconds."

The KHDZ blurb kicked in. The announcer's voice was a cross between Darth Vader and a BBC news anchor. "This is KHDZ, the source for news and entertainment, serving Hades and surrounding suburbs."

A twangy, irritating commercial jingle started up and John decided that he had more important things to do. He left Hector and walked to the hallway that led to the front lobby.

The lobby was long and narrow. Entering from the station floor, the only other door was set into the wall opposite, glass double-doors with a sign above it that read "Not an Exit".

Emily the Receptionist sat behind the counter facing the glass doors. She was a young woman with the constant look of boredom about her.

"Good morning, Emily," said John. "Anything come in for me this morning?"

Emily spoke flatly, exuding an air of indifference. "No."

"Has anything come in for Mr. Henderson about me?"

"No."

"Would you have told me if anything had in fact come in for Mr. Henderson about me?"

She gave a bored shrug. "Why not..."

"But it's been three days."

"I've been here two hundred years," Emily droned. "I've never gotten anything."

"But... I'm *expecting* this. As soon as the paperwork is cleared up—"

"Uh huh."

John Smith and Emily the Receptionist stared at each other in silence for several seconds. Emily's was blank. John's expression was tinged with anxiety.

He finally turned away from the counter in frustration.

"Thank you, Emily."

"Uh huh..."

Mr. Henderson was working at his desk when he heard a knock on his door.

"Come in," he said.

John entered the station manager's office and closed the door delicately behind him.

"Good morning, Mr. Henderson. Can I speak with you?"

Mr. Henderson glanced up from his paperwork. "I understand you've been annoying Emily."

"Uh..." Geez, that was fast.

Mr. Henderson leaned back in his chair. There was a hint of frustration in the manager's tired expression.

"John Smith. *Sir*. The bureaucracy in which you find yourself, in the very best of circumstances, is excruciatingly slow. The simplest of requests can take decades to see resolution. Now then... Sir... we come to your particular dilemma, for which there is no precedent. There is no process in place in which to resolve such a situation."

"But—"

"How long have you been here?"

"Three days."

"Three days." Mr. Henderson groaned a tired sigh. "Mr. Smith, it takes the bureaucracy of which I speak ten times three days to pass gas. It may be a thousand times three days before your situation rises to the top of some low-level administrator's overstuffed in-box. It may be a thousand times <u>that</u> before it arrives at the desk of someone who has even the slightest inkling of where your situation should actually be directed."

He leaned forward across his desk. "Shall I go on?"

"But sir—"

"I shall go on. At that point in the journey, your situation will have as yet even to be looked at. Still, we might choose to call it progress, as it will have by then at least made its way into the bureaucratic machine."

"Yes sir."

Mr. Henderson's gaze had just the faintest hint of empathy, but was mixed with impatience.

"You are going to be here while."

"Yes sir."

"Consider yourself fortunate that someone in this bureaucracy that we deride thought to put you here at the station to await resolution."

Mr. Henderson positioned himself over his paperwork, spoke one last comment as he returned to his work. "Reflect on the alternative; that you could instead be spending a few thousand years—"

"Yes. I know. Down the hall."

"Exactly. Down the hall."

John watched downcast as Mr. Henderson shuffled through files. The conversation was ended. The meeting was over.

John stood outside the manager's office, his back to the door. His shoulders sagged and he had a dejected look on his face.

He heard a woman's voice.

"Well that's just pathetic."

John looked up. Janice stood beneath the KHDZ sign, leaning on her broom. As ever, she was dressed in clean coveralls.

"Excuse me?" asked John.

"I don't think I've ever seen anyone come out of Henderson's office looking quite so pitiful. Did he eat your children?"

John didn't look as though he was going to respond to Janice's sarcasm, but finally put on as brave a face as was possible given the circumstances. "He clarified a few things for me," he said. "Thank you for your interest. Janice, is it?"

Janice gave a slight nod of the head and pushed off her broom, taking a step nearer to John. "Split a bagel?"

"What?"

"Not one of those rocks you get in the mess hall. I know a cave a few levels down that makes the greatest bagels ever." She planted her broom once again and leaned on it. "A quiet little café. Nice place to sort out any issues that might be bouncing around in your head."

"Sure," John said finally, stumbling for something, *anything*, a little wittier. But he had nothing. "Why not?"

They started toward the passageway. Janice spoke matter-of-fact as they walked.

"He's been known to do that, you know."

"Do what?"

"Eat children."

John and Janice sat at one of five small tables in the café, two coffee mugs and two halves of a bagel on the tabletop between them. One side of the little shop was open to the tunnel. Only one of the other tables was occupied; a man reading a newspaper. The paper was yellow.

The barista, a tall young woman with numerous piercings, stood behind the counter, appearing bored.

"I didn't know there were places like this," said John. "You know... in here, I mean."

"A café here and there, a deli or two, couple of shops." Janice lifted a brow and lowered her head conspiratorially. "Not officially, mind you. This is still a company town, after all; not really supposed to frequent non-sanctioned establishments. But then, if we had followed the rules, none of us would be here, would we? Present company excepted."

"Thanks." He pulled a piece of bagel off his half, put it in his mouth and chewed. "I still..." he fumbled for words. "A television station?"

"So you're okay with the idea of Hades, and that we're walking around in the afterlife, such as it is, but the concept of a television station somehow has you flummoxed?"

"No," he blurted, too quickly. "Yes... No, I'm not okay with any of this. None of it makes any sense."

"Haven't quite reached the acceptance stage," she stated knowingly.

John grew introspective. "Maybe I'm in a hospital," he thought aloud. "Back in the real world. I'm in mental limbo between life and death, and none of this is really happening."

"Speaking just for myself now, John, I can't say as I like that idea very much."

John Smith took another long sip of his coffee, glanced at the barista, at the man reading the newspaper, then out into the tunnel.

"Yeah, well, if I ever come out of it, I'll do my best to bring you out with me."

"Thanks. I'd appreciate that."

Chapter 3

John and Janice were still sitting at the small table. The bagel was gone, the coffee cups near empty. Behind the counter, the barista was resting her chin in an upturned palm.

The man reading the newspaper reservedly turned the page, folded the newspaper back and continued reading.

No one else had come into the café.

"If it wasn't so awful for you, it would be funny," said Janice. "I've been here over a hundred years... a hundred and twelve, actually... and I've never heard of such a thing."

"That's what Mr. Henderson said," grumbled John.

"He'd know. He's been around a lot longer than me."

"Just how long 'we talking, here?"

"Gotta be five, six hundred years, at least. He helped set up the station. That's been... sixty years?"

"And you've been here..." John shifted uncomfortably. "Janice, what did, uh—"

Janice quickly held up a silencing hand.

"Couple of unspoken rules here, John. Call it Hades etiquette. First, don't ask what brought someone down here. The reasons are usually messy; well, except for yours. Which is mildly amusing. But, you understand."

"Sure." *No I don't...*

"And some of us really are trying, each in our own small way, to make up for what we did topside."

"I understand."

Janice stared down at the remnants of her bagel, nodded slowly. "Well, even if you don't now, you will before too long."

"No, really. I get it."

"Good... good." She smiled thinly. "Second rule, guideline really, but strongly encouraged. We don't usually talk about what things were like up there at the time of our *relocation*."

"Okay... why?"

"You see, we all come here from very different times. The world was very different when I left it than when you left it."

"Sure, but why don't you want to know what's new up there?"

Janice took a moment, finally shrugged on shoulder. "We see enough. You can tell a lot, observing people when they come in."

"But there have been so many changes."

"I know that. Hey, the very existence of the television station. But... we're here. Forever. Really, what's the point?"

John studied the face across the table from him. At first he thought he might have an answer her question, but in the end he held his silence.

Judge Roy had a look that implied he had led a wild, maybe even dangerous life. His face was weathered and deeply lined; sharp, piercing eyes beneath heavy brow. Long, dark hair. He sat alone at a small table just in front of Miss Constance' Up All Night program set, empty now but for the gaudy purple couch that was the centerpiece of her show.

It was late at night, dark throughout the studio but for a few dim lights that managed to create more shadows than light.

Mr. Henderson stepped up to the table, sat in the chair opposite with a tired groan.

"One helluva day, Judge." He glanced about, up at the darkened stage, out into the shadows. "How was Miss Constance tonight?"

"Brilliant, as always," said the judge matter-of-factly.

"Yes, well, that's why she makes the big money, eh?"

That brought a low chuckle from Judge Roy, the hint of a smile.

"So, Henderson..." he started. "What's up with the new guy? Connie's... *producer*." The word 'producer' sounded unseemly.

"Smith? Smith's all right."

"A mistake in the paperwork?" he asked accusingly. "I don't think so."

"Looks legit on the face of it. That's what counts, what with the way of things. Assigned as my associate producer before Miss Constance grabbed him up. Hell, I didn't know what to do with him. Glad to give him to her."

"Come on, Henderson. Sent down my mistake? I don't buy it for a second. Do you?"

A shrug of a shoulder from Mr. Henderson. "Well, he for sure doesn't belong here, and that's for a fact. Now, as for the mix-up in the paperwork? Yeah... that's not something you see every day."

"My point exactly." Judge Roy grumbled.

Mr. Henderson let out another long, heavy sigh. "Doesn't matter. However he ended up down here, he's ours now."

"There's ways to take care of that, my friend."

"You keep your hands off, Judge," said Henderson, his voice low. He thought a moment. "For now."

Judge Roy growled to himself, shifted slowly about in his chair. He frowned.

"I'll not go out of my way," he said grudgingly. "But there's no promise, should he cross my path."

"Geez, Roy. What's got you all worked up?" He studied the judge a moment. He grinned. "You're not thinking he and Miss Constance—"

"Nothing to do with Connie," Judge Roy stated sharply. "I just don't trust him. You said it yourself. He doesn't belong down here."

"Well, don't you worry. Looks to me like Janice has him all wrapped up. He won't be straying far."

"Janice, huh?" Judge Roy had to smile at that. "The boy know what he's in for?"

"He may have an idea."

"You know damn well it wasn't her anarchist leanings got her sent down, Henderson. That woman has some serious issues."

"This coming from Captain Jonas Roy, terror of the seven seas."

Judge Roy shrugged. "It was a living."

Mr. Henderson leaned back in his chair, grew thoughtful.

"Truth be told," he said quietly. "If he'd taken any serious thought to the matter of all his newfound friends and colleagues, he'd be huddled in a corner about now."

Judge Roy now also leaned back, let out a contented sigh.

"That works for me."

The "Debbie's Kitchen" program set consisted of a high stone counter and a massive stone hearth set into the back wall of rough-hewn rock.

Debbie stood behind the stone counter, the hearth rising up behind her. She looked like she was in her twenties, but of course appearances were very misleading.

She was petite, had a child-like face, brown hair with bangs. She had a bubbly personality.

"Hello, everybody! Welcome to Debbie's Kitchen. I'm Debbie. Do I have a great show for you! I sure do."

She leaned against the counter and smiled. "Today we're going to shine the bright Debbie Light on a problem we've all had to face again and again and again." She gave an exaggerated knowing nod. "Some of you may already have guessed what I'm talking about, yes?"

Debbie paused for a calculated two seconds. "I'm speaking of the historic dilemma of ten hot dogs and eight buns. Uh-huh! You set out to prepare a nice meal, and if you're like me, you want everything organized just so..." As she talked, Debbie simulated the actions that she was describing. "You place your package of hot dogs on the counter. You place your package of buns right beside your hot dogs. You open the hot dogs, you open the buns, and what do you find?"

Debbie looked as if she was expecting an answer from the unseen television audience.

"Ten hot dogs, eight buns." Heavy disappointment. "I mean, really... what do you do now?"

Another two seconds of calculated pause, and Debbie perked up, straightened up, and put on a big Debbie grin.

"Well, I have the answer! When we return, I'm going to show you what to do with those two extra wieners. Stay right where you are! I'll be right back!"

Out on the station floor, John and Janice stood in front of the television monitor mounted high on the wall. Behind them, Hector sat at his desk, diligently going about his work.

John had a slightly stupefied look on his face, while Janice looked somewhat bored. To her, it was all quite familiar.

"That's Debbie," she said, in a flat, unemotional tone.

"Yes," John said numbly.

"I don't think she's all there."

"No." They turned away from the monitor, started across the station floor. On the far side of the floor, Debbie's set was visible. "It's all a joke though, right?"

They passed by Hector, who spoke without looking up from his work. "Remember where you are," he said dryly.

"Not many people care one way or the other about her show," said Janice. "Even if they did, no one is going to say anything."

They stopped in front of Mr. Henderson's office. Janice leaned close to John. "Rumor is that Debbie is Mr. Horn's daughter."

John turned his head sharply in the direction of the heavy wooden door to the office of the opposite wall. He looked then across the room, to the opposite wall. Debbie was standing behind her kitchen counter holding a limp hot dog in one hand.

He turned back to Janice. "You're kidding."

Janice shrugged noncommittally. "That was the rumor going around when the station started up."

John looked again across the cavernous room. Debbie was waving the hot dog above her head.

John came out of the station manager's office, wandered over to his desk.

Hector was sitting on the edge of his own desk, arms folded, eyes glued to the television monitor. John stood beside him, curious to see what had Hector so enthralled.

Hector was watching the soap opera "Moments of Our Nonexistence".

Bill and Joan were on the screen...

"Bill... oh, Bill..." said Joan tearfully, dramatically.

"Joan, Joan..." said Bill, just as dramatic.

"Oh, Bill..."

"Joan... why do you turn from me?" Long pause. "Joan?"

"You know why, Bill! You know why!"

The program cut dramatically to the soap opera's blurb, spoken smoothly and eloquently by the show's unseen narrator:

"Like lava through the flume, so flow the mindless Moments of Our Nonexistence."

Hector used the remote to mute the television, stood and returned to his chair behind his desk. He sat, a satisfied look spreading across his face.

"Hey, John," he said, almost as if noticing John for the first time. "So, what did Mr. Henderson have to say? Is he finally puttin' you to work?"

John dropped down into his own chair. He leaned over his desk, his expression much more somber than Hector's.

"That depends very much on your definition of the word work."

"Yeah," said Hector, a faint smile spreading across his face. "Miss Constance gettin' what she wants, is she?"

"He was glad to have something to assign me to."

"Yeah, well... *temporary*, right?"

John ignored the sarcasm, with some difficulty.

"The extent of my duties," he began. "Come up with a crappy movie for Miss Constance to '*offer up to her audience*' each night, see to it that she has strawberries or cherries or grapes or something to munch seductively on while she 'heavy breathes' to said audience... and, finally, see that she has an appropriately alluring night garment to wear each night as she lounges upon her purple couch."

"Sounds like an associate producer to me," said Hector.

"Really?"

"Come on man. Hell if I know." Hector began sorting through papers on his desk. "At least I don't have to do it anymore."

Chapter 4

John stepped through the narrow archway from his bathroom into the main room of his small quarters. He was dressed in pants and no shirt, had a bath towel over one shoulder and his hair was wet. A hint of warm moisture hung in the air.

He stopped short at the sight of Troy lounging comfortably across the bed, resting on one elbow.

"What the—"

"Good morning, John Smith!" Troy said, as pleasant as could be.

"Troy, what are you doing in my room?"

Troy pointed to a sport jacket that was draped over the back of the only chair.

"Miss Constance asked me to bring that to you," he said, then winked slyly. "She wants her producer to look snazzy..."

"Yeah? That doesn't really answer my question, though, does it?"

Troy sat up. "I don't know what you mean."

"You can't just come into my room," John said sharply.

Troy looked truly perplexed. "Why not?"

Which truly startled John Smith. "Because I said so."

"Really?"

"Yes. Really."

"You don't like me?"

"That's not the point." John pointed at the door. "You knock on the door. If I'm here, I'll open it. If I do open it, I'll ask you in."

Troy thought about that for a moment, intently and very seriously.

"I see," he said at last. "Seems an odd way to go about it, if you ask me."

"I'm not asking you."

Troy slid to the edge of the bed and slowly stood. He gave John a genuinely hurt look, lowered his head and started toward the door.

"Troy..." John sighed loudly. "Troy, I'm sorry. It's just..."

Troy gave a half-glance back to John, but continued his slow, plodding march to the door.

John tried again. "Listen, I have a thing about my space, and this room is my space. That's important to me. All right?"

Troy reached the door. He hadn't yet recovered from the hurt. "Sure, John Smith." He gave a nod to the sport jacket. "I'd wear that, if I were you. You hurt Miss Constance' feelings, you'll regret it. Know what I mean?"

"Sure," John said cautiously.

Troy opened the door, took one step through the threshold and stopped. He poked his head back into the room.

"I hear you're spending time with Janice," he said soberly.

"Is that a problem?" asked John, back on defense.

"No." Troy managed a half-smile. "No, I suppose not. But you might want to stay on your toes with that one."

"Why?"

"I like you, John Smith." Troy shrugged his pointed shoulders. "I wouldn't want to see you get hurt."

"That's ridiculous."

"Just sayin'."

John watched the door close. He looked over at the sport jacket that was so carefully draped over the back of the chair.

After a quick glance at the door to make sure that Troy wasn't going to unexpectedly return, he stepped over to the chair and lifted up the jacket.

It wasn't bad... not gaudy, not too flashy, not too conservative. A bit of quality and class with just a hint of restraint.

Hector came out of Mr. Henderson's office, walked over to his desk and sat down. Across from him sat John Smith, dressed in a nice sport jacket, a stack of DVDs on his desk. John absently set another atop the stack.

"Picked one out for tonight?" he asked John.

John spoke wearily. "Thought I'd go with 'Vampires from Bikini Island'."

Hector smiled approvingly. "Oh, I may just have to stay up for that one."

"Don't toy with me, Hector."

"Come on, John... you gotta learn to get into your work. You have to do whatever it takes to keep the job fun and interesting."

"You say so..."

"Hey. Look around. You're here. Who knows for how long? Years at least. Could be centuries. Could be—" he gave a questioning shrug of the shoulders. "Ya' know? Might as well make the best of it."

"Peachy." John looked warily at the stack of DVDs on his desk.

Troy appeared on the station floor, coming in from the hallway, and continued on the walkway. He looked a bit agitated. He stopped midway along the wall, near the massive wooden door to Mr. Horn's office.

He looked into the center of the station, tilted his head slightly as he considered Hector and John. He smiled then, visibly relaxed, raised a hand and waved.

Hector and John both waved back. John's wave was cautious and uncertain, while Hector's was casual.

Troy lowered his hand and turned his sharply in the direction of the main hallway from where he had just come. He frowned, turned and stalked out of the room, disappearing back into the hallway.

Hector had already turned his attention to the papers on his desk.

John, however, was carefully eyeing the threshold through which Troy had just passed.

"Hector..." questioningly.

"Yeah..." absently.

"What is it with Troy?"

Hector grinned but continued digging through his paperwork. "He is an odd one, isn't he?"

"I found him in my room this morning," said John.

"Yeah?" Hector leaned back in his chair, tossed a folder aside. "Yeah?" He didn't seem surprised.

"I came out of the shower, and he's laying there on my bed."

"That would be Troy," said Hector, nodding. "I once found him actually in my shower. He's got access to just about everywhere; here and down the hall."

"He can go anywhere he wants? Just walk in and put his feet up?"

"Pretty much." It didn't seem to bother him.

"But..." John fumbled for a word, frustrated. "How?"

Hector said nothing. He waited for John to come up with the reason.

John glanced in the direction of Mr. Horn's heavy wooden door. "Is it true that he's, you know... He and ..."

"Connected?" Hector slowly sat forward, placed his arms on the desk in front of him. "Troy has been around as long as anyone can remember. Before the station. Back when we were—" His face darkened faintly, as if shadowed from a memory. "Mr. Horn brought Troy up with him when we were first getting this place set up."

"And they're related..." John stated.

"That's what people say." Hector shrugged. "Cousins or something. Whatever substitutes for that down here."

Seems to be a lot of that, thought John. He was dully bewildered. "Troy is annoying, but I haven't seen anything that would make him... like... you know..."

"Hey, man, we all got it in us." Hector managed another very faint smile. "I mean, we're here, right?"

"Right," John frowned. "I think I'll sleep with one eye open."

"I do."

The *'Tell it to Judge Roy'* set was a small, high-ceilinged cavern. Dominating the room was the judge's reddish brown stone bench. It towered over the plaintiff's rickety wooden witness podium.

There was a small raised platform to one side of the judge's bench where the silent, ever-present bailiff stood. On the opposite side was a small wooden table at which sat the also silent, also ever-present recorder.

Judge Roy, moderator for the *Tell it to Judge Roy* program, sat high up on his stone bench. He looked coolly down on Edward, today's first plaintiff, who stood nervously at the plaintiff's podium.

Edward was a nondescript middle-aged man who had the anxious look of someone who has recently come to realize that just maybe it had been a mistake to have volunteered to appear on the Judge Roy program.

The unseen narrator spoke the program's blurb in a voice deep and serious.

"You think you've been wronged?

"You think you've been screwed?

"Well stop your whining, Citizen.

"You know what ya gotta do...

"That's right..."

The studio audience joined in with the last line:

"Tell it to Judge Roy!"

This was followed by the sound of applause from the unseen audience.

The narrator waited for the applause to end.

"We'll be right back to introduce our first plaintiff."

This was followed by the sound of an annoying commercial jingle. All the while, the camera remained focused on the nervous Edward.

The commercial jingle ended.

"We're back," the narrator said somberly.

More light applause from the unseen audience.

"Meet Edward," said the narrator. "Edward thinks he's been screwed by the system... Let's listen in."

"All right, Edward," said Judge Roy from high above the plaintiff. "Let me hear it."

As he listened, Judge Roy silently read through the pile of paperwork concerning Edward's case.

"Yes, sir," said Edward. "I filed an appeal concerning my case some time back, and I have every reason to believe the appeal was denied for reasons of prejudice. Sir."

"Appeal..." Judge Roy said absently, again without looking at Edward.

"Yes, sir. I appealed my uh... the decision that... that placed me here rather than up, uh—"

"I get it," Judge Roy said impatiently.

"Judge Roy, I don't think they looked at the appeal at all. They didn't consider how I had turned things around. I believe they were prejudiced by the... circumstances... of the *incident*, and never looked beyond that."

The judge nodded several times and finally looked up from the paperwork. He spoke very precisely.

"Two points of order here, sailor. Both of 'em are biggies," he began. "An incident such as yours is what <u>gets</u> people sent here. It is the <u>reason</u> for this place. Using it as an argument against the decision to send you here isn't likely to help your case. Second, the decision to send you here wasn't made here. It was made upstairs. And you know this."

Judge Roy held up a pile of papers. "This is isn't your first appeal. You've filed three, going back eight hundred years. Two of them upstairs. They were both summarily tossed out. You filed a third downstairs, knowing full well they had no jurisdiction."

Judge Roy carefully placed the papers back onto the stack in front of him. "You waste my time, Edward. The determination made regarding your situation is no more within my purview than that of anyone else down here. You knew that coming before me."

"No, sir!" cried Edward. "I swear I—"

"And now you would mock my intelligence."

"I'm sorry, sir. I never—"

"I find you to be a thoroughly offensive individual."

Edward started to protest yet again, but wisely decided against it.

Judge Roy leaned back until he was barely visible to the plaintiff standing at the podium below him. He came to a decision, let out a long, noisy sigh.

"Unfortunately, in and of itself, being offensive isn't a crime. However, I can hold you to account for the knowing and wanton consumption of the time that my staff and I have expended on your behalf." He lifted and dropped his gavel. "So be it."

Edward looked shocked and dismayed. "But I came to you for help! I came to you for help!"

Judge Roy had already dismissed this abuser of his time. He calmly set Edward's files aside and reached down to take a new set that was being silently offered to him by his bailiff.

"Next case," he said.

At that, two large, burly guards came into the room and stood to either side of Edward. He looked fearfully at one and then the other, then turned frantically to Judge Roy.

"Judge Roy!" he cried desperately. "Judge Roy, No!"

Judge Roy opened the file of the next plaintiff and began reviewing the case.

The two guards reached calmly for Edward.

"And we'll be right back..." said the narrator.

John came out of his room and closed the door. He took one step, then quickly reached back to make certain the door was locked. Satisfied, he started down the long hallway.

After four or five steps, he began to hear nightmarish sounds coming from behind him, coming from...

...*down the hall.*

He slowed his step, finally stopped.

He turned and listened.

Cries of anguish... coming from somewhere beyond the bend in the hall.

He started toward the sounds. He took a step, and another.

He stood in a darkened hallway. There was a flickering red glow beyond another bend in the tunnel ahead of him.

Empty, echoing hollow sounds...

Troy stepped up beside him.

"What is that?" asked John.

"It is whatever you imagine to be."

Neither said anything more for several moments.

"I don't belong here," John said at last.

"It was a mistake that brought you here, John Smith, but this is where you need to be."

"Why?"

"You must be here."

A long pause... a long, tired sigh.

"I had a life. It wasn't great, but it had meaning. It had purpose. This... this is..."

"It is necessary," Troy said smoothly. "You must be here."

"Must be? Must be? I'm not supposed to be here at all."

There was another long pause. John's expression slowly faded to inevitable surrender.

"How long? When can I go—" John hesitantly pointed heavenward. "Up?"

"I do not know."

"Ever?"

"Yes, John Smith," said Troy confidently. "One day."

When John got to the café, Janice was waiting, sitting at the same table where the two of them had sat before. The only other person in the café was the barista, who was quietly going about her business behind the counter.

John had a studious look on his face as he sat down opposite Janice. He could see that the coffee mug on the table in front of her was half empty.

Janice glanced up. "You wear your emotions, John."

"Do I?"

"You do. What's up?"

"Interesting phrase."

"What?"

"Nothing."

"Sure." Janice shrugged one shoulder.

John again groped for words. "Janice... do you ever go down the hall?"

Janice had appeared to be prepared for whatever John might say, but this was unexpected. It took her a moment or two to respond.

"Now and then," she said finally. "My job."

She turned her coffee mug absently, picked it up, set it carefully back down. "I spent some time there myself, you know; before the station opened."

John said nothing. He hadn't thought about that. There were a few moments of uncomfortable silence.

He looked over at the barista and managed to get her attention without calling out to her. He indicated that would like the same as whatever Janice was drinking. The barista nodded silently and set about preparing John's order.

John turned his attention back to Janice.

"I'm hearing a lot more..." he decided not to specify what it was that he was hearing a lot more of. "From down there. Lately."

"Yes, I suppose you would," she said flatly. "Founder's Day coming up soon."

"What?"

"Founder's Day. They're getting ready."

"What does—"

"Some of the activities... they're practicing."

John looked unsettled. "I see."

He of course did not see. He was glad when the barista brought his mug and set it down on the table. It was a welcome distraction from his thoughts.

"Oh, I almost forgot," he said. "I submitted my name to Judge Roy."

"You did what?"

"Judge Roy. I put my name in."

"Withdraw it."

"What? Why? They said I have a good chance of getting on the show. They've heard of me."

"Of course they've heard of you. They've heard of everybody. You go down there and you pull your name out."

John couldn't understand why this had Janice so upset.

"Why should I?" He leaned across the table. "I don't plan to spend the next thousand years down here waiting for some bureaucrat to put my paperwork in the right in-box."

"This won't help. They're not about winning, John. They're about ratings."

"And you don't think my getting outta here won't make ratings?"

"Don't be an idiot. They ain't got that kinda' pull. Nobody down here has that kinda' pull."

John stared down at his coffee. "One way or another, Janice. I'm getting out of here."

"What? You gonna escape?" She sounded incredulous. "From Hell? From what I've been able to observe in my limited time down here, the place is pretty much escape proof."

John's expression turned slowly from defiance to crestfallen. He slumped back in his chair. "I can't just sit back and wait."

"I'm really, really sorry, John." Janice's words were softer now. "I'm telling you. There's one way in, and there ain't no out. And Judge Roy... he'll burn ya'."

Chapter 5

It was late at night and the station floor lights were turned down low. The only significant lighting came from the Up All Night program set.

John stood in the shadows, watching Miss Constance. She was lounging on the purple couch that was the centerpiece of her set. She wore a long, flowing nightgown that showed everything while showing absolutely nothing.

She munched playfully on purple grapes.

Hector came up from behind John, rested a hand on his shoulder.

"Not bad, John," he said.

"Thanks."

"One thing, though. I wouldn't go grapes with vampires."

"You wouldn't."

"No. No, I wouldn't," said Hector. "Cherries, I think. Yeah, definitely cherries."

"I'll remember that," John said, half-hearted. "Cherries with vampires."

"Good man."

They watched Miss Constance in silence for few moments.

"What kind of work did you do topside, John?" asked Hector. He continued to watch Miss Constance toy with her unseen audience.

"I thought we weren't supposed to talk about our lives topside?"

"Why not?"

"Janice. She said—"

"Janice told you that?"

"One of the rules, she said. We don't talk about what got us sent here, and or what things were like up there when we left."

"Well that doesn't make much sense. Miss Constance' movies show us what things are like."

"Not so much," John smirked.

"Okay, but you know what I mean," Hector said sheepishly. He watched Miss Constance pop a grape with her teeth. "One of the reasons Mr. Horn likes this show is it lets the citizens see what they're missing."

"I suppose that makes some sadistic sense."

"Exactly," said Hector. He turned his attention from Miss Constance to John. "Janice has a long list of rules; rules for everything. They help her feel she has some control, down here where we have very little."

"She's a purposeful woman."

"Not letting you talk about what you did means that you can't ask her about what she did."

"What <u>did</u> she do?"

"Never heard. See?"

"Troy seems to know something."

"Yeah, well Troy knows something about everything."

On the program set, Miss Constance lifted a seductive shoulder and let out a catlike purr.

Hector nodded in her direction. "A real firecracker, that one," he said. "No one knows what she did either but she was hanged as witch."

"Then she's been here a while."

"I suppose. Mr. Horn brought her up to the station early on. Same with most of us."

Hector admired Miss Constance a moment more, turned to leave.

"Good job with the show," he said.

John watched him take a couple of steps. "Hey, Hector..." he called out softly.

Hector stopped and turned back. "Yeah?"

"This Founder's Day thing... pretty big around here?"

"Nothing bigger."

"Big."

"What else you got down here? You plan, you build, you create... The big day comes, you do your thing, you walk around and see what everyone else is doing."

"Like what?"

"I don't know, man. Booths, games, speeches, the parade." His thin smile was almost sad. "And don't forget the television specials."

"I see what you mean; sounds like a living hell."

Hector looked confused at first, then let out a quiet laugh and smiled broadly.

"Hey, not bad, man. Good to see you getting into the swing of things."

Hector turned about again and took several more steps before John again called out to him, still working to keep his voice low. Hector stopped yet again and turned. This time he waited silently for whatever it was that John wanted now.

"I was a teacher," said John.

It took Hector a few moments to realize that John was answering the question that had started this whole conversation going.

"That a fact?"

"School for troubled kids," said John.

"Good man." Hector stepped into the dark.

John turned his attention back to Miss Constance, who pulled a grape from the bunch with her teeth and drew it seductively into her mouth.

John stood alone and silent in the darkened station, the glow of the Miss Constance program set just reaching his feet, painting his silhouette in half-shadow.

Troy sat alone in one of the chairs in the waiting area outside Mr. Henderson's office, spindly legs crossed, hands clasped and resting on a bony knee.

He gave a slow, casual nod to Hector as he came into the station, passing the waiting area on his way to his desk.

"Good morning, Hector," he said.

"Troy," Hector answered guardedly. He took another couple of steps, stopped and looked back. "Something going on?"

"Not really, no." Troy stared at Mr. Henderson's closed door and frowned. "John Smith is not a very patient man."

"Ah. Right." Hector looked to Mr. Henderson's office. "Right."

Mr. Henderson leaned forward across his desk, fingers tightly intertwined. He refused to look up at John, standing directly in front of him.

"I told you last week, and the week before that. There is absolutely nothing I can do. No paperwork. No request for an audience. Nothing. You are here until you are told not to be here."

"It's not—"

"I don't care that you don't belong here," said Mr. Henderson. "No one cares that you don't belong here. It doesn't matter one damn bit that you don't belong here."

"Maybe Judge Roy…"

Mr. Henderson laughed, leaned back in his chair. "Yeah. You do that."

"Why not?"

"Have you ever actually watched that show?"

"Once or twice," answered John, defensively.

"Really? And have you ever seen anyone come away happy?"

"Well no, but—"

"Oh, right... you're different."

"I am different. I don't—"

"All right, stop. I've had enough." Mr. Henderson shoved himself forward, looked piercingly up at John. "Now you listen and you listen good. It doesn't matter that you were sent down my mistake. It doesn't matter that you were a wonderful person when you lived in the sunshine. You are here now. You died. You went to hell. Welcome, sir. Want cake?"

Troy stood as the station manager's office door opened and John Smith came out.

"Good morning, John Smith."

John gave a tired nod in response as he closed the door slowly behind him.

"John Smith, I—"

John quickly raised a hand, jabbed a shaky finger.

"Don't – you – say it."

"I just—"

"Don't. I don't want to hear it."

John stood there a moment more, hands shaking. He pushed himself away from the waiting area, out of the station.

Hector watched from his desk, his face fraught with empathy. Troy let out a sympathetic sigh.

"He makes it so difficult."

"Yeah," said Hector. "Good thing you're on his side."

"Yes. Fortunate."

John was sitting on the floor of the dark hallway, just before the bend in the tunnel, from beyond which came the haunting, hollow echoing sounds of empty caverns and the occasional cries of suffering souls.

Debbie came down the hall from the direction of the station. She stood somberly before John, her back to the opposite wall. She studied him a few moments, then slid down until she was sitting on the floor directly in front of him.

"Hey," she said flatly, uncharacteristically non-chipper.

"Hey." John glanced across at her. "Debbie? Debbie's Kitchen?"

"Yep," said Debbie. "John? Just here until the paperwork gets sorted out?"

"Yeah," wearily. "That's me."

Debbie leaned forward and held out her hand. "Hello, John. Pleased to meet you."

John looked at the offered hand, finally reached out and they shook hands.

"Hello, Debbie," he said impassively.

"I'm surprised we haven't crossed paths sooner. The station's not that big a place."

"I work the night shift these days," said John. "I've seen you around. Interesting show."

"Uh, huh." Debbie gave a slight grin.

"Yeah, well..."

"So what has you moping out here in the hall?" She glanced in the direction of the bend in the tunnel. "At this particular spot?"

"Just wandering. And feeling sorry for myself."

"I see," she nodded. "You do a lot of that?"

"Oh, yeah. Lots. Lots and lots."

"Hmm. I see. And which you figure gives you the most satisfaction, John? The wanderin', or the self-pity?"

John lifted his gaze at that, looked directly at Debbie. Debbie met his gaze head on, waited for an answer.

"I find both to be revealing," he finally said. "And neither particularly satisfactory."

"I would imagine."

John rested a wrist on one knee, pointed a finger in Debbie's direction. "You're not exactly the perky thing you let on, are you?"

Debbie gave a quick half-smile. Again they studied one another. Again Debbie patiently waited.

John looked to his left, down the hall leading to the main part of the station. "I've been exploring these tunnels all day, gone into every nook and cranny. And ya' know what I found?"

"Sure," said Debbie. "A few shops, a handful of cafés, and lots of tunnels with lots of doors with room numbers on 'em."

"Yeah. Pretty much."

"And all that wanderin' and self-pity brought you right back here."

John looked carefully at Debbie and furrowed his brow.

"Who the hell are you?"

Debbie took a moment, then climbed to her feet. She held out a hand for John to take.

"C'mon," she said. "I want to show you something."

John looked at the hand, reached out then and let Debbie help him to his feet.

Debbie led John around the bend in the tunnel.

They stepped out onto a ledge overlooking a pit hundreds of feet deep. The bottom glowed orange and red and purple. There were shifting shadows, but nothing definitive. The hollow, empty echoes were louder here, and there were faint whispering sounds, as of a shifting wind.

The only feature on the ledge was a rough-hewn stone bench.

"Ya' feel that?" asked Debbie.

John's face turned a dull gray. "Oh, geez," he mumbled, suddenly overcome.

Debbie took John's elbow and guided him to the bench. They sat, and Debbie laid a comforting hand on his arm. John took a long, shuddering breath.

"What is that?"

"Give it a minute," she stated. "It'll pass."

They sat in silence on the stone bench. Debbie rested her hands in her lap. A minute passed; maybe more.

"Better?" she asked.

John managed a trembling breath. He nodded, took another, longer breath.

"What... what is it?" he asked again.

Debbie settled back, stared down into the pit.

"Hopelessness," she said quietly.

"Oh, man."

Shadows of burnt orange and purple slithered across the walls. A hollow, empty whisper rose up from the pit.

"I see things sometimes," said Debbie. "Hear things. It reaches up to me. Takes hold of me."

"Then why do you come here?"

The expression on her face drifted from internal suffering to a haunted gaze.

"I was there, down there, for so, so long," she said, not much above a whisper. "I'm never going back. Not ever. I would do anything. Anything." A twinge of a smile then, though a bit forced. "Even Debbie's Kitchen."

"You don't like doing the show?"

"Oh, God no. I thought you said you've seen it?"

"Yes." John grinned slightly, briefly. "But I still don't—"

"Coming here... does something. It sets things right in my head."

John looked away, looked forward, in the direction of the pit.

"I think I get it," he said. A long pause, then. "The wiener episode. Particularly good, I thought."

"Thanks." Debbie grinned pleasantly. "We worked hard on that one."

Another long pause...

"So," John started. "You and... you're not, are you?" It was a statement of fact more than a question.

"No. We're not."

"Then why—"

"I don't know whether you've noticed. He likes his games."

"I'm getting that."

"You wouldn't believe what I've had to deal with, folks looking to get an in with Daddy."

"Well, I'm glad you're not, you know, daughter of Satan."

"Yeah."

"And thanks." John wiggled a finger at their surroundings. "For the tour."

Debbie's face softened. "No problem."

John stood before the doors in the reception lobby, gazing out. There was nothing beyond the glass. Emily watched indifferently from her post behind the counter.

Janice came in from the hall and crossed the lobby, cast a knowing nod at Emily along the way.

"Hello, John." She stood beside him. "Whatcha doin'?"

"I've been thinking," he said thoughtfully. "When I came through these doors, I was so scared."

"Most understandable," she said. "Not anymore?"

"I'd be crazy not to be scared. Let's just say, I'm starting to gain my footing."

"That's good."

"Hmm," grunted John.

Janice looked about; at the room about her, Emily behind them, behind the counter. At the doors, the sign above the doors that read 'Not an Exit'.

"We didn't have this when I came down," she said. "Didn't have the TV station back then."

"Hmm," John said again. He was on his own line of thought. "Did you leave many folks behind when you died?"

"I told you, we don't—"

"Me, I had this on-again, off-again relationship going. Her name's Carol. She's a good person, but... we don't really have much in common." He thought a moment about that. "I don't think it ever would have worked."

Janice didn't say anything. She was actually a bit frightened.

John continued.

"My sister and I are pretty close. She's a teacher, too. Same school." He smiled at some fading memory. "She has a couple of really great kids. Five and six."

In the glass of the doors then... moving images, faint at first, then sharper, clearer, mixing with the reflections of John and Janice.

A birthday party, young children around a table; a boy smiling in front of his cake and candles. A woman in the background, hint of sadness.

"Eddie had a birthday," sighed John. The image began to fade. "Guess he's seven, now."

The long, drawn out silence was heavy. The glass in front of them now showed only their own reflections staring back at them.

"No," said Janice. "I didn't have anyone."

John turned to her. A warm glance, a soft smile. He reached out, took her hand. She accepted it.

It was a warm moment.

"Let's take it elsewhere, people," said Emily.

John came into his room carrying a portable television and set it down on the bed, leaving the door to the hall open. He looked around the room, then went over to the dresser and dragged it across the floor until it was in a better position to place the TV and be able to watch it from the bed.

He took the television then and set it on the top of the dresser, knelt down and was reaching behind it to plug in the power cord when Janice appeared in the open doorway. She stopped one step inside the room and spoke pleasantly.

"Didn't you say something about there being nothing worth watching?"

John finished plugging in the power cord and stood up. He reached around behind the television and began hooking up the cable.

"Still true," he said. "But Miss Constance is insistent. I don't have to be on the floor all night, but she expects her producer to watch her performance."

Janice looked side-glance at the bed, then back at John. There was a sparkle in her eye and a smirk on her face.

"I see."

John positioned the television for viewing from the bed. "I'm surprised to see you here. I seem to remember you saying something about not spending time in private quarters."

"I think it was more along the lines of 'I seem to spend a lot of time alone in my <u>own</u> quarters'. That doesn't preclude the occasional visit to other quarters."

"I see."

Janice hopped onto the bed, slid back until she could sit with her back to the wall. "What are we watching?"

The lights were off, leaving only the flickering glow of the television to illuminate the room, creating shadows that danced from bed to table to dresser and across the rock walls of John's cell.

He and Janice were lying atop the covers of the bed, watching 'Up All Night with Miss Constance' on the television. They were dressed comfortably, John wearing lounge pants and undershirt, Janice dressed in a loose pullover and short-shorts.

Janice's coveralls were on the nearby chair.

"Where did you find this horrible movie?" she asked.

"Same place I find all of 'em," said John. "In a big box labeled 'Really Bad Movies'."

"Maybe you should find the box labeled 'Not So Bad Movies'."

"That probably misses the point of where we are."

"Why, Mr. Smith. I do think you might finally be getting it."

"Is that so?"

At that, Janice gave John a gentle jab in the side, followed by a light, pleasant kiss. This started to lead to something more when...

On the television, the program cut to an intermission and Miss Constance appeared on the screen. She was lounging playfully on her purple couch and began teasing her audience.

"So, what do you think, my sweeties? She is quite the little vixen, is she not?" Miss Constance gave a come-hither look. "I bet you'd like to try a little of that..."

Janice mumbled, "Not really, no..."

"Well, you might just get your wish, my darlings," Miss Constance continued. "In honor of this year's Founder's Day, I'm sending out a special invitation just for you."

She sat up oh-so-slowly and leaned closer to the unseen camera. She spoke in a husky whisper. "How would you like to spend a night with Miss Constance?"

"What?" Janice blurted.

"Not what you think," John said absently.

"That's right, sweetie," said Miss Constance. "You just drop by the Miss Constance booth and slip me a little piece of paper with your name on it. Who knows? You might be the lucky boy that I choose to have snuggle up here beside me, keep me warm through the long, cold night on an upcoming episode of Up All Night With... *me*."

Miss Constance giggled like a playful kitten.

"You're kidding," groaned Janice.

"She does enjoy her work," said John.

"I'll see you in person this Founder's Day. Come on by."

Miss Constance shifted position and tone of voice. "Are you ready for more of tonight's feature? Mmm, me too. Oh... but before we do, I want to give a *very special* thank you to someone *very special* out there. You know who you are, my sweetie."

She slid back to a lounging position and gave another of her playful giggles. "Now back to *The Spy Wore Heels*."

Miss Constance winked as the television image slowly faded and returned to the night's movie feature.

"Just what did she mean by that? Someone very special?" demanded Janice.

"That's very, <u>very</u> special."

Janice was not amused. The glare was withering.

"C'mon Janice," said John. "You know Miss Constance. Always teasing, always leaving them wondering."

"This was more than that. I know her."

"What are you saying?"

"You know very well what I'm saying."

"No. I don't."

"If I find out that you and her—"

"Oh, God no."

"Don't bring Him into this." Janice jabbed a finger at John. "You mind what I say."

She slid off the bed, grabbed her coveralls off the chair. John looked pleadingly after her as she walked toward the bathroom.

"Janice..."

Janice disappeared into the bathroom. If there had been a door to slam, it would have slammed.

John watched the empty threshold for several moments before looking back at the television. A young, leather-clad woman was kicking the bejeezus out of two hapless foes.

"Damn," John grumbled under his breath.

Miss Constance stepped down from her set. She pulled on a less revealing, quite sophisticated housecoat as she approached a small table with two chairs. A serving tray on the table held a small pitcher, several glasses and a dish of cookies.

Judge Roy waited in one of the chairs, watched admiring as Miss Constance sat in the other.

"Good job with the show tonight, Miss Constance."

"Thank you, Jonas." Miss Constance poured herself as glass of juice. "What has you up and about so early? You're not much of a morning person, as I recall."

"Bit of trouble sleeping."

"Well, that's not like you at all."

Judge Roy pointed at the pitcher. Miss Constance nodded and waited patiently as the judge poured himself a glass, took a cookie from the dish, and leaned back in his chair.

"How's that *producer* of yours working out?" he asked.

"Just fine."

"Rather an odd sort, isn't he? This John Smith?"

"How so?"

"I don't know. Bit out of his element, isn't he?" Judge Roy brushed at cookie crumbs on his shirt.

"He's settling in all right." Miss Constance eyed the judge warily. "The wellbeing of my producer has you tossing and turning?"

"Just making conversation." He took a drink of his juice, set the glass down on the table. "I suppose you know he was signed to appear on my show."

"Is that so?"

"All sealed and delivered. Then out of the blue, he's taken out of the lineup. Not a word of explanation."

"Really? That's too bad."

"Yes it is."

"He would have made an interesting plaintiff, I would imagine."

"He certainly would have." Judge Roy finished off the cookie, rubbed the crumbs from his fingers. "You wouldn't have had anything to do with Mr. Smith being pulled, now would you, Connie?"

"What would make you think such a thing?"

"Protecting your boy?" He brushed at crumbs on his shirt. "You've obviously taken a shine to the lad."

"I like him just fine, but what he does in his off hours is no concern of mine."

"Oh come on, Connie. There's nothin' happens 'round here without your blessing."

"Dear Jonas, you give me way too much credit. I'm just another tunnel dweller trying to get by."

Judge Roy gave a loud, hearty laugh at that.

"Oh, woman! Would that were so!" He leaned forward, and the missed crumbs rolled onto his lap. "A word from you and the lights don't burn. Shows don't show. Folks I pass in the hall one day, gone the next."

"I believe you're mistaking me for someone else," she said heavily.

"No. No, not at all. I know you. I know you better than anyone knows you."

"That was a very long time ago, Jonas."

Judge Roy sat back again. His expression and the sound of his voice went melancholy. "It certainly was, my dear Connie."

He slowly got to his feet. He picked up his glass, took another drink and set it back onto the table.

"You stand so very close to the flame, Miss Constance. If I thought in a million years that you would listen, I would tell you... but then—"

"I'm fine."

"I'm sure you are." He started away, stopped and looked back. "And with young Mr. Smith under your protection, I have no doubt that he is fine, as well."

"As I said," she spoke hesitantly. "You give me too much credit."

"My apologies." Judge Roy nodded politely.

Hector sat at his desk, his full attention to the television mounted on the wall.

Troy was at John's desk, leaning back in the chair, feet up.

"Moments of Our Nonexistence was on. Bill and Joan were in deep, dramatic conversation.

"Joan, Joan..." said Bill. "You can't possibly think that I would ever be with... with... *someone else*."

"Oh, Bill... Bill," said Joan. "I know all about... her. I know all about... the Other Woman!"

"No, Joan. No!"

"Yes, Bill. I know all about... Alicia!"

"No Joan! No! Joan, don't turn away from me. Please, Joan!"

"I'm sorry, Bill. I'm sorry! I can't bear to look at you. Not knowing... not knowing what I know. Not knowing that..."

"What, Joan?" Bill asked pleadingly. "What is it?"

"I can't... I can't..."

"Tell me, Joan! You must tell me!"

"Alicia is..."

"What are you trying to say, Joan? Please, Joan. Look at me and tell me!"

"Alicia is... Alicia is... *with child!*"

Dramatic closing music, followed by the program narrator, the words spoken smoothly and eloquently... *"Like lava through the flume, so flow the mindless Moments of Our Nonexistence."*

"Why doesn't Joan just kill him and be done with it?" Troy sneered.

Hector clicked the remote in the general direction of the television.

"Because, Troy, in spite of what Bill has done, Joan still loves him."

Janice approached the desks, dressed in her clean coveralls, broom in hand. Troy ignored her, sat up and continued his conversation with Hector.

"But the man is the cause of all Joan's sorrow. Killing him is the only real option." He jabbed a crooked finger. "And she should take out that Alicia bitch while she's at it. A large rock upside the head should do the trick nicely."

Janice sat on the corner of the desk. "You've been down here a long time, haven't you, Troy?"

Troy slid the chair back and stood up. He gave a curt nod in Janice's direction.

"A pleasant day to you, Janice," he said, a hint of menace in the tone. He looked back to Hector. "I shall see you later, my friend."

"Yeah, man. Next time."

Janice watched Troy leave, then dropped down into John's chair. She swung it around until she was facing Hector, her broom held out to one side.

"What's up, Janice?" asked Hector.

Janice shrugged, frowned, said nothing.

"Yeah. Same here," said Hector. He slid his chair forward and began sorting through paperwork on his desk. "How you and John getting on?"

"All right," said Janice. A thoughtful pause, then, "He say anything?"

"Nah. But he's got the look."

"What look?"

"Ya' know. The look." He glanced in her direction. "Kinda' like the one you got."

Janice gave a solemn, almost meek smile.

"Well, maybe not that one," said Hector.

"Sorry," said Janice through a soft chuckle.

"Don't worry about it." Hector smiled sympathetically. "You make a cute couple. Talk of the town."

Chapter 6

John sat alone at the same table that he and Janice used most often. There was a single mug sitting on the table before him.

The man with the newspaper was at the next table, the front page facing away from him revealed the headline 'Founder's Day Today'.

The barista behind the counter looked rather bored.

John appeared dejected.

He smiled though when Janice finally came into the café from the open tunnel.

Her manner was difficult to read at first. She might have been angry, she might have been sorrowful.

John stood as she approached the table. "Good morning, Janice," he said. "I was afraid you weren't coming."

They both sat down at the same time. Janice got the attention of the barista, who nodded and began preparing Janice's order.

"Listen," John went on, "I'm really sorry about the other night."

"No, John. It wasn't your fault. My fault. All my fault. I overreacted. I always overreact. I'm sorry."

"Well, I'm glad you're here."

"Hey, it's your first Founder's Day." Janice's words sounded forced. "Gotta give you the special tour."

"I'm looking forward to it," said John. "I have a few things to get squared away at the station, and after that I'm all yours."

The barista brought Janice her coffee. She waited until she started back to the counter.

"Of course you are, John." She turned the cup about, slowly lifted it up and took a cautious sip. She smiled thinly as she set the cup back down. "And I appreciate that. I appreciate that very much."

Janice walked down the hallway, rounded the corner and stopped.

Troy was blocking her path. He did not look happy. He had a dark, menacing look on his face.

"Get out of my way, Troy," said Janice.

"Or what?"

"Just get out of my way." Janice sounded more bored than frightened.

Troy took a step closer. "You leave him alone."

Now Janice looked startled. "What?"

"You may have played the freedom fighter topside, but down here you're just another tunnel dweller. You step out of line, you'll find yourself on the long march down the hall."

Janice's expression shifted to uncertainty. "I don't know what you're talking about."

"I won't let you take John Smith down with you," Troy said in a dark, ominous tone. "He belongs <u>here</u>. He belongs at the station."

"I would never do that to John."

"*Love*, Janice?" Troy smirked. "That happened once before, did it not?"

"I—"

"That is what got you sent down here, is it not?"

"That was different."

"Quite disturbing, if I understand correctly. Most, most unsettling."

Janice appeared crestfallen. Her tone changed to one of surrender. "I've spent a hundred years atoning for that."

"That makes everything okay, then?" Troy moved in close and had to tilt his head to look up at her. "Nothing you do here goes unnoticed. All is seen. All is heard."

He went in for the final turn. "You are watched, my little revolutionary."

Janice made a final attempt to stand up to the little man. Her words were cool and precise.

"I know that," she said.

Troy's expression oh-so-slowly morphed into cool satisfaction. He let Janice dwell on her situation a moment more, then calmly stepped around the woman and disappeared down the hall.

Alone now in the empty tunnel, unmoving, Janice looked frightened, broken. She fought against an uncontrollable trembling.

Debbie rounded a corner and found the open door of the janitorial closet, almost lost in the lower levels of the maze of hallways.

It was a small room; a shelf of supplies, a rack with brooms and mops, a metal cabinet, a small table and a single chair. Janice was sitting with her elbows on the table, rubbing her face with both hands.

Debbie spoke from the doorway.

"Janice. Is everything all right?"

Janice sat up straight, wiped her face a final time and managed a thin smile.

"Debbie," she said. "What brings you down to my neighborhood?"

"Poor life choices."

Janice couldn't help but grin at that.

"Right." She pulled herself together, worked to push down her emotions. "You ready for today?"

Debbie moved nearer and to one side. She leaned back against the shelves, studied Janice.

"Problems, huh?"

"My little ol' issues brought you here?"

"An acquaintance of an acquaintance caught a bit of your exchange with Troy."

"Of course," Janice said, frowning. "About what I'd expect. Skulking in shadows."

"They were worried about you. I wanted to make sure you were all right." She half-grinned. "You and me, we've been here a long time."

Janice clasped her hands on the table, glanced down at them.

"Yeah... that might be changing."

"That bad, huh?" Debbie shifted about again. "I know Troy can be difficult. And it is sometimes hard to know where he's coming from."

"Well, him and me, we've never really gotten along. And now, something's got a big, fat bug up his butt."

"John Smith."

Janice nodded thoughtfully at that, silent agreement. After a few moments, then...

"I've never really fit in here. Anywhere, for that matter. Topside, I was always out of place. And trying to fit in up there only made things worse." She shrugged. "Look where it got me."

"Janice, you're as much a part of the station as anyone." She moved forward, came up close to Janice. "You just be careful."

Janice looked to Debbie, her expression firm.

"I can't change who I am. I can't change how I face this place. I just can't."

A sad smile from Debbie.

"Hey, you wouldn't be our Janice."

John and Hector stood in front of the television monitor. The narrator was speaking in a smooth, bold voice.

"When you can't be out there celebrating, you need to be right here with us. We'll be feeding you Founder's Day programming all day and all night."

"Yes, we will," said Hector, quite matter-of-factly.

The narrator's tone shifted then to heavy solemnity. "In keeping with the solemnness of the occasion, this afternoon we'll be bringing you a very special *'Tell it to Judge Roy'*. Believe me, this is one you won't want to miss."

"No, you won't," Hector stated calmly.

The narrator's tone shifted again. "Now back to Hot Seat LeGrande, a Founder's Day edition of your show and mine, The Hot Seat!"

"And here we go," said Hector.

The Hot Seat returned, and Jim, host of The Hot Seat, was talking to Bob.

"This is it, Bob. This is your chance. Today... Founder's Day. You could win it all." Dramatic pause. "All right. You know how this works."

Hector spoke pointedly to the television.

"Give it to me, Jim."

"One more question, Bob," said Jim. "This is today's final question."

At that moment, Janice stepped up beside John. "You ready to go?"

"Uh..." John was unable to take his eyes off the television monitor.

"Uh?" asked Janice.

"Shhh," hissed Hector.

Jim on the television: "Are you ready, Bob?"

"Oh, he's ready," said Hector.

John pointed weakly up at the monitor. "One second, Janice. Bob might win."

"Hey. I'm trying to hear this," said Hector.

"Bob might win?" Janice was near to fuming. "You hate this show. You hate all these shows. We're supposed to be going to the midway."

"Just one sec," said John. "Just ... one..."

"I'm supposed to show you Founder's Day." Janice suddenly sounded more hurt than angry.

"Hey…" cried Hector. "I missed the question!"

"Janice, I promise," pleaded John. "I just want to see—"

"Okay, John," said Janice, very coolly.

She turned away.

"Janice!" John called after her as she stalked away.

"That's right, Bob!" Jim cried out. "That is absolutely right!"

There was loud, ecstatic cheering from the unseen audience.

"You have done it!" Jim continued to cry out, near screaming. "You have done it! You have taken it on! You have faced it down! And you have beaten it!"

Janice continued to stalk off.

Hector looked painfully up at the monitor. "Aw, man."

John hurried after Janice.

Hector pointed numbly up at the monitor. A sad, empty gesture.

Jim, the host of The Hot Seat, had to speak over the roaring cheers of the unseen studio audience.

"This is ab-so-lute-ly phenomenal!" he cried. "Oh, my goodness! Ladies and Gentlemen, this moment will live in KHDZ history FOR-absolutely-EVER!"

"Aw, man," said Hector.

The tunnel holding the Founder's Day midway was wider than most. This allowed for booths to line one side and still permit the crowd of people to pass comfortably through.

Several dozen people were milling about. John and Janice were among them, each with a small bag of popcorn in hand. Their body language made it very clear that Janice was in control of the situation.

They were near the 'Drown the Clowns' booth; a row of squirt guns targeting a row of clown heads. Booths further down the line included Whack-A-Joel, Cupid's Arrow and the Dunking Machine.

"D'you notice?" John was saying, "This popcorn is all right, but… it does have an odd aftertaste. Don't you think?"

Janice drifted closer to the Drown the Clowns booth.

"Consider the heat source that popped it, John,' she said absently.

John looked down at his bag and grimaced, tossed the almost full bag into a nearby trash bin.

The booth had a row of six squirt guns mounted to the counter, each corresponding to a clown head at the back of the booth. An empty balloon was sticking out of the top of each clown head.

But instead of plastic clown heads, these were real heads, real clowns.

A carnie sat in a raised chair behind the counter. He was a scruffy looking middle-aged man with a week's unshaven face.

"Come on up, people," he said, "and have a seat. Take aim, fill 'em up, bust the balloon, win your prize."

John looked apprehensively at the squirt guns. He leaned near Janice. "It is water, right?" he asked.

Janice leaned over the nearest gun. She looked up at the carnie, who wrinkled a single, caterpillar brow.

Janice cautiously touched the end of the gun with a finger, calmly rubbed the fingers together.

"Well?" asked John.

Janice sniffed at her finger, lightly touched her fingertip to her tongue.

"Janice!"

Janice looked coolly at John, finally stuck out her undamaged tongue.

The carnie shook his head and turned his attention back to the milling crowd. "Let's go folks. Take a seat, shoot the clown."

Another midway visitor sat down at a pistol station, leaving only one seat open.

Janice nudged John. "Go for it, John," she said.

John looked uncomfortably at the row of living clown heads at the back of the booth.

They looked calmly back.

"I don't think so," he said.

Janice quickly slid into the last empty seat. "Wuss." She settled in and made ready for the contest.

"We've got our six marksmen, people," said the carnie. He shifted about and placed a hand on a big red button. "Everybody ready... Everybody aim..."

He pushed the button and a metallic alarm sounded. "Everybody fire," he finished.

Janice and the others pulled the triggers of their mounted pistols. Water streamed out, striking the faces of the clowns, occasionally making it into their open mouths.

As the contest progressed, each of the clown heads sputtered and choked. The balloons protruding from the top of each slowly filled with air.

Janice called out to the clown head that she was targeting. "Keep your mouth open, Brad!"

Brad the Clown Head sputtered and choked like all the others. "Damn you, Janice," he said amid the sputtering. "You bit—"

Janice got in a good, long stream of water that choked off the end of Brad's comment.

"Open up!" she said sharply. "Open!"

There was a loud pop as the balloon atop a clown head several heads down the line from Brad popped. All the water streams faded to nothing and the balloons atop the other clown heads slowly deflated.

"Winner at station three!" said the carnie. He reached up and grabbed a small stuffed doll, tossed it to the winner.

Janice stood up, glared across at Brad the Clown Head.

"Thanks a whole lot, Brad," she said.

"Go to hell, Janice," said Brad the Clown Head.

Brad the Clown Head started laughing, and then all the Clown Heads started laughing.

The carnie rose up from his chair grinning. "All right, you clowns," he called out to his staff. "Let's try and keep it professional."

There was more laughter from the clown heads. Walking away from the booth, John was grinning but Janice did not appear pleased.

"He did that on purpose," she said.

"A friend of yours, is he?"

"No friend of mine."

The sign over the next booth read 'Whack-A- Joel'. It consisted of a table with eight holes cut into the top, each large enough to fit a head through. A big, burly carnie stood behind the table, arms folded, a wooden mallet held in one hand.

Janice looked down at the table, then up at the burly carnie. "Where's Joel?" she asked.

"He's in there," said the burly carnie. He sounded bored.

Joel poked his head up through one of the holes. Janice smiled down at him.

"Hello, Joel."

"Hello, Janice," said Joel.

A second head, also Joel, popped up through another hole in the table. "Hey, Janice," he said.

A third Joel Head popped up through yet another. "Janice!"

"Hello, Joel," said Janice. Then, "Hello, Joel."

John looked ill at ease, and perhaps a little queasy, as he eyed the collection of Joels. Still, he tried his best to maintain his composure.

"Do you know everybody here?" he asked Janice.

Yet another Joel popped up and smiled happily up at Janice.

Janice smiled back at the latest Joel. She held her hand out to the burly carnie, who handed her the wooden mallet. She looked down at the table. Eight Joel Heads, one in each hole, were smiling up at her.

"You guys ready?" she asked.

"Ready!" said all the Joel Heads.

"Let's do this."

All eight heads dropped down into their holes.

Janice readied herself. She bent her knees slightly, held the mallet at the ready. She glanced briefly up at the burly carnie, then focused her attention on the tabletop.

She nodded curtly. With that, the carnie unemotionally lowered a hand down on his big red button.

The Joel Heads started popping up through the openings, one at a time. Each stayed up for less than a second before dropping down again.

Janice began whacking them on the head with the wooden mallet.

The Joels began popping up and dropping down more and more quickly. Janice whacked them more and more quickly, the action growing faster and faster.

John and Janice climbed into a colorful cart that was sitting outside a tunnel entrance. Above the entrance was a sign that read 'Tunnel of Love'.

Once settled into the cart, it started forward and slowly disappeared into the darkness within.

The cart came out of the tunnel a few moments later.

John hurriedly jumped out even before the cart could come to a complete stop. He looked anxiously, and with some panic, horror, and utter disbelief, back at the tunnel.

Janice was laughing gleefully.

John and Janice stood in front of an elaborately constructed Dunking Machine. Janice prepared to throw a red ball at the target that was hanging beside a terrified looking woman sitting on the drop shelf.

Five or six others stood about, all eagerly watching and waiting.

John stepped up to the half-wall that encircled the dunking machine. He looked down into the pit that the victim would be dropped into if Janice hit the target.

Janice threw the first ball... and just missed. Several in the crowd groaned. Several others threw up their arms in frustration.

John looked up at a sign that hung on a post beside the machine: "Drop her into the Pit of Despair".

Janice threw the second ball. The ball hit the target. The victim dropped into the Pit of Despair, disappearing quickly from sight.

The small crowd went crazy, dancing and cheering. Janice jumped up and down triumphantly.

John caught a quick glimpse of Debbie. She stood unmoving amongst the cheering, dancing crowd.

John glanced hesitantly over the half-wall and down into the pit.

Looking up again, away from the pit, into the crowd... Debbie was gone.

Debbie was sitting on the wooden bench across from the Clown Heads squirt gun booth. Midway-goers were passing before her, but she wasn't paying attention to any of the goings-on; her thoughts were somewhere distant.

Troy approached, sat down beside her. He said nothing at first. He crossed his legs, clasped his knees and watched the citizenry pass by.

He spoke then without turning to her.

"Have you been enjoying the festivities, my dear?"

"I do not believe that is a requirement, is it?" she asked, responding without looking at Troy.

"A requirement, no. But it is recommended."

"By whom?"

"Ah, yes," Troy said, smiling. He looked side-glance then to Debbie. "I suppose that could be an important consideration."

"They are all important considerations."

Troy nodded at that, looked forward then.

"I suppose that is so," he said, thoughtful.

They grew silent then, together watched the activities at the booth across the way. The players were squirting streams of water at the cloud heads.

"What do you want, Troy?" asked Debbie.

There was a winner at the Clown Heads booth; cheers. The carnie tossed the winner a stuffed animal.

Troy continued to observe the scene about them. He put on a genuine smile. He took a satisfied breath, let out a long, contented sigh.

Serious, then...

"It is necessary that John Smith remain here," he stated.

"Necessary for whom?"

Troy turned and looked directly at Debbie. "For the station," he said.

"For you, then."

"As you wish," Troy said with a shrug. He looked again across the way, then at passers-by. He offered a friendly nod to one and then another. "We understand each other, you and I."

"We always have."

Across the way, the carnie was encouraging another group of citizens to take a seat at his booth.

"I would ask that you support John Smith." Troy half-turned his head to Debbie. "Hold his hand, as it were, through whatever difficult times may lay ahead."

"I would do that in any case," said Debbie.

"We are of like minds, then."

"We are not."

Troy leaned near, placed a bony hand on Debbie's leg.

"The station is important to you."

Debbie shifted position, clasped her hands in her lap. "It is," she said.

Troy gave a slight knowing smile, as if in answer. He straightened, stood up calmly. He looked about at the activities going on up and down the midway.

"Oh, I do so enjoy Founder's Day."

John and Janice sat at their favorite table in the café, each now with a personalized mug. For the first time, all the other tables were occupied, and there were several people standing at the counter.

John looked as though he wanted to be having a good time, and for Janice's sake was trying to appear as though he was actually having a good time. Coming through this false front that he was putting up was the fact that he just didn't get it.

Janice, on the other hand, looked to be really enjoying the day.

"I think this year's boat race may be the best I've seen," she said. "And I've seen my share."

She watched John struggle with a smile. "You don't think so?" she asked.

"You can't go by me, Janice. My first year."

"But you ought to know if you liked it or not."

John struggled to come up with a satisfactory answer, or at least a safe one. "It was pretty good, I guess," he said at last. "I mean, maybe it really wasn't my kind of thing, ya' know?"

"How can you say that?" Janice was perplexed. "It had everything. Wild fans, suspense, seat-of-the-pants thrills."

"Of course. You're right..." said John. "You're right..."

Janice studied John suspiciously. "You didn't like it at all."

"It was fine." John surrendered under the pressure. "I'm sorry, it's just... Janice, it was six people hurtling their boats at full speed into a wall. First one to splat wins."

Janice looked stricken. "What about the Cupid's Arrow booth?"

John was obviously afraid to answer, but finally, grudgingly, "You shot that girl in the heart with an arrow."

"John," she stated defensively. "I begged you to be my target."

"Yes! To be shot in the heart with an arrow!"

"And you would have loved me forever!"

"I don't need to be shot with an arrow to love you, Janice."

"Oh, how sweet..."

John stared down at his personalized mug.

"And that girl?" he asked.

Janice picked up her own mug and took a long drink, finally set the cup carefully back onto the table, turned it label out.

"She'll love me forever, of course," she said softly.

"You're okay with that?" When Janice didn't answer right away, he asked another question. "You're okay with all of this?"

Janice looked uncomfortable; really uncomfortable for perhaps the first time. It took a long time for her to answer.

"It's all in fun, John," she said, a bit guiltily. "I mean, ya' gotta give us something."

"Janice, I—"

"I accept where I am. I deserve to be here. I know that. We all deserve to be here."

"I—"

"But I gotta push back," Janice cut him off. "I have to. I have to resist. It's just... it's who I am."

"I can see that," he said. "I'm all right with that. But what does it have to do with Founder's Day?"

"Nothing," Janice admitted. "Not really. But it does. It all does. Everything does. It's all the same thing."

"I don't understand."

"I know." A melancholy smile. "I think that's why I'm drawn to you."

Now John had to smile. "I like you, too."

Janice leaned back in her chair and grew introspective. Her words were spoken as if to herself.

"There is no winning, here," she said. "There is no fight, really. The most you can do is struggle against the ties. That's what I do. I resist, even knowing that in the end... in the end, we are where we are."

She struggled with a silent, internal demon. Her tone then was one of acceptance. "But that's not you, though. Is it?"

John spoke fretfully, words stumbling. "I'm just here until—"

"Yeah, I know," said Janice. "Paperwork."

The viewing stand was a raised wooden platform, eight feet by ten feet, with wooden rails that had been decorated with colorful paper streamers. In the center of the platform were two chairs. Sitting in the chairs were the announcers for the Parade of Souls: the Mayor and Mike Johansen.

They were broadcasting the parade to the television audience. Each held a microphone. As always, there were no cameras visible.

"Mr. Mayor," said Mike Johansen. "If what I've seen so far of this year's Founder's Day is any indication of what to expect here, the Parade of Souls promises to really be something special."

"Absolutely, Mike. Everyone involved in this year's celebration receives a hearty '*well done*' from me," said the Mayor. "But then, I expected no less. I believe I stated on your very program that this would be the best year ever."

"You certainly did," Mike smiled and shook his head dramatically. "I must admit, though, with some of the great Founder's Days I've experienced in past years, I seriously doubted that you could pull it off. My hat is off to you, sir. A superb job."

"Thank you, Mike."

"So, with the parade set to begin at any moment, what can we expect?"

"Surprises, Mike. Thrills, chills... and surprises."

John and Janice approached Miss Constance's 'Up All Night' booth. Her purple couch was there, positioned beneath a colorful silk canopy. Miss Constance was lounging comfortably, and a line of fans waited anxiously to approach, small pieces of paper held tightly in hand.

Miss Constance playfully inspected each fan that stepped forward and apprehensively deposited their strip of paper into a large glass jar.

She smiled demurely when she saw John and Janice watching from out in the midway. She lifted a hand and wiggled her fingers in an inviting hello.

John lifted a hand to wave back, but Janice tugged at his arm and dragged him along. The two of them continued down the midway, but John did manage one more curious look back.

Miss Constance was waiting. She gave him a playful wink, then turned her attention back to the line, contentedly continued attending her adoring admirers.

Mike Johansen and the Mayor looked expectantly to the parade route. There was movement at the far end of the wide, high-ceilinged tunnel, and they could hear the sounds of an appreciative crowd of spectators.

It had begun.

"Mike," said the Mayor. "This year our Parade of Souls is led by a virtual 'royal court' of colorfully dressed jesters. Upon reaching their destination, the gates will open to the sounds of gaiety."

The parade route, decorated with bright streamers and banners, was lined on either side by dozens of spectators. Leading the parade were a dozen men and women dressed in colorful jester costumes. As they traveled the route, they danced and laughed and waved to the spectators.

John and Janice moved through the crowd and approached the sideline. Janice clapped happily, her face glowing as a child seeing her first parade. She waved excitedly when she saw someone among the jesters whom she recognized.

"Looking good, Darren!" she called out.

Darren the Jester waved a hearty hello to Janice, shook the balls on his hat and continued marching.

Janice continued clapping as Darren led the way for the rest of the parade as it progressed forward.

Something happened, then...

Janice's expression slowly darkened... Her clapping slowed... Her smile faded until finally her face showed no emotion at all.

She spoke softly. "Wait for me."

John could only just hear her over the background noise of the crowd. He wasn't really certain that he understood what she said, but before he could respond, she turned and walked away.

John was left to watch her disappear into the crowd.

Mike Johansen and the Mayor continued to broadcast the parade to their unseen television audience, through the as always unseen cameras.

"Wonderful, Mr. Mayor," said Mike. "Just wonderful."

The mayor wore a bright grin. "It is just the beginning, Mike. Just the beginning."

Mike straightened suddenly. This was... this something completely unexpected.

"What is this? Am I seeing things?"

The Mayor beamed proudly, barely managing to keep his silence, to allow the sight itself to speak for itself.

"Mr. Mayor. Is that... is that Bob?"

"That's right, Mike," the Mayor said at last. "A favorite of yours, I do believe. This year's King of the Parade of Souls; on his way to an existence that we can only imagine."

"Oh, a splendid choice, Mr. Mayor," whispered Mike.

John watched from the sidelines.

Four men in leather harnesses, bound together by thick ropes, pulled a large, wooden cart. The wheels of the flat cart were four feet in diameter and made of solid wood. The heavy wheels ground noisily over the gritty floor of the tunnel.

Bob from the Hot Seat television program sat atop the flatbed cart in a large, high-back chair: a cheap throne. He wore a paper crown and held a wooden scepter in one hand.

He smiled and waved to the crowd with his free hand.

The cheering crowd called out to him.

"Bob, Bob!"

"We love you, Bob!"

"I wanna have your baby, Bob!"

John was distracted, anxious, his attention drawn more to the crowd than the spectacle of the King of the Parade of Souls.

He searched the crowd for any sign of Janice.

The sound of Mike and the Mayor speaking, then.

"And now, Mike, and to all of you who couldn't be with us today, I bring you... the Lost Souls."

Behind Bob's cart walked a somber gathering of men and women. Each had a haunted expression, an empty gaze. They plodded slowly forward, oblivious to those who watched.

And those who watched grew solemn and quiet. Those who wore hats took them off.

"A humbling sight, dear sir," came Mike's voice.

The Mayor's voice again. "May those who walk before us today find peace where they tread tomorrow."

"Well said, Mr. Mayor."

A moment later, the expression on John Smith's face turned to bewilderment.

Amongst the lost souls walked Janice, following behind the King of the Lost Souls. As all the others, she was oblivious to those around her.

John pushed between the two people standing in front of him. "Janice! Janice!"

Janice didn't respond.

John stepped out in front of the crowd.

The spindly arms of Troy reached out and grasped tightly to John.

John didn't seem to notice. "Janice! No! Janice!"

The tiny figure of Troy stepped fully beside John.

"No, John Smith." Troy pulled John backward.

"Janice!" John struggled to free himself from the little creature, to get to Janice. "This isn't right! Janice! I have to—"

"No, John Smith," Troy said sternly.

"But—" John looked desperately at Troy.

"You cannot," said Troy. "She is lost to us. They are all lost to us, now."

John looked from the Parade of Souls to Troy and back, frantic to do something, anything...

The last of the souls passed.

"You are safe, John Smith," said Troy.

"What?" John turned sharply to Troy.

"You belong here."

As John looked down at the little creature, trying to sort out what Troy meant, the sound of Mike Johansen's somber, respectful voice could be heard.

"What an amazing sight, Mr. Mayor. Stunning. I find myself speechless." More chipper, then. "And I do believe there are a record number of participants this year."

Chapter 7

Judge Roy came onto his program set, dark but for some unseen faint illumination. It was late evening and all was quiet.

He looked about the set, his expression melancholy. Ahead of him was the plaintiff podium, beyond that the judge's bench towered above all.

There was movement then in the shadows atop his bench. Judge Roy's expression turned dark, his words a deep growl.

"What are you doing here, creature?"

Troy, lounging on the judge's bench, sat up, casual and unconcerned. His legs dangled over the edge.

"Jonas," he said. "An enjoyable celebration this year. Do you not think so?"

"Get off my bench."

Judge Roy walked to the steps beside his bench, took the steps. He eyed Troy sliding around to face him as the judge reached his chair and sat down.

"Waddya want, creature?"

Troy crossed his legs and clasped his hands around his knees.

"Ya' like it here, don't ya' Jonas?"

"Judge Roy to you."

"A position bestowed upon you by our little system here."

"I earn it. Every day."

A smile from Troy. "And you enjoy it."

Judge Roy eyed Troy, studied him.

"Things could be worse," he stated flatly.

Troy nodded, grinned in satisfaction.

"I have a talent, dear Jonas. I have an eye that sees. That eye sees all. And what it sees, my friend, is that you are very much at home here. The others endure, they may even appreciate that *things could be worse*, as you say. But you... no. You thrive here." He leaned near the judge. "You, sir, are a *creature* of this realm so much more than I."

"Where are you going with this, Troy?"

Troy leaned back, hesitated. His expression lost all humor.

"Word is that you have issues with our newest arrival at the station."

"John Smith? I can take him or leave him. What's it to you?"

"I would prefer that his time with us be... untroubled." Troy let that sit for a moment, then finished coolly. "Hands off."

Judge Roy reevaluated his earlier assertions. He sat back, frowned, his jaw tightened.

"Pulling him from my line-up. That wasn't Connie's doing. It was yours." A thoughtful pause. "What are you up to, creature?"

"I have plans for him," said Troy, glancing outward.

"And... what say Mr. Horn?"

Troy brought his gaze back, looked once at Judge Roy, looked away and didn't respond.

"Oh..." Judge Roy said softly. "You be sailing in very dangerous waters, little man."

"Such is the realm in which we find ourselves, Jonas."

Judge Roy had a sudden thought.

"It was no mistake, was it?" he asked. "You' the one got him sent here. But how?"

"Come now, Jonas. You more than anyone knows what is possible here and what is not. And that, sir, that most certainly is not. I simply see opportunities and I act upon them."

Judge Roy leaned forward, looked carefully at the creature sitting on his bench. Troy was probably telling the truth. He saw no way that anyone could have manipulated circumstances and had this John Smith character brought here intentionally.

So Troy was simply taking advantage of the situation.

"I don't get it, creature," he said. "To what purpose? John Smith is no one."

"John Smith has a place here at the station," Troy stated sternly. His tone turned menacing. "He has a role here. As much as you; or me. I intend to see that he fulfills that role. I trust you understand."

Judge Roy let out a long, slow breath. "I begin to. That I do."

Mr. Henderson and Miss Constance walked the hallway toward the station floor. It was late, there was no one else in the passage.

"Another Founder's Day in the books," said Mr. Henderson.

"Tomorrow we begin planning for next year," droned Miss Constance.

They walked in silence for a few steady paces. Mr. Henderson finally broke the quiet, speaking almost to himself.

"If we ever needed proof as to where we are," he said despondently.

"Yes, well..."

"I was sorry to hear about Janice. Young Mr. Smith is no doubt taking it hard."

"Word has come from half a dozen directions that it was the lady's relationship with Mr. Smith that got her a ticket to the parade."

"Troy," grumbled Mr. Henderson. "I thought as much. He's taken a shine to our latest staff addition. Any ideas on what he's up to?"

They stopped at the bend in the hallway; the station floor beyond was in late-night shadow. They could just make out the figure of John Smith sitting at his desk.

Miss Constance slowly shook her head no.

"Whatever it is, Troy needs to watch his step. There is only one in the realm with any real power, and it isn't him."

"I don't know about that, Miss Constance," he said doubtfully. "I've been surprised by what he manages to pull off so many times, my surprise has been greatly diminished."

"As may be, he works cross-purposes to Mr. Horn he going to find himself walking the same walk as our lady janitor."

"The same might be said of you, Miss Constance. From most any perspective, you and our friend Troy might be said to have very similar roles here at the station. I would argue that the two of you are on the same side."

"There are no sides in Hades, Mr. Henderson," said Miss Constance. "And whatever Troy may be up to, I have but one purpose. To survive one more day."

The station floor was illuminated only by the light of the 'Up All Night' program set at the far end of the cavern, where Miss Constance was just setting about to begin her show.

John leaned back in his chair, stared out across the room, lost in thought and absently fumbling with a pencil.

Mr. Henderson saw John when he came into the station.

"A long day, Mr. Smith." Mr. Henderson cleared one corner of John's desk and sat.

John put on a melancholy half smile without looking up. "Most definitely a long day, Mr. Henderson."

Mr. Henderson gave John a long, understanding gaze.

"It's been quite some time since my own, but I do see it in others," he said.

"What's that?" John absently tossed the pencil onto the desk.

"Your first Founder's Day." Mr. Henderson paused, looked across the cavern at Miss Constance, who was joyfully going about her show. He continued then without looking down at John. "It can be a traumatic experience, one's first."

"It doesn't make any sense."

"I don't think it's supposed to make sense, John."

John looked up at Mr. Henderson for the first time. "People actually enjoy it?"

"This is Hades, son. We're not meant to enjoy anything."

"Janice seemed to think so."

"That a fact." The statement was noncommittal.

"It's all in fun," John quoted. "That's what she said. You have to give us something."

Mr. Henderson looked away from John, a peculiar grin forming on his face.

"Janice was never one to open herself up to people, but with you, she was trying." His tone turned darkly serious. "Founder's Day is a game, my young friend. A very serious, very emotionally manipulative game."

Mr. Henderson stood, straightened the items on the desk that he had pushed aside.

"Yes, it is all 'in fun'." He nodded toward Mr. Horn's office. "His. Not ours. Everything you saw today, was driven by him, was for his benefit."

"He's not even here."

"He is always here." Dead calm then. "Don't you ever doubt that."

John Smith visibly struggled to sort out what this all meant.

"What was it all about? What is any of this about?"

"We can never know what he's trying to accomplish. That's all part of what he's created here. What we try to do is play against that." Mr. Henderson was speaking more as a professor than a station manager now. "This reality may have been his design, but we took it and wrapped it all up in a pretty package. We do our best to turn it in on itself; as much as he'll let us, and maybe just a little bit more. How else could we possibly get through it, year after year?"

"And the parade?"

"The reason for Founder's Day. The grand culmination of all that comes before it." Mr. Henderson held up a hand. "Before you ask, I have no idea how the Lost Souls are chosen. Sometime during the parade, they just... *know*. It could happen to any of us. Each year, it might be any one of us."

"What happens to them?"

"No one has ever come back, so no one really knows."

"Some place worse than..." John couldn't finish.

"Who's to say?"

"Then how do you know it's not a way out of here?"

"I don't. One can hope."

Mr. Henderson started away from John's desk, but turned back after a few steps. "Janice rule number four. Never talk about what underlies Founder's Day. Doing so would burst the bubble."

He turned and continued away, spoke over his shoulder. "*You gotta give us something...*"

A thin mist hung in John's cell, the last remnants of his earlier shower. He could be heard in the bathroom beyond the threshold as he prepared for the day.

The television on the dresser in the main room was turned on. The morning newscaster was reporting on the previous day's Founder's Day celebration.

"Thank you very much for that thoughtful report, Jeff. An interesting story that should not be lost in all the excitement of yesterday's myriad of Founder's Day activities."

He focused then on the audience and the next of the Founder's Day stories. "By all accounts, this year's celebration was the finest we've had in these parts in a long, long time. This from the mayor late last evening."

The Mayor's voice came over the tiny speaker of the television. "In every respect but one, this is without a doubt the most thrilling Founder's Day in all my years as mayor."

"He was referring, of course, to the absence once again of Mr. Horn," said the newscaster. "The mayor went on to express his sincere hope that the busy founder will be able to attend next year." A change in tone then, as he continued through the stories. "As every year, the grand finale of yesterday's numerous events was the Parade of Souls. Procession-goers were witness to a record ninety six participants, several from right here in the KHDZ studios."

After a moment's hesitation, "We wish them all the best."

There was a knock at the door. John came out of the bathroom buttoning his shirt. His hair was still wet and was combed straight back.

The newscaster continued unabated. "In other related news, three participants in this year's boat race—"

John reached over and turned off the television, shutting down the newscaster's voice with a loud click.

He opened the door. Troy stood in the hallway.

"Troy... good morning." John stepped aside. "Come in."

"No thank you, John Smith." Troy sounded as somber as John felt. "I bring you a message."

They stared at one another for a long moment.

"So..." John said finally. "The message?"

Troy gave a half-bow. "Your presence is required at the station."

"All right. I—"

Before he could finish his sentence, Troy turned precisely and left, stalking stiffly away on his thin, spindly legs. John watched after the little creature, then slowly closed the door.

Hector sat at his desk, attentively watching the television mounted on the far wall. He glanced very briefly at the approaching John Smith before returning his full attention to the news program. The newscaster's words and tone and turned cool and professional.

"We are unable to verify exactly when he arrived," said the newscaster. "But it is believed to have been sometime late last night and, as is his custom, he returned to us without fanfare. Once again, this late-breaking news; Mr. Horn returned sometime late last night."

Hector spoke calmly to John without looking at him. "You really shouldn't keep him waiting."

"I don't know what—" John stood beside his desk. "I was just told that—"

Hector lifted an arm and pointed in the general direction of Mr. Horn's office.

John tried not to look at the heavy plank door. "You mean—"

Hector used the remote to turn down the volume on the television, returned to the paperwork on his desk.

"Yep," he stated quietly.

The walls of Mr. Horn's large office were covered in thick panels of rich, dark woods. A large, heavy desk was at the far end of the room facing the door.

There was a solid knock on the door.

An oddly familiar voice responded to the knock.

"Come in," said Mr. Horn.

The door opened and John Smith stepped hesitantly into the room. There was a heavy, hollow thud sound when he closed the door behind him. He was confused when he saw who looked like a well-dressed Nicolas Cage sitting behind the desk.

"I'm sorry. I was looking for Mr. Horn." John stumbled over his words.

"Hello, Mr. Smith. Please. Sit down."

"Aren't you... but you... I didn't even know you were, you know... wow. You're down here?"

John's attention was drawn to a long, leathery, barbed tail curled around the side of the desk. Mr. Horn smiled thinly and the tail slid back out of view.

"Is it all right if I call you John?" He indicated the guest chair. "Please, John. Do sit."

John again fumbled for words as he sat in the offered chair.

"But aren't you—"

"Call me Mr. Horn." Mr. Horn / Nicolas Cage smiled brightly and leaned back in his maroon-colored leather chair.

"John," he continued. "I would like very much for us to start out on the right foot. How about you? Wouldn't you like for us to start out on the right foot?"

John nodded numbly but said nothing.

"Good, good. After all, the situation in which you and I find ourselves is no reason for us to be less than civil with one another, is it?"

"No."

"Very good. I'm so glad you agree."

"Yes, sir."

Mr. Horn, wearing a perfectly charming expression, carefully studied his guest.

"It must have been a helluva shocker, finding yourself down here. Eh?"

"Yes," said John. "It certainly was."

"With your fine record. Teaching our troubled youth, no less. And all that volunteer work!"

Mr. Horn leaned forward and placed his forearms on his desk. He clasped his hands together.

"Yet, here we are. All to the good, from my side of the ledger. A soul on the books that I wouldn't ordinarily have, a new set of eyes here at the station; and, from what I hear, a damned fine producer for one of my favorite programs." Another broad smile. "Great, eh?"

"S'pose so."

"Oh, come now, John. Don't be glum. It could have been so much worse, could it not?"

"So I hear."

"My, yes. You could have been sent... " Mr. Horn used his fingers in an exaggerated air quote gesture. *"down the hall,* as they like to say around here."

"Yes." John mumbled almost silently.

"You would have been miserable, John, and I would never have had the benefit of your expertise as producer of Miss Constance' fine television program. So." Another bright smile. "We both win. Right? Everyone wins. Eh?"

"I guess so."

"You guess so? John, John." He spoke earnestly. "Show me the error in my logic."

"I'm not supposed to be here."

Mr. Horn's tone grew no-nonsense and more stern. "But you are here. That is a fact, my friend. I can see you. You are sitting right in front of me. Is that not so?"

"Yes."

"I can do nothing to change that. You can do nothing to change that. It is completely out of our hands. We must make do, as best we can, until the Powers That Be see fit to correct their little mistake."

There was a long pause, and when Mr. Horn / Nicolas Cage spoke again, it was with a firm finality. "So. John Smith. Welcome to the KHDZ family. If there is anything that I can do to make your time with us more... agreeable... please do not hesitate to ask."

The conversation was unmistakably at an end.

John Smith heard the slithering sound of Mr. Horn's tail sliding across the floor. Mr. Horn continued to hold his charming, shining smile.

John stood up with some uncertainty.

"Yes, sir." John walked toward the door. He stopped midway across the room and turned about to face the figure of Nicolas Cage sitting at the large desk.

"Mr. Horn?"

"Yes, John?" Mr. Horn leaned back comfortably.

"The parade... the Parade of Souls."

"Yes, John." He looked as though the very mention of the event gave him tremendous pleasure.

"Where do they go? The Lost Souls."

"Oh, John," Mr. Horn offered a gentle smile. "To a very, very special place."

John waited a moment more, hoping for more of an answer. There was nothing more.

"Yes, sir." John started toward the door again. He reached it. He opened it.

Nicolas Cage spoke to the receding figure...

"Good day to you, John."

"Yes, sir."

Hector shifted paperwork around on his desk and looked askance at John Smith as he sat slowly down in his chair.

"Everything all right?"

John shrugged in answer. He looked dazed. He finally reached down to a cardboard box sitting on the floor beside him and set it on the desk.

The words "Really Bad Movies" were handwritten on the side. They had been written with a feminine hand.

Hector couldn't help but smile. He nodded at the box.

"Janice did that," he said.

"What?" John sounded numb, lost.

"That." Hector pointed at the box. "She wrote that."

John turned the box around and saw what Janice had written.

Hector's expression turned sympathetic. "Hey, man. You never know."

John nodded imperceptibly. He took a handful of DVDs out and set them on the desk, then set the box back on the floor.

"Hector?" he asked. "Mr. Horn..."

"Yeah?"

"He was... an actor. He was... Nicolas Cage."

"Oh. That." Hector leaned cozily back in his chair and rolled his pencil between his fingers. "I don't know this Nicolas Cage guy, but I can say with confidence that our Mr. Horn is not Nicolas Cage."

"Okay. But he—"

"A while back, a guy said Mr. Horn was someone named Angelina Jolie. Again. I wouldn't know. Me, I've seen him as Napoleon, Andrew Jackson, a lot of people." He sat forward again. "Just something he does. Someday you'll walk into his office and you'll be looking at you."

Hector returned to his work.

John looked distractedly at the DVDs on his desk. He was unable to bring himself to delve back into it.

"Listen, man," said Hector. "He's been observing us for thousands of years. He studies how we think, how we deal with problems, how we relate to one another. What we argue about."

He gave a guarded glance to Mr. Horn's door.

"I don't think he'll ever figure us out. He's too different from us." He tapped at his temple. "His mind doesn't work like ours."

"But what's with—"

"Hell, I don't know. Maybe he thinks that if he looks like us, sounds like us, that he can understand us. Who knows? Maybe he just likes dressing up in our clothes." He turned his attention to his work for good. "What's to figure? We're just here to play the game, man."

"Right," John said under his breath. "The game."

He looked away from Hector when he sensed movement across the room.

The barista came into the station from the hall. She was dressed in clean coveralls and was carrying Janice's broom.

The opposite side of the station, Debbie stepped up onto her program set.

"She's here bright and early," Hector said absently.

John looked in the direction of the program sets. Debbie moved unhurriedly about her set, preparing for this day's Debbie's Kitchen show.

She took a moment to look across the station floor. She saw John. After a long moment, each offered the other a slow, sad smile.

Hector gave another quick glance to Debbie, then spoke conversationally as he returned to his work.

"She must've done something right. Finally moved her to the time slot she's been wanting all these years" He gave John a wily side-glance. "Ya' do what ya' gotta do, right?"

Chapter 8

One Hundred Years Later

Maria Cordoba sat in one of the two chairs in the waiting area outside the office of the station manager. There was a manila folder in her lap. She looked out of place here and a little uncomfortable.

Troy sat in the other chair. He crossed his impossibly thin, spindly legs. He smiled at Maria. It was a friendly smile.

It nonetheless made Maria even more uncomfortable, but she managed an awkward smile in response.

Troy finally broke the silence.

"Helluva day, eh?"

Maria attempted another smile. She was only partially successful.

"It could have gone better," she said.

Troy nodded slowly, knowingly. He let out a long, drawn out sigh.

"Ah... yep."

Maria looked anxiously toward at the station manager's door, as if silently willing it to open.

Stenciled on the frosted glass inset in the door were the words *"John Smith Station Manager"*.

"You'll like him," said Troy.

"Excuse me?" Maria had a frightened, confused look on her face.

Troy pointed a long, crooked finger at John Smith's office door. "John Smith," he said. "Good man."

"Oh."

"Been at this a long time." Troy nodded sagely. "Knows his stuff. He'll take good care of you."

Maria didn't have a clue as to how to respond.

"Thank you," she said.

The station manager's door opened.

John Smith stuck his head through the opening. When he saw Maria, he stepped fully out of his office. He looked at Maria with some sense of puzzlement.

"Who are you?" he asked.

Maria stood up. "Maria. Maria Cordoba."

"That a fact," John Smith stated flatly. Seeing the folder, he held out a hand and she handed it to him.

John spoke to Troy as he opened the folder to look at the contents.

"Don't you have work to do?" he asked.

~ End

Broken Sky

Prolog

The empty plain stretched out to the horizon. The alien sky overhead, awash in reds and purples, sat over the featureless landscape like a glass shell. The world was still and silent.

A sudden explosion of light and color and sound. The mountain range burst into existence, cutting across the panorama and replacing the thin thread of horizon with its jagged ridge line, a shadowy silhouette of dark blue.

Nestled in the mountains, at one end of a narrow valley, a smooth, gleaming white wall, set against a hillside, stood in contrast to the forest around it. A big man with sharp features and a hard gaze stood atop the wall, at the edge of an unadorned, flat rooftop. Karl lifted his gaze from the forest and out to the horizon, then above him to the reddish shell of sky overhead.

He appeared... satisfied.

Chapter One

Mannie Alvarez awoke in a small room of faded, roughhewn walls. A red shimmering glow pushed its way through the thin curtain that hung in the only window. He rose up from his cot, trudged over to an old sink and turned on the faucet. The pipes grumbled noisily, but the water came out clean.

Mannie was in his late thirties. His medium complexion hinted at a Hispanic heritage. He was a good looking man, but the life he had been living recently made him look tired all over.

He washed his face and hands, then walked through the narrow threshold between his bedroom and the main room of his two-room shack. He took a long, well-worn coat from its hook on the wall, put it on as he crossed the room and stepped out on a simple porch.

His shack was one of a dozen buildings that made up the tiny community. It had the appearance of a small, old-west town that had been dropped onto an alien world. The newly arrived mountain range was just visible as a dull shadow on the far horizon. The unearthly, cloudless sky above was a smear of reds and purples.

He watched a solitary figure in a hooded cloak walk across the street near the far end of town. Carla climbed the steps of the community hall and disappeared inside. After a few moments, Mannie stepped off his porch and started down the street.

The front room of the community hall was cluttered with several couches, small end tables and coffee tables, and a couple of round dining tables. It was lit by a handful of oil lamps sitting on tables and hanging on walls. Nothing in the room matched, as if it had all been collected haphazardly over time.

Mannie took off his coat and hung it beside Carla's cloak.

There were several other people in the room. Some glanced up at Mannie before returning to whatever they had been doing; most did not.

Yolanda Yates was a black woman in her early fifties. She wore khaki trousers and a heavy shirt; her hair was pulled back tight and bound in a bun.

The General was in his sixties. His short hair was gray around the ears, salt and pepper on top. His clothes, despite being civilian, hung on him as if they had a military cut.

Ben, a young boy of about nine, was playing a game of checkers with Professor Westin, a tall, thin man in his late sixties. The Professor's graying hair looked as though it used to be neat and trim, but had since grown shaggy.

Carla was standing before a small, tattered chalk board. She erased the number "21" that had been written on it, carefully wrote "22". Setting the piece of chalk back in the tray, she glanced silently at Mannie. She was in her early forties, and in a different life would have been considered attractive.

She turned about and disappeared through the door beside the chalk board.

Young Ben looked up from the checker game as Mannie started across the room. He spoke softly so as not to disturb the muffled hush that lay over the room.

"Mrs. Johansen says breakfast will be ready any minute."

"Thanks, Ben." Mannie followed Carla through the door.

Carla was at the counter mixing up a pitcher of milk.

Mrs. Johansen stood at a wood-burning cook stove, looking down into a pot of oatmeal. She had the look and dress of a middle-aged pioneer woman, strong but weathered by a harsh life.

"Good morning, Mannie," she said.

"How are you this morning, Mrs. Johansen?"

"The oatmeal will be ready in a minute," she said. "We could use more wood for the stove."

Mannie picked up the empty basket beside the back door. Stepping outside, he let the door swing slowly closed behind him.

The back walls of the buildings to either side of the community hall were lined up with that of the hall. Looking outward, the landscape ahead was wide open. No buildings, no trees, nothing.

Mannie walked over to a scattering of cut and split firewood that lay strewn about on the ground; all that remained of the wood pile. He knelt down and picked up the few scraps, tossed them one by one into the basket.

He heard the sound of the door opening and saw Carla step outside. She stood silently near the door, glanced once at Mannie before turning her attention to the barren landscape.

Mannie picked up the basket, walked slowly over to her and set the basket down beside her.

Carla folded her arms across her chest, glanced again at Mannie, again looked away and stared out across the landscape. The quiet was oppressive. The tiny cluster of buildings and the handful of people living in the small community were utterly alone in the alien isolation.

Mannie could see Carla's apprehension, the thinly veiled look of concern on her face. He didn't ask her what was bothering her. He turned away, tried to ignore her unease.

Young Ben burst through the door. "They're back!"

Mannie gave Carla a quick, heartening smile and started toward the corner of the building, disappeared between the community hall and the building beside it.

Those who had been in the community hall now stood out in the dusty street in front of the building, their attention focused up the road.

Two figures were visible in the distance, approaching on foot. John Devon was pulling a small cart, Robin Hanley walking beside it.

Devon looked like someone plucked out of middle-America; white, late thirties, a wife and two-point-five children waiting for him in a three bedroom home somewhere in a quiet, middle-class neighborhood in a quiet, middle-class community.

Robin was in her early twenties, but could pass for a teenager. Her long, medium brown hair was pulled back into a ponytail.

Both looked as though they had been on a long trek.

They drew nearer, and at some unseen signal those who had been waiting rushed forward to greet them. Within moments, the new arrivals were surrounded by relieved friends who began bombarding them with "we thought we'd lost you...", "Are we ever glad to see you...", and most notably "what'd you find?"

Mannie remained outside the group and waited. Devon eventually left the cart and pushed his way through the crowd. Approaching Mannie, he shook head in a silent 'no'.

Mannie indicated that they should walk. The two started toward the alleyway between the two buildings opposite the community hall.

"Wish I had better news," said Devon.

"Not one to get my hopes up."

"We did come across two new creeks, a grove of trees. That's about it."

Once through the alley, they continued on toward a wooden water tank sitting on a raised platform seven feet above the ground. A hand pump brought water up from a well and into the tank. A hose wound down one of the corner posts to a faucet.

Devon set his pack down and turned on the faucet. They continued to talk as he washed up.

"We went ten days out before turning back. I swear, those mountains never got an inch closer. How is that possible? I mean, no matter how far away they are, shouldn't they have appeared closer after ten days march?"

"In the real world, maybe," said Mannie. "You brought back wood, anyway."

"We stopped at that grove of trees on the way back." The wood would be green, but there wasn't much seasoned firewood left. It was better than nothing.

Devon finished washing. He took an old, worn towel from its hook near the faucet and began to dry his face and hands. "Where the hell are we, Mannie? What is this place?"

"Wrong guy to ask... I don't even know who *you* are." *I don't know who <u>any</u> of you are.*

It was a welcome home celebration. Two tables were set up in the main street, and all ten residents of the community were there.

Lee Takahashi, a middle-aged Asian man with a pleasant face, friendly eyes and a calm smile had missed that morning's return, having been on a short foraging trip in the other direction. His half-day excursion had netted the group a handful of potatoes and a small, wooden box.

There was a bustling of activity as the residents passed dishes of food back and forth, speaking animatedly to one another in lighthearted voices. The food was lacking in quantity and color and variety. There was a pot of thin stew, a serving plate containing something gray and mashed that was most likely the potatoes that Lee had brought back, a basket of pale colored bread rolls, and a pitcher of watered down powdered milk.

Mrs. Johansen stood in front of the pot of stew. She began filling bowls and passing them down.

"Looks like we'll all be sleeping with full bellies tonight," the General said cheerfully, setting his bowl down in front of him.

Devon held up his glass of milk. "I thank everyone for this fine welcome home." He took a drink as others held their glasses out in toast.

"We're glad that you and Robin are home safe, Mr. Devon," said Mrs. Johansen.

Robin sighed contentedly. "Everything looks delicious."

"And it tastes magnificent," said the General. "Well done, Mrs. Johansen."

"Thank you, General." Mrs. Johansen nodded to Lee Takahashi. "And the potatoes should round out the meal quite nicely."

Lee nodded politely.

Mannie studiously watched as those around the two tables began spooning their stew, taking bites of their rolls, and scooping up their small portions of mashed potatoes. Conversations grew more muffled as everyone began eating in earnest.

Half an hour later, Mannie stood near the community hall porch observing the after-dinner activity going on at the tables. Devon and the Professor moved away from the others and started in his direction. He acknowledged their approach with an easy nod and a soft-spoken greeting.

"Waddya say, Professor?"

The Professor took a drink from a faded plastic cup before answering. "I say that despite efforts to the contrary, I am anticipating an increasing state of hunger amongst the populace."

"A distinct possibility."

Devon smirked. "You're dampening the happy mood, Professor."

"Mood be damned," said the Professor. Then in a softer tone, "I understand we have serious matters to discuss." When Mannie and Devon said nothing, the Professor pushed ahead. "We're going to have to send out another team."

This time, Mannie managed to give a noncommittal shrug.

The Professor frowned. "What other choice is there?"

"I doubt it's going to be enough."

"Then what are you suggesting we do?"

"You know what he's suggesting," said Devon.

With that, the Professor frowned and let out a low growl. He looked over at the group gathered around the tables, then turned back and looked sharply at Devon and Mannie.

"You're talking about abandoning the town."

"It's an option," said Mannie.

Devon nodded. "It's already being talked about."

"Where would we go?"

"To the mountains," Mannie stated flatly.

"Mr. Devon has already tried that," said the Professor.

"The mountain range is there," said Mannie. "We can see it."

"We just can't get to it."

"Of course we can."

Devon threw Mannie's earlier words back at him. "In the real world, maybe."

Mannie smirked at that, but the Professor was not amused. He gave Devon a stern, professorial look.

"Can we reach it or not, Mr. Devon?"

"I don't know," Devon said, after a long pause. "But we're going to have to try something, and we're going to have to try it soon."

The three of them stood silent then. They all knew that something had to change. The Professor finally nodded in the direction of the General, who was holding court over by the dinner tables.

"What does the General have to say?" he asked.

"I haven't talked to him about it," said Mannie.

Devon sounded doubtful. "I don't think he's all that keen on leaving."

"He's been here longer than any of us," said the Professor, "and he has experiences to draw on that none of the rest of us have."

"Hey, I'm not all that keen on leaving town either," said Mannie. "If he has another option, I'd be interested in hearing what it is."

"Good," said the Professor. He spoke then to both of them. "I agree that our situation is growing increasingly dire. We must have a stable food supply. And, yes, our time to take action is limited. As our existing stores diminish, any such action may become more difficult."

Over at the tables, the others of the group were in light, animated conversation; stark contrast to their surroundings and the mood of the three at the steps of the community hall.

It was nearing dusk, and the strange colors in the sky were growing darker. Mannie worked the pump handle beneath the water tank, bringing water up from the well and drawing it into the tank above him. It was a regular chore that usually fell to him or Devon.

He saw Carla approaching, kept pumping even after she reached him and looked silently down at him.

"Is another team going out?" she finally asked.

"I suppose." His tone was matter-of-fact. He kept working the pump. He could hear the water being drawn up through the pipe and into the tank.

"Supplies are low," said Carla.

"I know that."

"People are getting nervous."

"I know that, too."

Carla wrapped her arms around herself, looked around them in frustration. She frowned then. "Are we going to abandon the town?"

Mannie straightened, locked down the pump handle. He looked as though he had just finished a round at the gym.

"Not my decision, Carla."

"That's not what I asked."

"Yeah, well, it's all I have."

"Yeah, *well*, it's not good enough." Carla gave him a sharp glare. "You know what it was like before we had the town. As bad as things are, this is better than... *out there.*"

"Like I said. Not my decision."

Carla was about to respond with a carefully thought out biting retort when something caught her attention. She turned away from Mannie. He sensed it then as well. He looked around them, then looked to the sky. They both looked to the sky...

The sky darkened. The faint breeze that had been blowing stopped.

The world held its breath.

The Professor stood on the porch of the community hall. He was looking up at the same sky as Mannie and Carla. Mrs. Johansen came outside and stood beside him.

The sky exploded in blinding light and color. It lasted for several heartbeats. There was a deep, resonating boom.

And then it was over. The two standing on the porch listened and waited.

"West?" Mrs. Johansen suggested, breaking the brief silence.

"North, I think," answered the Professor. "Any guesses as to what we might find, Mrs. Johansen?"

"Pray it's food, Professor."

"Think big, madam. A restaurant. A roadside establishment that serves decadently large portions."

Back at the water tank, Mannie and Carla were looking to the north.

"North again," said Carla.

"Looks like it." Mannie started walking back to the cluster of buildings that was home. Carla followed beside him. They moved casually, as if nothing had happened.

"Sure hope it's food," said Carla. "A long way off, though."

"Couple a' days at least."

It was morning, an hour or so past dawn; or what passed for dawn. Mannie walked from his bedroom into the main room of his shack, carrying a partially filled canvas pack in one hand, a balled-up shirt in the other. He set the pack onto a small table and stuffed the shirt into it.

Devon stepped into the open front doorway from the porch.

"I wish ya luck."

Mannie walked over to a shelf and picked up a small, leather pouch. He returned to the table and continued packing. He gave a muffled grunt of a thank you.

"Yeah," Devon mumbled back. "You sure you don't want me to go with you?"

Mannie lifted the pack over one shoulder. "You just got back. We'll be fine." He started toward the door and Devon backed out to give him room.

Out on the porch, they could see the wooden cart parked in front of the community hall. A small group had gathered around it.

"You sure you want to take the General?" asked Devon.

"Tough old bird is gonna outlive us all," said Mannie.

"You know that's not what I meant."

Mannie's grin broadened as he stepped down into the street. Devon followed after him and they started in the direction of the others.

"You should probably start making plans," Mannie stated flatly.

"I am."

"Whatever we find on this trip, if anything, won't make a bit of difference in the long run."

"But in the short run, we may get something to eat," Devon said calmly. "Who knows, maybe a change of clothes?"

This time, Mannie's grin wasn't quite as broad. "And that's why I'm going." He lost all humor. "You and I both know there's not enough coming in to sustain us. We stay, we starve."

"You really think you can convince everyone to leave?"

"Their choice. They can leave or stay." Mannie looked side-glance at Devon. "What about you?"

"Oh, I'm convinced we can't stay." He nodded in the general direction of the purple silhouette on the horizon. "I'm not convinced that we'll ever reach those mountains."

Mannie looked back to the crowd they were approaching. "Not my place to make anyone leave. Anyone wants to stay, I got no quarrel. That includes you."

"But you're going." It was a statement. There was no question in the tone.

"Planning on it. Unless the General has something up his sleeve."

They reached the others and Mannie tossed his pack into the back of the cart. Devon held his hand out and he and Mannie shook hands.

"We should be back in a week," said Mannie.

"I'll see what I can do." Devon stepped back. So did several others. The General started around toward the front of the cart, and Carla and Lee Takahashi followed.

"Let's get at it," Mannie said to the General, and the two of them began pulling the cart, Carla and Lee walking beside them.

The Professor and Ben stood in the middle of the dirt street and watched the search team pull away. The others drifted slowly in the direction of the community hall.

They switched out every few hours, Mannie and the General pulling the cart for a while, then Carla and Lee Takahashi. The wheels rolled smoothly over the flat plain of short, yellow grass, the landscape stretching away unchanged all the way to the horizon, where the mountain range was little more than a purple smudge. The sky overhead was as alien in appearance as always, but away from the town it seemed all the more artificial, like a colorful dome set into place over them.

After a short break for lunch, Carla and Lee took up cart duty, following the General and Mannie who walked twenty paces ahead of them.

"What are you hoping we'll find, Lee?" asked Carla. They estimated they were two days from the materialization site.

"We find what we find, Miss Masterson." Lee Takahashi didn't talk much, and when he did, he kept his comments brief.

"Very profound, *Mr. Takahashi*, but there must be something that, if you could ask for anything, would be waiting for us up there."

Lee gave it thought. "Then," he stated succinctly, "I would wish for shoes for the boy."

"Shoes?"

"Yes."

"That's it... Shoes for Ben..."

"The boy needs shoes."

"Hmm," she said softly. "That's cool." She turned her attention back to the task of pulling the cart. "But then, why not wish for a whole crate of shoes?"

"Because he does not need a whole crate of shoes."

And with that, they trudged forward in silence.

By midday the following day, most of those in the group were growing increasingly ill at ease, though perhaps not all for the same reason.

Lee and Carla, walking some distance ahead, said nothing to each other. This was to be expected of Lee, but it was surprising that Carla said nothing.

The General and Mannie were taking their turn at the cart. The General had been talking about one thing or another for over an hour, leaving Mannie to half listen and free to let his mind wander.

Eventually even the General fell into an uncomfortable quiet. After more than a dozen steps, his silence began to make Mannie feel uneasy. He was about to ask the General whether there was something bothering him when the older man spoke up.

"I believe we should have reached the site by now, Mr. Alvarez."

"We haven't missed it, General," said Mannie.

"And to what do you attribute such confidence?"

At that very moment, Carla turned her head and called out to them. "Something up ahead," she said.

Mannie fought down a grin. "To an unfailing sense of direction, General."

Fifteen minutes later Mannie and the General drew the cart to a stop. Carla and Lee were already walking carefully around and through a number of items scattered about the site.

Among the debris was an office chair, a wooden desk, and a small side table. Carla gave the chair a slow spin as she walked past it.

Lee squatted down and picked a book up from a pile lying on the ground and began paging through it.

The General moved away from the cart, took several steps forward, stopped and glanced down at several binders that were lying on the ground. One lay open, papers fluttering in the slight breeze. He stood with his hands clasped behind his back. "What do we have, Miss Masterson?" he asked.

"It could be better, General."

The General studied what appeared to be the remains of an office. "We can dismantle the furniture for fuel," he said. "If no one needs the items, of course."

"I think we already have all the office furniture we can use," said Mannie.

Lee stood then, tossed the book that he had been looking at back onto the pile. "I don't think much of the gentleman's reading habits."

"Your opinion notwithstanding, Mr. Takahashi," said the General, "I would imagine the previous occupant of this office might miss his reference materials."

"These reference materials have nothing to do with business, General."

It took a moment, but the General finally realized what Lee Takahashi was inferring.

"Ah. I see."

Mannie watched Carla approach the desk. "Anything in the desk?" he asked her.

She rummaged through the drawers, mumbling the names of the items she found. Pencils, pens, notepads... She opened a side drawer, pulled out a portfolio and set it on the desktop. She opened it, pulled out a business card and read it silently. She spoke then as she tucked it back into the portfolio.

"Mister James Barstow, from Jackson, Oregon; an accountant, apparently."

Mannie raised a brow. "How exciting for him."

The General continued his survey of the relocated office. "His life has no doubt recently grown a tad more stimulating."

Carla sighed noisily. "At least the poor guy wasn't sitting at his desk when it suddenly vanished from Jackson, Oregon."

"You see anything else?" asked Mannie.

Carla flipped through several pages that were tucked into the side pocket of the portfolio. "Nothing much. Except... these all have dates from about two years ago."

"Interesting," said Lee.

"But what does it mean?" asked Mannie.

"It could mean any number of things," said Lee. "But it is interesting."

The General spoke in a smooth, observational tone. "How so, sir? We have previously collected things that have to all appearances come from other times."

"*Appeared to*," Lee noted. "We find a piece of furniture made thirty years in the past, it may have come from thirty years ago, but it may have come from any time since it was originally manufactured. This is more definitive. Our friend Mr. Barstow isn't likely to carry letters all dated two years ago and nothing sooner, nothing later."

Mannie stepped over to the pile of books that Lee had been looking at and started rummaging through them. He opened one, checked something on one of the first few pages, tossed it aside and looked at another, then another.

"Copyright dates correspond to the letters. Some older, but none newer than two years ago."

The General nodded curtly at that, then surveyed the scene around them.

"Information that we may be able to use down the road," he said. "I suggest that we gather what supplies we may be able to use—writing materials, wood for our fires, and so on. We have a three day journey home."

The little town was awash in muted evening colors. Mannie crossed the street and approached the community hall. Climbing the steps up to the porch, he could hear the low rumbling of conversation going on inside.

All the residents of the community were gathered in the main room, a few standing, the rest sitting in the mismatched couches and chairs.

"Good evening, sir," said the General.

"General." Mannie took the one step down into the room. He nodded at Lee, who was standing out of the way, his back against the far wall.

"We were just discussing our options," said the Professor.

"And what have you come up with?" asked Mannie.

Carla spoke up in a calm monotone. "We can leave, or we can stay."

The Professor smiled patiently. "If we leave, there is the small matter of where to go. Do we go to the mountains? Or perhaps somewhere else? If we stay, do we choose to stay indefinitely? Do we set a timetable or some other milestone before choosing to leave?"

"And what is the consensus?"

Devon piped in. "We haven't gotten that far."

"What if we don't reach a consensus?" asked Carla. "Do some go and some stay?"

"Each chooses their own path," Mannie stated coolly.

The light coming in through the window continued to grow dim. Mrs. Johansen set about to turn on the lamps. The Professor watched her for several moments before turning his attention to the group as a whole.

"I believe that prior to a decision being made, we should hear the General's views on the matter."

"Waddya' say, General?" Devon asked almost cheerily. "You've been unusually quiet."

The General stared straight ahead, giving away nothing of what he might be thinking, but looking as though he was gathering his thoughts.

The Professor tried to encourage him.

"You have been here longer than any of us," he said. "You've seen things that none of us have seen. You were the first to find this town, back when it was just three buildings and nothing else."

"None of that gives me more insight than any of you as to what we should do."

"Nonetheless, I would very much value your opinion, General."

"I appreciate that, Professor." The General shifted position, seemed to look inward. "I have watched our community grow; watched as each of you, in turn, found your way here and found some solace in residing within a collection of boxes with windows and doors... and chose to stay.

"And yes, I have seen some things out there, things quite extraordinary, even by the standards of where we now find ourselves. I have no doubt that all of you have witnessed things just as unusual as any that I have seen."

The General grew quiet. The others waited, and when he spoke again, he was very introspective. "This is not a world in which to be alone. The isolation can be quite overwhelming."

"You were alone a long time," said Carla.

"Yes, Ma'am. About four years, best I can figure. Maybe three years out there, another year here in town." The General turned to the boy. "And then you showed up, son. I haven't had a moment's peace since."

The boy grinned. The Professor watched and waited for what he believed to be a politely appropriate amount of time. "So what do we do, General?"

"I don't believe we have a choice, Professor."

"Are you suggesting that we leave?"

"We are seeing far fewer of the materializations, at least within a reasonable distance of town. Of those we can reach, we are finding less and less food."

"But to just leave..." said Carla, almost pleading.

"I don't like the idea any more than you, Miss Masterson." Such as it was, this collection of broken down old buildings had become home. For all of them.

Robin Hanley, who had spoken very little throughout the meeting, leaned forward, crossed her arms and held her elbows in her hands. "Where would be go?"

"Yes, General," the Professor said firmly. "Do you recommend the mountains, as Mannie has suggested? Or do you share the concerns that several others have voiced? That they cannot be reached..."

"They can be reached. They are like any other materialization."

"A mountain range is more than a couch," said Carla.

The General tiredly shook his head. "There was nothing there, girl. Then there was a crack in the sky, and the mountains fell through."

There was a long moment of silence before Mannie said softly, "Just like a couch."

The dull gray light that had been coming in through the window had continued to fade until now there was only darkness beyond the glass. The few lamps in the room glowed yellow, pushing shadows across the already darkened faces of the group.

Chapter Two

Carla stood just inside Mannie's open front door, the alien world behind her bathed in darkness. She saw his familiar canvas bag on the table, now half full. There was a small wooden crate beside him, once used to carry fruit, of late used to hold Mannie's few possessions.

Mannie came into the room from the bedroom, rolling up his blanket as he walked over to the table. He saw Carla standing in the doorway, but said nothing.

"You aren't taking much," said Carla.

"Not much to take." Mannie placed the tightly rolled blanket into the wood-slated box. Studying the canvas bag and the crate a moment, he finally picked up the bag and set it into the box with the odds and ends. "Not much more than I came with," he said thoughtfully.

"You have a roof over your head."

"I won't argue this with you, Carla." Mannie looked frustrated and slightly annoyed. "I'm not in charge here. I'm not ordering anyone to go."

"But we are going, though, aren't we?"

"You can stay."

"No. I can't."

Mannie picked up his box and started toward the door. "I'm sorry."

Outside, the shell of the predawn sky overhead was a deep, dark blue. In front of the community hall, the cart was nearly filled with assorted boxes, bags, long-handled tools, and other supplies. Lee Takahashi was methodically shifting the contents about, attempting to make more room.

Robin Hanley stood to one side, wrapped tightly in a long blanket. She didn't appear all that comfortable with recent events.

As Mannie approached the cart, Lee spoke without looking up from work.

"I'll take that."

Mannie handed him his box. "Need any help?"

"I just about have it."

Devon stepped out of the community hall and onto the porch, carrying a box of pans and metal plates.

"Nice timing, old boy." He climbed down the steps and handed the box to Lee. "That's the last of it, Lee." He turned then and gave a despondent look in the direction of the porch just as Mrs. Johansen stepped through the door. "The General was right, Ma'am. This is no place to be alone."

"Thanks just the same, Mr. Devon," said Mrs. Johansen. "Out there... that's not for me."

"What we've left for you won't last long."

"You've left me more than my share."

Mannie approached the foot of the steps. "You know the direction we've taken, if you change your mind."

Robin wrapped herself more tightly in the blanket. "We'll be watching for you."

Mrs. Johansen gave Robin a gentle smile, said nothing more.

Devon gave up and turned away, moved around to the front of the cart, to where Lee was waiting. The General stepped out ahead and led the way as Lee and Devon began pulling the loaded cart. Ben and the Professor followed behind.

Robin stood silent in the center of the street. Carla looked up again at Mrs. Johansen, suddenly rushed up the steps and the two women hugged.

Mannie and Yolanda waited at the base of the steps.

"They've been together a long time, those two," said Yolanda. "I'm surprised Carla is leaving without her."

"She hasn't left yet," Mannie mumbled.

Yolanda gave Mannie a parental smirk. Carla and Mrs. Johansen reluctantly pulled apart and Carla took the steps down from the porch. She gave Mannie a hard look as she passed him and followed the others. Mannie and Yolanda followed a safe distance behind.

Robin had yet to move from her spot in the middle of the dirt road. She continued to look up at Mrs. Johansen, who remained stoic on the community hall porch.

"Go, child," the woman said, and gave Robin a reassuring nod.

Robin turned finally and slowly trailed after the others.

The travelers sat in a circle on the ground beside the cart. A lantern was set in the center of the circle, pushing a dull light out to the group but not much further. The night sky was a dark blue, with no stars, but there was a glow to it.

Some had finished their dinner, and their empty metal plates were on the ground beside them. Some held metal cups in hand. The conversation was light.

Yolanda looked out on the emptiness that surrounded them. "It's always so quiet out here," she said. "I think that's what bothers me the most. Not the weird sky or the fear of going hungry, or even the arrivals. It's too quiet. It's not right. It's not normal."

"There's nothing normal about this place," said Devon. He sat with his back against one wheel of the cart.

The Professor set his cup down beside his empty plate. "Tell us, Miss Yates, what did you do back in the real world, before you were snatched away and brought here?"

Yolanda put on a sheepish expression and didn't answer right away. Seeing this, Devon grinned.

"This must be good," he said. "And why have we never heard your story before?"

"Come now, Mr. Devon," said the Professor, stepping in to defend Yolanda, using his most fatherly tone. "As our most recent resident, we must give Miss Yates time to grow comfortable enough to tell us her tale."

"She's been with us quite long enough, Professor. We've all told our life stories... *ad nauseam*. It's long past time for something fresh."

"I don't mind," said Yolanda. "I just don't have much reason to talk about it."

"And so?"

"I... told fortunes."

"Ya what?"

The Professor pursed his lips. "I see."

"For the tourists," Yolanda stated more firmly. "I did rather well."

"Monetarily, or...?" asked Devon.

"The money."

"Hmm," the Professor sighed.

"Tourists expected to see a black woman in full regalia dispensing fortunes. They went home feeling like they got what they came for."

"Of course." The Professor changed the direction of the conversation. "Where were you when you were taken?"

"At the breakfast table, in the back room of my store. I was eating a bowl of cereal."

"A pleasant memory, then?"

"I enjoyed the quiet time before the day got noisy," said Yolanda. There was a hint of nostalgia in her voice. "I guess I didn't really know what quiet was."

There was a long pause then, before Yolanda came out of her reverie. "How about you, Professor? What of your exit from the real world? I don't suppose you were standing in front of your class, to suddenly vanish from the podium, leaving your students befuddled?"

"Nothing so dramatic, I'm afraid. I was in my office, grading papers."

Devon repositioned himself, finding a more comfortable spot against the cart wheel. "I didn't know professors did that any more. I thought they left that to assistants."

"I like to get my hands dirty, every now and then, Mr. Devon." The Professor managed to speak down to Devon, as a Professor softly giving a student a verbal slap on the wrist.

Yolanda turned to Devon. "How about you, John? What were you doing when you were taken?"

Mannie, who had been listening to the conversation from a distance, chuckled lightly. Devon gave him a disapproving look before answering.

"Well," he muttered, "as most of you know, I was in the shower."

It took a moment for Yolanda to realize what that meant. When she did, she tried not to appear startled, but the surprise was evident in her tone and expression.

"You came here naked?"

Mannie answered for Devon. "Bare-assed and baby fresh."

Devon grumbled. "Shampoo in my hair."

"Oh my," said Yolanda.

The entire group grew quiet. Most had slight smiles, thinking on Devon disappearing from his shower, arriving here, out on the open plain, wet and soapy.

Then came the realization that Devon's situation hadn't been funny at all. No food or water was bad enough; but no clothes...

And the smiles faded.

"Oh my," Yolanda said again.

And the smiles slowly returned. And then light laughter from those sitting around the glow of the lantern.

§

Lucas stood unseen in the shadows beyond the camp, observing the group gathered in a circle around the lantern, the cart parked to one side. The glow of the light from the sky overhead illuminated the landscape just enough to distinguish his features. He was in his twenties, slim and small featured, below average in height. There was the hint of a boyish appearance about him.

He watched the group; intent, focused. His attention wasn't menacing, but there was something ominous about his gaze.

The sounds of laughter reached out to him. A slight smile shown on his face.

Back in the camp, a curious, unsettled look crossed Yolanda's face. The smile born from the laughter moments earlier slowly faded.

She turned her head, looked beyond the camp. She looked in the direction of the unseen observer standing in the shadows just beyond the reach of the light.

She saw nothing. And yet...

"Yolanda?" asked Devon. "What is it?"

Yolanda gazed out beyond the camp a few moments longer, shook her head uncertainly.

"I don't know," she said softly. She turned back finally to the others, tried to bring back her smile, but now it was forced. "It's nothing... Like I said, it's too quiet out here."

In the shadows beyond the camp, Lucas hadn't moved. He watched, studied. There was a sparkle in his eye; a reflection from the glow reaching out from the camp.

The group started out again a little after dawn the next morning, taking two hour shifts at the cart, always marching in the direction of the smudge of silhouette on the horizon. The day passed as the day before, and the next passed as the day before that.

Five days, each like the one before it. Late afternoon; the Professor and the General were pulling the cart. Mannie and Lee were several hundred feet out in front, with the rest trailing behind.

Carla and young Ben walked together. They talked some of their lives before coming to this strange place, particularly about the people they had known. Ben spoke of his family. Carla had heard it all before, but she responded as if she was hearing it for the first time.

The conversation eventually came around to the woman they had left back in town, now all alone.

"I wouldn't worry about Mrs. Johansen, Ben. She's a tough lady. She got along well enough before she met up with the rest of us."

"Yeah, but times are different," said Ben. "That's why we left, isn't it?"

"Yes, that's true," said Carla. "But now she only has herself to care for. She doesn't have to mother hen all of us."

Up ahead, Lee and Mannie had been walking in silence since they took over point almost two hours earlier. Neither was all that adept at making light conversation.

Now, Lee Takahashi began making subtle facial expressions as if he intended to speak. He finally cleared his throat.

"Mr. Alvarez," he began, then paused.

Mannie waited for Lee to continue, finally urged him on. "Yeah?"

"Mannie," Lee began again, pushing ahead. "Perhaps we should consider going to three-quarter rations."

"We need all our energy, Lee."

"We're going through our supplies more quickly than anticipated."

Mannie's brow scrunched up in thought. "We figured we had what, fourteen days?"

"Yes. And after five days, we have consumed at least half of our rations."

"That's not so bad, really."

"The mountains are no closer."

"They're closer," said Mannie. "They just don't look closer."

"Of course," Lee said patiently. "My mistake."

"We shouldn't expect to see them any closer for at least another five days, maybe more. We know that much from Devon's trip."

"I understand that," said Lee. "It is for that reason that I believe we need to begin conserving our supplies. If we do not, we will be out of food long before we reach the mountains; even by your own estimations."

Lee and Mannie marched forward in silence for several long seconds. Mannie stared straight ahead, in the general direction of the bluish silhouette of the mountain range.

"All right," he said at last. *Damn. He's right.* "Three-quarter rations."

The General and the Professor were walking point, Carla and Yolanda pulling the cart ten paces behind. Far behind the cart, the others marched in pairs.

The General looked slightly to the left. Something caught his eye. At least, he thought so. He said nothing, but continued glancing to the left as he and the Professor continued trudging forward.

A shadow appeared in the distance a few degrees off the direction in which they were marching. The shadow slowly formed into the shape of a man.

The General caught the Professor's attention and indicated the figure coming toward them.

The Professor nodded and they continued walking. Behind them, the rest of the group quietly followed, with only the sound of the cart's wheels turning on their axles breaking the silence.

Details formed on the silhouette and they could see then that the man was Mannie. They continued ahead for several more minutes before stopping to let Mannie finish closing the distance, settling in for a break.

When Mannie reached them, he let his pack slide down from his shoulder and tossed it into the cart. "There's a gorge two days ahead," he said. "Cuts right across our path."

"Now what?" asked Carla.

"We go to the gorge."

"And then what?"

Mannie turned in the direction he had just come from. The only thing visible was the mountain range, looking exactly as it always had.

"You can't see it until you get right up to it," he said. "But down inside, it's like a forest."

"Water?" asked the General. Water was in very short supply.

"Has to be. I didn't go down, but I did find what may be the only route." He gave a curt nod. "And from the gorge, the mountains look closer. A lot closer."

Mannie and Devon approached the edge of the gorge. It appeared as a deep gash in the earth; in the distance far beyond, the mountains were indeed visibly closer, if only a little.

They stepped to the very edge of the precipice and looked down. A cool breeze rose up to brush across their faces. The gorge below was filled with dark green forest, the canopy far below the lip of the canyon-like walls. The only sound was that of the cart coming up behind them as the rest of the group drew nearer.

"Okay," said Devon, breaking the silence. "Not something you see every day." He stretched out beyond the edge, studied the sheer walls below them. "Where's this way down?"

Mannie nodded to their left. "That way; not far." He looked back at the others, now only a matter of yards away. "We'll have to leave the cart. Carry what we can."

Once everyone had a chance to have a look at the wide chasm that cut across their path, they turned and started along the edge. It took only a few minutes to find the way down, such as it was; a switchback trail never more than two feet wide, often much narrower.

It took some time to sort through the supplies and decide what to take and what to leave behind, but eventually everyone had a full pack and they started down. Perhaps they could come back some day and collect up what remained, most likely not.

Mannie led the way down the canyon wall. They found themselves slipping and sliding as much as walking and climbing. The forest canopy was far below, an indication of the depth of the gorge and just how far they had to descend.

Midway down, with the treetops still some distance below, the sky above exploded in a violent storm of wind and light and color. It was as if the *materialization* was opening up right there amongst them. Half the group lost their footing and began sliding. Those that managed to stop themselves grasped and held onto those sliding past.

Once the world around them had once again quieted, Carla steadied herself. "That was..." she started, but was unable to finish.

Lee Takahashi spoke in a matter-of-fact tone. "I believe there was an arrival quite near here."

"Ya think?"

"An arrival?" Ben asked anxiously. "Right here?"

"Very near," said Lee.

Those below Carla began moving again. "We'll be all right, Ben," she said, and once again started the descent. "We just need to keep moving."

The Professor continued to see things from an academic perspective. "This entire gorge is no doubt the result of materializations; the forest as well."

"Thanks for that, Professor," Carla said sardonically.

The rest of the climb down was quiet. The trail, such as it was, wound back and forth, sometimes quite steep, at other times an easy descent.

Mannie reached the floor and stepped away from the foot of the cliff wall. The clearing at the base was narrow, and opposite the wall stood a nearly impenetrable growth of trees and brush. As Mannie studied the vegetation for the best route in, the others gathered behind him one at a time as they reached the floor.

"Oh, man," said Devon, dreading going into the brush even more than he had dreaded the climb down.

"Well put, Mr. Devon," said the Professor.

Mannie turned his head slightly and looked first at Devon, then at the Professor.

Carla, however, spoke up first. "Well?"

"Onward then?" suggested the Professor.

"Let's get at it," said Mannie. He started forward, pushing into the brush where it looked most accessible. There was no trail that they could find, but the way was passable. Mannie used his sense of direction, which was in fact better than most, but they also managed to capture glimpses of the far wall of the gorge now and then whenever the trees thinned out enough to give them a clear view.

An hour after reaching the gorge floor they came to a meandering brook. They stopped to fill canteens and water bags, and rested for a while, before again pushing on. They stopped again at midday when they came to a clearing. Packs rested where they were dropped.

The General drank from a leather water bag, and handed it to Lee.

"How far do you estimate?" he asked Lee.

"Not long now." Lee put the cap back on the water bag and handed it back.

The Professor stepped out of the woods, having taken care of business. "One step forward, two steps back," he said. "I feel we may be going backward."

"I believe that we have, once or twice," said Lee.

At that moment, the sky suddenly turned very dark, followed seconds later by flashes of light and explosive booms.

The Professor looked at Lee with some concern. Devon looked over at Mannie, who tried to appear calm but was clearly unsettled.

The moment passed. The world grew quiet once again.

"That's the fourth arrival since we've been here," said Carla.

Third, actually, thought Lee. "I believe that with each, the forest grows thicker," he said.

Ben said aloud what everyone was thinking. "What happens if an arrival happens here? Right here?"

After several seconds during which no one answered, Yolanda stood up.

"Let's not find out," she said flatly. She picked up her pack and began to slip into it. Others came to their feet. Everyone was up then and picking up their gear, although most were deliberately calm about it.

They spent another hour struggling through heavy undergrowth beneath the thick forest canopy. The line of travelers stretched through the brush, Mannie continuing in the lead, making a rough path for the others to follow.

There was an explosive boom, but any visible display was hidden by the canopy. Carla pushed up near Mannie.

"We have to get out of here, Mannie."

"I'll take your request under advisement," he grumbled.

"If an arrival happens where we're standing—"

"I know that, Carla."

They entered a section of the forest where some of the trees and some of the bushes looked to have grown within one another; sharing the same space.

Carla's resolve hardened. "Mannie."

"I know." He didn't need any encouragement. He knew damn well what could happen. This gorge was a nightmare made real.

The sky darkened and the bizarre world of the forest floor turned incredibly black. There was an explosive splash of color and the hollow boom denoting another arrival. This time, however, the sounds of the arrival were accompanied by a shattering, wood-splitting noise as trees and brush suddenly appeared in the woods beside the group, taking up the same space as the vegetation that was already there, and shards of wood were blasted in all directions.

Everyone in the group dropped to the ground. With the splinters and dust still settling, Devon called out to Mannie. "I'm with Carla," he said in a forced calm. "I think we should get the hell out of here."

"I concur," came the voice of the General from somewhere beyond Devon. "Heartily."

"Well... so long as everyone agrees," said Mannie. He pushed forward, everyone else following right behind. They moved as quickly as the vegetation allowed, which wasn't always as fast as they would have liked. Twice more the sky darkened, followed by the flash of bright, explosive color and the boom of the materialization; both times accompanied by the earsplitting sound of splintering wood.

Mannie stepped out of the forest and into a narrow clearing that ran between the wall of trees and cliff wall rising up from the floor of the gorge. The others came stumbling after him. They spread out, hurrying quickly away from the treeline and as far from the trees as the wall of the gorge allowed.

There was another darkening, another bright crackling of color and then the thunderclap.

Yolanda looked around at the others. *Someone is missing.* "Where's Lee?" she asked.

Each in the group scanned the faces and figures of the others, as if Lee might somehow be hiding in their number. Mannie dropped his pack, spoke with some trepidation.

"Wait here," he said, and started back toward the wall of trees.

In spite of Mannie's suggestion, Carla dropped her own gear and hurried after him. She kept him just within sight. Behind her, several of the group could be seen moving about in clearing.

Mannie stopped. Carla continued forward with a sense of dread. When she reached him, she moved up cautiously beside him.

She saw what he saw.

Part of Lee's head was protruding out of the trunk of a tree. One arm hung limply out of one side.

Yolanda and Ben stood a few yards from the treeline, waiting anxiously for Mannie and Carla to return with news of Lee. Yolanda had an arm around the boy's shoulders.

Robin and Devon sat on a wide, flat stone at the base of the cliff wall, several yards from one another, looking as if they were already certain of the news that Mannie would return with.

The General and the Professor stood well off to one side, speaking quietly amongst themselves.

"The fact that this strip is clear," said the General, "would indicate that we are relatively safe. For the moment."

"We have no idea whether the arrival pattern that we are currently witnessing is normal for this area or is a new phenomenon."

"I agree with your observation, Professor, but not necessarily with the conclusion that you wish to draw from that observation."

"I draw no conclusion. On the contrary, General, it is you wishes to draw suppositions with little or no evidence."

The General calmly placed a hand on the Professor's arm as he looked back in the direction of the others. They watched as Mannie and Carla stepped out of the woods.

Mannie said nothing. Carla looked stricken.

"Oh, dear," the Professor said softly.

Yolanda gripped tightly about Ben's shoulders. Her expression was blank. Ben looked up at her, then wrapped his arms around her waist as if to give her comfort.

Devon lowered his gaze and stared down at the ground between his feet.

Robin stood stiffly, wrapped her arms about herself, as she often did. "He was always off by himself. I don't think we ever said more than a couple of words to one another." She stared down at the rocky ground beneath her feet. "Always busy going about doing something for somebody without being asked. Just did it."

The General cleared his throat. "Good man."

Carla moved over to a dirt mound and dropped down to a sitting position. The Professor walked over and stood beside her, rested a comforting hand on her shoulder.

Mannie stood away from the rest of the group, studied the face of the cliff. He sensed Devon's approach, heard him sigh in a tired way.

"How does it look?" Devon asked.

Mannie only shook his head, took another couple of stumbling steps to one side.

Devon followed, indicated the forest behind them. "I'm not going back in there, Mannie."

"So don't."

"Then don't give me that sad shake of the head." Devon nodded sharply at the cliff. "How does it look?"

"Looks good," said Mannie.

Devon gave an exaggerated nod. "That wasn't so hard, was it?"

Mannie breathed noisily then, looked left along the base of the cliff. A hundred feet further along, the trees grew closer along the wall. He turned his attention again to the cliff directly in front of them.

"We can't go up here," he said. He pointed to the right. "That way is no better."

With that, they both looked again to their left. The forest was thick right up to the base of the cliff. Devon tried to sound optimistic.

"Maybe it's clear again, once we get beyond that stand."

Mannie looked as though he was trying to see through the trees and beyond.

"Maybe. Hope so." He looked then over at the rest of the group.

"Come on," he said, and they walked back to the others. They gathered up their gear as they encouraged everyone to their feet. Within minutes they were traveling along the base of the cliff, a few yards apart, one behind the other.

They stayed close to the cliff, occasionally had to dodge rocks that broke loose from above and rolled down, some splintering as they hit bottom, some crashing noisily into the woods.

Mannie continued looking for a viable way up the cliff, the others willing to follow blindly along, letting him search for the best route up.

It was another hour or more, and getting close to dusk, before Mannie came to a hesitant stop. He stepped back, head back, and studied the rocks and shadows that hovered above them.

At this spot, the treeline was about twenty feet from the cliff. The cliff itself had a much more gradual slope here than what they had been seeing up to this point.

Devon came up beside Mannie. "Not too bad," he said.

Mannie looked at the sky overhead. It was still clear. The cliff wall, however, was in early evening shadow.

"We'd never make it to the top before nightfall."

"I don't want to spend the night down here," said Devon. They had experienced another arrival just a few minutes earlier, and not far inside the trees.

"You'd rather climb a cliff in the dark?"

"Yes," Devon said emphatically. "Yes I would."

Carla came up and stood between them. "Me too," she said.

"That's crazy," said Mannie.

"I don't care," Devon said firmly.

Mannie studied the faces of Devon and Carla as carefully as he had studied the face of the cliff. He looked then at the others, now coming in close.

The General examined the sloping wall towering above them. "An easy climb at the base," he said, "though it is difficult to see what it may be like further up." He turned to Mannie, an apologetic look on his face. "I'll go along with the voice of the majority on this one, Mr. Alvarez. I agree wholeheartedly with your assessment as to the foolishness of starting up at this time of day, but my gut says to get the hell out of here."

Devon gave a sharp nod. "I think his gut speaks for all of us."

"It does," Carla said shortly. "Definitely."

Mannie shook his head sadly, but adjusted his pack with a surrendering shrug of his shoulder and began the climb without comment.

The General spoke up again, directing his words up to Mannie's receding figure.

"If we travel quickly, and if the way is not too terribly formidable, perhaps we could make it to the top before the fading light becomes a danger."

"Whatever," Mannie mumbled without looking down.

Midway up the cliff. Mannie slide-stepped horizontally along a narrow ledge, looking for a way to continue upslope. The sun had set and the evening was gray and beginning to fill with shadows.

Devon was beside Mannie, the General several paces beyond Devon. The others trailed quietly beside and below the General, each two or three paces beyond the other, the line of climbers disappearing around a jut of rock.

Mannie stepped out onto a wide flat ledge, thirty feet deep and sixty feet across. At the back of the ledge, the cliff wall rose straight up to the darkening sky.

Mannie took a few moments to shake out the jitters and then began looking for a possible way up. He could see nothing in the maze of shadows. The top of the cliff was still another hundred yards above them.

Devon stepped up beside him, and the General came up on his other side a moment later. Both dropped their gear at their feet.

Back along the trail, someone set some rocks loose. They heard the sound of stone striking against stone, the gloomy resonance fading into the shadows below, all the way to the floor of the gorge.

The General quietly cleared his throat. "I would not be averse to spending the night right here," he said.

"Nor I," said Devon, choosing not to look directly at Mannie.

Mannie only nodded a silent affirmative, walked slowly toward the back of the ledge and dropped his pack at the foot of the next rise of cliff.

The General turned to the group at large, most of whom had now made it safely onto the ledge. "It is growing much too dangerous to continue," he said authoritatively. "We will be spending the night here and going the rest of the way up in the morning."

"Is that such a good idea?" Robin sounded anxious about spending the night halfway up a cliff.

"We should be safe enough here," said the General.

Devon couldn't let it go at that, and spoke out to no one in particular. "I would suggest that if you are a restless sleeper that you make your bed near the back."

Once settled and as comfortable as they could be in their situation, they ate a light dinner of cold rations and watched the sky finish its transformation to the now familiar alien night; a tapestry of dark blues, purples, and blacks.

There was little conversation, and it wasn't long before, one by one, each set about to get what sleep they could, curling up under the thin blankets they had brought with them.

Mannie woke after only a few hours, and when he was unable to get back to sleep he quietly stepped away from the others and walked out to the lip of the ledge. Sitting on the very edge, legs hanging over the side, he let the scene envelope him.

Overhead was the shell of plum colored night sky. Below him was the canopy of the bizarre forest that covered the floor of the gorge, now in shades of black. And across the gorge, he could see the sheer face that was the far wall. Beyond, spread out beneath the alien sky, stretched the flat plain, shimmering faintly against the glow of the night.

Carla rose up from one of the shadows at the back of the ledge. She approached the edge of the shelf and sat down beside Mannie. At first neither spoke, and when Carla did finally say something, her voice was low, so as not to disturb the others.

"Looks like the arrivals have finally stopped."

Mannie gave a slight nod. "Can't sleep?" he asked.

"Not very well."

"Me neither." Long sigh. "I think I miss my shack."

Again silence. In the long pause, they heard someone snoring peacefully back in the shadows.

"Mannie," Carla said softly, "whatever I may have said, whatever happens, it was the right choice... us leaving town."

Mannie replied with another silent nod.

"I didn't know it then, consciously, but... I never would have left if I hadn't believed, somewhere deep down in this brain of mine, that it was the right thing to do." She gave his arm a soft pat. "You're doing a good job... natural leader."

"I'm not the leader," he grumbled. "I'm not in charge."

Carla grinned. "If you say so."

"I say so."

They again fell silent. Mannie had nothing to say, and Carla struggled with what to say next.

"Would I have liked you back in the real world?" she finally asked.

"I don't know. Do you like me now?"

"Don't know for sure. 'spect so."

"Well," Mannie was starting to grow uncomfortable, "I'm the same now as I was then."

"I doubt that. This place changes people." Carla looked directly at Mannie. "You were a school teacher, right?"

"Third grade."

She took a moment to process that. "You don't seem much like a school teacher to me."

"You're seeing me a bit out of my element."

The comment faded into a long silence in which neither looked at the other. A minute passed before Carla sighed imperceptibly. "I wonder how Mrs. Johansen is doing," she said quietly.

They continued to sit there in the quiet of the night, the strange alien sky overhead, the gorge in shadows below them, the flat plain in the distance beyond the far wall.

Mannie brought his hands up and nudged himself over the top of the cliff, brought his knee up and pushed himself up to his feet.

And he found himself looking at a man sitting on the ground some forty feet away, legs crossed and hands resting in his lap, fingers intertwined.

It was Lucas, the mysterious young man who had observed the group from the shadows back on the plain. He showed no emotion at Mannie's appearance.

Mannie pushed back his surprise and started forward, approaching the stranger. Behind Mannie, Devon climbed up from the gorge, quickly sorted out the scene and followed Mannie.

"Well, well," he said, perhaps to Mannie, perhaps to the stranger.

Mannie stopped three paces from the stranger. Not taking his eyes off the man, he let his pack slide from his shoulders and fall gently to the ground.

"Good morning," he said.

"Good morning," said Lucas, looking calmly up at Mannie.

Mannie glanced behind the stranger, saw only scattered scrub brush, a few trees here and there, and the mountain range, much closer now.

"You live around here?" he asked, turning his attention back to the man.

"Nope." With that, Lucas shifted position and stood up.

"So what are you doing here?" asked Devon.

Lucas smiled and held his hand to Mannie. His physical appearance was non-threatening, but the smooth calmness and the glittering gleam in the eyes were unsettling.

"I've been waiting for you," he said. "The name's Lucas."

Mannie took the hand and shook it. "Mannie Alvarez."

Lucas nodded greeting, then reached a hand out to Devon. Devon gave it a cool study before finally accepting it.

"John Devon," he said.

"Hello," answered Lucas. The others in the group had by now made it off the cliff face and approached. Lucas shook hands with some, gave a friendly nod to others.

Mannie wasn't ready to be friends just yet. "What do you mean, you've been waiting for us?"

Lucas indicated Yolanda. "Specifically, for her."

Yolanda stiffened. "Excuse me?"

"What the hell does that mean?" Mannie asked sharply.

"Sorry," Lucas smiled sheepishly. He struggled for the right words. "I get, well..."

"Well, what?"

"Sorry. I've never had to put it into words before." He gave an apologetic shrug. "Visions, I guess you'd say."

"Huh?" Devon cocked his head to one side.

"What he said," said Mannie.

"Pictures." Lucas fumbled. "Images. In my head. The last few days, I've been getting them from her."

"These pictures, they told you we were coming?" Mannie didn't sound as though he was believing any of this.

"Sort of. Like I said, it's difficult to put into words."

"So it would seem."

"The images that I get from people, from some people, usually have some meaning that I can interpret."

Devon sounded almost as doubtful as Mannie. "And what did these postcards from Yolanda tell you?" he asked.

Lucas gave Devon an uncertain smile. "Pardon?"

Mannie grew increasingly impatient. "Having a great time, wish you were here... yada yada yada. And?"

Lucas lost his smile and spoke matter-of-factly. "You left your town a few weeks ago. I don't know why, but it was important that you leave." He turned his head to look behind him. "You're going to the mountains."

"Yeah." Mannie was hesitant.

"If it's all right with you, I'd like to go with you."

Mannie didn't look particularly surprised at this. He glanced over at Devon, who shrugged noncommittally. Mannie then looked back over his shoulder. The General was frowning.

The Professor appeared more accepting. "We were all strangers at one time," he said.

The General grunted loudly in the general direction of the stranger.

"What information can you provide regarding our destination, sir?"

The Professor tried to soften the tone. "Are you hungry?" he asked. "We don't have much, I'm afraid, but what little there is, we will share."

Lucas spoke up before anyone else could chime in. "That's very kind of you." He reached into his coat pocket and pulled out a small apple. He tossed it to Devon.

Devon grabbed it out of the air, studied, smelled it. He held it out for the others to see, finally tossed it to young Ben.

Lucas nodded at Ben and the apple. "I can take you to more of those," he said.

It wasn't the prettiest apple that Devon had ever seen, but...

"Lead on, my man," he said.

They travelled through grassy, gently rolling foothills. Scrub brush was now more common, as was short, twisted oak and alder.

Rising above them, yet still some distance away, were the taller, more rugged mountains.

Lucas led the way. Mannie and Yolanda walked beside him, the others following along behind, forming a straggling line fifty yards long.

Lucas answered a question from Yolanda. "No, it isn't a matter of reading your thoughts or your mind," he said. "I'm not getting into your brain. I only receive what you project out."

"I'm sending out images?"

"I believe Mr. Devon called them postcards." The word 'postcards' sounded foreign coming from Lucas.

"I had no idea," said Yolanda. "I mean, my grandmother was said to have visions and the like, but I never. Do you send out... postcards?"

"I don't think so. But then, I really don't know. I've never met another receiver, like me. So, who knows?"

"Then I might receive as well as send," said Yolanda, wondering.

"Perhaps we can find out?"

They group wandered down into a wild, overgrown apple orchard. The trees were misshapen from years of unmanaged growth. The apples were small and discolored.

Robin pulled one from a low branch and bit into it.

"Not too bad," she said through a mouthful of apple. She quickly finished it off, tossed the core aside, and picked another. The others began pulling fruit from the lower branches.

Twenty minutes later, everyone was scattered about the orchard, most sitting, paired off and talking quietly.

Mannie sat alone with his back against the trunk of one of the apple trees. His eyes were closed, but he opened them when heard someone approaching.

Devon eased himself down. "Lucas says that we should head for a valley not too far off, not too high in the mountains."

"Why," asked Mannie.

"Food, water."

Mannie leaned forward a little and looked in the direction of Lucas, who was sitting with Yolanda. The two of them appeared to be in pleasant conversation.

Mannie furrowed his brow. "If there's a nice little valley in the mountains with food and water, and Lucas knows about it, then what is he doing out here?"

"Couldn't tell ya', Mannie. You think he's up to something?"

"Of course he's up to something."

"That doesn't mean he doesn't have our best interests at heart."

Mannie was not amused. "No doubt." He gave a long, serious look across the orchard at Lucas. "He's a strange one, and I'm not talking about that weird connection he has with Yolanda."

"But that is peculiar."

"Yeah, but... he has... a familiarity... with this place."

"Maybe he's been around here a lot longer than the rest of us."

Mannie slowly shook his head.

He's way too comfortable here... thought Mannie. He slowly shook his head. "It's not just that. This comes from... knowledge."

Mannie continued to watch Lucas and Yolanda. Lucas seemed to sense that he was being observed. He looked in Mannie's direction. He gave a friendly nod, completely innocent, then returned to his conversation with his new friend.

Chapter Three

From a distance, the waterfall was a thin ribbon of silver slicing through a growth of dark green covering a steep mountainside, threading down to a misty pool at the base. The top of the fall looked to be borne from the sky.

The group hiked and climbed a rugged path that wound its way up the slope, following close to one side of the waterfall. They climbed in silence, the roar of the waterfall a constant backdrop suppressing any other sounds.

As they climbed up over the lip of the waterfall, an alien landscape stretched out before them; a wide valley with rolling hills bordering either side that spread away, reaching out into the distance. The floor of the valley was a grassland with a meandering river in the center that fed the waterfall. A fog-like mist hung low above the river, spread to either side over small meadows. Unfamiliar species of trees clustered together in small groves.

The sky directly overhead was steel blue, a low dome hovering over the valley. As the setting receded toward the far end of the valley, the color shifted to shades of purple, then of deep red.

A large structure sat on a towering rise at the far end of the valley, its tall walls gleaming white against the daylight.

Lucas stepped out ahead of the others, striking out down the center of the valley.

Mannie didn't look happy. After a few moments to take it all in, he started determinedly forward, marching after Lucas.

Devon put on a light, mocking grimace and leaned nearer the General.

"Lucas is in trouble," he snickered.

Lucas reached a slight rise and stopped, stared in the direction of the structure at the far end of the valley. Mannie came up beside him, glanced sharply at the scene set out before them and then turned to face the odd little man.

"What the hell's going on?"

Lucas continued looking at the structure that dominated the end of the valley. "A beautiful sight, isn't it?"

"Lovely," Mannie said impatiently. "What is it?"

Lucas smiled, but there was a hint of uncertainty in the expression.

"Home?" he offered, self–questioning.

"You're not sure?"

Lucas was so long in responding that Mannie didn't think he was going to answer.

"I have been away for a very long time," he said finally.

"But you live here? *Lived* here?"

The General and Devon came up beside Mannie and Lucas.

"I think you owe us an explanation, Lucas," said the General.

Lucas now finally did look away from the scene, looked directly at the General. "Why?" he asked.

"Sir." The General was momentarily taken aback, but quickly regained his composure. "You came to us. You asked to join us, and we welcomed you. You then guided us to this location, suggesting only as to the presence of food and water, while knowing full well what we would in fact find. Now, sir. What is this place, what is that structure, what is your relationship to it—" The General paused a moment, but the others knew that he was not quite finished. "—and why did you think it necessary to seek us out and bring us here?"

Lucas had listened patiently, his smile very faint. Once the General had finished, the smile broadened, just a little, and Lucas rolled his head back and looked to the sky, then the valley, and then the gleaming walls of the structure in the distance. He spread his hands out and took it all in.

"This place. This place is my world," he said. "This valley, the gorge that you passed through, the plain that you crossed over, the town in which you lived. My world." He let his head roll back around to look again at the General, then at the group that had gathered around them. "You are guests here."

Devon leaned forward, looked pointedly at Lucas. "That, my man, would imply that we can leave."

Lucas slowly, with an air of quiet assurance, turned away from the group and looked again in the direction of the distant structure.

"That might be possible, Mr. Devon."

Most were gathered now around a small campfire, the glow reflecting off those sitting nearest it. They had set up camp for the night near the river. The dusk overhead was a wash of dark blues and purples, and there was a bright shimmer to it that shone down on the valley floor.

Lucas sat on the nearby rise, looking out over the valley and the structure in the distance, his silhouette visible against the strange sky.

Mannie stood some distance from Lucas, some distance from the camp. Devon approached him, coming from a brief conversation with Lucas. He gave a faint shrug.

"He grew up here; in this valley, in that castle, or whatever it is. According to him, there's some kind of a *confrontation* looming."

"What is it with him?" asked Mannie. "What's with all the mystery?"

"I don't know."

"What does he want us for?"

"Don't know."

Mannie frowned, looked back at the group gathered around the campfire. While most of the others were looking into the flames of the small fire, Yolanda was looking at Lucas.

Mannie eyed the woman. "She might be able to get more out of him than you did."

"You think she can do what he can do?" asked Devon. "Remember, he doesn't read minds, he only picks up what she sends out."

"Even if that's true, and I'm not saying that it is, how do we know that he isn't sending out too? Sending out exactly what we want to know?"

Devon looked from Yolanda to Lucas, back to Yolanda. He held out a hand then in a silent '*after you*', and followed Mannie as he started to camp. They settled in beside Yolanda, sitting on either side of her. She gave a knowing nod and smiled somberly.

"You would like to know what Lucas is up to," she stated.

"Hey, she's pretty good," Devon said snidely.

Mannie ignored the sarcasm. "Yes. We would like to know what Lucas is up to; and what he wants with us."

Yolanda slowly shook her head. "He's blocking me."

"You've tried, then?" asked Devon.

"Of course I've tried." Yolanda glanced in Lucas' direction. "And he knows it."

Mannie was also looking at Lucas. "He must have known from the start that you had the ability to pick up images as well as send them."

"How can he be blocking you?" Devon asked. "I thought he could only pick up what you sent out. Wouldn't it be the same in reverse?"

"I don't know. I mean, I think it's just as he said, but I can see that he's putting up something, and it's preventing me from seeing what's there."

As they watched, Lucas turned his head and looked at the three of them. A calm had settled over him.

Yolanda sounded lost, almost frightened. "Listen you guys. This is all brand new to me. I just tell fortunes. I tell tourists what I think they wanna hear. This? This stuff is weird."

"Maybe this place turned on some latent powers you didn't know you had," suggested Devon.

"Or maybe he did," said Mannie. He spoke without turning away from the man's gaze. "I'm not going to blindly follow this guy."

"I agree," said Devon. "Although, I must admit... this valley? Not too bad."

"Maybe."

"What maybe?"

"I don't know." Mannie looked out into the increasing darkness, then up at the sky. "I half expect a dragon to suddenly swoop down breathing fire."

Now it was Devon's turn to look anxiously upward.

Damn it, I hate when he does that...

Mannie was asleep near the dead embers of the campfire. The predawn morning was very quiet. Lucas knelt down and rested a hand on Mannie's shoulder. When he opened his eyes, Mannie somehow managed to not look surprised.

"You need something?" he asked, looking calmly up at the face hovering over him.

"Can we talk?" Lucas asked in answer.

With that, Mannie slowly sat up and swung himself around. He saw that everyone else was still asleep, forming a circle of blanketed bodies a few yards out from the dead campfire. He pushed himself to his feet and followed Lucas out beyond the perimeter of the camp, pulling on his jacket as he walked.

Lucas watched him approach, but said nothing once the two were standing side by side. Mannie stuffed his hands into his pockets.

"What can I do for you, Lucas?" he asked. He tried to look and sound casual, kept his eyes on the scene before them and not this strange man.

Lucas took another moment, breathed in their surroundings.

"Strange world this is, huh?" he asked finally.

"You could say that."

"Anyway, it's what I've heard. I wouldn't know."

Mannie said nothing. There was nothing to say.

Lucas pushed ahead with his thought. "I was brought here when I was a baby." He indicated the large structure in the distance. "I lived there most of my life."

Something about that statement struck Mannie as wrong. It took a moment for him to realize what that was. "But these mountains... they just showed up a few months ago."

"That's right."

"So how can you have spent your life here?"

"Interesting, huh?" Lucas' smirk said *now you're starting to get it*.

Mannie was really not happy. He wasn't getting it. He wasn't getting it at all.

"What do you want from us, Lucas? We're not going any further without some answers."

Lucas put on the same 'this is my world' look that he had the day before. He took a step in the direction of the structure. "My brother is in there," he said. "No doubt watching us."

"All right. I take it you and he had a falling out."

"Karl left me here. Alone."

"And?" *What does any of this have to do with us?*

"He's reshaping the world into something of his own making."

"Is that what the *arrivals* are all about? These materializations?"

"He is creating tears in the fabric of space, using pieces of parallel universes to build his own little empire here in this world."

"Your disagreement... it wouldn't have anything to do with who is going to run this empire, would it?"

"I like this world just the way it is." Now it was Lucas who sounded frustrated. "If I can't stop him, my brother will destroy it. And just where do you think that would leave you and your friends, Mr. Alvarez?"

Lucas was leading the way up the center of the valley, Mannie walking beside him. The others trailed along well behind them.

As Devon had said, this wasn't such a bad place. The valley floor green meadows, small groves of trees and the ever-present meandering river. It was all very different than what they had become accustomed to, living out on the plains.

Carla came up beside him. "I thought we weren't going to follow this guy anymore," she said. "Not without some answers."

"He made a compelling argument," said Devon. He wasn't looking at her, wasn't looking at the two walking ahead of him. "You got someplace else you gotta be?"

"This doesn't feel right."

Devon didn't respond, but now Carla had ruined the mood. His expression changed subtly, not that she noticed.

"There's something really wrong here," she went on. "And it's getting more wrong by the minute."

Devon again said nothing, at least not at first. When he finally did speak, his voice was low and he still couldn't bring himself to look at her.

"Yeah," he sighed. *Damn it...*

They continued in silence for another hour before stopping for a break. Lucas wanted to keep going... no reason to stop... *come on, let's go...* but Mannie insisted. He wasn't about to let Lucas run everything.

They stopped again at midday and had a cold lunch. Lucas' impatience drove everyone crazy and they started out again after only a few minutes.

Mid-afternoon. They passed a children's playground, the kind that one might see in a small neighborhood park. There was a swing set, a small merry-go-round, teeter-totter, jungle gym, bars.

Set into the hillside high above the playground loomed the gleaming white castle.

Lucas was giddy with excitement.

Lucas stepped through the great double doors and into the main hall of the castle, Mannie immediately behind him. The room was large, with a high ceiling that allowed a mezzanine at the top of the staircase directly opposite the main doors. The walls and ceiling were bright white. The furniture consisted entirely of a handful of small tables set against the walls.

Lucas rushed toward the stairs as the others came up behind Mannie.

"No place like home, eh?" said Devon.

Mannie didn't answer.

Robin shook her head slowly, speaking barely above a whisper. "I don't much like it."

Lucas ran back and forth along the mezzanine, calling out for his brother, disappearing now and then as he searched the rooms.

"Karl! Come out, come out!" He disappeared then from view and the room grew quiet.

Mannie lowered his gaze and looked around at the others in the group. Some began moving away from the front door and were cautiously exploring. They looked through the occasional door, though for the moment no one left the main hall.

"What do you think, Mannie?" asked Devon. "Nobody home?"

Mannie gave a noncommittal shrug. Lucas reappeared at the top of the staircase, paused a moment, then half bounced as he stomped down the stairs. He turned quickly and hurried to his left, disappeared through another set of double-doors.

Mannie was watching the doors, waiting for Lucas' return, when a movement drew his attention back to the mezzanine.

Karl stood stoically at the top of the staircase. His imposing figure was in stark contrast to that of his brother Lucas. He had an air about him that defined him as the master of the house.

He watched silently as everyone worked their way back to the center of the main hall. Once all were gathered together, Mannie took several steps forward.

Karl appeared to inspect each member of the group before finally speaking.

"Welcome," he stated coolly. The single word denoted nothing in the way of Karl's feeling at this invasion of his home.

"Thank you," said Mannie. "You must be Karl."

Karl took two steps downs the stairs, slow and confident. His presence dominated the room.

"You must be friends of my brother," he said.

"Friend might be too strong a word," said Mannie.

Karl smiled knowingly. "I understand completely."

Midway down the staircase, Karl stopped and watched Lucas come back into the main hall. When he spoke to his brother, it was both friendly and ominous.

"Lucas, my boy. So good to see you."

Lucas paused, then took another two steps. His physical presence changed, his self-confidence draining. He tried to get it back, struggled within himself and fought to put on the face of confidence.

"Karl... kind of you to make an appearance."

"Oh, Lucas. Actually, I've been waiting for you. So looking forward to getting together, reminiscing over old times." Karl took another step down the staircase. "How has the world been treating you? You look well."

"It could have been worse."

"I'm so glad." Karl turned then to look at the group as a whole. "Refreshments?"

With that he descended the stairs and walked casually to the set of doors opposite those that Lucas had taken. He expected the others to follow.

The room they entered was glass-domed, the ceiling a hemisphere of metal ribs and thick plates of glass that reached down nearly to the floor. The alien sky was visible overhead; the valley below stretched out to the horizon.

The floor of the observatory was concrete, with cobblestone pathways wandering in and around tables, benches, and several telescopes on tripods. Plants grew in raised beds that lined the paths.

Karl stepped behind a serving table. On the table were several glass pitchers, a number of glasses, and a tray of cookies and breads.

Karl lifted a pitcher and began filling glasses.

"I find this particular juice to be very refreshing," he said. "I trust that you will as well."

Mannie was wary, but the Professor moved in and picked up a glass. He took a cautious sip, nodded appreciatively. Several others then moved forward and reached for glasses of juice and cookies.

The Professor indicated the spread of drink and snacks. "You were expecting us," he said.

Karl silently indicated the scene outside, with the view of the valley floor and the path they had taken to reach the castle.

"Of course," said the Professor.

Devon washed down a mouthful of cookie with a big swallow of juice. "Helluva a layout you have here," he managed to say.

"My father was quite the architect," said Karl. "This observatory... this was for my mother."

Karl glanced over at Lucas then and there was a very uncomfortable moment. The look from Karl was one of disappointment; the look from Lucas was one of suppressed anger, but also of apprehension.

"You live here all alone, now?" asked the General.

Karl again looked at Lucas, this time more sharply, before responding to the General.

"That's right," he said unemotionally.

"If I might ask, sir, how is it that you are here? I have the impression that you did not arrive in the same manner as the rest of us."

"That is correct. Our father brought us." Karl smiled at Lucas. "Is that not right, dear boy?"

"I wouldn't know," stated Lucas.

"Of course you do." Karl turned to the entire group. "But then, Lucas was quite young when Father created this world."

This last statement took everyone by surprise. Devon was the first to speak up.

"What's that?"

"And Lucas and our father never did get along," continued Karl. He lifted a brow and eyed Lucas. "Would you not agree?"

"Got along well enough."

Devon tried to interject, looking for an answer to his question. "Excuse me. About this whole 'creating the world' thing..."

"Yes. Quite," adds the General.

Karl feigned genuine surprise. "Are you saying that Lucas never mentioned it?"

"Not in so many words, no," said Devon.

"Not in any words," the General stated.

"I see," said Karl. "Yes. I can understand why he might not want to broach the subject of our father." He again looked over at Lucas. There was clearly something unspoken going on between them.

Lucas, for his part, had managed to regain at least some of his self-assurance, but his negative emotions were making it difficult for him to maintain a clear head.

Karl took a long drink, then held the glass out before him and looked at it appreciatively.

"This world did exist in some fashion, of course," he said. "This alternate plane was here. What my father did, what our father did, was to bring together the elements necessary to construct this physical reality that you see now all around you."

The Professor was dumbfounded. "Absolutely amazing," he managed to get out.

"Or absolutely insane," said Carla.

"Father is a genius, my dear," said Karl, smiling softly. "Intensely brilliant. But I grant you that he is quite... eccentric."

Carla fell silent under Karl's glittering gaze, the man's smile taking on a painted look.

The General spoke up. "But why on earth would anyone do such a thing?"

"Come now, General..." the Professor interjected. "The man created a world."

"And look what he did with it." The General was not as awestruck by the achievement as the Professor. "We were kidnapped, literally wrenched from our lives, and brought here to squalid lives of meager existence, barely able to survive at all."

Karl stiffened and his face grew dark. "That, sir, was not my father's doing."

"Of course it was," Lucas jumped in. "His and yours."

Karl looked studiously at Lucas, finally gave a subtle nod. "Lucas, Lucas... what <u>do</u> you have in mind? Do you think to somehow remove *me* as well?"

Mannie, who had been standing near the glass wall, moved nearer to Karl and the rest of the group. "What happened to your parents, Karl?" he asked.

"Ah. A very important question. The answer to which unravels the mystery."

"He killed them," said Lucas, spitting out the words.

"I don't think so," Mannie said calmly.

"Very perceptive, sir," said Karl.

Carla looked from Karl to Lucas and back again. "Lucas killed them?" she asked.

"They live yet," said Karl. "At least, I believe they do."

"What happened to them?"

Karl looked carefully at the drink in his hand, set it down and looked sadly at Lucas. After several moments, he turned back to Carla.

"There are an incalculable number of unfinished worlds, like this one, each existing in an alternate plane, empty but for these barren wastelands of planets." He nodded in the direction of Lucas. "My brother sent our parents to one of these."

Mannie took another step nearer Karl. He wasn't about to be drawn into an emotional tug-of-war. He spoke quickly to his own line of thought.

"When?" he asked.

"Some time before the first of you would have arrived."

"That's a lie!" Lucas said sharply.

"I don't think so." Mannie remained calm.

"I went looking for them," said Karl.

"And you took this castle with you," said Mannie.

"And this valley. And these mountains."

The Professor understood. "So that they would be able to see you, even if you were not able to see them."

"Yes."

"And now you're back," Devon piped in, "and the mountains are back."

"You weren't able to find your parents?" asked Carla, though it was more of an observation than a question.

"No. I am afraid not."

Mannie, Devon and Yolanda stood near the glass wall that looked out across the valley. The others were scattered about the observatory in small groups.

Mannie looked across the room at Karl and Lucas. The two were in a heated discussion. Lucas looked angry, while Karl was apparently trying to keep things civil. He lifted a hand and rested it on the smaller man's shoulder. Lucas shoved it aside.

Devon let out a questioning sigh. "Waddya think, Mannie?"

"I'll believe Karl before I'll believe Lucas, but I wouldn't trust either one."

"You seemed to connect with big brother."

"What he had to say made sense, but that doesn't mean he's not keeping something from us; something that could hurt us."

"There was truth in his words," said Yolanda. "I could sense it."

Devon grinned. "You mean that weird connection of yours?"

"Simple intuition."

"Not... uh..."

Yolanda only shrugged, and Devon nodded thoughtfully and looked back at the brothers on the other side of the observatory.

"Well, if he is telling the truth," Devon went on, "and he's not asking anything of us, I'm going to have to side with Karl."

"He's telling a truth, not necessarily the truth."

"Don't start slicing words on me, Yolanda," said Devon.

"Who says he's not asking anything of us?" asked Mannie. "Give him time."

"Will you two give me a break?" groaned Devon. "I don't even know what we're doing here."

Mannie lowered his gaze and gave Devon a somber look. "Lucas asked for our help." It may have been an accusation, but was more likely a simple observation.

Before Devon could come up with a witty retort, the General stepped into the conversation. "Which he has yet to call us on. In what manner was this assistance to take?"

Devon jabbed a thumb in Yolanda's general direction. "Something she was supposed to do."

"I don't think he's ready." Yolanda looked curiously in the direction of Karl and Lucas. "Whatever he was expecting here, he got something different."

"Well, you keep your mind in access mode, or whatever it is," said Devon. "And listen out for what either one is up to."

With that, the four grew quiet. They could just hear the harsh tones coming from the heated discussion continuing across the room, but couldn't quite make out the words.

Mannie turned and looked out at the darkening sky. When he spoke, it was little more than a mumble.

"I'm thinking there might yet be a dragon coming out of the sky, breathing fire and vengeance down on all of us."

It took everything that Devon had not to turn and look out at that same sky.

Damn it, enough with the dragon crap, already...

The hallway was wide and lined with dark, heavy doors. Several brass lamps hanging on pale walls provided an iridescent glow.

Karl had already shown most of the others to their rooms. Behind him, Carla was just disappearing through the door beyond Karl and Mannie.

Karl opened the next door.

"And this would be yours, Mr. Alvarez," he said.

Mannie stepped past Karl and started into the room. "Thank you."

"My pleasure. Sleep well."

Doubt that, thought Mannie. He heard the door close behind him.

The room was clean, almost antiseptic. There was a single bed, a chair, and one table. Drawers were built into one wall, beside a sliding panel.

Mannie moved toward the panel, pulled it aside. As he did, a light within the compartment came on. It was an empty closet.

He slid the panel closed and stepped away, moved toward a glass door in the far wall. He came out onto a private balcony, moved to the railing and rested his forearms on the top bar, leaned forward and admired the scene before him.

The night sky was a very dark blue, with no stars; but there was a glow to it that illuminated the valley that was splayed out before him. The river meandering down its center had a flickering luminosity, the hills to either side of the valley were hovering, dark silhouettes.

Carla stepped out on the balcony beside Mannie's. They acknowledged one another, but neither broke the eerie silence that seemed to lay heavily over them.

At the center of the wide, flat roof was a workstation surrounded by an encircling, three-foot high glass-walled perimeter. Above the roof, above the workstation, was the same great shell of night sky that Mannie and Carla were admiring.

Lucas stood within the workstation. He glanced only briefly at the approaching figure of his brother Karl. He casually flipped one switch, then another. Nothing happened.

Karl didn't appear to be overly concerned with Lucas' actions. He walked into the workstation area, glanced at one panel, then another, not really interested in what he was seeing. He pulled a tall stool toward him and slid onto it.

"What are you after, Lucas? What do you want?"

Lucas flipped another switch, flipped it back, without looking at his brother.

"You stole my home from me, Karl," he said.

"You stole my family from me, dear brother."

"Yeah, well..." Lucas smiled modestly. "We could have accomplished a lot together. The world we could have built."

"We don't want the same world," Karl said tiredly. "I intend to make things right. I am going to rectify the damage that you have done."

"Return this world to that empty existence we had before? I don't think so." Lucas absently flipped the switch back and forth, again and again. Nothing happened, but then he didn't expect it to.

"Think as you wish, brother."

"There is much left to do." He indicated the workstation around them. "I can now continue my work."

Karl tapped at his temple. "Not without the key."

"Yes. I know." Lucas grinned. "Your *integration* into the system."

"It won't work without recognition."

"I have not forgotten," said Lucas, fully confident now. "It was a nice upgrade. You had me for a while."

Karl chose to say nothing. *Let the boy hang himself.*

Lucas' grin broadened to a full smile. Now he tapped at his temple. "I am not without resources... *dear brother.*"

Karl shook his head sadly. "There is no other way in, Lucas."

Lucas could see Yolanda in his mind, sharp and clear. She was in her room. She was asleep.

"I know," he said. "Your key will do."

Yolanda's eyes fluttered opened. *Fear...*

"That will never happen," said Karl.

"It already has."

Yolanda was unable to move. Panic... *oh my god...*

Lucas was in control. "A simple matter, really."

He flipped a switch.

Karl could see it, could feel it.

"Lucas. No."

The world around them exploded in a tremendous shattering of color. In a flash then, all color beyond the rooftop washed to black.

Everything around them vanished.

Mannie stepped cautiously out onto his balcony. The scene was surreal. The castle they were in was now suspended in a black void. Scattered out in the distance were fragments of landscape hovering in the black.

Several cracks of lightening sent blazes of bright blue across the surface of the fragments before the shadows washed back over them.

Carla stepped out onto her own balcony. She moved slowly to the railing.

"What is this place?"

Mannie shook his head uncertainly. *How the hell would I know?*

"What happened?" Carla asked, as much to the void around them as to Mannie.

This time, Mannie had an answer. "The dragon..."

Lucas took a step back from Karl, kept himself just out of the reach of his brother.

Karl took a step closer. "Take us back," he said sharply.

"Oh, I have no intention of staying here," said Lucas.

"Don't play games, boy."

Lucas lost all sense of joviality. He was now quite serious in tone and manner.

"No games," he said. "I'm going back. You are not."

"Don't do this." Karl spoke firmly. He would not show doubt or fear.

"The woman has your mind imprint," said Lucas. "I have our father's toys. I have my home."

"Lucas..."

"What more? Time to go." Lucas felt something akin to joy. "I have a world to build."

Karl took another step nearer. This time, Lucas didn't step back. He glanced at the work panel, which was now midway between the two of them.

Karl smiled menacingly. "I think we have a point of contention that needs sorting out, don't you? Dear brother?"

Lucas didn't look as confident as he did just a moment earlier. The dominating air of big brother pushed threateningly at him.

Damn him.

His gaze shifted quickly from the panel and back to Karl. He started to think that he might just lose control of the situation.

Damn him, damn him...

Karl let the menacing look fade, leaving a coldly dead calm. "Did you really believe that you could just walk in and take all this away from me? I am not as weak, nor as naïve, as our father, dear boy."

He lifted his hand several inches, held it out so that it hovered near the panel. A visible spark jumped from his fingers down to the Plexiglas. Several small indicator lights flickered.

Lucas realized what was about to happen. He jumped at the panel and slapped at the controls.

"No!"

He wasn't in time, not that he could have done anything about it. Blue lightning cracked overhead, spidering across the great shell that enclosed the world, bathing the rooftop in the bright, blue glow.

Karl and Lucas were seized in a fractured moment in time.

The fragments of worlds hanging like ornaments in the black void rushed in on the vortex of the lonely white castle.

Yolanda was unable to move, was uncertain even that she still existed. Her terror was visible only in the glimmer of her eyes.

Lucas screamed out in anger and pain. Karl's face stiffened in fierce determination. The universe around them filled with the rush of fragments of worlds coming from a thousand different realities.

Mannie and Carla stood as silent observers on the tiny balconies, awash in the blue glow of the flashing of the blue lightning. Shadows drifted across their silhouettes as world fragments rushed toward them and past them.

All grew suddenly very slow and deathly quiet. The inrush of small worldlets toward the castle, the center of this bizarre fulcrum, gradually slowed to a near stop.

Carla turned her head in slow motion and stared at Mannie.

Mannie sensed that she was looking at him, slowly turned from the magnificent scene in front of them and looked at Carla.

Neither knew what to say, what words to speak to break the enchantment they found themselves at the heart of.

Yolanda, alone in her room, felt the paralysis ease. The muscles throughout her body, the taut lines across her face relaxed. She let her head roll slowly to one side...

She stood in the middle of an open plain. She turned her head slowly, completing the movement begun a moment before.

She turned her body; slowly, very slowly...

So many different views from so many different worlds. Each line of sight revealed a different sky, a different horizon.

In some worlds there were people. In most worlds there were not.

All the worlds... all at once.

Yolanda stopped.

Something was wrong... something was very wrong...

Please no...

Not Yolanda.

Lucas...

Lucas stood two paces from Karl.

Shock, surprise... horror shown on Lucas' face.

Karl spoke softly, but there was no remorse.

"Sorry, boy."

Alone in her room, Yolanda screamed out in agony.

Taking a shuffling step back from the balcony railing, Mannie watched the sky before him shatter into millions of tiny pieces, each a glittering blue.

A moment later the universe turned completely black.

On the rooftop, Lucas collapsed forward. Karl stepped up quickly and took hold of him, eased his brother to the floor. He stood then and moved into position before the work console. He held his hand over the panel. Again a spark jumped from his fingers.

Mannie watched as the black void beyond the balcony dissolved to the scene of the valley.

Everything looked exactly as it had earlier.

"That's some dragon," said Carla. Her hands held tight to the railing of her balcony.

Mannie started to grin, but realization swept over his face. He turned about and hurried from the balcony.

Coming into the hallway, he saw the Professor enter Yolanda's room, the General right him. The room was crowded by the time Mannie got there. He found himself standing inside the door.

Robin was sitting on the bed beside Yolanda. When she glanced up at Mannie, she looked lost.

Carla came in, pushed her way through and approached the bed. "What's going on?" she asked, not to anyone in particular.

"I think she's in a coma," said Robin.

"But how?"

"If I had to guess," said Devon, standing with his back against the wall, "I'd say that Lucas has done whatever it was he was planning; whatever he needed her for."

Mannie didn't need to see anymore. He turned about and left the room. Devon followed him several seconds later.

Carla continued looking down at Yolanda. "What could have happened?"

The Professor spoke for the first time. "I have no doubt that Mr. Devon is correct. That Lucas fellow used Miss Yates to nefarious purposes, most likely to overcome the power of his brother." He looked anxiously at the door, then at the General. "Perhaps we should follow Mannie."

At that moment, Ben came into room.

"You two go ahead," said Carla. "We'll catch up."

Mannie came into the main hall from a side door, Devon right behind him, just as the Professor and the General started down the staircase from the mezzanine.

"No sign of them?" asked the Professor.

"It's a big building," said Devon.

The four of them met at the foot of the stairs. The General looked about them, his expression dark and his tone of voice darker.

"Perhaps we should call out in some manner," he stated. "Alert our host to our desire for a dialog."

Karl appeared at the top of the stairs. "That will not be necessary, gentlemen." He looked then to his right as Carla came out onto the mezzanine, Robin and young Ben right behind her. Karl accompanied them downstairs. Once gathered together, he made a quick visual sweep of the group.

"I apologize if the disagreement between my brother and myself alarmed anyone," he said.

"It did much more than that, sir," said the General.

"Something's happened to Yolanda," said Robin.

Karl looked genuinely surprised, though not particularly upset. "That is unfortunate."

"That's it?" Carla spouted, an accusation more than a question.

"What would you have me do, Madam?"

"What was all that?" asked Mannie. "What happened?"

Carla wasn't finished yet. "What happened to Yolanda?"

Karl studied both Mannie and Carla, as if trying to decide which question to respond to. He let out a thoughtful, if calculated, sigh.

"My brother attempted to wrest control of... *of this*... from me." He indicated the world around them. "He used your friend as a conduit to gain access to the system. Connected the way they were, it would seem that Lucas brought her down with him."

"Then your brother—" Devon started.

"What was it we saw?" Mannie cut him off.

"All the worlds, all at once," said Karl. He turned an eye to Devon. "My brother is dead, Mr. Devon."

Chapter Four

Most of the group had gathered in the conservatory, all but Carla and Robin, who sat with Yolanda in her room. Mannie stood at the glass wall, looking out at the valley. The sky outside was splashed with this world's idea of evening colors. He could hear the Professor and the General, sitting together on a nearby bench, arguing in hushed voices.

Devon came up beside Mannie, looked through the glass and saw the same valley that Mannie saw. "What do we do now?" he asked.

"I don't have the slightest idea," said Mannie.

"We can't stay here."

"I'm open to suggestions." Mannie looked side-glance at Devon.

"That dude whacked his brother, and I don't think he minded doing it," said Devon. "He's as batty as Lucas ever was."

"At the moment, we have nowhere to go; and I'm not leaving Yolanda behind."

Devon grimaced at that. "Carla says she's the same."

Mannie had already heard the same. He looked over at the General and the Professor. They had stopped their discussion and were looking over in Mannie's direction. He glanced back at the one and only door. He looked hard at Devon.

"We need her," he said. "She may be our only way home."

Mannie stepped out onto the rooftop and started across toward the workstation enclosure. Karl stood in its heart, moving calmly from panel to panel. He acknowledged Mannie's arrival without stopping what he was doing or even looking up from his work.

"Good evening, sir."

"Karl," Mannie said calmly.

"You have questions, Mr. Alvarez."

"A few."

Karl continued his work. "Concerns," he stated.

"A few."

Karl lifted his attention from one of the panels and looked at Mannie for the first time.

"You are hoping to return home... you and your friends," he said. "I am guessing that Lucas promised this in return for your assistance."

"Something like that."

"With Lucas no longer among us, you are afraid that your way out has been closed to you."

"If such a way ever actually existed."

Karl's grin was unsettling. "The key question. The answer to which all else rests."

"And whether or not you will help us."

Karl dropped his gaze from Mannie down to the panels of the workstation. He spoke as he returned to his work.

"If such a thing were possible, what manner of host would I be to deny your request for assistance? Unfortunately, it is not possible. I cannot return you to your world. I am sorry."

With that, Karl flipped a switch, straightened and backed away from the panel. He stepped out of the workstation and walked several paces. He stopped then and looked out to the horizon.

There was no sound, but there was a visible burst of color and light far in the distance.

Karl spoke over his shoulder. "It will take much for me to repair the damage done by my brother," he said.

Mannie looked from the horizon back to Karl.

"But you had this equipment with you all this time," he said. "How could he have caused all this?"

"In addition to stranding our parents on some half-formed world, Lucas managed to set a number of things in motion before I was able to stop him. Most of what you see beyond the valley was created, and is still forming, from the seeds that he planted years ago."

Karl turned about and returned to the workstation. Stepping inside, he again hovered over the panels. "I must locate each of these seeds and undo what they have borne."

"Then why can't you undo our being brought here?" asked Mannie. "Send us back?"

Karl spoke in short, curt words. "Because I don't know where you come from."

Mannie was startled. He stiffened, lifted a hand and pointed in the direction of the horizon they had been looking at a minute earlier.

"Then what are you doing with all that?"

"I am removing from my world that which does not belong."

The General and Devon stood just inside the door of Mannie's room, watched Mannie come out of the bathroom wiping a wet cloth across his face.

Devon looked frustrated. "What the hell did he mean by that?" he asked Mannie.

"He thinks Lucas fouled up the pristine world that their father created, and he plans on setting it right."

"So send us home."

"He says he doesn't know how."

"And you think he's telling the truth?"

"I don't know."

The General was frowning. "Do you think Lucas really knew? How to send us back?"

"I don't know that either," said Mannie.

"If there is a way," said the General, "we need to find it."

Devon let out a dark, tired sigh. "Right now, that needs to be second on our 'To Do' list."

"Yeah," sighed Mannie.

"I suppose you're right," said the General.

"Of course I'm right. I'm not going to be *removed* without a fight."

At that moment there was a knock at the door and the Professor stuck his head in.

"Yolanda is awake."

Mannie was the last to make his way into Yolanda's crowded room. He pushed his way through the others and stood beside the bed. Robin was sitting beside Yolanda, who looked up at Mannie.

"Waddya say, Yolanda?"

"I say hey."

"How are you feeling?"

"Not too bad."

Mannie looked for a spot and sat down on the bed next to Robin.

"Did they tell you what happened?"

Yolanda took his hand. "They told me."

"Do you remember much of it?"

Yolanda looked carefully at Mannie, and it looked like she was mentally trying to put everything into place.

Robin leaned protectively nearer. "She's been through a lot, Mannie."

Mannie ignored her. "Yolanda?"

Yolanda nodded as if the gentle movement hurt. "I remember all of it," she said.

"You happy now?" said Robin.

Mannie pushed ahead. He needed to know and he needed to know sooner rather than later. They may not have a later. "Did you see what Lucas saw? Do you know what Lucas knew?"

Yolanda put on a brave smile. "You're not gonna like it."

Devon stepped out onto the balcony and stood beside Mannie.

"She's asleep," he said.

Mannie placed his hands on the railing, but said nothing. Devon turned and leaned back, looked toward the glass doors.

"The Professor says she's not going to be in any shape to move for some time."

Mannie looked out across the valley, almost as if the answer to all their problems somehow lay out there.

Devon folded his arms. "So, what are we going to do?"

"What choice do we have?"

It was an answer more than a question. Devon took that in, let it sit, then nodded and let out a surrendering sigh.

"So..." he said. He looked at Mannie, but Mannie was still looking out at the valley.

Devon turned around and leaned forward, looked out and tried to see what Mannie saw.

"Okay," he said. "We can't wait for him to *remove us from existence*."

"There's not much doubt about what he meant."

"No. There's not." Devon gripped the rail, looked down at his whitening knuckles.

Karl was standing near the edge of the roof, staring out at the horizon. It was a beautiful day, and after several hours of hard work, he deserved a moment to take stock of his accomplishments.

Mannie came out onto the rooftop, took several slow steps and stopped, realizing Karl wasn't at the workstation. He saw him then, and started toward him. Devon, Carla and the General appeared from the stairwell then and followed him.

As Mannie stepped nearer to Karl, the others moved to either side, spreading out across the roof.

Karl spoke without turning. "Your friend is better?" he asked.

Mannie stopped, still four steps away. He eyed Karl suspiciously.

"A bit."

"That is good."

"She had some interesting things to say."

Karl said nothing at first, continued to look out at the world that was spread out before them. His world...

"Did she?"

"I'm guessing you knew that," said Mannie. When Karl ignored the comment, Mannie continued. "We can't go home."

"I did tell you that, Mr. Alvarez."

"Yes you did. You said that it was because you didn't know where we came from," said Mannie, and he took a step closer. "Now that's not quite true. Is it?"

Karl now did turn about and looked at Mannie. He was calm, almost tranquil. His gaze quickly took in the others standing in a wide semicircle several paces beyond Mannie.

"I have no idea where you come from," he said. "You each come from different worlds, perhaps even from different times."

"That has nothing to do with not being able to send us home."

Karl turned back again to look out at his world. The discussion no longer interested him. "A pleasant evening, is it not?"

"The reason you can't send us home is because home no longer exists."

"Those worlds still exist," he said with a light sigh. "It is Time that has been shattered."

"What does that mean?"

"That is a complex—"

"Dumb it down for me," Mannie said sharply, cutting him off.

Karl turned about smoothly and gave Mannie a thin smile. "My father, the brilliant man that he was, created an interconnecting web consisting of Time and parallel layers of space; a very delicate, very carefully constructed web. My brother, in his ill-conceived attempt to strand me on some half-formed world, destroyed that web. Forever."

Karl looked indifferently at the others of the group, turned his attention back to the colorful horizon, seemingly unconcerned about any possible danger.

"Not his intention, to be sure," he stated.

What a beautiful, beautiful day, he thought.

"Is this where you try to kill me?" he asked. "I should tell you, I am not without defenses."

Devon was several steps behind and to one side of Mannie.

"That had been the plan," he said.

"We find, however, that it will not be necessary," said Mannie.

Karl turned precisely at the unexpected statement. His eyes darted from Devon back to Mannie. He had anticipated something different.

"Is that so?" he asked, for the first time truly curious.

"That is quite so," said the General.

"I see." Karl did not see, though he tried to maintain good form.

Mannie spoke evenly. "Remember that connection your brother established between Yolanda and that system of yours?"

"More accurately, she helped form the bridge between Lucas and the system."

"Whatever."

"That bridge still exists," said Carla.

"Between Yolanda and your machine," said Devon.

Karl smiled thinly. *All is well.* He tapped his temple with a finger.

"I changed the key," he hissed.

"Yeah," said Mannie. "And that would probably mean something if Yolanda wasn't already inside."

Karl's face paled only slightly. He was still trying to maintain control of the situation, but doubt was creeping in.

"Is that so?" he asked, a little less certainly.

"That's so," said Devon.

It took a few moments... *Something... what is that?*

A look of confusion washed slowly over Karl's face. He glanced down at the open palm of his right hand. He rubbed his fingers together.

Something is wrong...

He glanced up at Mannie.

Something is wrong...

"No." he mumbled. *Realization...* "Please."

"I'm sorry."

Karl vanished.

There was a brief, hollow sucking sound, and hair and loose clothing were drawn toward the empty space where Karl had been.

Mannie, Devon, Carla and the General were alone on the roof.

Chapter Five

Mannie approached the children's playground at the base of the hillside, the gleaming castle structure towering overhead. He wore a light jacket, a backpack slung over one shoulder, both fairly new.

He came up to Devon and Carla, standing near the swing set. A hundred yards beyond, the General, the Professor, Robin and young Ben were standing in the heart of a patch of freshly turned earth. Robin and Ben were working the soil with shovel and rake. The Professor and the General looked to be doing more discussing and arguing than working.

Devon stepped away from the swing set. "You sure you don't want me to go with you? Only take me five minutes to get my gear together."

"I'll be fine," said Mannie.

"All right, if you're sure. I just hope you're not wasting your time."

Mannie gave a faint shrug. "I know I'll find at least one."

Devon grinned. "You think you can pry her away from that dusty old town?"

"You better," Carla ordered.

"For sure." Devon's grinned broadened. "Mrs. Johansen is the only decent cook in this whole world."

"I'll do my best," said Mannie. His own smile was sad.

"You do that," Carla said, this time more softly. "I'll keep a light on for you."

Mannie looked as though he was going to reach a hand out to Carla, instead shifted the weight of his backpack. "Don't wait up," he said.

Carla reached in close and gave him a light kiss. Mannie looked uncomfortable, but not displeased.

Devon waited for Carla to step back.

"How long you figure you'll be?" he asked.

"Don't really know. But if there are others out there, I need to find 'em. Without the arrivals, they'll be living off the land, what's out there."

"Not possible," stated Devon.

"Exactly."

"Send 'em to us," said Carla.

Mannie appeared ready to go. He glanced over at the group preparing the garden bed.

"Fresh vegetables."

"Eight to twelve weeks, they say," said Devon.

"I might be able to make that."

"We may have stores enough for years—" Carla started.

"—but fresh," Devon finished the thought, "now that's worth coming back for, eh?"

"Absolutely," said Mannie. *There's so little of anything out there.*

The three grew silent. Mannie looked at Devon, then Carla. She again leaned forward and they hugged awkwardly. He turned and shook hands with Devon.

"Don't send us any whackos," said Devon.

"I'll tell 'em the mountains are full of dragons."

Mannie started away. After several steps, he looked ill at ease. He stopped, turned back to the others.

"I never would have let her do that," he said, "if I'd known."

"I don't know that she knew," said Devon.

"I'm sure she's all right, Mannie," said Carla. *Wherever she is... With Karl? They couldn't know. Not for sure.*

"Yeah..."

He started walking again. He looked over at the others toiling in the garden as he passed by.

Robin and Ben stopped their work and waved. The Professor and the General each gave a slight bow.

Epilog

Mannie walked down the center of the dusty street, casually glanced at each building that he passed, looking for any sign of life. The small backpack was strapped to his back; a canteen hung on his belt.

The little town hadn't changed much. Actually, it hadn't changed at all; a handful of weathered buildings with worn, faded siding. He could see his small shack at the end of the row of buildings on his right.

He had the strange sensation of returning home. How odd. He had never thought of this rundown collection of old buildings as home when he lived here. But more than half his time on this world had been spent in this town. He had felt some sense of safety during his time here.

And he hadn't been alone. Here he had found a family of sorts.

He had never thought he needed anyone. He had never been one to have a lot of friends, had never reached out to anyone. But, if pressed on the point, it had been... comfortable... having others nearby, sitting down to dinner with other people... sharing the situation with comrades.

He drifted toward the community hall. He paused only a moment at the foot of the steps, climbed up onto the porch and went inside. He was back out on the porch half a minute later. He stepped onto the top step and looked out at the town. The only movement was dust blowing across the main street.

Mannie appeared to be alone.

He took the steps one at a time, walked down the street to his shack. He left his gear inside his front door, then walked around back and over to the water tank.

It still worked. The running water seemed louder somehow. He washed his face and hands, took a drink, then took the towel and dried his face. He folded the towel neatly and placed it back on its hook.

Mannie stood on the porch of his old shack. He was dressed in fresh, if well-worn clothes. The sky had taken on the dusk colors common to this world. The reds and blues were darker, the shadows murkier.

The town was enveloped in a haunting emptiness.

Mannie's world was a very quiet, very lonely place.

He straightened then, slowly, and looked at a flicker of movement in the distance. As he watched, a silhouette took shape.

Someone was approaching town.

Mannie stepped off the porch and faced the approaching figure. Not until the person was within a hundred yards did Mannie's expression change.

Mrs. Johansen was carrying a large sack over one shoulder. She smiled as she neared, stopped two steps from Mannie and slowly brought sack around off her shoulder and set it down in front of her.

"Good evening, Mrs. Johansen."

"Hello, Mannie," she said. "Good to see you."

"You too." He smiled as he indicated the sack. "D'ya bring me anything?"

Mrs. Johansen reached into the sack, rummaged around and pulled out an orange. She straightened, eyed Mannie, and handed him the orange.

Mannie smelled it appreciatively. There wouldn't be many more of these.

"Very nice. Thanks."

"You're welcome."

Mannie reached down with his free hand and picked up Mrs. Johansen's sack. The two of them walked down the center of the street. A slight breeze blew dust across the scene.

"So, Mrs. Johansen. What are your thoughts regarding carrots?"

"That depends. Cooked or raw?"

"Yes. I suppose that makes a difference, doesn't it?"

"Does to me."

~ End ~

The Caravan

The fourteen wagons of the Carver caravan formed a long column that stretched out across the grassy, rolling plain. Each had a driver and a passenger riding shotgun. More than a hundred men, women and children walked alongside. A security team rode on horseback, on left and right flank, front and rear.

The Carver Family wasn't the largest caravan in the North Region, but it was well-organized, well-armed and well-supplied. The wagons included an armory, chuck wagon, children's nursery, medical wagon, supply wagons. They looked a lot like the wagons of the old west, centuries past, but these had been infused with the characteristics of those of the traveling circus and of Gypsy caravans. Most had been modified to include wooden enclosures.

The members of the caravan dressed in contemporary, rugged outdoor clothing, but of many different styles and fashions.

Austin had been with the Carver Family for seven years, almost since its inception. He had been riding shotgun for three years, most of that on the lead wagon. During that time, the caravan had been attacked four times while on the trail. Each assault had been successfully beaten back.

When he saw the silhouette of a city skyline shimmering purple on the horizon, Austin knew they were only a few hours away from the end of another long trek. Not long after, he saw one of the three forward scouts turn his horse about and begin to drift slowly back toward the main body of the caravan. It took only a few moments for him to identify the rider as the leader of the caravan.

"Wonder what Mr. Carver wants," said Marley, the driver of the wagon. Rob Marley had been a member of the Carver Family even longer than Austin. He was in his late forties, a good ten years older than Austin, and was a bit out of shape, though not overly so.

"We'll soon find out," said Austin, though he had a pretty good idea.

John Carver stopped a dozen yards ahead and waited for the wagon to approach. "Two hours," he said. "Keep a sharp eye."

Austin nodded silently.

The Family never brought their caravan fully into any of the long-dead communities they visited, choosing instead to make camp outside the town perimeter and send teams in to search for supplies. Nonetheless, coming up on a town was always precarious. While the way had been scouted several weeks earlier, and they knew where they were going and what they expected to find, there was the chance that marauders, or another band, either from within the city itself or from another caravan, might be laying in wait for them.

Austin's wagon continued forward and John Carver patiently waited for the next wagon in line. Carver was a big man, strong muscled and broad shouldered. He had a sober disposition and his demeanor suggested that he took his responsibility as leader of the caravan very seriously.

"Be great to get off the trail for a while," said Marley. He stared dully ahead. "Wouldn't mind settling in for a month or two."

"If supplies are as good as they say, I expect you'll get your wish," said Austin. While the city had most certainly been gone through a number of times over the years, it was a big place. Preliminary searches indicated that there was a lot yet to bring out. They expected to fully supply the caravan and Austin had heard talk that they might be wintering there. He hoped so. Traveling through the wet season was not pleasant.

He sensed movement and glanced down at the set of mirrors that gave him full range of view of the procession behind him.

Those on foot immediately behind the lead wagon were beginning to draw nearer, no doubt anxious to get where they were going now that Carver had made it official: they would be there well before nightfall.

After glancing quickly to the tree line far to their right and noting the flank guard, he turned and looked back at the woman and her son walking beside the wagon.

"Any word on what Saul is cooking up for us?" he asked.

Sandi shrugged and said nothing.

"Fish," said Daniel. Daniel Carver was nine years old, the grandson of John Carver. His father had been killed five years earlier.

"Okay. Fish sounds good."

"Yup," said Daniel.

The chuck wagon was designed so that Saul could do a lot of his preparations while on the move, and complete the meal once they stopped and set up camp. They traveled three hours in the morning and three in the afternoon. This gave them plenty of time in the morning and evening to take care of the day-to-day affairs that were best dealt with when not moving, and they usually spent an hour or so midday relaxing over lunch. They were in no real hurry. They usually had all they needed, and they would get where they were going when they got there.

Rob Marley grumbled from his place beside Austin.

"My god, man, how much more of that do we have to endure?"

Austin turned and grinned. "Oh, come on, Rob. Waddya got against fish?"

"Nothing. You know that's not what I'm talking about."

"Oh, that's funny."

Daniel spoke up then. "We caught a lot."

"And you did your part, Daniel. Your first time out, too." Austin turned to Daniel's mother. "Ain't that right, Sandi?"

Sandi Carver showed little emotion. "That he did."

Austin heard Marley chuckling under his breath and turned about sharply.

"Just what are you laughing at?"

"Nothing at all, my man. Nothing at all."

"You just mind where you're going, Marley."

"Not a problem, Austin. Not a problem."

Austin settled back into position and returned to performing his duty as shotgun for the lead wagon. They traveled in silence for a long while. Austin glanced occasionally at the mirror reflections of Sandi and the boy, then at the tree lines in the distance to either side of them, and back to the figures of the two riders several hundred yards ahead of them.

John Carver rode past on his way back to the forward scouts. A few minutes later a pair of riders rode up from mid-caravan and hurried past. They would be going on ahead to scout out the encampment site one final time, making sure that all was safe.

As they neared the outskirts of the abandoned city, Carver directed the wagons from his position on horseback, calling out to the drivers and indicating where they should draw their wagons.

The configuration was always the same, so once Rob Marley had brought the lead wagon to a stop and Austin had jumped down, those coming up behind needed little direction. Carver watched it all with a careful eye and occasionally barked out orders to move forward or back.

Even before Rob Marley had guided his wagon into final position, security watches had begun moving to their posts under the direction of Mr. Brown, the security team leader who had scouted the area weeks before with the survey team.

Once stopped, the wagonmasters climbed down, took a few moments to stretch and make shrewd comments to their fellows, and then set about to take care of their animals. The horses would soon be under the control of the animal master, but not before they had been groomed and brushed and cared for by the drivers.

Everyone had a job to do. There was the mess hall to set up, the sleeping quarters and the latrines. As this was to be not just an overnight encampment, they would also be establishing the supply depot, medical tent, children's nursery and school, and much more. All facilities would be set up in anticipation of a "long-stay".

Being part of the security team, the shotguns went on defense immediately upon arrival. Austin started across the clearing with two weapons in hand: the shotgun and a rifle. He maneuvered his way through the controlled chaos to reach the armory wagon. The side of the wagon was already open, exposing the weapons lockers. The armorer and an assistant stood before the lockers.

Austin handed over his shotgun without a word.

"Thank you, Austin," said the armorer, and with that turned about and set the weapon in its place in the locker.

Austin had already started toward his designated post, his rifle cradled across his folded arm.

Permanent security posts would be constructed over the coming days, but for now they were set up as a daily stop. Austin's position was a small, cleared area set just in the shadows at the edge of an open meadow. A thousand yards across the large field were the outskirts of the abandoned city.

There were no major skyscrapers, but there was a core downtown area from which a number of buildings rose up, several of them eight to ten stories tall.

The building nearest Austin was an office building, three stories tall with lots of dark windows. It sat at the outer edge of the city, bordering the field that spanned the distance between the city and Austin's outpost. It was surrounded by what had once been a parking lot.

Far to his right, Austin could just make out the line of an old highway that cut across the field on its way into the city. The road was grown over now, long since encroached upon by the surrounding vegetation, but the telltales were there: the straight line of a narrow, smooth band of terrain and the occasional road sign still standing.

Austin saw no movement within his watch area but for advancing shadows and the occasional bat darting about in the early evening sky. From behind him came the sounds of the camp coming together. They would be putting up the wood framing and raising tents, building campfire pits, digging latrine trenches, and going about a dozen other activities that needed to be done before they would settle down for the evening.

The dusk had almost turned to dark when Mr. Brown approached from the direction of the camp.

"Austin," he said.

"Good evening, Mr. Brown."

Mr. Brown stood silent a moment, looking in the direction of the city. "It's quiet."

"Not a sound." Austin indicated the camp behind them. "How're things looking?"

"About set for the night."

"So... waddya think? A *long-stay*?"

"Already prepping for it."

"Marley's hoping for two months."

Mr. Brown gave a sage nod. "I believe Mr. Marley will get his wish. We may be laying in for the entire season."

"You won't hear any complaints from me," sighed Austin.

Mr. Brown continued to look coolly across the open field. The two men were silent for a few moments, and when Mr. Brown spoke again, he did so without taking his eyes off the city across the way.

"All depends on what we find in there. Prelims look good. I expect there's a bit in there we can use."

"And we have a good location," said Austin. He didn't much like the thought of winter travel this far north. He was familiar with this area. He'd grown up about a week's travel to the east.

"We're here for a fortnight no matter what the foraging teams come out with." Mr. Brown's manner changed then, suggesting that he was getting ready to relieve Austin. His tone of voice suggested the same.

"You may stand down, Austin. You are relieved."

"Sir?"

"I have eyes and a workable trigger finger. I'll do well enough till your relief gets here. Go get yourself some dinner while there's still something left. It's fish tonight."

"Yes sir." He started away rather uncertainly. "Thank you sir."

Austin walked across the partially established camp, his weapon cradled familiarly across his arm. Inside the camp perimeter, within the circle of wagons and animal pens, were the rows of individual tents and a number of family-size tents. A handful of campfires were scattered about the central commons.

Along one side of the camp were the larger tents and pole buildings that would be the supply stations, medical station, school, nursery, and work stations. For now, most stood empty or contained boxes and crates waiting to be unpacked.

Austin nodded silent hellos and waved to several people as he crossed the center of the camp and worked his way to the mess tent; two rows of poles holding up a canvas canopy. Inside were eight folding tables with benches, enough to hold a third of the population. The far wall of the tent was formed by Saul's chuck wagon, the side of which was open now and exposing the kitchen within. The lowered side became an L-shaped work counter, behind which Saul now stood. Food was laid out on the counter around him, and a short line was slowly progressing along one side.

Austin worked his way across the mess and toward the chuck wagon. There were a dozen or so people sitting at several of the tables. John Carver was at the corner table with his daughter Sandi and young Daniel.

"Hey Saul," said Austin, picking up a plate and waiting at the end of the line.

"A pleasant good evening, Austin." Saul smiled in his direction, continuing his work. He was spooning the last of the boiled potatoes into a serving dish. There were only a few servings left of some of the food items.

"How's the fish, tonight?"

"Absolutely wonderful, dear sir. I haven't heard a single complaint."

"Who would dare?" Austin moved forward, near enough now that he could reach the first food dish, the green beans. "Full spread tonight, I see."

"Absolutely."

Austin looked down at the flat tray upon which lay slabs of some pale, fleshy, skinless fillets.

"I don't know how you do it, Saul," said Austin. "You are the master of your profession."

"You are too kind, sir."

Austin worked his way through the line and took his plate to an open seat at one of the tables. He ate in silence, watching the dinner crowd slowly thin out. Very few came in after him, mostly the last of those coming off security detail.

He could hear the sounds of the camp settling into evening: singing, laughing, campfire chatter. It was all faintly muffled by the hollow silence that seemed to press in from beyond the perimeter.

His attention was continually drawn to the table at which Sandi Carver sat with her father and her son Daniel. He was just finishing up when Bennett came into the tent and walked hurriedly past him. He returned to Austin's table a few moments later with two cups of coffee.

"Hey, Austin," he said, sitting down beside him. He slid one of the coffees over to him. "What say?"

Bennett was about thirty, had a rugged appearance. There was an independent air about his manner. He was good-natured, but there was always the sense that he was just waiting for something better to come along. Despite this, he and Austin had become good friends.

"I say hey, Bennett." Austin pushed his plate aside and picked up the offered coffee, though his attention was still on Sandi, not so much on Bennett. "You off duty already?"

"'til morning. You going in tomorrow, ain't ya?"

"Team One." Austin would be going into the city with one of the foraging teams. He would be serving as security, allowing the foragers to focus on getting supplies. Bennett would also be doing security. He was one of the Security Riders, riding flank when the caravan was on the trail.

"Team Two. Should be fun," he grinned.

"I just want it to be uneventful," said Austin.

"Oh, don't say that, my friend. A surprise or two would be quite nice after such a quiet traverse across the wilderness."

Austin took another drink from his coffee, set the cup down carefully and mumbled, "No surprises."

"Aw... warehouse full of pretty new clothes? Or how about a couple a' dozen cases of MREs?"

"That'd be great," Austin said mildly. "And that's not what you meant."

"Loosen up, old boy. Whatever comes is comin'."

There was a moment's pause in the conversation, then Austin frowned.

"Mr. Brown is in another of moods," he said.

"The kindly uncle, am I right?" Bennett smirked. "He's a strange one, for sure. Damn good security chief, though."

Austin nodded in silent agreement. Bennett's smile turned conspiratorial.

"You know what I heard?" he asked. "Long time past... maybe four, five long-stays back, I don't remember exactly where..."

"Wha'd you hear?" Austin asked, though a bit distracted.

"I heard that Mr. Brown was a school teacher before. Little kids." Bennett took a sip of his coffee, kept pattering on. "He hardly seems old enough. Does he to you? I mean, I hardly even remember before. Just a kid, myself. You?"

"I thought he was a sergeant in the army."

"That was before he was a teacher." Bennett shrugged. "Maybe it was after."

Bennett finally grew quiet. Both were looking over at Sandi, who was in deep conversation with her father.

Bennett leaned over close to Austin. "You ever plan on gettin' in on that?"

"Don't be crude," said Austin.

Bennett straightened and tried his best to look offended. It only lasted a moment, though, and then he got serious.

"Listen, man. Mourning period is long, long over. Being John Carver's daughter doesn't give her any special privileges."

"If she's not ready, she's not ready," Austin said flatly. "I'll respect that, if it's all the same to you."

Bennett now put on his most tired, sad expression. "Oh, dear boy, dear boy... my poor, deluded dear boy. What am I to do with you?"

"You could give me some peace, for a start."

"Mr. Carver's grandson needs a daddy."

"Daniel has Carver. That'll do for now."

"Oh, Austin. What are you afraid of? Do Brian's shoes seem so large in your eyes that they cannot be filled?"

Now Austin gave Bennett a hard look. He spoke in a cool, almost menacing tone.

"When have you ever known me to be afraid of anything, Bennett?"

Bennett leaned back and held up both hands in a mocking defensive gesture.

"Hey. "I'm just sayin..." Now Bennett's expression turned darkly serious. "If you don't move in on that, someone else will."

As Austin watched, Sandi turned briefly away from her conversation with Carver and looked distractedly in Austin's direction. It was almost as if she had sensed that he had been watching her.

Her expression didn't change, and she turned away without acknowledging him, returned to her quiet discussion with her father.

Young Daniel looked at Austin. The boy gave him a slight smile and a brief wave. Austin gave a half-wave in return before Daniel turned back to his mother and grandfather.

Bennett looked admiringly at Daniel when he spoke again to Austin.

"Somebody's gonna be that kid's daddy. If it ain't you, then somebody else."

Austin spoke without taking his eyes from Sandi and Daniel. "Shut up, Bennett."

chapter two...

Austin stepped out of his small, one-man tent just before dawn, his rifle in hand. The camp glowed faintly in predawn gray, illuminated somewhat by the glowing embers of the numerous campfires that were still smoldering. Fingers of fog slowly crawled between the tents and across the central compound.

He could see lanterns burning in the mess tent. He pulled on his jacket and started toward it. Bennett joined him halfway across the compound and they entered together.

Two women, Jones and Jennie, were already there, seated at one of the tables.

Jones was about thirty. She dressed sharp and efficient, wore her long, black hair pulled back tight across her scalp and hanging down her back in a braided tail. She was quiet by nature, but this quiet had a dark, shadowy feel about it.

She was a member of the survey team that had performed the earlier recon of the city they would be going into.

Jennie was Saul's assistant and his niece. She was in her early twenties and had a natural attractiveness. She did her best to take some of the pressure off her uncle, and was quick to come to his defense when she thought someone was trying to take advantage of his kind disposition.

Austin and Bennett reached Saul. He offered them each coffee and they returned to Jones and Jennie with cups in hand.

"Morning, ladies," said Austin as they sat down.

"Good morning, Austin," said Jennie.

Jones nodded her 'good morning' silently.

"So what do you think, Jones?" asked Bennett, a bit too loud for so early in the morning. "You've been in the city. You did the early recons. What are we going to be taking out of there?"

Jones seemed less than thrilled at the prospect of giving Bennett a rundown on the inventory.

"Clothes, kitchenware, tools..."

"That much still in there?" Bennett urged. "After all these years?"

"Books too, she said," said Jennie.

"Yeah? What kind of books?" asked Austin.

Jones was nodding in calm agreement. "Saw some how-to books we could use. And repair guides, stuff like that."

"And school books for the children," said Jennie.

"That's pretty cool," said Austin.

The remaining members of the two foraging teams began trickling into the mess tent: Madsen, Thomas, Carl, Talbot, Rawley, Takemura.

John Carver was the last to come in. Saul poured a fresh cup and had it ready by the time the leader of the caravan had reached him.

"Thank you, Saul." He turned about and faced the room. "Good morning, everyone. I trust you are all ready for today's foray, eager to be about it."

Most of the room offered a 'good morning' in return, sprinkled with 'absolutely' and 'yes sir'.

"I want you all to be careful in there," he said. "Take it easy this first trip."

His eyes fell on Austin and Bennett. He gave them a sharp look. "You two don't take any chances with my people. You have any concerns at all, you pull 'em out. There's nothing in there worth risking lives over."

"We'll take care of 'em, sir," said Austin.

"Count on it, Mr. Carver," said Bennett.

Carver acknowledged their responses with a sharp nod before turning to the rest of the group. "And the rest of you... you know the drill. You listen to your security. It's what they're there for. It's what they're trained for."

He looked over at Jones. He put on a rare smile, nodded in her direction. "My surveyor here tells me there's a lot of good stuff in there. Right, Jones?"

"Yes, sir."

"So bring me some," he told the group. There was more 'yes sir' and more 'absolutely sir', before Carver ended his pep talk. "Good luck, then. I'll see you this afternoon when you get back."

With that, everyone rose up from the tables and began moving toward the exit. Saul called out to his niece just as she reached the tent flap.

"Jennie! Bring me back some salt!"

"You got it, Uncle." Jennie leaned close to Austin, grinned and spoke in a mumble. "We better damn well find salt."

Two small, open supply wagons waited outside the mess tent, each being pulled by a single, stout horse.

Austin and Jennie started toward the forward wagon. Madsen moved up to the horse and took hold of the lead. After a brief conversation with Carver, Jones moved out ahead of the first wagon and started forward, and Madsen started the wagon forward.

Austin looked back to the Team Two group, still milling around the second wagon.

"Thomas! You coming or not?"

Thomas finished up his conversation with Talbot and double-stepped to his own team.

Bennett stood to one side of the team that he would be protecting. He gave a strong nod to Austin and Austin replied with a slight wave of two fingers, settled his rifle across his arm, and followed alongside his team.

Madsen led the horse down the center of the asphalt thoroughfare, following the double-yellow line that had once been used to separate vehicles hurtling towards each other at forty miles per hour. The horse's hoofsteps echoed loudly down the empty manmade canyon with its strange walls of glass and brick and concrete.

Jones, guiding the team from one supply location to the next, kept pace a hundred feet ahead of the wagon. Austin followed directly to the left of the wagon, staying on the concrete sidewalk close up against the buildings. Jennie and Thomas followed several dozen paces behind the wagon, watching the darkened windows and doors and the mouths of the alleyways for any signs of danger.

All on the team had strapped on sidearms before entering the city perimeter, though Austin was the only member who actually had a weapon at the ready, his rifle resting on his right forearm, his left hand resting on the trigger guard. His shotgun and several other weapons were in the back of the wagon.

Up ahead, Jones entered the next intersection. She stopped, pausing to look to her left and right, scrutinizing the scene in both directions. Above her, dead traffic lights hung low and still on metal cables. Satisfied that all was safe, she started forward again, continuing across the intersection and down the street.

They had been in the city for three hours, and they had not seen any signs of life. They had visited three locations that Jones had mapped earlier, and had come upon several others by chance. The wagon was half full, mostly children's clothing, though they had also found some writing supplies and kitchenware. They had even found horse tack that had been left behind in a ransacked pawn shop.

"Hold up, Madsen," said Austin. He stopped in front of a large window. The bottom floor of the building housed a department store; the upper floors appeared to be offices or living quarters.

Austin could see that the store had been gone through more than once over the years by other foragers. Nothing had been left undisturbed.

"Waddya see?" asked Jennie. She walked calmly towards him, her hand resting casually on the butt of her holstered pistol. Thomas waited out in the street.

Austin waited for her to come up beside him, then pointed to a shadow in the store.

"There."

"I don't..." Jennie started, then smiled thinly, "Ah."

A large dog sat in the shadow of an empty display case. It was looking directly at them, but showed no emotion. It didn't appear angry or frightened, but it didn't look happy to see them, either. Austin looked away from the dog, carefully examining the rest of the floor, what could be seen from the window.

A staircase in the far corner was half hidden behind several empty shelves that had been shoved to one side, as if by chance. The stairs themselves looked partially blocked by empty boxes and large drums.

"There," he said quietly, indicating the staircase.

Jennie nodded silently. Meanwhile, Madsen had left the horse and wagon and came up behind them.

"What's the big attraction?"

"Somebody's living here," said Jennie.

"Yeah?"

"Trying not to show it," Jennie said matter-of-factly.

"Let's move," said Austin.

"Come now, Austin," said Madsen. "That's not very neighborly."

"You want to invite them over to meet the family?"

"Why not?" Madsen gave the building another look-over. "Too pushy?"

"Maybe another time."

Jennie looked from the staircase to the dog. "Looks like a nice dog."

Madsen smirked. "You're on this side of the glass and he's on that side." He put his forehead up close to the window pane and studied the interior. "They've gone to a lot of trouble to hide their presence. That's for darn sure. No signs of traffic comin' and goin', not a spec a' dust outta place. They're good."

Austin turned at the sound of a sharp whistle.

Jones had stopped and had come back as far as the intersection. She held out her arms in a questioning gesture. Austin gave a wave to Jones and nodded to the others to move out.

Bennett stood guard outside a windowless building as the rest of Foraging Team Two brought out boxes of children's clothes. Their wagon was in the middle of the street directly in front of the open door, already more than a third full.

Rawley came up beside Bennett, cardboard box in hand. He lifted out a cute outfit for a young girl and held it up for Bennett to see.

"Check this out, Bennett," he said. "My sister's kid would love this."

Bennett hardly glanced at the outfit, his attention focused on their surroundings. He was watchful, but not overly anxious.

"Yeah, it's cute, Rawley."

Talbot approached Bennett as Rawley continued on to the wagon. He turned to the door, his back to the street. He spoke calmly.

"You see him?" he asked.

"I see him."

Behind Talbot, in the alley across the street, the silhouette of a human figure slid deeper into the shadows.

"Waddya think?" asked Talbot.

"Just curious, most likely. Wouldn't you be?"

Takemura came out of the building carrying a box of clothes. Talbot nodded curtly at the man as he passed by on his way to the supply wagon.

"I would," said Talbot, in answer to Bennett. "I might also have already sent someone to bring back a bunch of my friends."

Bennett studied the shadowy silhouette in the alley as it shifted into and out of the other shadows.

"He knows we know; doesn't seem to mind that too awful much." Bennett glanced at the wagon, gave a quick look back at the door to the warehouse.

"How much longer, you figure?"

"Why? What are you thinking?"

Bennett nodded to Carl, the surveyor for the team. Carl moved to stand nearer to the wagon and take up watch.

Bennett started across the street, spoke over his shoulder to Talbot.

"I think I'll go have a chat with our new friend."

"You're always the one to reach out a hand, Bennett."
"Hey. Could be fun."

Team One was moving down a narrow, heavily shadowed street. The buildings had dark brick facades with large doors and few windows.

As before, Austin walked on the sidewalk to one side of their wagon. Madsen led the horse. Up ahead, Jones led the way.

The sound of a distant rifle shot echoed down the canyon-like avenue.

Madsen stopped the horse and wagon. Ahead of them, Jones gradually moved to one side of the street. Jennie and Thomas calmly moved up close to the wagon, their hands resting on their weapons. The wagon would provide some minimal cover, should the need arise.

Austin calmly studied the second-storey windows for indications of movement. He saw none.

"Bennett's ought-six," said Jennie.

Austin gave only the briefest affirmative nod in reply. He was listening for anything further that might tell them what was happening with Team Two. All the while, they watched for any sign of trouble in their surroundings.

Finally, Jennie visibly relaxed. "Guess he got what he was aiming at," she said.

A few moments more, then Austin took a step off the sidewalk. He looked in Jones' direction and the two of the made eye contact. At some silent agreement, Jones turned about and started forward again.

The rest of the team followed.

John Carver was helping put together the framing of what would be the schoolhouse. Two others of the Carver Family were working with him.

He stepped back, hammer in hand, and admired their work.

Coming along just fine, he thought to himself. He sensed movement on his left and turned to see Mr. Brown coming toward him. *And just when I was starting to enjoy myself.*

"Let's break for lunch," he told his coworkers.

The two men left just as the security chief reached him.

"We may have a problem," Mr. Brown stated.

"Problems can lead to good things, Mr. Brown; if properly managed."

"Yes, sir." Mr. Brown was frequently confronted with such clever observations. He didn't look all that convinced.

Carver moved to a table and set down his hammer. "That gunshot we heard earlier?"

"It could be related. As likely not."

Carver took a moment to consider what that might mean. When he saw his daughter and grandson approaching, he decided not to dwell on it. He would find out soon enough.

"Okay, Mr. Brown. I'll be right there. Give me a minute to get cleaned up."

Sandi looked anxiously at the receding figure of the head of security as she and her son reached Carver.

"Everything all right, Father?"

"Nothing to worry about, I shouldn't think. We may have some entertainment before long."

He smiled encouragingly down at his grandson, placed a strong hand on the boy's shoulder. "You two go enjoy your lunch. Make my apologies to Saul. All right?"

"Yes sir," said Daniel.

Austin and the rest of Team One approached the small, downtown city park right at midday. The lawn and shrubs had long ago become overgrown, and the once neatly manicured landscape now had a wild, natural look.

When he saw Team Two approaching the park from another street, he slowed down to wait for Bennett, letting his team move on into the park. When near enough that the two could talk comfortably, Austin spoke in a jovial tone.

"Shooting at rabbits?" he asked.

"Ah..." Bennett sighed. "The idiot freaked on me. I was just lookin' to talk, maybe gain a little intel."

"That's too bad." As they continued forward, he indicated the teams up ahead of them. "How are your foragers doing?"

"Lotta stuff for the kids. Brand new." He swung his rifle around and rested it on his shoulder. "Man, I am so ready for lunch."

The two wagons stood in the heart of the park beside a small playground that was still open and clear. Scattered about were several benches and a couple of round wooden tables.

The horses were being seen to by Madsen and Talbot. Rawley was at one of the tables, distributing the lunch of bread and cheese that Saul had put together for them.

Austin took his with him and stood watch at one end of the park. He had a clear view of an intersection formed by the main streets that met up at the south side of the park.

Looking back over his shoulder, he could see the playground, the wagons, and the members of the two teams settling in around the tables and benches. Beyond, Bennett was stood watch at the opposite end of the park.

Jennie stepped away from the playground and started in his direction. He turned about, munched on bread and cheese and waited for her to reach him.

"Not a bad morning, all things considered," she said.

Austin nodded calmly, took another bite of cheese and gave a half-smile. "No salt for Saul."

Jennie chuckled lightly. "There's still time, Austin. Best not go back without the salt."

"That depends on how badly he needs it."

"Ya' can't salt the fish without salt."

There was a long pause then as Austin tried to come up with something else to say.

"We can use those clothes," he said finally.

"I can't wait to see them on the children." Jennie stared in the direction of the empty street bisecting the park. Nothing was moving. "Quiet town," she said. "Except for Bennett's rabbit."

Austin mumbled in agreement without really saying anything.

"You think many people live here?" asked Jennie.

"Not many."

"S'pose not... 'cept those over the store, of course. They can't be too pleased with us showing up."

"I wouldn't think so."

"I wonder if Bennett's rabbit was part of that group."

"If I had to guess one way or the other, I'd say it was likely. Can't know for sure."

Jennie accepted this, and the conversation shifted.

"Think we'll get a chance to do much fishing while we're here?"

"Don't know. Maybe," said Austin. "We're pretty well stocked up. Besides, you haven't found Saul's—"

"Yeah, yeah," she said quickly, cutting him off.

A bright flare suddenly rose up into the sky, high above the city skyline. A faint tail of smoke trailed away behind it.

"Damn," growled Austin. He absently tossed the piece of bread that he hadn't quite finished and vigilantly monitored the perimeter of the park.

"Problem," Jennie stated flatly. "What do you think? The camp under attack?"

"Couldn't say. Could be anything," said Austin. "Could be an attack, could be some kid coughed up a fur ball and Doc's afraid it's contagious."

"Or they're telling us that the foraging teams are in danger," said Jennie. "Maybe we stirred something up. That rabbit, maybe."

Austin looked back at the rest of the group. They were calmly preparing to head out. Jones caught his attention and gave the signal.

"Let's go," he told Jennie.

Jones led both teams through the city. She stayed twenty yards ahead of the two wagons, which traveled half a dozen yards apart. Austin walked flank on one side of the group, Bennett on the other. Everyone was armed and ready for anything.

When they reached a small freight office, the wagons were taken around to the side of the two-storey building by the wagonmasters while the rest of the team went inside.

Austin, Bennett and Jones went up the stairs while the others settled in to wait.

Coming out onto the roof, Austin spoke over his shoulder to Bennett as he started across.

"Check the city."

Austin approached the west side of the building, dropping into a crouch the last few feet. Once in position behind the short façade, he reached into his jacket pocket and pulled out a small pair of binoculars.

Jones scrambled up beside him. She looked out across the grassy terrain with the naked eye.

They weren't directly opposite the camp, but rather a ways south. With his binoculars, Austin could see the individual tents and wagons, the fire pits, and the movement of the family members.

Everyone in the camp appeared calm but resolute.

"Looks like stage one defense," he told Jones, then handed her the binoculars.

Bennett came up beside them. "The city's quiet."

"Looks like the threat is to the camp," said Austin.

Jones handed the binoculars back to Austin. "I don't see anything, but they're preparing for something, all right."

Bennett took out his own pair of binoculars. He saw John Carver come from around the back of the mess tent on horseback.

Carver swung his right leg around and slid from the saddle. Rob Marley, just coming out of the mess tent, took hold of the horse's halter.

"Let me take care of her for you, Mr. Carver."

"Thank you, Rob."

"Helluva a day."

"It has its good and bad, Mr. Marley. As do they all." Carver gave his horse a gentle hand on the shoulder. "Ask Jonas to give her something special."

"Will do."

Inside the mess tent, Saul was waiting for John Carver with coffee cup in hand.

"Dear Saul," John sighed appreciatively, taking the offered cup. "You always know just what I need."

Saul waited for Carver to take several swallows. "Any idea what we're dealing with?" he finally asked.

"Twenty or thirty of them, I'd say. Well equipped, but a lot of Old World techno."

Saul shook his head sadly. "Our way... our way is best. Better not to become dependent on that which we cannot maintain ourselves."

Carver rested a hand on Saul's shoulder.

"My mentor, my conscious, dear friend; as you have been since the beginning."

"Our way has served us well."

"That is true," John nodded as he took another sip of Saul's fine coffee. "As the Old World fades further into the past, the techno of the past seems less important."

His smile then took on a faintly devious quality. "And yet it seems that we continue to forage through the dead cities of that past for much of what we need."

Saul wagged a crooked finger. "We do not bring out techno." He had the look of a wizened old professor deriding a student who has gone astray.

"Quite right, quite right." There was an uncomfortable pause, and then Carver held his coffee cup up between them. "Such is our way."

"It is the way. Truth is truth."

"Is it?" Carver took a moment then, glanced into his cup, studied it as if the answer lay there. "It is all a matter of selecting truths that best suit our needs, is it not?"

"We choose philosophies of our own design in order that we might survive."

"Yes, and thereby we create our own truths." Carver could see Saul's increasing distress and gave him a comforting smile. "Do not fret, old friend. You and I are in agreement on this."

He spoke soothingly, gave the older man another pat on the shoulder. "In the long term, our adversaries' reliance on Old World techno will be their undoing. Of more immediate concern is the likelihood that it may give them short term advantage."

"You shall deal with it, John... and we will be all the stronger for you having done so."

"As you are so frequently prone to point out."

"Absolutely." Saul ceremoniously took the half-empty coffee cup from John Carver's grasp. "And you best be about it."

Carver smiled again and turn about to leave. "Yes, sir. I'll do that."

Austin shifted his weight from one leg to the other, continuing to watch the camp from his position on the roof of the building, behind the short facade. Bennett and Jones were sitting beside him.

"There he is," he said. He watched as John Carver came out of the mess tent and walked to the central campfire in the main compound. He stood, unmoving then, and stared down at the few flickering flames in the fire pit.

"Well?" asked Jones.

"Hold on."

Almost a minute went by, and then Austin watched Carver walk slowly around the fire, stop again, and kneel down. He took the poker and began stirring the almost-dead coals.

"North side," Austin said calmly.

"Marauders, then," said Bennett.

Carver had given them the signal. North side of the fire pit meant they were dealing with marauders. He jabbed the poker into the ground as he stood and started slowly away, walking to his command tent.

Austin turned away from the scene and squatted down beside Bennett and Jones. They took only a moment to finalize their plans. Bennett and Austin would take their teams via alternate routes to meet with the security team that would by now be running operations from the established post several hundred yards from the camp. There they would get what information they needed prior to whatever assault on the bad guys was being planned.

"The kids'll have to wait on their new clothes," said Bennett. He had a barely suppressed grin.

"Not for long," said Austin. His tone was more ominous. With that, he led the way from the rooftop down to the rest of the group waiting downstairs. They grabbed only what they would need for the coming confrontation and left the building. Leaving behind the wagons and horses, they traveled several blocks together before splitting into the two foraging teams.

By separating, they hoped that, should they come unexpectedly upon anyone, that at least one team would reach the security post.

Austin and his small group traveled quickly and silently. He took the lead and Jones brought up the rear. They moved at an easy jog about six paces apart.

Marauders; Austin didn't know how many or where they were, but based on what he knew of their surroundings, he suspected a small woods beyond the hillside to the west of the camp. They could have come in unseen from the other side, arriving by highway from the northwest.

Based on past experience, Austin could assume there were anywhere from ten to fifty of them. While fewer than ten could inflict a lot of damage, the existing camp security was well-equipped to handle such a threat without going to stage one. Carver would have dealt with the trouble straightaway. As for more than fifty, there were very few marauder groups of that size, and these were well known. Austin didn't believe any of them were in this area.

He led his team across the parking lot that he had stood watch over earlier and on into the thick vegetation on the other side. He followed a well-used animal trail that ran along the base of the slope until he came to a small clearing, passing a sentry along the way.

Most of the security detail had already gone into position. Only Mr. Brown and his two lieutenants were in the clearing.

Mr. Brown sent Jennie, Madsen and Thomas off with one of the LTs without a word or an explanation. When he nodded to his other LT, she took Jones by the arm and led her away.

"You with me," he said then to Austin. When Austin glanced quickly around the now empty clearing, Mr. Brown nodded in the direction of the animal trail and the unseen sentry. "He'll see to Bennett when he shows up." He then turned and started uphill without another word.

Austin followed Mr. Brown up to a grass-covered ridge. Down slope on the opposite side of the hill was a field of yellow grass with a scattering of short, scrubby bushes, giving a clear view of a wide clearing at the base of the hill.

Three figures were in the clearing, standing beside an old Jeep with a hard canopy. A thousand yards beyond the clearing were two other vehicles. Austin could just make out figures moving about the vehicles.

Mr. Brown indicated the woods far beyond the second group.

"Their camp is in there," he said. "Eight or nine more power rigs; a flatbed carrying fuel drums."

Austin took that in. One vehicle below, two more a thousand yards out, nine more in the trees, and a fuel rig.

Where'd these guys come from? he wondered.

"Any idea who they are?"

"Don't recognize 'em. Could be new, could just be new to the area."

Austin saw one of the three directly below them speak into a hand radio of some kind.

Motor vehicles, communications equipment.

Techno.

They must have it pretty good. High cost of living, though, and with each passing year, more and more difficult to maintain. And with each passing year, more and more difficult to find fuel.

Better our way...

Some of that stuff would make living so much damned easier... why not use it while we can?

Austin knew what Saul would say. "You depend on it now, what are you going to do when it's gone?"

Oh, I don't know... adjust, maybe...

"Their techno is going to give them an edge," he said.

"I doubt that." Mr. Brown was a true believer. He was studying the scene through a rugged pair of binoculars. "Everyone knows what has to be done. What needs saying has already been said."

Austin let the matter drop. The security team leader was probably right. This was nothing they hadn't faced before, and they had always come out on top.

"Here we go," said Mr. Brown. Down below, John Carver was approaching the Jeep on horseback. The three men watching him approach spread out so that they were standing a few yards apart, presenting themselves as more difficult targets.

Austin brought out his own small pair of binoculars and slid into position beside Mr. Brown.

John Carver let his horse plod slowly forward, offering it little guidance or direction. It could see where its rider wanted to go, and could sense that it wanted to take its time getting there.

When it got to within twenty feet of the three men, now forming a line across its path, the horse stopped.

This is where its rider wanted to be.

Carver studied the faces of the three men, the way they stood, the positions of their arms and the way they held their hands.

He already knew there were no others in the power rig behind them.

He already knew there were two vehicles a thousand yards to his left and that there were five people waiting there.

He knew that further away, camped in the shadow of the trees near the foot of the nearby hills, the rest of the marauder band waited.

Carver looked directly into the eyes of the man that he took to be, by manner and position, the leader of the group. He held his silence. His horse breathed out a bored blubbering noise.

The leader of the group stared back at Carver, confident in his situation. He assumed that sooner or later this throwback would introduce himself.

John Carver did not.

After a long, increasingly uncomfortable silence, the man standing to the leader's left couldn't take it anymore.

"Ya' know how to speak, dipstick?"

Carver smiled inwardly. Outwardly, he showed no sign of having heard the man.

However, the leader's expression changed subtly.

What the hell, Thompson?

Now he was going to have to take the time to turn this conversation back to his favor.

"You in charge of the parade camped outside my city?" he asked.

"John Carver," he answered smoothly.

"Yeah. Whatever. Simple question. *Are you in charge?*"

"That would be me."

"See? A simple answer. That's all I asked for." The man sighed wearily. "Jesus."

"John."

"That's cute," said the leader. "I don't much like cute."

"And I don't imagine you see much of it," said Carver. He let his horse finish another blubbering spell. "What do you want?"

"Now that's more like it. Right down to business." The man put on a thin grin and there was a sinister twinkle in his eye. "The name's Morgan."

Carver didn't acknowledge the introduction, as if he was waiting to hear an answer to his question and anything else was irrelevant.

"How 'bout climbing down off that sack of dog food," said Thompson, the man to Morgan's left.

Carver again ignored him. He continued watching the leader. When Morgan saw that Carver intended to stay on the horse, he too ignored Thompson, as if the man hadn't just given this John Carver character an order.

"You and your little caravan have incurred several fees that need to be addressed," he said. "At your earliest convenience."

"I see."

"Yes. First of all, there's a toll charge for traveling through our territory. Not insignificant, I'm afraid. And then there are fees incurred for camping on our property. Oh, and of course the foraging fees related to entering our city and retrieving supplies."

"Sounds like a lot of fees," said Carver. "I had no idea."

"I suspected that was the case," said Morgan. "I even suggested that very possibility to my colleagues. How could you know, I asked. How could you possibly know?" Another thin grin. "And yet, there it is."

"There it is," said Thompson.

"To continue," Morgan went on. "The toll charge. This is based on the number of wagons and personnel in your party. As I said, not insignificant. Camping fees, again based on the size of your party, and the intended length of your stay. Now, the foraging fees are normally calculated against the quantity and value of goods that you bring out of the city."

"Of course."

"Being that I'm in an understanding mood, we'll drop the fines normally associated with failure to get a permit."

Carver nodded solemnly, grew thoughtful. At length, he said simply, "And these fees can be addressed at my convenience."

"*Earliest* convenience," the leader smiled again. After a moment, the smile faded. "Delay of payment could result in severe penalties."

Saul stood waiting outside the mess tent with Sandi Carver. Sandi took the horse's reins from Carver.

"Welcome back, Father," she said coolly.

"Thank you, Sandi."

"How'd it go, John?" asked Saul.

"As expected," said John Carver. "Food, ammunition, horses."

"Horses? What would technos want with horses?"

"Food. For their dogs, apparently."

"Oh, that's just disgusting," said Sandi. Her father's horse snuggled its head up close to Sandi and she absently gave the animal a pat on the neck. "And I assume they threatened to take everything if we don't pay up."

"Seize everything; take the women, kill the men, sell the children."

"How much time do we have?"

"I told them I had to meet with my council to discuss the arrangements. They didn't buy it, of course, but they did give us until morning to gather together their fee."

"Excellent," said Saul.

"I thought so."

"Should offer a refreshing distraction," said Sandi. There was a hint of a smile on her face. "Don't you think so, Father?"

"Yes, daughter. I certainly do."

chapter three...

Morgan sat down in the wooden folding chair that was waiting for him near the campfire. There was movement and noise all around him; music, laughter, arguments, dancing, fighting. The marauder camp was alive.

A slave girl handed him his coffee and quickly disappeared. Morgan took a swallow of the coffee and set the cup on the small table beside his chair.

The sound of a nearby generator was little more than white noise, almost drowned out by the music coming from the entertainment center that had been set up at the far end of the camp. Speakers were mounted high up on the surrounding trees. Ropes strung from tree to tree hung heavy with kerosene lanterns.

The camp perimeter was lined with power rigs: cars, trucks, buses, 4x4s. Guards stood watch in the darkness beyond.

The slave returned with a plate of food. Morgan took the plate, watched the girl turn about and make her way back through the dozens of people that were bustling about the camp. He couldn't remember her name; *Janice or Janet or Carol...* something like that. He had kept her when they had sold the last group of captives. She was in her twenties, wasn't all that much to look at, especially with that ugly scar on her cheek, but she did her job and the figure wasn't bad. And there was just enough to hang onto with a little extra to make things comfortable.

He hadn't decided whether to throw her in with the next collection they would be bringing in from this latest caravan.

Thompson approached from the command tent, grabbing a chair along the way. He set the chair beside Morgan's and dropped into it.

"We're all set," he said.

Morgan grunted acknowledgement, absently scooped a spoonful of food into his mouth and chewed. He was still pissed at his second in command for the way he had handled himself at the meeting with that John Carver character. He had made Morgan look foolish. Worse, he had made it look as though Morgan couldn't control his people.

Thompson sensed the simmering anger but chose to ignore it. He looked at his large wristwatch with the scratched face and worn and faded wide leather band.

"Smitty'll be moving on their camp in forty minutes." He snickered. He always got a kick out of surprising the quarry. It got 'em every time. *You said tomorrow... you said tomorrow...* they would whimper, on their knees, preparing to die. Great stuff.

The second team, following ten minutes behind Smitty's, would handle cleanup. Then Thompson's own group would go in at daybreak and collect supplies and slaves.

"Fine," said Morgan. He set his plate down on the side table and picked up his coffee. He took a swallow. It was getting cold. He tossed the contents of the cup into the campfire, held it patiently out to one side. Janice or Janet or Carol or whatever-the-hell-her-name-was made a quick appearance, coffee decanter in hand. She filled his cup and was gone.

"What the hell's her name?" he asked.

Thompson shifted about, looked back toward the kitchen.

"Don't recall. Got her up north, right? That dirty little town by the river? I think she had a brat with her." Thompson shifted back again, settled into his chair. "Didn't we sell it off to that farmer?"

Morgan had already lost interest. He stared into the distance. A furrow slowly formed on his brow. "There was something odd about that guy."

"What guy? Carver?"

"Something different, somethin' not right. I can feel it."

"All over, soon enough." Thompson glanced around the camp, back at his watch. "Wonder where Jeffries is."

Jeffries, their head of security, liked to check on all the guard posts this time in the evening, particularly when they were settling into a new camp. After making his rounds, he usually dropped by for a cup of coffee with Morgan.

Morgan shrugged, sipped at his coffee, and leaned back in his chair. But Thompson's casual observation stuck with him. Where was Jeffries? He was seldom this late.

Without shifting position, he began studying the shadows beyond the perimeter. At first, he could see nothing, having to give his eyes time to adjust. He had been staring into the fire, and initially the shadows were just shadows.

Movement...

Morgan was certain that he saw one shadow passing in front of another. He tried not to react.

"Crap," he grumbled.

"What?"

"Not sure. Could be nothing."

Thompson had no idea what that meant. Morgan's mood being what it was, he decided to wait for more information.

Morgan continued to look into the darkness beyond the perimeter. Those damned kerosene lanterns were as bad as the flames of the campfire. He was having difficulty seeing anything.

And why should he have to? That was what he had the guards for.

The shadows looked unmoving but for reflections of firelight dancing against the trunks of the trees.

Maybe that was all it had been. Maybe he had been mistaken.

Thompson suddenly jumped up out of his chair and said something unintelligible. He took a step, stopped, and stumbled slightly. Morgan watched him turn slowly about and look down at him, a perplexed look on his face.

A thin wooden shaft was protruding eight inches out of his chest. He looked down at it, then back at Morgan.

"Wha..." he started, stopped. He raised a hand, as if to take hold of the object. When his hand was within a few inches, it went limp and fell away. Thompson dropped slowly to his knees, then fell forward.

Morgan was on his feet. "Intruders!"

No one seemed to understand what he meant, those who heard him at all through the din of the camp. A moment later, it didn't matter. The perimeter of the camp suddenly burst with life as a wave of attackers rushed out of the shadows and waylaid into Morgan's people.

For several seconds, Morgan could only watch, mesmerized by the method of the assault. The attackers were insane, coming at those in the camp like berserkers, screaming and crying out, waving swords like pinwheels, slashing with long knives, lunging with spears.

Arrows continued to streak into the camp from the trees. Morgan heard one feather past his ear and he dropped to the ground, crawled hurriedly around the campfire and scrambled to a large table. Kneeling beside the bench, he looked quickly at the scene around him.

How can this be happening?

His people were being slaughtered. They were hardly even fighting back. With the perimeter guards apparently either dead or incapacitated, and the assault team moving in on the Carver caravan, *and probably walking into an ambush*, those left behind were defenseless.

The whole world shattered in a blinding light and deafening roar as the fuel drums on the flatbed exploded. A bright, orange mushroom rose up through the trees. The heat rolled through the camp in a wave, tossing aside chairs and tables and knocking people to the ground. Morgan felt the blast of heat against his face and quickly shielded his eyes against the glare.

Slowly lowering his arm then, struggling to look into the hell in front of him, Morgan saw the silhouettes of Austin and Mr. Brown moving against the backdrop of orange and black flames, stalking their victims, slaying anything that moved.

The figure of a slender young woman stepped into the golden glow of firelight, a thin sword held in each hand. Jennie turned her head slowly and her face shimmered orange and gold. Her eyes were wide and white and shown bright with insane bliss. The expression on her face was one of absolute euphoria.

Oh my god... thought Morgan. *We're all going to die...*

Austin and Mr. Brown walked on either side of the small group of prisoners. Austin had a rifle resting on one shoulder, a blood-spattered sword across the other. His clothes were covered with blood, and there was a smear of red across his left cheek. The sun was just coming up and the warm, reddish rays felt good against his face. His smile was a contented smile.

Amongst the half a dozen prisoners was Morgan. He didn't look like he was trying to hide in the crowd; rather he wore what dignity remained to him on display for everyone to see. He had a few superficial injuries, and there were spatters of blood on his clothes.

Behind Morgan walked the slave girl. Her name was Lydia. She appeared no different now that she was a prisoner of the Carver Caravan than she had when she was a slave to the marauders; she was neither more submissive nor less.

As they approached the perimeter of the Carver camp, a security detail came out to meet them.

"I'll take 'em in, Austin," said Mr. Brown. "You get yourself cleaned up."

"Thank you, Mr. Brown." One of the security team silently offered to take Austin's sword. Austin continued alone into the compound. The camp appeared calm, quiet, unaffected by the previous night's events.

Bennett came out of the mess tent, cautiously sipping at a cup of hot coffee.

"Austin, old boy. Aren't you just a mess?"

The two walked to the washing station together. Austin leaned his rifle against a post, then carefully took off his blood-soaked shirt and began cleaning himself up.

"I take it things went well here?"

"Like a dream, my friend," said Bennett. He had been part of one of the teams that had lain in wait for the inevitable attack by the marauders. "It doesn't look as though I got quite as deeply into the night's events as you."

"I doubt you lacked for diversion." Austin took a towel and began drying himself. He was going to have to go to his tent for clean clothes. First, though, he took Bennett's coffee from him and took a deep swallow, then handed the cup back.

The six prisoners were led toward a high-fenced enclosure behind the row of community tents. As they approached the gate, Morgan heard John Carver call out to the guards.

"Hold up a minute, if you please, Mr. Brown."

Mr. Brown noted Carver's focus of attention and took Morgan by the arm. He pulled him aside as the other prisoners continued into the prisoner enclosure.

Morgan glanced once at the boy standing at Carver's side. The kid had no expression at all. He looked back to Carver.

"Carver, isn't it?"

"John Carver."

"Yeah... John Carver... what are your plans for my people? What few I have left."

The last of prisoners were led into the enclosure and the gate closed.

"As a general rule, we don't execute prisoners."

"I'm surprised you ever have prisoners."

Carver gave a slight smile. So did the small boy.

"Not as a general rule."

The two men eyed each other warily.

"So... plans?" asked Morgan.

"They will be given adequate supplies and will be sent on their way."

The two were again silent.

Mr. Brown stood stoically, disinterested of the conversation but wary of whatever Morgan might attempt to do.

Daniel continued to watch, outwardly unemotional, the exchange between his grandfather and this leader of the marauders.

Morgan hadn't missed the careful wording of Carver's comment.

They will be sent on their way.

"I'm grateful for that, at least."

Carver gave a slight nod to Mr. Brown, who turned Morgan about and led him along the path behind the community tents, away from the prisoner enclosure.

Carver looked down at his grandson. "Are you hungry, Daniel? I smell breakfast cooking."

"Yes, Grandfather."

From within the prisoner enclosure, the slave girl Lydia detachedly watched Carver and the boy walk down the path, side by side, the man's arm around his grandson's shoulders.

She watched with much greater interest as Morgan was led away in the opposite direction.

chapter four...

Three days later, the camp looked much more complete, more permanent. Structures were up, boardwalks were laid out. The small, wood-framed schoolhouse had a sign over the door that read 'school'.

Austin sat before the central campfire, which was set into a permanent stone fire pit. He was sitting in what had once been Morgan's wooden chair. Two other chairs, placed on the other side of the small table next to Austin, were empty.

He finished up a plate of food, set the plate onto the side table just as Rob Marley and Jennie came up and sat in the waiting chairs.

"Well, they're on their way," said Marley.

"More than they deserve," grumbled Jennie.

"Be nice, Jennie."

"You know the routine," said Austin. All prisoners received a knapsack of supplies and a full canteen, and were sent on their way.

"Considering what little we got from the encounter, they got the better end of the deal," said Jennie.

Austin indicated the chair that he was sitting in. He rubbed a palm appreciatively across the smooth wood of one of the arms.

"We got some furniture."

"Some weapons and ammo," Marley added. "Armorer is happy as can be. Hell, he almost smiled at me this morning."

Jennie was not to be appeased. "We spent half a day yesterday destroying all their techno."

"Rules is rules, Miss Jennie," said Marley.

"I don't care a fig about the techno. It was half a day wasted, time we coulda' spent foraging in the city."

"You were in the city almost the entire afternoon."

"We have all winter, Jennie," said Austin. He settled more comfortably into the chair. He appeared to be enjoying the early evening. "You're just upset because you haven't found Saul's salt."

"That's not—"

"You'll not ruin my mood." Austin laid his head back.

"Besides," said Marley. "We'll get something for Morgan, and it could be considerable. He's a real piece of work, that one. I bet a lot of folks are eager to get their hands on him."

"We'll see," said Jennie. "In the meantime, we gotta feed him. We gotta take care of him."

"Have patience, dear girl," said Marley. "Have a little patience."

Something caught Rob Marley's eye. Looking across the compound, he saw Sandi Carver and Daniel coming out of their family tent. The boy was leading a dog on a leash. It was the same dog that had been standing guard in the department store days earlier.

"And what do we have here?" Marley spoke with one eye to Austin. "It appears that young Daniel has a new pet."

Austin sat up and looked across the camp. "What the—

"We took the hideout today," Jennie answered matter-of-factly. "Wasn't much of a fuss, really."

"And?"

"Bennett said he knew just the person to take care of the dog."

Austin stood up slowly. "Did he?"

Rob Marley shifted back around and spoke in a faintly mocking tone. "He made quite a show of givin' the animal to the boy, so I hear."

Austin looked uncertainly across the compound at Sandi and Daniel. After a few uncomfortably long seconds, he absently nodded a silent 'see you later' and started away from Marley and Jennie.

Jennie gave Marley a reproachful look. Marley grinned.

"No choice, dear girl. Absolutely no choice."

"Don't give me that, Rob Marley."

"The lad takes pushing."

Jennie grew thoughtful. She leaned back in her chair, frowned.

"So I noticed. Why, do you suppose?"

"Simple, Miss Jennie. He pines for love long lost."

"Austin?"

"Not much younger than you when... well, when the world changed. They survived it, the two of 'em. Struggled to make a go of it. Times was much harder then, back before the tribes."

"I was just a baby when Uncle Saul took me in," said Jennie. "I've only known the caravan."

"Best that way." Marley stared into the fire. "Right before he joined with Carver, Austin and his wife, pregnant then, I think... a gang got to 'em."

"How awful. Geez, and she was pregnant?"

"Don't really know much about it. He doesn't talk on it. But I know it went real bad." Marley watched sympathetically as Jennie looked back toward Austin. "Our friend Austin deserves some happiness, yes? Even if it takes a bit of shoving to get him where he needs going?"

Austin walked casually, trying to look as though he just happened to be heading in the same direction as Sandi and her boy. He met up with them just outside the mess tent.

"Hello," he said. "Good evening... Sandi, Daniel."

"Good evening," said Sandi.

"Hey, Austin." Daniel wore a big grin. "Look at my dog."

Austin held out his hand for the dog to sniff before giving the animal a gentle pat on the head.

"Yes, I see."

"Bennett gave it to me." Daniel gave the dog a brisk rub and a pet.

"Did he?" Austin managed a faint smile.

"They took the store today," said Sandi.

"Ah..."

"I understand there was a lot of stock," she continued.

"Hmm."

Sandi sensed the awkwardness in the situation, and grew a bit uncomfortable. She finally indicated the mess tent. "I guess we should be going in."

Austin nodded, but quickly knelt down in front of the dog. The animal looked at him a moment, then suddenly gave him a lick on the face. Austin took it without comment.

"She likes you," said Daniel, grinning.

"Yes." Austin stood up. "So I see."

Sandi hid her own grin. "Well, like I said... dinner waits. My father."

"Of course." Austin watched Daniel tie the dog's leash to a newly installed stake outside the door flap. Sandi gave Austin a final half-glance before she and the boy went inside.

When Austin returned to the campfire, Marley tried to ignore him, but Jennie raised a brow, a knowing smirk on her face.

"Bennett movin' in on it, is he?" she asked. She quickly continued before he had a chance to respond. "Yeah. He said something about it when we got the dog."

Austin was clearly not pleased by the turn of events. He stood in painful silence, uncertain what to say.

Marley was still staring into the fire. "It's going to be a long winter," he said calmly. "Longer for some than for others."

Austin looked studiously down at the wagonmaster. Rob Marley continued watching the short, flickering flames. Austin looked once then at Jennie, who was watching him somewhat expectantly. He quickly turned his attention back to Marley, who was diligently keeping his focus fixed on the fire.

"I suppose that's true," Austin said quietly. He shifted his weight from one foot to the other, then back again. After several more moments, he turned and walked calmly way from the campfire. He walked unhurriedly yet determinedly across the compound in the direction of the mess tent.

Rob Marley looked rather pleased with himself.

Jennie leaned casually back in her chair. "You are quite the bastard, Mr. Marley."

"Quite a nice assist, Miss Jennie." Marley's grinned broadened just a little.

Austin entered the mess tent. He saw Sandi and Daniel walking over to the corner table, dinner plates in hand. Carver was already there, quietly eating his dinner.

Austin approached the table just as Sandi and Daniel were settling in. He took a moment to acknowledge them, then spoke to Carver.

"Mind if I sit down?" he asked.

Carver indicated the bench. "Not at all, Austin. Pull up a bench." He glanced deliberately at his daughter, then returned to his dinner.

chapter five...

The slave girl, *Janet or Janice or Carol or something*, stood stoically on the rooftop, looking in the direction of the Carver camp in the distance. There was a calm, cold emotion emanating from her, from her stance, from her facial expression. The ugly wound on her face was only just starting to show signs of healing.

It had been a week since she had been let go. Lydia no longer wore the same dirty, tattered clothes she had been forced to wear since first being taken captive by Morgan and his marauders. She was now efficiently dressed in quality clothing: new pants, shirt, jacket and boots.

She wore a utility belt on which she had attached a canteen, a knife, and a holster with pistol. At her feet rested a quality backpack.

Lydia lifted an expensive pair of binoculars to her eyes and studied the Carver camp. Lowering them again, she bent down and picked up the backpack. She stuffed the binoculars into a side pocket and slid the pack over one shoulder.

She looked again in the direction of the camp. There was nothing kind or warm or fuzzy about her gaze. There was the air of a predator about her.

Lydia turned about and walked smoothly across the rooftop.

The sky overhead was slate gray and threatening snow. Several inches of snow lay on the ground. The tents and buildings were spotted with patches of it.

A month had gone by. The camp was neat and orderly. Delicate plumes of smoke rose up from several campfires. Light was visible through the slightly open door flaps of the mess tent.

Two children appeared suddenly, laughing giddily as they rushed out from between two of the larger family tents, one chasing the other. Both were dressed in warm, winter clothes.

As they ran past the mess tent, they almost ran into Austin, who was just stepping outside.

Austin was dressed in a warm coat and was wearing heavy boots. He braced his rifle against his leg, buttoned his coat, and then shouldered his weapon.

Jennie stepped out of the tent behind him, a plate of food in hand. She wore a lighter coat, and looked as though she didn't plan on staying outside for long.

Austin looked down at the plate in her hand.

"I'll take that to him, Jennie."

"You sure?"

"Absolutely. I'm headed that way." He took the plate.

Jennie looked at the camp around them, and at the threatening sky overhead.

"Looks like winter is finally here," she said.

"We're ready for it."

"I suppose so." Jennie grimaced against the cold. "I've never been on good terms with cold weather."

"I don't mind the cold so much, but I hate the wet. Miserable stuff. Especially if you have to travel in it."

"At least we don't have that to deal with. We're snug as bugs, right where we are."

"Well, bug..." Austin smiled at that. "You should get back inside before you freeze your antennae off."

"I'll do that." Jennie wrapped her arms around herself, turned toward the tent flap. "Thanks for taking that over."

"Glad to be of assistance."

Austin waited until Jennie had gone back inside and then started away, working his way around behind the tent. He followed the wide path that ran behind the row of large community tents. The air glowed a dull, silvery gray. Somewhere up there the sun was trying its best to push through.

Up ahead, a lone figure stood in front of a small, high-fenced enclosure. Within the enclosure was a tiny, wood-framed shed with canvas roof. There was just enough space in front of the shed for a man to take two steps in either direction.

Morgan was sitting in a chair in front of the little shed.

The guard watched Austin approach. He looked unconcerned, and silently acknowledged him when Austin reached the enclosure.

Austin held up the plate for Morgan to see. Morgan rose slowly up from the chair. He was gaunt, with shadowy gray skin. He appeared listless and there was no sparkle in his eyes.

"Austin," he said softly. "They have you on kitchen detail, now?"

Austin slid the plate through a narrow, horizontal slot in the wire fence. "We all do what we can, Morgan."

Morgan took the plate and returned to his chair. He used his fingers to pick through the small pieces of food. He showed little interest in his meal, appeared to simply be going through the motions. He spoke without looking up.

"What's the word?" he asked.

"Six days."

Morgan held a gristly piece of fleshy meat up where he could get a good look at it, grimaced, tossed it aside. "Lookin' forward to it."

"Last of the runners came back yesterday. Word is, you're downright popular."

"Is that so?" He had little interest.

"That is so. It should be a lively auction."

"To be followed soon after by the execution."

"What the winner does with you is none of our affair."

There was a long moment of silence, when there seemed to be no sounds coming from anywhere. Morgan continued to pick through his food, eating the vegetables and tossing out most everything else.

"No. Of course not."

"I don't mean to kick a man when he's down, but I doubt the execution will come as quick as you might like."

"That so?"

"I'm thinkin' they'll be wanting to take you back with 'em, put you on display for a while, show everyone there's some justice in the world."

"That's nice," Morgan said flatly. "Very touching. I'm all emotional. See?"

Austin heard footsteps, turned to see young Daniel hurrying up the path toward him. When the boy reached him, he came to a stop. His attention was drawn to Morgan. He eyed the prisoner dispassionately.

Morgan gave him a slight side-glance. "Morning, boy... pulled off any fly wings lately?"

"What is it, Daniel?" asked Austin.

Morgan grimaced again at another piece of meat that he'd lifted from his plate.

"Yes, Daniel," he grumbled. "Just what is this vile stuff you and yours keep feeding me?"

"We got fish!"

"Fish? Hell, boy, there hasn't been fish since long before you were born."

Daniel's expression turned hard. "We got fish."

"Whatever you say, boy."

"Daniel, what do you need?" asked Austin.

"Grandfather wants you in the compound," he stated firmly. "The foraging team got attacked again."

Austin's muscles tensed in a mix of anger and frustration.

Morgan managed to keep his smirk under control. "Tough break, eh?"

"Anyone hurt?" Austin asked Daniel.

"Some."

Austin started down the path. "Come on."

Morgan watched them leave, the strange boy following eagerly after Austin. He looked down at his plate again, delicately picked up another disgusting looking piece of meat. He glanced up at the guard, who was watching him from outside the fence. He tossed the meat aside, wiped his fingers on his pants and continued picking through vegetables, all that remained on his plate.

A crowd had gathered in the center of compound when Austin came from around the mess tent, Daniel following behind him. Talbot, one of the foragers, was being carried away on the stretcher. Bennett and Jones stood to one side, talking with Carver. Jennie and Saul were there.

Carver looked as though he might not be able to restrain his anger. He spoke in cold, precise words.

"This stops," he said. "This stops today."

"Yes sir," said Jones.

"She comes and goes like a ghost," said Bennett. "And there's no reason behind it."

"I'm not pointing blame, Bennett." said Carver. He was seething. This was the fourth attack in as many weeks. "Two more wounded."

"That makes six by my count," sighed Saul. "I suppose we should be grateful that no one has been killed."

Carver looked then at Austin.

"End this," he said, then turned to Jones. "The foraging teams stand down for now."

"Yes, sir," she said. "Sir? I would like to go back in. This witch... I'd like to help."

"Coordinate with Austin."

"Yes sir."

Carver's gaze reached beyond the camp. *What the hell is this woman after?*

Bennett stood near the perimeter of the compound, rifle resting across his arm. Behind him, Jones and two others were just leaving the camp.

He watched Austin and Sandi as they said their good-byes in front of Sandi's family tent. Austin placed a hand gently on her arm and gave her a light kiss. She looked silently after him as he walked away.

Austin shouldered his rifle as he approached Bennett, spoke as he passed by.

"Let's go."

Bennett looked back once more at Sandi, then turned to follow. "You two still aren't together, though... right?"

"Shut up, Bennett."

"I mean, not *really* together."

"Shut up, Bennett."

Bennett grinned. "Uh, huh..."

Most of the buildings that lined the street in this section of the warehouse district had dark brick facades and wide, metal doors. Austin and Bennett walked on opposite sides of the street, their weapons cradled loosely across their forearms.

Bennett stopped at a narrow door leading into an office of one of the warehouses. The sidewalk at his feet was stained with blood. He waved for Austin come over.

"This was the site of the third attack," he told him. "Where Rawley took it."

Austin gave a silent half nod as he studied the surrounding area. Bennett indicated the dark alley on the other side of the street.

"One shot, from over there." he said. "I went in after her. Got close... followed her out onto the next street. Thought I had her, too, for a while, but..."

"And this morning?" asked Austin.

"Two blocks up, one block over."

Austin took all of this in. This crazy woman had hit his own group not far from there, just a few blocks over.

Bennett wondered aloud. "You think she's protecting territory?"

"Maybe... Be a mistake, though. It could help us pinpoint where she's nesting."

It just didn't seem right. Austin continued to look around them; at the shadows, at windows, at doorways. "She seems smarter than that. Don't you think?"

"Suppose. I mean, she knows how to handle herself, all right." Bennett looked sheepish then. "She knows how to lose someone when she wants to."

"Yeah... yeah, that's what I get. I think she knows what she's doing."

"Okay. So?"

"So then, what's she after?"

"She could be leading us right where she wants us to go. What choice do we have?"

"None." Austin started walking. "None just yet."

Bennett sighed and tossed a hand lightly in the air before following about him.

"Lead on, sir," he said, then under his breath as he looked warily around them, "Lead on, lady."

From a vantage point high atop a warehouse roof, Lydia coolly watched Austin and Bennett as they walked guardedly down the narrow street. She stood unmoving against a cool breeze that brushed gently across her scarred face and her long, straight, clean hair.

The two men in the street below eventually passed beyond her view.

Lydia silently slipped away from the edge of the roof.

One of Mr. Brown's lieutenants was pulling a guard post detail. He stood diligently at his station, looking out at the abandoned city across the field.

He was surprised by a rustling sound coming from the nearby brush. He quickly brought up his weapon and pointed the barrel in the general direction of the sound.

Jones stepped into view very near the lieutenant.

"Hold on there, mister," she called out.

"Damn you, Jones."

"Should I go back into town and alert the others to beware of possible friendly fire?"

"You might warn 'em not to creep up on a person." With that, the hint of realization suddenly crossed the lieutenant's face.

Where were the other two who had gone in with her.

"Where are they?" he asked. "Are they all right?"

"They're fine. We split up," said Jones. "Have you seen Austin and Bennett?"

"They didn't come this way."

Jones grew circumspect. "I imagine they'll be a while, yet. They were working the warehouse district." She started to leave. "My team is probably an hour behind me. Don't shoot 'em. I'm going to be needing them again tomorrow."

Lydia watched the exchange between Jones and the lieutenant from the shadows in the nearby brush. Jones started away then, and Lydia saw the guard give the woman a sharp glare before turning back to maintain his watch.

Lydia followed parallel to Jones as Jones moved from the guard post and through the perimeter vegetation that surrounded the Carver camp.

John Carver, Mr. Brown, and another of Mr. Brown's lieutenants stood around a wooden table that had been moved into center of the compound.

Jones entered the compound and walked over to the table and those gathered around it.

A shadow moved unseen in the brush just beyond the perimeter.

Morgan stepped out of his tiny shed and into the even smaller yard within his prison enclosure. He took a moment to stretch the muscles in his back.

He noticed that his ever-present guard wasn't at his normal station.

Probably taking a leak...

Morgan calmly took the two small steps to the front of his enclosure. Standing directly before the wire mesh, he glanced from side to side.

The guard was sitting on the ground a few yards to the right, his back against a stack of wooden boxes. He was slumped over to one side.

The slave girl, *Janice or Janet or Carol or something*, stepped unexpectedly into view, directly in front of Morgan.

Morgan did his best not to look totally taken aback, and was only partly successful.

"My oh my," he whispered, letting out a stumbling breath. "I must say, I am genuinely surprised."

"No doubt," said Lydia. The statement was short and clipped.

Morgan again glanced from side to side, then looked more carefully at the body of the dead or unconscious guard. He turned his attention again fully to the slave girl standing before him. He couldn't help but be a little bit impressed.

"To what do I owe the pleasure?" he asked. Then, "Just what is your name, by the way? If you don't mind my asking."

"Lydia."

"Lydia. Not Carol, then... and the purpose of your visit, Lydia?"

"I haven't decided yet."

"So it is vengeance, then."

"Something like that."

"It really couldn't be anything else, now could it? You had your freedom. You could and should have left here long ago. And yet... here you are."

"Here I am." She studied Morgan, as if she might somehow get the answers she was seeking from his wrinkled brow, the dark shadows under the eyes, the unshaven cheeks and neck. "I'm torn between two options. The first is to kill you now and be done with it."

She took a moment to relish this first option before continuing. "The second is to take you back, return you to face justice."

Morgan gave her a tired, sympathetic smile. "I'd go with the first option, if I were you."

"That is my inclination."

Morgan continued to look calmly at Lydia, apparently unconcerned as to his fate, whatever that fate might be.

"And so?" he asked. "Option number one?"

"I have a problem," she said, hesitating. "You see, while not many of my caravan survived the attack, there were a few. I shouldn't take all the pleasure for myself. They deserve a piece of you as well."

"Then by all means, dear lady, let us be on our way." He shifted about and sat down in his chair. He looked gaunt, as if their conversation had drained him of what little energy he had. "Make your choice and be done with it. Either is fine with me."

"Are they not treating you well?" Lydia smirked.

"Can't say as they are, Lydia. An interesting bunch. Real spirited. Perhaps you've noticed."

"I noticed."

"Yes, I suppose you have." Morgan paused to take a breath. "I'm guessing that's you causing all the fuss in town. Though the reason eludes me."

"I was having a spot of trouble getting in here. And I figured getting you out was going to be worse yet."

"All that bother? A diversion? Really?"

"Now they're looking out, not in."

"Oh, they're jumpy all right. No doubt on that score."

"And they have their best people in town."

"And you... you are here."

"With you."

"You're a cool one, I'll give you that."

"Patient, too."

Morgan stood slowly, took the one step to the fence and looked Lydia in the eye. "Listen, these people are not what they seem. I most strongly suggest that you get out of here. Don't waste your time with me. Go with option one." He gestured shooting himself in the temple. "And leave."

Lydia returned Morgan's gaze, struggled to come to a decision.

"I can't do that," she said, finally.

"I'm being straight with you now, Lydia. Stop playing games with these people. They're dangerous. Not like me kind of dangerous. I mean, really not like me. These people are really, seriously scary."

"And I should take advice from you?"

Morgan's tone was increasingly ominous. "It's not what they do, or even what they've become. It's how good they are at it, how well they've adapted. But mostly? Mostly it's because they enjoy it."

Austin walked across the concrete floor of the warehouse. It was empty but for a few empty barrels, some torn cardboard boxes, and strewn paper trash. Evening light shone through yellowed pane windows that spanned the top of one wall.

Up ahead, Bennett stepped through an office door. Austin followed him in.

A wooden desk had been pushed against one wall, making room for a narrow cot. The blankets on the cot were in disarray.

A few supplies sat on the desk and in several boxes sitting on the floor.

"Her nest," said Bennett. "This is definitely where she's staying."

"Not much." Austin glanced into the boxes and over at the supplies on the desk.

"Doesn't need much," said Bennett.

Austin nodded absently at that, moved over to the cot. He sat down, placed a hand onto the bedding.

"She slept here last night. But..."

"What are you thinking?"

What am I thinking? Austin wondered silently. He wasn't sure.

"Nothing, I guess." He frowned, hesitated, stood finally and started toward the door. "Okay. Let's get the others over here."

He hesitated again when he got to the doorway. He studied the room a final time. Bennett watched him curiously, an uncertain look on his face.

"Oh, damn," Bennett droned. "What is it?"

"No..."

"No? What, no?"

"Let's get back to camp."

"What? Austin... what are you... what?"

"This feels wrong."

"Waddya mean, it feels wrong? This is it. You said yourself that she slept here last night."

"We shouldn't have been able to find it. She let us find it." Austin's expression hardened. "She wanted us to find it."

"So... good. I'll get the others."

Bennett looked to get around to the door, but Austin stood unmoving in the threshold.

"She's leading us away, Bennett. She's drawing us away." Austin backed out of the office and into the warehouse. "We have to get back to camp."

chapter six...

Lydia led Morgan along the narrow path that ran behind a row of one- and two-person tents. Morgan's hands were bound, and a six foot lead of rope ran from the bindings to Lydia's grip. She held a pistol in the other hand, her holster now empty.

Morgan looked as though he was willing to accept whatever fate waited in store for him.

In the main compound on the other side of the tents, a handful of people moved about, some preparing campfires for the evening.

Lydia stopped short. The silhouette of a woman appeared suddenly from between two tents and blocked her path. The woman stepped nearer, and Lydia could see that it was Jones, a pistol held comfortably at her side. She had a cool expression and a confident stance.

Lydia chose to avoid the confrontation. She stepped quickly between two tents, pulling Morgan with her. As she came into the main compound, two people stopped abruptly, surprised at this strange woman's sudden appearance.

They didn't seem overly frightened, though, not even when Lydia held her weapon up at them. They simply stepped calmly aside and waited to see what she would do next.

Lydia turned about as Jones stepped through the line of tents and stood again in her path, still holding her pistol down at her side.

Lydia pulled at the rope lead without taking her eyes off Jones. Morgan stumbled forward and fell onto his knees behind her.

"This is mine," she said. "I'm taking him with me."

Jones said nothing. She didn't move.

John Carver approached from behind Lydia, stopping four paces away.

"I'm afraid not, Miss," he said calmly.

Lydia turned to face this new danger. She raised her weapon up until it was aimed in his general direction.

Carver was unarmed. He held his palms out to show that he was not a threat.

"He belongs to us," he said. "You'll have to leave him."

"No," Lydia said sharply. "He has to face up to what he's done."

"There are others who feel just as you do."

"Not my concern," she said, but she sounded just a little uncertain. "I'm taking him back to my caravan, to what's left... of my tribe."

"If you want him, you have to bid on him; just like everyone else."

"We don't have anything left." Lydia yanked on the rope lead. "He took it all. He took everything."

"I understand," said Carver. "I really do. But your loss is far from unique. My dear, why are you more deserving of dispensing retribution than any of his other victims?"

"What gives you the right to decide that I'm not? What gives you the right to auction him off to the highest bidder?"

Carver's smile shifted subtly, grew less friendly and a hint more threatening. He lowered his arms. "Young lady," he said smoothly. "We own him."

Other members of the Carver caravan had begun to gather, continued to appear, coming slowly out of their tents, from the mess tent, from other social structures, from beyond the compound. They silently and methodically drew nearer, forming a wide circle around John Carver on one side, Jones on the other, and Lydia and Morgan in the center.

Carver's expression turned subtly sad.

"What will we do with you?" he sighed.

Lydia was growing increasingly uneasy. She had yet to show fear, but she understood that her situation was dire.

For the moment, she said nothing.

Carver continued, now more formally. "You have committed significant acts of violence against us, and we have done you no harm. We did, in fact, gain you your freedom. Did we not?"

"That changes nothing." Lydia yanked again on the lead and pulled the kneeling Morgan toward her.

"I suppose not," Carver ceded.

Sandi Carver took a step from the circle and approached Carver from behind.

"Shall we take her, Father?" she asked.

Carver looked to Saul, who was standing to one side, observing. The older man was wearing a bloody apron and was using it to absently wipe blood from his hands. Saul shook his head negatively, albeit reluctantly.

With that, Carver spoke to his daughter while turning his gaze back to Lydia.

"It would appear not, my daughter. The larders are full. We do not take more than we can use."

"Perhaps a party," she pleaded, near crestfallen. "A celebration... the attacks are ended."

"We will celebrate," answered her father. "But we have all the fish that we can use."

Austin and Bennett stepped into the circle. Carver gave them a "good work" nod. Austin took a step closer to Lydia. He stopped, stood in motionless silence.

Jones continued to wait several paces behind Lydia.

"We are a patient people," said Carver, "but I grow weary of this."

"Then let me go." Lydia yanked hard on the lead. "With this."

Enough is enough.

Carver spoke precisely. "He is staying with us. Of that, let there be no mistake. The only issue remaining before us is the question of your future."

"That is of no concern to me."

"Your concern, or lack thereof, means nothing to us," Carver responded with increasing impatience. "We might be willing to take into account that no one has been killed. I can assume that was intentional?"

Lydia said nothing. Her stance and expression made it clear that she had nothing more to say.

Carver now appeared to be bored with it all. "We are done with this, then," he concluded.

From near Lydia's feet, Morgan let out a morbid chuckle.

"My dear... it looks to be Option One after all."

There was no change in her expression. With only the slightest movement, and without taking her eyes from Carver, she shifted her pistol and pulled the trigger.

The loud, booming gunshot echoed hollowly in the silence of the camp. The sound reverberated away from the compound in all directions, fading into the distance.

A cloud of pink and white burst from the side of Morgan's head, seemed to hang suspended in the air.

Lydia, still looking with dead calm at Carver, held on the rope lead for several seconds. When she finally let go, the body of Morgan crumpled to her feet.

Austin and Jones both raised their weapons and targeted Lydia.

Carver looked dispassionately at Lydia. "Oh, dear," he said.

Lydia tossed her pistol onto the ground in front of her.

epilog...

It was a bright, clear day. The camp had been struck, the buildings were gone, the tents were packed up and put away.

The wagons formed a circle in the center of the clearing that had been their home for the last four months. Austin and Sandi stood next to the lead wagon, holding hands, Daniel beside them absently gnawing on a stick of jerky.

A number of men and women on horseback were already starting out of the site. Carver guided his horse forward and turned about to face the caravan.

"Let's move out," he called.

Those on foot started forward, following Carver out of the clearing.

Marley called down to Austin. "Come on now, buddy."

Austin and Sandi held hands a moment more. They pulled apart then and Austin climbed aboard. Looking back down at her, they shared a smile. She laid a hand on her belly. She was just beginning to show signs of being pregnant.

Austin looked at Marley. "Well?" he urged.

"Well nothing, let's do this."

The fourteen wagons of the Carver caravan traveled in column across the grassy, rolling terrain. More than a hundred men, women and children walked alongside the wagons.

Marley was driving the lead wagon. Beside him, Austin rode shotgun.

Sandi Carver and young Daniel walked beside the lead wagon. When Sandi glanced up, she saw Austin looking down at her. The two shared a furtive smile, then Sandi pointedly turned away and focused on the way ahead.

Austin grinned and turned his attention back to his duty. He ignored the faint smirk that appeared and then faded from Marley's face.

"Gotta tell ya', Austin," Marley said in a casual, conversational tone. "In spite of everything, this is without a doubt the best *long-stay* I can remember."

"Yeah. Yeah... 'spect so."

"Yeah, that too," Marley said with a light chuckle.

"Yeah... 'spect so..."

The Carver caravan had spent the entire winter camped outside the city. The members of the tribe were rested, healthy, and ready to move on after the *long-stay*. The caravan was well-stocked. The abandoned city had provided them with all the supplies they needed, including Saul's salt.

Something in the distance caught Austin's attention. Without drawing notice, he turned his head slightly and studied the wooded shadows at the outer edges of a grove of trees in the distance.

He saw it, then. A figure silhouetted against the trees.

It was Lydia. She stood stoically, watching the Carver caravan as it moved slowly across the open plain.

Austin relaxed, though he continued to keep an eye on her.

There was nothing threatening. She simply stood there... observing.

Austin's calm gaze drifted from Lydia back to Sandi, then forward.

The caravan rolled on, the sound of wheels turning on their axles, wood striking wood, canvas slapping.

We do not take more than we can use...

~ *End*

The Christmas Cave

Prolog

December 27, 1960

Jenny Miller led the way down the dark tunnel. She held an oil lantern cautiously in front of her, the dull yellow glow pushing out ahead of them. Her younger brother Bill and their friend Mike followed close behind, each carrying a bulky flashlight. The light beams danced as bright sabers, slicing the air and stabbing at the rock walls of the tunnel.

They had been exploring these tunnels for months, spending most weekends here in the dark, ever since Jenny's thirteenth birthday party and they heard those stories of that kid from decades earlier.

Jenny had brown hair braided in long, loose pigtails, wore blue jeans with the cuffs folded up, a flannel shirt and light jacket. Her brother Bill, twelve years old, dressed similar to his older sister: blue jeans and flannel shirt, his brown hair trimmed short.

Their friend Mike was fourteen years old. He was a tall, lanky black kid, dressed in dark jeans and light colored jacket.

Jenny came to a sudden halt, forcing the others to come up short behind her.

"What is it, Jen?" asked Mike.

Jenny held up a hand for quiet. She listened intently.

Bill pushed up beside his sister, looked sharply down the tunnel.

"Is this it?" asked Bill, a harsh whisper.

"Shhh!" Jenny hissed. "Quiet, Bill."

They listened. There was only silence.

"I don't hear anything," said Bill.

"Me neither," said Mike.

Jenny studied the tunnel ahead of them.

Something...

She turned down her lantern until there was only a tiny pilot of flame.

"Turn those off," she mumbled.

Bill and Mike turned off their flashlights. The little flicker of light from the lantern wasn't even enough to show their faces.

There were only the dark silhouettes of their bodies in the tunnel.

And the sound... the whisper of a breeze...

Very faint then, from beyond a bend in the tunnel: a shimmering light, blue and red and yellow.

"Mike?" Jenny asked over her shoulder.

"I see it."

"That's it," said Bill. "We found it."

He started forward, moving quickly past his sister. She reached out and took hold of his arm, pulling him to a stop.

"Oh, no you don't, little brother."

"What?"

"We go together," she stated.

"Then come on." Bill pulled free and started forward.

Jenny turned up the lantern, a frustrated big-sisterly look on her face. She stalked after him, Mike beside her.

"Bill," she hissed. "Don't you get lost."

Her brother disappeared around the bend in the tunnel.

Chapter One

A late-model sedan, nice but not extravagant, traveled alone along the winding two-lane mountain highway. The trees covering the rolling hills on either side were a mix of evergreen and deciduous, most of those having lost their leaves several months earlier. The sky overhead was clear and bright.

Mom and Dad sat in the front seat, Dad behind the wheel. Tom and Olivia Harper were typical middle-class parents from a typical middle-class environment back home. They were dressed casual and comfortable, ready for Christmas vacation.

Jack, thirteen, and his twelve year old sister Amanda were in the back seat, Jack eyeing his smart phone in frustration. He was a typical suburban kid just entering his teens; all arms and legs, bushy, sandy-colored hair.

He had the look of a boy unaccustomed to mountains and streams and trees beyond the occasional family camping trip, whereas kid sister Amanda, while from that same suburban neighborhood back home, looked as though she might be a bit more comfortable out in the woods; tomboyish, and with her blonde hair cut short to keep it out of the way.

Jack frowned and stuffed his cell phone into the side pocket of his light jacket.

"Still nothin'," he grumbled.

Dad glanced once in his rearview mirror. "Sorry about that, Jack," he said. "It'll probably come and go up here." He didn't know where there might be towers up here. The last time he had been here, there hadn't been a single one.

Mom gave a sympathetic smile, but she was inwardly pleased that Jack might not be able to spend the next two weeks hovered over his smart phone.

Amanda was watching the scene passing her window, Jack his own window. Neither looked all that upset about their situation, but neither appeared particularly excited either. They'd spend the holiday at their grandmother's, and that was fine with them.

"Anything to do up there?" asked Jack, still looking out his window.

"Sure," said Dad. "Lots of things."

Mom shifted position. "Just remember, Jack... we're here to spend Christmas with your grandmother. You be nice. You behave yourself."

"They'll be fine, Liv," said Dad. A strange look on his face then. "You know my mother. It's not her we need to worry about. Or the kids." A hint of ominous overtone. "It's us."

"I suppose you're right," Olivia smiled, but the smile faded. "I wish we could spend more time with her." *The kids are missing so much,* she thought.

"She'll never move off the mountain, and as much as I'd like, there's no way we can move up here."

"I know," Olivia sighed. She admired the passing scenery for a few moments. "I can't believe... so many years. The kids were just babies the last time we were up here."

"I know. And now..." His words trailed off. He couldn't finish the thought.

"It'll be all right, Tom," his wife stated. "I'm sure it will."

In the back seat, Jack had his cell phone in hand yet again. He frowned, yet again, and put the phone back in his pocket. He spoke to the back of his dad's head.

"Like what?" he asked.

"What, like what?" asked Dad.

"What is there to do?"

"Ah," said Dad, glad of the opportunity to redirect his thoughts. "There's fishing, swimming, hiking. And you know, I think the Madsen's have a son just about your age."

Amanda piped up for the first time. 'Will there be snow?"

"Could be," said Dad. "We're too low in elevation to catch much of the heavy stuff, but I remember snow most Christmas mornings."

"Cool." Amanda turned her attention back out her window.

Dad grew nostalgic, the look on his face much more pleasant than a few moments before. Olivia smiled warmly at her husband.

Tom glanced over at his wife, gave her a warm smile in return.

"I do miss this place," he said.

§

Jenny Harper stood waiting on the porch of large mountain cabin. Now in her sixties, she was a handsome woman, her hair gray-streaked and pulled back in a long ponytail. She dressed in jeans and a comfortable flannel shirt. There was a gleam in her eye, a smile on her face. She was smart, quick-witted, strong willed and independent, all of which showed in her free-spirited manner.

The entire front of her house was fronted with a covered deck. The open area before her was dirt and grass, with the occasional shrub, and beyond stood the barn and several smaller outbuildings. Forested hills encircled her property.

The sedan pulled into the yard. She took the top step down from the porch, put her hands on her hips and waited for the family to start climbing out of the car.

"There ya' are," she said. "How was your trip?"

Tom started across the yard as Jenny took the rest of the steps down from the porch.

"Hey, Mom." They met at the foot of the steps and hugged. "Took about five hours. Not too bad. Traffic was light most of the way."

Olivia reached them then, more hugs.

"How are you feeling, Mom?" she asked. Olivia had thought of Jenny as a second mom since the day she and Tom first started dating.

"I feel fine," said Jenny. "Really. Just fine."

The kids were out of the car and standing halfway between car and cabin. Jenny put her hands on hips once again and grinned. "My, my," she said.

"Grown a bit, haven't they?" Tom observed.

Jenny's grin broadened and she called out to the children. "Well, come over here, you two!"

Jack and Amanda trudged over. Jenny reached out and pulled them both in close.

"Hey, Grandma," they both mumbled in unison.

"Oh, my." She held them out at arm's length. "The last time I saw you two, you couldn't a' been more'n a foot tall."

"Oh, Grandma," Jack groaned.

"You say that every single time," said Amanda.

"Do I really?" Jenny gave them each a pat on the shoulder, indicated the surrounding hills. "So waddya think of the old homestead? Your dad grew up here, ya' know. He spent his days out there. Not in front of a television."

"I love it," said Amanda.

"Me, too," said Jack.

Jenny gave them a wary eye. "Good answer. Bright children."

Olivia had to snicker. "Oh, they're going to love it here, Jenny."

"Hmm." Jenny eyed their clothes, their footwear. "I hope they brought along some decent hiking shoes."

Tom had made his way back to the car.

"I made sure of that, Mom." He opened the trunk, began pulling out travel bags and suitcases. "Okay, guys. Let's get this stuff inside."

Jenny turned Jack and Amanda about and all three worked their way back to the car, Olivia following closely behind them.

Moments later Jenny led the way into the house carrying a basket of peaches. "These look wonderful," she said, setting the basket on the table. "They must have been hard to find, this time of year."

"You know how Tom is about his peach cobbler," said Olivia. She set a travel bag onto a wing chair.

Jack set his own travel bag next to his mom's, then pulled his cell phone out and anxiously sought a signal.

"Might as well turn that thing off, Jack," said Jenny. "No signal within five miles of here."

Tom looked nostalgically around the room. It was a large room with living and dining areas; walls and furniture of heavy woods, a large fireplace, thick curtains pulled open and revealing large windows.

"Man, I sure miss this place."

"Whose fault, boy?"

"Yes, Mom." He nodded then at the couch. "I see you finally replaced the old couch."

"Last Spring. I thought I mentioned it."

"You did, Mom," Olivia said apologetically. "And you sent us pictures of the new one."

"Oh, that's right," Tom said sheepishly. He picked up the two bags he had carried in. "Think I'll unpack." He motioned to the children. "You two, end of the hall."

"Jack on the left, Amanda on the right," said Jenny.

Once Tom and the kids had disappeared down the hall, Olivia joined Jenny at the table, pulled out one of the chairs and sat down.

"You sure you're up to this, Mom? We're a handful."

"Absolutely," said Jenny. "You stop worrying."

"Like that's going to happen."

"At least keep the worrying to yourself," said Jenny. "I don't want to hear it. This is going to be a wonderful Christmas. Let's not spoil it."

"You're absolutely right." Olivia reached out and placed a hand comfortingly on Jenny's arm. She missed Jenny. Long conversations on the phone weren't enough. It wasn't the same.

Amanda pulled a pair of pants from her travel bag and took them to the dresser. Her bedroom was small, with just enough room for the twin bed, the dresser, and a desk under the window; but it was also bright and cheery.

Jack came through the door and plopped himself onto the bed, looking dejectedly at his cell phone.

"Poor Jack," said Amanda, and she pulled her bag over. "Looks like we'll have to be a family. You know, like, talk to each other?"

Jack slid back until he was against the headboard.

"I can live with that; for very short periods."

"Uh, huh." Amanda looked over at the window. The forest was visible through the glass. "I think we're going to have a great Christmas. Grandma looks good, considering."

"Yep. She does."

"Better than I expected."

Jack gave a heavy shrug. "Probably a home turf thing."

"What?"

"Home turf," said Jack. "Home territory. Like Dad says, Grandma doesn't like to leave the mountain."

Amanda drifted over to the desk and pulled out the chair. She sat, leaned nearer the window. The view was amazing.

Can't blame her for that, she thought.

Jack stared down at his smart phone.

Nothing.

Chapter Two

After dinner, Tom and Olivia settled into chairs out on the porch, a pair of coffee cups on the small wooden table between them. The evening was warm for December, but it was still a bit cool, so both wore jackets.

Tom reached over and picked up his coffee. He glanced once through the window behind them before turning back, cup in hand. Jack and Amanda were inside, sitting at the dining table. They were playing a board game.

Jack is doing just fine, despite being disconnected from the rest of humanity...

"That was a great dinner, Liv." Tom took a sip of his coffee.

"I didn't have much to do about that."

Tom smiled. "Mom can be a bit controlling in the kitchen."

"The kitchen?" Olivia reached over and picked up her coffee, settled back into her chair, warmed her hands with the mug. "She's holding up well. She's strong."

"No scrawny brain tumor is going to beat Jenny Miller Harper."

"It'll certainly know that it's been in a fight."

That's for sure, thought Tom. *Well, we'll enjoy the holiday. Afterward, we'll take Mom down the mountain, they'll cut the thing out, and we'll have her back home before the nurses can turn on her.*

Tom had to grin at that.

Olivia saw the look on his face, and was about to ask him what was so funny, when Jenny came out of the woods, her tall hiking staff in hand. She came across the yard toward the house and stopped at the foot of the steps.

"Another wonderful evening," she stated. "A bit warm for December, really."

"It's beautiful," said Olivia. "And so peaceful. The only sounds are nature's sounds."

The sound then of the kids arguing over one of Jack's dice rolls came rolling out through the window, right on cue.

Those outside ignored it.

"You were gone a while, Mom," said Tom. "You must've gone all the way to the creek."

"I dropped in to see a friend."

A friend? thought Tom. *In the woods?*

Jenny climbed the steps, reached the porch. She turned and looked out at the surrounding hills. Her mountain. The sounds of the game going on inside continued to reach out onto the porch. It somehow made the evening all the more pleasant.

"I think I'll see if the kids are up to a game of cards," she said suddenly.

Olivia watched her turn about and go into the house. Tom could only grin that grin again as he continued to look out at the evening shadows that were reaching in ever closer.

He took another sip of his coffee.

The morning was bright and sunny, promising to be another nice day. Jenny came out onto the porch, waited for Olivia to follow her out of the house. She handed her a list.

"If they're out of buttermilk, they never keep enough on hand, get plain yogurt. But it's gotta be plain yogurt."

"Got it." Olivia put the piece of paper into her shirt pocket.

Tom came through the front door then, stepped around the women and started down the steps.

"We're going to drop in and see Carl and Emma on the way back, Mom. But we should be back by noon."

"I'll have lunch on the table," said Jenny. She called out to them then as they reached the car. "You tell Emma she still owes me three dollars."

"Yes, Ma'am." He grinned at Olivia. "Poker."

Jenny watched from the porch as Tom circled the car about in the yard and started down the dirt drive to the highway. The sound of the car faded and within moments nature crept back in. She looked warmly out at the forest-covered hills, enjoyed the morning breeze, the sunshine.

A sharp, sudden pain... she grimaced, pressed the heel of her hand to her temple.

She quickly lowered her hand at the sound of the door opening behind her.

Jack and Amanda stepped outside dressed for a hike: jeans and warm shirt, hiking shoes. Each wore a light daypack.

"Okay, Grandma," said Amanda. "We're ready."

"Let me just have a look," said Jenny. She inspected their clothes, turned them around, adjusted their packs. "Very good," she stated, quite precisely.

"Are there any wild animals?" asked Jack.

"Of course."

"Really?"

"Of course. Cougar, bear, deer, porcupine, skunk, rabbit... all manner of creature."

"Are they dangerous?"asked Amanda.

"Killer rabbits," joked Jack.

"Them and others," said Jenny. "Just don't surprise 'em. Don't be too quiet. Don't make a racket out there, but don't be sneaking around, either."

"Ma'am?"

"Ya' gotta give 'em a chance to get out of your way. And don't ever come between a mama and her babies. If you do come face to face, don't run, but don't stare 'em down; just back away."

"Okay," said Jack, more anxious than he wanted to let on.

Jenny took a compass out of her pocket. "Either of you know how to use a compass?" she asked.

"Yes, Ma'am," said Amanda. "I do."

Jenny handed the compass to her. "You stay on this side of the creek, don't cross a road," she pointed, "and keep that mountain to your south. Do that, you can't get lost."

"Got it," said Amanda.

"Off you go, then." Jenny motioned them off the porch. "Be back before noon."

They thanked Grandma as they took the steps down from the porch, started across the yard toward the trailhead between the barn and the larger of the two lesser outbuildings.

They found themselves walking along a winding, well-traveled path, the vegetation pushing in on them from either side. After a few minutes the trail turned up the hillside and grew steadily steeper. Jack and Amanda began to climb. They were glad when the trail suddenly leveled off, then opened onto a large, wide open clearing.

They stepped to the edge of the clearing. A panoramic vista was spread out before and below them. From here they could see sweeping mountainsides of forest, open meadows, and clear blue sky.

After a few minutes rest, they started again, following the trail back into the trees. Another twenty minutes and they could hear the placid sound of water coursing over rock. They came up to a creek, followed the bank without crossing.

Sometime later the trail veered away from the creek, turning more directly uphill where the creek continued to flow its gentler course. They nonetheless decided to follow the path, and within a few minutes entered another clearing.

Directly ahead of them was a small cabin; rustic, some of the rough-hewn siding planks older than others, revealing that it had been patched and repaired piecemeal over the years.

A string of Christmas lights hung loose on the front eave, turned off. The bulbs were a mix of colors: green and blue and red.

The mountain rose up directly behind the clearing. Another trailhead next to the cabin led to away and continued up the hillside.

"Do you think anybody lives here?" asked Jack.

Amanda walked up the cabin, leaned up close to a window. Inside was a table and one chair, a narrow bed against a wall near a fireplace. On the other side of the fireplace was a wall of shelves with books and odds and ends. In the near corner were a sink and counter and small refrigerator.

"I think so," she said. She stepped back, noticed a switch mounted next to the front door. She reached out and flipped it up. The string of Christmas lights turned on. Several bulbs weren't working. Several others flickered a few times before remaining on.

One bulb suddenly went out.

A man's voice then, deep and not entirely friendly. "Waddya kids want?"

Mike stood just inside the trailhead beside the cabin, hiking staff in hand. He was dressed in rawhide pants and jacket, a heavy plaid shirt. A graying black man, sixty six years old, his face several days unshaven. There was a haunted, absent gaze in his eyes. He set his small backpack onto the wooden workbench built against the side of the cabin.

Jack and Amanda took several steps back from the cabin as Mike moved around to the front.

"Sorry, mister," said Jack. "We didn't know anybody lived here."

Mike flipped the switch and the Christmas lights went out.

"You know it now." He gave the kids a careful gaze. "You belong to Jenny?"

"She's our grandma," said Amanda.

"Heard about that," Mike grunted. "You here for a couple of weeks, then. Christmas."

"That's right," Amanda stated.

"You know Grandma?" asked Jack.

"Course I know her." He looked from side to side, examining the front of his cabin as if to make sure nothing was missing or damaged. "Known her all my life."

There was a long pause then. Mike eyed his uninvited company. His company shuffled nervously under the gaze.

"You two best be off," he said.

Dinner was a warm, pleasant atmosphere. The family sat around Grandma's long dining table, Jenny at one end, Tom and Olivia on one side, Jack and Amanda on the other.

"Oh, that's just Mike," said Grandma. "That's his cabin."

"Is he dangerous?" asked Olivia.

"Oh my, no. Not at all. Mike's a darling."

"He has a cabin up here?" asked Tom. "I didn't know he had moved back." He obviously knew of Mike.

"Couple of years now," said Jenny. "He bought a patch of land up near the mouth of the caves."

"Caves?" Amanda perked up. This got her attention.

"You mean the—" Olivia started.

"Yes," Jenny answered.

"What caves?" Jack asked, as curious as Amanda. *Caves?*

"There're caves up here?" asked Amanda.

Tom looked distractedly at Jenny, at Olivia, gave a quick glance to the kids. He looked back to Jenny.

"After all these years?" he asked his mother. "Is he still—"

"Yes. Yes, I'm afraid so."

There was a hint of sadness in that, and it was reflected in Tom's own expression. He turned slowly then back to the kids. "Mike is a friend of your Grandma's," he said. "They grew up together. At least till Mike's family moved away."

Jack wasn't about to let the conversation shift away from what was important.

"What caves?" he asked.

"You never told the children about the caves?" Jenny asked Tom.

"The subject never came up."

Jenny put down her fork. She leaned over her plate. "Well, it's front and center now."

"Mom," Olivia spoke thoughtfully, "I'm not so sure—"

"Oh, what's the fuss?"

"Mom..." Tom sighed.

Jenny turned her focus back to Jack and Amanda.

"I was thirteen," she said. "We had been hearing stories about a special cave for as long as any of us could remember. A secret place deep in the mountain where it was always Christmas. Of course, Mike and I didn't believe the stories, but my little brother Bill was certain there was some truth to them." She leaned an inch nearer her grandchildren and grinned slyly. "We were happy to go along with it. After all, exploring the caves was fun. It was exciting. It's a real maze in there. Those tunnels go on for miles. We explored 'em off and on for most of a year. Got lost more'n once."

"Lost?" Amanda perked up.

"Oh, we always managed to find our way out again," she said dismissively. She smiled at Tom, who frowned, a sparkle in her eye. She leaned back then, continued her story. "Two days after Christmas, nineteen hundred and sixty. We were deeper in the mountain than ever before, in a section of the caves we had never been in before. We saw a light up ahead, beyond the bend... where there should be no light. Flickering red and green and blue."

"Like Christmas," Amanda whispered.

"Just like Christmas," Jenny said softly. She grew silent. Her expression grew solemn. Tom reached a hand out and rested it comfortingly on her arm. She gave a gentle smile, patted the back of his hand.

"Bill rushed ahead of us," she continued. "I tried to stop him, but then, that was Bill."

"What happened, Grandma?" asked Amanda.

"He disappeared around the bend. About then the lights went out. Mike and I ran after him, but by the time we got there... he was gone. There was nothing there."

"Nothing?"

"Nothing. Just more tunnel. We followed it, searched for hours; ended up completely lost. Took most of a day to find our way back out."

She went thoughtfully silent again. Jack was about to ask her what happened when she started again, her voice more soft than ever before.

"A rescue party went in to search for him. But they never found him. Never found anything. Not a sign."

"What do you think happened, Grandma?" Amanda asked.

"Who's to say, sweetie. Maybe he found the Christmas Cave. I'd like to think so." She again grew quiet, and while the kids wanted to know more they could sense that now was probably not the time to pursue it.

Jack slid his chair back and stood up, gathered his plate and silverware and took them into the kitchen. Amanda followed his lead, and moments later they headed down the hall to their rooms.

When Jenny took her own dishes into the kitchen, Olivia leaned forward and rested on her elbows.

"They're going to end up in those caves, you know," she said, her voice just low enough to keep her children from overhearing. "How can they not, now that they've heard the stories?"

"Kids gotta be kids, Olivia," said Tom.

"It's dangerous."

"It's not that bad. Geez, every kid on this mountain ends up in the caves, me included. It's almost a rite of passage."

"Just... don't encourage them," said Olivia. "We're their parents. We tell them to stay out. We need to be together on this."

"Of course, Liv," Tom gave his wife a pleasant smile.

"I mean it, Tom." Olivia spoke firmly. "You were lost in there for two days."

"Day and a half. And I was eleven."

"They're not much older. And you could have died in there."

That last lay heavy in the room. They heard Jenny in the kitchen, putting leftovers into bowls and the dishes in the sink. From down the hall came Amanda's voice. It sounded like Jack should have knocked first.

"So what happened to Mike, do you think?" asked Olivia. "How did he become so obsessed?"

"I don't know." Tom shrugged. "Maybe he felt responsible." His mom had told him more than once that Bill had followed Mike everywhere.

"You don't think..." Olivia wondered, "He can't believe that Bill is still alive."

"Who's to say?" Tom wondered right back. "You heard Mom. After Bill was lost, rescue teams went over those tunnels with a fine-toothed comb. Never found a trace of him. Or of the Christmas Cave."

"Oh, but you don't think it really exists? That he actually found it?"

"No. Of course not. But Mike might."

After Bill went missing, Mike had snuck off every chance he got to go searching in the caves. The sheriff even tried boarding up the entrance, but that didn't stop him. His parents got so worried that they finally moved away, took him off the mountain.

Jenny didn't hear anything of him for fifteen years. Then he started showing up summers. He'd spend a couple of weeks on the mountain, going into the caves for days at a time.

"The poor man," said Olivia. "Searching for a lost little boy, year after year."

Jenny came out of the kitchen and settled again at the table.

"I thought Mike was married," said Tom.

"Mary passed away the winter before he moved back up here for good," said Jenny. "His son has a family of his own, lives back east somewhere. I don't think he ever hears from them." She looked up from the tabletop, to Tom, to Olivia. "It's just Mike."

"Not true," said Olivia. "He has you."

"Yes, he does." Jenny took a long, soft sigh. "He certainly does."

Chapter Three

Jack and Amanda followed the bank of the small stream, the narrow trail drifting in and out of the woods that shadowed the brook. The morning was almost as nice as the day before, perhaps a little cooler.

They came out into a meadow. A boy sat on a rise in the bank where the stream running beside the meadow widened out to form a pool. He had a fishing pole in hand, the line running into the water.

Daniel Madsen was twelve years old, had dark red hair, dark freckles on the bridge of his nose. He wore jeans, well-worn hiking shoes and a long-sleeve shirt.

He looked up at Jack and Amanda's approach but said nothing.

"Hey," said Jack, as much a 'good morning' as if he actually said good morning.

"Hey," said Daniel, indifferent to the greeting. He looked back to his fishing pole, lifted it, let the line shift in the water.

"Fishing, huh?" asked Amanda. "Catch anything?"

Daniel leaned over, lifted a chain that ran into the water, revealing two fish on the line. He lowered the fish back into the water, focused his attention again on his pole.

"You visitin' Mrs. Harper?" he asked.

"Our grandma. I'm Jack," said Jack. He pointed a thumb in Amanda's direction. "My sister."

"Amanda," said Amanda.

"Daniel. Madsen." He looked up at Jack and Amanda, shaded his eyes. "Your mom and dad came by the house to see my folks yesterday."

"Suppose so."

"Your dad grew up here, same's my dad." He turned back to the stream. "He moved to the city, I hear. That where you're from?"

"Yep," said Amanda. "So you live here. You like it?"

"Yep."

"You know Mike?" asked Jack.

"Lives in the cabin over yonder? Sure. What about him?"

"Just wondered."

"We met him yesterday," said Amanda.

Daniel looked carefully at the fishing line in the water, lifted and lowered the tip of the rod.

"Nice enough fella," he said. "Bit odd, I guess. Dad says he ain't been right in the head since he lost his friend in the caves."

"That's what I hear," said Jack.

"It was our grandma's brother that got lost," said Amanda. "They were looking for the Christmas Cave."

Daniel gave a slow, knowing nod. "Twarn't the first that got lost in there. Doubt he'll be the last."

"You been in the caves?" asked Jack.

Daniel only shrugged, stared at his fishing line.

"Have you looked for the Christmas Cave?" asked Amanda.

"I know about it. Ain't really done much searching for it."

"What'cha hear?"

"Well... supposedly, not that I believe it, mind you, but supposedly, some kid came out of the caves after being lost in there three years. Said he'd been living in a cave full a' wondrous sights and lots of bright colors. Them's his words. Said it was the Christmas Cave." Daniel gave a slow sigh. "People been lookin' for it ever since."

"But you ain't gone in?" asked Jack.

Daniel gave another shrug. "Like I said. Don't believe it." He turned an eye up to Jack. "You goin' lookin'?"

"Considerin' it."

Daniel nodded, looked back at his fishing line again, dipped his pole up and down yet again.

"Expect you should talk to Mike, then," he said.

Mike was sitting at his table, coffee cup in hand, when there came a light knock at his door.

He gave a curious look at the door. A knock on his cabin door was a rather uncommon occurrence. He had very few visitors. Only one, really. Jenny. That certainly wasn't Jenny's knock.

He stood and took the two steps to the door, opened it.

Jack, Amanda and Daniel looked up at him.

He looked tentatively apprehensively down at them.

"Yeah?" he asked.

"Hey, Mike," said Daniel.

"Daniel."

"We'd like to talk to you," said Jack.

"About what?"

"The Christmas Cave," said Amanda. "We want to talk to you about the Christmas Cave."

Mike studied Amanda for a long time, his expression giving away no emotion.

He stepped back then, motioned for the kids to come in, turned about and retreated into the cabin. He settled into his chair at the table as his guests sought places to sit down. There was only one other chair and the bed.

Daniel chose the chair, while Jack and Amanda stood before a large, hand-drawn map hanging on the wall.

"Wow," said Jack.

The map detailed a complex maze of tunnels and caverns. Quadrants and divisions reflected different sections and multiple levels.

"This is what you've been doing up here?"

"Used to come up here summers. Full time now."

"Wow," Amanda said, repeating her brother's observation.

Daniel slid back in his chair. "I told 'em that if they wanted to know about the caves, they should talk to you."

"Nothin' to know, 'cept stay out of there."

"You're not taking your own advice," Amanda observed, indicating the map.

"I got a job to do."

"To find Bill?"

"That's right."

Jack turned around and looked at Mike. He spoke as he settled onto the bed.

"After all these years?"

"That's right."

Amanda pointed to a spot on the map. "What are these?" she asked.

"Collapsed tunnels," said Mike. "Tremors bringing down the ceilings."

"Earthquakes?"

"Doesn't take much. Tunnels are hundred years old and more. Little bit o' shakin' can bring down whole sections."

"You get a lot of earthquakes up here?" asked Jack.

"Some. Now and again. You can feel 'em in there more'n out here." He looked across the room at his map. "It makes the searchin' tougher."

"But after all these years, you still haven't found it? The Christmas Cave?"

Mike gave a sharp nod in the direction of the map. "I know where it should be. I know where it was."

"Waddya mean, Mike?" asked Amanda.

Mike stood, took one long step and leaned forward. He reached out and slowly pointed to a spot on the map.

"It was right there."

"But—"

He drifted back and returned to his seat at the table. "That's where it was."

Jack stood up again, cocked his head and studied the map.

"You mean, it was there before, and it's not there now?"

"I was standing there two days ago," he stated flatly. "But it looked just like it did that day. Nothing. Just tunnel."

Amanda stepped away from map, sat down on the bed beside her brother.

"That day you and Grandma followed—"

"That's right," said Mike. "Nothing there. More tunnel. But that's where it shoulda' been."

Jack stared at the map.

He studied every feature, every line, every tunnel and cavern.

Chapter Four

Jack and Amanda sat on the top step of the front porch. Out in the yard, near the car, their mom was saying good-bye to their dad.

Grandma came out onto the porch and stood behind the kids.

"A shame," she said.

"We get it a lot," said Jack, his chin resting in his hands.

"It's his work," said Amanda. "An emergency is an emergency."

"Well, it is important," said Jenny. "His foundation helps a lot of people."

"We know," said Amanda.

Tom looked over and called out to them.

"I'll be back in a couple of days," he said. "Three days, tops."

"Don't you worry, Tom," Jenny called out. "You just do what needs doing and get back to us safe." She spoke then to Jack and Amanda. "There you go, children. We'll see your father again well before Christmas."

Down in the yard, Olivia watched Tom drive off. Once the car was gone from sight, she turned and walked slowly over to the porch.

"Are you two all right?"

"It's okay, Mom," said Jack. "Really."

"You know your father's work." She looked apologetically up at Jenny. "The foundation runs on a shoestring as it is. They can barely—"

"Don't apologize, Olivia. The work is important. No one's being deprived here." She nudged Jack from behind. "Right?"

"Nothing we can't handle," said Jack with a grin.

"Right," Jenny said firmly.

"Right," agreed Amanda.

"Right," sighed Olivia. "So, what are your plans for this afternoon?"

"Daniel is gonna show us his secret swimming spot," said Jack.

"The Madsen boy?" asked Jenny.

"They met him this morning," said Olivia.

"I heard he was coming home. I didn't realize he was already back."

"He said he lived here," said Jack.

"He does. Or he did, up until, oh, about two years ago. Carl and Emma have really been looking forward to having him back home."

"That's right," said Olivia. "The boy was ill, wasn't he? I had completely forgotten about that. He certainly looked well yesterday. And they didn't say a word."

"I'm afraid he's not well at all."

"I'm so sorry to hear that."

"What's wrong with him?" asked Amanda. Daniel hadn't looked sick to her, either.

"Leukemia, I'm afraid," said Grandma.

"Leukemia?"

"Cancer, sweetie," said Mom.

Jack turned about. "Is he gonna be all right?"

"There's nothing more they can do for him, Jack. It was decided he should spend what time is left here on the mountain, long as he's able." She looked up, out at the surrounding mountains. "I am glad to hear he's home."

Jack, Amanda and Daniel peered over the top of the ridge. Mike's cabin was visible in the clearing below. For the moment there was no movement, no sign of Mike.

Jack glanced sideways at Daniel. Other than being a bit pale, maybe a bit short of breath, Daniel didn't appear all that sick.

"There he is," said Daniel.

Jack turned back quickly and looked down at the cabin.

Mike stepped from the trail and into the clearing, wearing a knapsack and using a tall hiking staff. He walked around to the front of the cabin. He went inside.

"That's the trail he left by this morning," Daniel continued. "I'll bet ya' nickels to donuts it'll take us right to the caves."

Amanda frowned. "I told you, Daniel. We can't go into the caves."

"Why not?"

"Because our mom told us to stay out of 'em."

"Well," said Jack, "It was more of a suggestion, really."

"Jack..." Amanda frowned yet again.

"She didn't actually order us not to go into the caves. She just doesn't like the idea of the caves on general principal."

"You know what she meant, Jack."

"C'mon, Amanda. Let's at least have a look."

Amanda gave him a cool stare, then looked at Daniel. He had the hint of a soft smile, but didn't look to be forcing her one way or the other.

"I don't know," she said.

"You guys do what you want," Daniel said with a shrug. "I gotta do this."

"I thought you didn't believe in the Christmas Cave," said Amanda.

"I'm willing to consider the possibility."

Amanda figured Jack's excitement over this had infected poor Daniel.

Jack's gaze was almost pleading. She knew he wouldn't go without her. If he got into trouble over this, better to have his little sister along to share the pain.

"Just a quick look," said Jack.

Her resistance collapsed. They were both going to be grounded for a month over this.

"Maybe just a quick look around." She glanced up at the sky. "But not today. We have to get home. I am not going to be late."

"But we go first thing in the morning."

"Yeah, all right," Amanda grumbled.

Jack turned to Daniel. "We'll meet you back here, get an early start. Right?"

"Right-O."

"Okay, then." He pointed a finger at Amanda. "And no backin' out."

"I said I'd go, didn't I? Geez." She lowered her head. "Oh, I just know I'm going to regret this."

It was late afternoon before they made it back to the cabin. Jenny and Olivia were decorating the tree when they came in.

"There you are," said Mom. "Did you have a good time?"

"Yeah," Amanda shrugged.

"S'pose," said Jack.

"Did Daniel show you his secret swimming hole?"

"Yeah."

"So? How was it?"

"It was okay."

Grandma looked the two of them over with an experienced eye.

"You didn't go swimming?"

"Nah."

"It was too cold for swimming," said Amanda.

"Oh, that's too bad," said Mom.

"That's all right," said Jack. "We went exploring."

Olivia and Jenny gave each other questioning looks as Jack and Amanda disappeared down the hall.

"I wonder what they're up to?" asked Olivia.

"They're up to being kids, I expect." Jenny stiffened suddenly, pressed her fingers to her temple.

"Mom?" Olivia took a step toward Jenny. "Are you all right?"

"I'm fine, sweetie." Jenny tried to shake it off. "Just a bit of a headache."

"Maybe you should sit down."

"No, I'm fine." Jenny reached for a decoration. She had difficulty focusing, tried several times to get hold of the ornament before finally giving up.

Olivia took another step nearer and held Jenny's arm. "Jenny? Come on, Mom. Sit down."

Jenny hesitated, finally gave a brief nod. "Maybe for just a minute, then." She smiled warmly at Olivia as she sat down.

Olivia slowly sat in the chair beside her. "Mom?"

"Better." Jenny waved a dismissive hand. "Nothing, really."

"It doesn't look like nothing to me."

"I'm fine, now." She took a long, deep breath, smiled reassuringly. *Not nearly as bad as the spell I had this morning,* she thought. *Seems to be worse in the mornings.*

"Maybe we shouldn't wait. Let me call the doctor. We'll move it up."

"No, no, dear. It'll pass. Always does. Let's just enjoy the holiday. All right?"

"Mom..."

"I'm none the worse."

Olivia wasn't ready to let this go. It took her a few moments to respond. "I'm not going to let you take any chances, Jenny. If I think—"

"Of course, of course."

Olivia doesn't look at all convinced.

"Honestly, dear," said Jenny, and she gave Olivia yet another comforting smile. "See? It's passed. Now let's get back to this tree."

Jack sat on Amanda's bed with his back against the headboard. Amanda was sitting in chair by the window, holding the curtain aside with one hand, looking casually outside.

"Daniel seemed okay," she said absently. "Kinda tired, maybe."

She lowered the curtain and looked over at Jack.

"Didn't he seem okay to you?"

"He seemed fine," said Jack.

"Yeah. I thought so too. I don't think he's as bad off as they say. I mean... wouldn't he have said something?"

Jack just shrugged in response.

Amanda turned back to the window, pulled aside the curtain. "Maybe we should have asked him about it. Maybe he was waiting for us to ask him about it."

"It's his personal business," said Jack. "He wants to talk about it, he'll talk about it."

"Maybe."

"They always make it out worse than it is." Jack was way past ready to change the subject. "Waddya think we'll find in the Christmas Cave?"

"I didn't say I was going to go into the tunnels, much less that I'd go looking for the Christmas Cave."

"Sure you're going in."

"I only said I'd take a look. Nothin' about going inside."

"Well, that doesn't make any sense," said Jack. "Ya' gotta go in. What? You gonna stand outside and stare at it? Besides, it's like, ya' know, Daniel's Last Wish."

"Oh, don't you go playin' the guilt trip card on me, Jack."

"I'm just sayin'."

Amanda gave her brother a chilling glare. "That's cold."

Jack settled in more comfortably, stared up at the ceiling and grinned. His work was done.

"All right," Amanda said firmly. "I'll go to the caves with you, and we'll have a look around inside. But I'm not promising anything."

"Of course. We'll just check it out. We'll see what's what."

Mom's voice came from down the hall.

"Kids! Come out here and help with the tree."

Chapter Five

Jack, Amanda and Daniel walked stealthily past Mike's old cabin in the early morning, started up the trail they had seen Mike come out of the day before. Each had a small knapsack on their back.

The trail wound through woods, meadow and open hillside, always upward. Misty fog rolled over grassy fields and through the trees. It would take the morning sun rising higher to burn it off.

An hour from Mike's place and they stepped out into a clearing of bare ground at the base of a steep rock face. There was a crevice between two tall rocks that formed a dark opening four feet wide.

A worn path led directly to the opening.

"This must be it," said Daniel.

"It doesn't look like much," said Jack, with a hint of disappointment.

"What'd ya' expect?"

Amanda moved in closer to the cave opening. "Looks kinda' menacing, if you ask me."

Daniel shrugged out of his knapsack, set it at his feet and opened it. The others followed suit. Each brought out a flashlight.

"You sure about this?" asked Amanda, gripping her flashlight.

"I'm not makin' you guys come with me," said Daniel.

"It'll be all right, Amanda," said Jack. "If you feel uncomfortable, we'll come back out."

"I already feel uncomfortable."

"Well ya' gotta give it a chance," said Jack. "We'll just go in a ways, have a look around."

"What if we get lost?"

"We won't get lost." He tapped at his temple. "I have Mike's map right here. I'll take us right to the Christmas Cave."

"All right, then." Daniel picked up his knapsack, flicked on his flashlight. "Let's go."

Amanda let out a sigh and gave a short nod. Jack grinned, picked up his knapsack and led the way to the entrance, turning on his flashlight as he stepped through the opening.

Inside, the opening to the outside world behind them was a bright glare, ahead of them the way narrowed quickly toward a dark tunnel.

"Okay," Amanda whispered harshly. "We finished here?"

"Funny," said Jack. "What say we give it just a little bit further?"

Daniel was a little more determined. "I'm taking this as far as it goes," he said. "Wherever it takes me."

"Don't you worry, Amanda," said Jack. "It'll be fine. Home before dinner."

"You promise me, Jack."

"I promise. You say the word, we'll go home."

Amanda studied her brother's face for a long time.

"All right," she said at last, and with that Jack led the way.

They were immediately engulfed in the darkness. Light beams from their flashlights danced like sabers, stabbing into the dark, reaching feebly into the black, creating shadows of the three of them on the tunnel walls.

Olivia stood at the side table in the living room on which the phone sat, the only phone in Jenny's cabin. She had the receiver to her ear.

"Okay Tom, I'm glad to hear it," she said, then listened. "Okay. Okay, we'll be waiting for you. See you soon... I love you, too."

She hung up the phone, looked across the room at Jenny.

"He's on his way back," she told her. "He should be here tonight."

Jenny walked toward the dining table, cup of tea in hand.

"That's wonderful, dear." She sat at the table.

Olivia walked over and sat beside her. "How are you feeling, Mom?"

"All the better for the good news." She indicated her cup. "The water's hot. Would you like me to fix you some tea?"

"That's all right." Olivia stood and gave a light pat on Jenny's arm. "I'll get it."

Jack continued to lead the way through the tunnels, Amanda and Daniel following behind.

"Not to worry," Jack said over his shoulder. "This is the way."

"Uh-huh," Amanda mumbled.

Jack tapped again at his temple. "It's all in here. Like a photograph."

"Jack, I've been lost before, and this is pretty much what it looks like."

"No, no. No worries. No worries."

Daniel, bringing up the rear, was more optimistic than Amanda.

"Hey, being lost is a good sign," he said. "I'll bet you can't find the Christmas Cave without being lost."

Not the support that Jack was looking for.

"We are not lost," he insisted.

"Jack?"

"Amanda?"

"Jack, this is where I feel uncomfortable and we head back."

"I'm telling you, Amanda, this is the way. It's all good. All good."

Jenny and Olivia headed outside after an early lunch. Olivia went to one of the outbuildings and brought out the ladder while Jenny untangled the string of Christmas lights.

They had been working at hanging them along the rain gutter for half an hour, Olivia up on the ladder and Jenny standing below, when a car came into the yard. The Madsen parents got out.

Jenny left the foot of the ladder and started toward them as Olivia stepped down.

Carl Madsen was thirty nine years old, medium build, hair beginning to thin. He dressed warm, ready for mountain weather. His wife Emma was a year older, thin and tired looking. She dressed as if she was from the city and only here on a visit. This, despite the fact that she had lived on the mountain most of her adult life, ever since her wedding day.

"Sorry to bother you, Jenny," said Carl.

"Don't be silly, Carl. You know you're welcome anytime."

Olivia stepped up next to Jenny. "Carl, Emma. Good to see you both again. Is there a problem?"

"Hello, Olivia," said Emma. "I don't suppose Daniel is here? Don't suppose you've seen him?"

"I believe he's with Jack and Amanda. They were going up to see Mike, then heading up the creek to some meadow or other."

"I'm sure he's all right, Emma," said Jenny. "They're just exploring."

Olivia could see very real concern on Emma's face.

"Is something wrong?" she asked.

"I'm sure it's nothing," said Carl.

"He didn't take his medicine with him," said Emma. "He's been gone all morning."

"Oh, my," said Olivia. "We expect them to be gone all day. They took sack lunches with them."

Jenny reached out and placed a hand on Carl's arm. "Would you like us to go looking for them?"

"No, it's all right. Just being overly protective. He's skipped his medicine before."

"Are you sure?" asked Olivia. "Really, we can—"

"No need. We do tend to smother him these days. And he hates the way the medicine makes him feel."

Emma smiled guiltily. "And we are constantly after him to take his medicine. It's probably why he spends so much time out there."

"Oh, I doubt the boy needs any encouragement in that regard," said Jenny. "You know I'm right, Carl. You remember these mountains when you were his age. Drawn to 'em like a magnet, you were."

"Yes, of course."

Jenny gave Carl's arm another pat, then reached over to Emma held her arm comfortingly.

"They'll be home well before dinner. Standing orders."

It was early evening before Tom made it back. He came in through the front door and set down his travel bag, smiled in Olivia's direction when she came in from the kitchen.

"Hey, Liv. Sorry I'm late. Hit some traffic."

They hugged and kissed, then Tom looked around the room. All quiet. Too quiet.

"Did I miss dinner?"

Olivia sighed. "The kids aren't home yet. I'm starting to get a bit worried."

"I'm sure they just lost track of the time, Liv. Where were they headed?"

"They said they were going to hike up the creek. Daniel is with them."

Jenny came into the living room from the kitchen. "Hello, Tom. Welcome home."

"Hey, Mom." He looked back to Olivia. "I'm sure they're all right."

"But what if they've gotten lost."

Jenny spoke out as she sat at the table. "They know the boundaries, Olivia. Tough to get lost so long as you stay in the boundaries."

"Not if they've gone into the caves, it isn't."

"There is that, of course." Jenny frowned. "Frankly, I'm more concerned that something may have happened to Daniel."

Tom looked curiously at his mother, then at Olivia.

"Carl and Emma were here earlier," said Olivia. "Daniel didn't take his medicine this morning, didn't take it with him." She folded her arms, held her elbows with her hands. "I think we should go looking for them. Don't you?"

"You say they went hiking up the creek?"

"That's what they said."

All three were quiet for several moments. Jenny finally placed the palm of one hand firmly down on the table and stood up.

"All right. Let's see if Mike has seen them. I'll get changed." She waved a hand at them. "You too, you too. Go on. You can't wander about the woods dressed like that."

The sun had set before they reached Mike's cabin. They knocked and waited, knocked again. When there was still no answer, Jenny opened the door and the others followed her in.

Inside, the room was dark. Jenny reached over to the light switch and turned on the light. Tom stepped into the kitchen area. Everything looked cold.

"He's been gone all day, at least."

"Look at this, Tom," said Olivia. She was standing before the large map on the wall. Tom took the few steps to stand beside her. Jenny spoke up behind them.

"That's his map of the caves. He's been working on it for years."

Olivia studied one specific location on the map. She pointed. "The Christmas Cave."

"He found it?" Tom asked.

Jenny stepped up beside him, spoke matter-of-factly. "He thinks so. But there was nothing there."

"Mother?"

"Mike's been there a couple of times the last few weeks." She and Mike had talked about it just the other day.

"Tom..." Olivia sounded really worried now. "What if the kids saw this?"

"Of course they've seen it." He stared hard at the map. He nodded at the location Mike had indicated. "That's where they are."

"Then I guess that's where we're going," said Jenny.

"Mom... maybe you should wait at the house. In case they show up there."

"What if they do?"

"They'll wonder where we are."

"So."

"Mom..."

"End of discussion."

Tom turned away from his mother, gave the hint of a nod and finally stepped over to the desk.

"All right," he said at last. "Give me a minute. I'll make a copy of the map."

Jenny took a last quick glance at the map before starting toward the door.

"I know the way," she said. She turned and started toward the door. She stopped then, hesitated. She reached out and grasped the door jamb. Facing away from the others, she fought back a grimace of pain.

Tom saw that something was wrong. "Mom?"

The pain slowly subsided.

"I know the way," she repeated. "Come on. Mike keeps a spare lantern in the shed."

Jack slowed and looked back at the others. The tunnel here was very narrow, was well lit by their flashlights.

Daniel appeared pale, short of breath; fatigued.

Jack stopped. "Let's take a breather."

"Good idea," said Amanda. She studied the features of this narrow stretch of tunnel. "We've been here before."

"No we haven't," Jack stated firmly.

Daniel took a deep breath, let it out. He looked forward and back, then at Amanda.

"How can you tell?"

"I can tell."

Jack was insistent. "We have not been here before."

Amanda shook her head sadly. "We are so lost."

"I'm telling you, this is the way out."

"You said before."

"And it's still true."

"But we're going down."

"We have to go down to go up."

Amanda leaned nearer Daniel, who appeared increasingly pale in the feeble light.

"Hey, you okay?" she asked.

"Sure." Daniel put on a weak smile. "Just give me a second."

Amanda turned to her brother. "Jack, we need to go back."

Jack looked at Daniel, didn't like what he saw.

"Yeah. Okay," he said. "I know the way."

Daniel shook his head sharply and pushed himself forward.

"Not going back. I'm ready. Come on."

"Amanda's right, Daniel," said Jack. "We should go back. We can try again tomorrow."

Daniel took another halting step, turned then and looked back at the others.

"No. No. You don't understand. This is it. This is my last adventure. I'm going on. No matter what." He took a moment to catch his breath. "Alone, if I have to."

Jack looked once to Amanda, turned slowly again to Daniel.

"No, man," he said. "Not alone."

Amanda surrendered to the majority, gave a grudging nod. She saw something then up ahead in the tunnel, beyond Daniel.

She grasped Jack by the arm.

"Hey..." she said, almost a whisper. "You see that?"

Jack and Daniel both looked ahead, tried to see beyond the reach of their flashlights.

"See what?" asked Jack.

Daniel slowly raised his arm and pointed.

"That." Up ahead, from beyond the bend... a faint light.

"Are we out?" asked Amanda.

"No." Daniel stated flatly. "Not out."

He turned off his flashlight. The others followed suit.

The tunnel was dark but for a colorful, flickering glow beyond the bend in the tunnel.

"Wow," Amanda whispered.

"Yeah wow," said Jack. "Come on."

They started forward, cautiously approached the bend. Beyond the bend, they came face to face with Mike, standing tall in the center of the tunnel.

He looked down at them, his lantern held up before him, a dull yellow glow.

"Oh," Amanda said curtly. "It's you."

"Yes. Me," said Mike. He looked at Daniel. "You okay, kid? You don't look so good."

"I always look this way. I don't get enough sun."

"I hear ya." Mike turned forward. "I got something better."

He turned off his lantern.

Several dozen feet ahead of them, the tunnel glowed in bright, colorful light.

Tom, Olivia and Jenny made ready to go into the caves. The sky overhead was gray and dreary. Night came fast here and it would be dark soon.

There was only one lantern between them, and Tom held it up as Jenny lit it. A hazy glow spread out across the ground. There were a number of footprints.

"They've been here, all right," said Tom.

Jenny saw larger footprints amongst those of the children.

"Mike's in there," she said.

"With them, do you think?" Olivia asked hopefully.

"I doubt very much that he would take them into the caves, but he may well have found them."

Looks like we're all headed to the same place, thought Tom.

"Are you two ready?" he asked.

"Oh, yes." Olivia gave her husband the hint of a smile. "Let's go ground some children."

Tom gave her a strong affirmative nod, then held the lantern out to his mother.

"Mom?"

Jenny took the lantern and led the way into the caves.

Chapter Six

Jenny turned down the lantern flame till there was only the lightest flicker.

"Well, I'll be," she said.

Several dozen feet ahead of them... bright, flickering light of red and blue and green.

She looked back at Tom and Olivia.

"I don't understand," she said. "It wasn't here. I swear, it wasn't here."

"Then it must come and go," said Olivia. "One day it's here, the next it's not."

Jenny looked back at the light. Tom placed an arm on his mother's shoulders. "That would explain why Mike hasn't been able to find it until now."

"After all these years. Bill." Jenny stared longingly at the shimmering colors in the tunnel ahead of them.

Tom took a moment to allow his mother to take it all in.

"After you, Mother."

"Yes," she said. "Thank you, Tom."

Jenny took a step toward the light, then another...

She stepped out of fractured, flickering light emanating from a wall of solid rock. She found herself standing on a narrow ledge forty feet up a cliff. Tom and Olivia came through the colorful, glittering portal and stood beside her.

The flickering behind them stopped.

The cavern was well lit. Phosphorus in the walls and ceiling created its own light, and the numerous other minerals reflecting the phosphorescent light created their own blue, red and green.

Bright, sparkling Christmas colors...

The cavern was hundreds of yards across. A narrow river ran from left to right, beginning midway up the cliff wall above them on their left, tumbling in a noisy falls. Reaching the cavern floor, it formed a river that ran across to an unseen outlet beneath the distant right wall.

"Oh my," said Olivia.

"Welcome to the Christmas Cave," said Jenny.

Mike climbed the steep, narrow path up a nearly vertical rock wall, the kids following close behind him. Daniel looked much healthier than he had before entering the cave.

They came out onto a wide landing. On the far side stood a shack with an open door and no roof. Mike took several more steps, enough to allow the kids to step off the path and come up onto the landing beside him.

"Hey." Jack spoke in a hushed tone. "Somebody lives here."

"Duh," said Amanda.

"Bill," said Daniel.

Amanda stepped out in front. "Who else," she said, and walked slowly toward the shack.

Bill, a slim man with gray hair and a long beard, came out of the shack. He took a single step and stopped. He wore shorts, shirt and sandals, all made of woven vegetation.

Mike placed a hand on Amanda's shoulder as he stepped past her.

"Bill?"

Bill looked taken aback at hearing his name spoken. He said nothing, remained fixed to his spot a single step from his shack.

"Bill?" Mike asked again. "Is that you? It's me. It's Mike."

Bill's gaze sharpened. He leaned his head forward, studied Mike, then ran his gaze to each of the children.

He looked back at Mike.

"Mike?" His lips quivered. His eyes teared up. He began to cry. "Mike?"

"Yeah, man. It's me."

"Oh, God. Oh, geez." He took a stumbling step forward.

"It's me, Bill." Now Mike began to cry. He blubbered as he staggered forward. "I found ya. I found ya. I knew I would. Danged if I didn't."

They reached each other, wrapped their arms around each other.

Jack, Amanda and Daniel didn't move. They couldn't move. Their eyes welled up. They worked hard at holding back the tears.

"I'd say this was a good day," said Amanda.

"Yeah," Daniel just managed to get out.

"S'pose it is," said Jack.

§

Tom, Olivia and Jenny approached the Rainbow Bridge, a V-shaped roped bridge that spanned the river, crossing to a landing on the opposite cliff wall. Hundreds of brightly colored stones were woven into the rope.

Tom appeared uneasy. He reached a hand out to the rope.

"It looks strong enough," he said.

Jenny grinned. "Ya' nervous, son?"

"I'm fine, Mother." He took a step. He looked at Olivia, then pointedly at Jenny. "You wait here until I get to the other side."

"Sure," said Jenny.

"I mean it, Mom." He started out, took it slow but steady.

He was midway across when Jenny leaned toward Olivia.

"Did Tom ever tell you about the rope bridge at Thornberry Creek?"

"I don't think so."

"Oh, you'd remember," said Jenny. "Thing stood for thirty years. Tom couldn't a been more'n six or seven years old. We were picnicking at the creek, the boy decides to cross the bridge. First time. Never crossed it before. He marches bravely out onto the bridge, we're all watching."

Jenny nodded in Tom's direction.

"He's about where he is now. Anchors pull out of the bank, bridge drops into the water."

"Oh, my. How terrible."

"Kid was as light as a small dog. Never would've imagined such a thing. I went in after him, pulled him to shore." A shadow seemed to brush across her face. "Darnedest thing..."

Tom reached the other side, turned and rested his hands on the supports.

"All right," he said. "Good and solid. Come on across."

"Thank you, son." Jenny called out. She looked side-glance at Olivia and gave her a wink and started out.

She stopped midway along the bridge, her hands grasping the hand ropes. She closed her eyes, smiled contentedly. Taking in the soothing sound and sweet smell of the river below, the aura of the enclosing cavern hovering above them.

"Mom?" Tom called out worriedly. "Mom?"

"Be quiet, dear," said Jenny, She kept her eyes closed, kept her contented smile.

Tom continued to look worried, but did as he was told. He kept quiet.

Jenny took in a calm, healthy breath, slowly opened her eyes. She looked... refreshed.

She started forward again.

Mike and Bill were alone in Bill's shack; four walls of twigs and bamboo-like stalks and hand-wound twine. There was no ceiling other than thin rope that ran from wall to wall every two feet to hold the structure together. One open arch served as the doorway.

Bill sat on a narrow cot, Mike in one of two chairs. There was a small table in one corner. The furniture was made of the same material as that of the walls.

"Interesting place you have here, Bill," said Mike.

"It's not much, but I call it home."

"I can't help but notice. Two chairs?"

"I could say I was expecting company," Bill said, smiling.

"Were you?"

"Nah. Gave up on that a long time ago."

"I am sorry," said Mike. "I tried. I've been trying my whole life."

"Hey, you're here. That's amazing."

Their conversation grew less awkward as they slowly became reacquainted.

Meantime, Jack stood on a small ledge above Bill's shack landing, looking out across the cavern. He called down to Amanda and Daniel, who stood outside the shack below.

"The river comes right out of the wall, over by where we came in." He hopped down in three short steps and came up beside them. They all looked down to the floor of the cavern. "It runs right below us, disappears under that far wall over there."

"Suppose there's fish in it?" asked Daniel.

"Maybe. Bill's been eatin' something all these years."

"You lookin' to go fishing?" asked Amanda.

Daniel looked almost eager. "Might just do that."

Something below drew Jack's attention. He leaned farther forward.

"Uh oh," he said.

"What is it?" asked Daniel.

"I think we're in trouble."

"What?" Amanda felt a tightness in her chest. "Jack?"

"It's Mom."

Chapter Seven

In the shack, Bill gazed off into the distant past.

"That was the Old Man's chair," he said quietly.

"I thought you were alone?"

"I am. Long time, now." Another moment's drift to another time. "He was here when I got here. Crazier 'n a bug, I thought at the time. He must'a been here years a'fore I showed up. Livin' here all by himself."

"Did he come through the way we did?"

"I guess so," Bill shrugged.

"Where was he from?"

"Don't know. He didn't speak English." From the expression on Bill's face, he seemed to enjoy those nostalgic moments, those journeys to the past. "I mean, after a few months we were able to understand each other, at least a little. He talked some about the village he came from, but it didn't sound nothin' like any place near the mountain."

"He came here from a different cave?" asked Mike. If the old man came in through a different portal, that could be important.

"I suppose it was a cave. We didn't talk much about outside. Mostly he talked to me about how things work, how to get food, how to make stuff."

So... what happened to him?'

"Died." Another shrug. This time, it was somehow sad. "Went to sleep one night, didn't wake up."

"Bill. I'm—"

"A long time ago. Long, long time ago."

They sat quietly then, each in his own thoughts.

Voices then, from outside the shack...

Jack, Amanda and Daniel stood looking across the landing as Tom stepped onto the ledge. Olivia and Jenny came up behind him, stepped up beside him. Seeing the children, Olivia rushed forward.

"Jack! Amanda!" She wrapped her arms around them. "Oh, my! Oh, my!"

"Hey, Mom," said Jack.

Olivia pulled away, looked over at Daniel. "Are you all right?" she asked. "Your parents are so worried."

"I'm fine, Mrs. Harper." He took a moment to endure a quick hug from Mrs. Harper. "I feel really good, actually."

"I'm so glad to hear that." She looked again at Jack and Amanda. "Oh, you two are so grounded."

Mike and Bill came out of the shack. Olivia wasn't surprised at all. She pulled the children aside, opening the view between Bill and Jenny. She smiled warmly at Jenny.

Jenny approached her long, lost brother. Bill haltingly approached his sister.

They held each other for the first time in more than fifty years.

Jack and Amanda sat on the edge of the landing, legs dangling over the side, looking out across the cavern. Behind them, Tom and Olivia walked casually across the ledge from the direction of the trailhead.

Amanda leaned forward, looked straight down below them. She could see Mike, Bill and Jenny walking along the base of the cliff far below, at the river's edge.

Jack glanced at Amanda, looked down at what Amanda was looking at.

"They're just like kids," he noted, smiling.

"They were just kids the last time they were all together," said Amanda.

Jack gave a light chuckle before turning serious. "Did you see Grandma when they first saw each other? I've never seen her cry before."

"She is one tough lady, I'm here to tell ya'."

"Heck of a reunion," said Amanda after a long time.

Behind them, Tom and Olivia continued their stroll, nearing the shack. Tom nodded in the direction of the kids.

"Just look at 'em, Liv. You'd think we were at a picnic.

"Some picnic." She let out a long breath, and there was a tremor in her words. "I was so worried."

"Yes, but we found them. And they're safe." He admired the scene around them. "And think of it. Just consider where we are."

"Consider just a little bit further, Tom." Olivia's words were cool now. Cool and precise. "We found the children. We found Bill. And yes, we found the Christmas Cave. It is amazing. I agree. It is all so amazing."

"It sure is."

"Yes. Now, how do we get home?"

"Well..." Tom falteringly waved a hand toward the opposite side of the cave, doubt already forming in his mind. "We go out the same way we came in."

"Tom... do you really think it's going to be that simple?"

"Absolutely."

"Really. Then explain to me why Bill has been here for fifty years."

Tom curled a brow, frowned. A long moment of uncertainty hung in the air.

"I don't know," he said at last. It took him another few moments to regain some sense of composure and confidence. "But I do know this. I am having Christmas dinner in the house I grew up in. And I'm having peach cobbler for desert."

Mike, Bill and Jenny walked slowly along the riverbank near the Rainbow Bridge. The stones woven into the rope sparkled.

Jenny took it all in; the river, the bridge, the walls and the domed ceiling.

"It's all so beautiful, Bill. I can see why that boy called it the Christmas Cave, so long ago."

"You're seeing it at its best, Jen. It'll lose some when the river dies back."

"What do you mean?"

"It only runs like this nine days a year," said Bill. "Rest of the time it's not much more than a trickle."

Mike stopped, studied the river. The others stopped and watch him. After what seemed like half a minute or more, Mike crossed his arms and frowned thoughtfully.

"What happens then?" he asked, his attention still on the river.

"The colors fade some. They don't go away, but the cave goes dim."

Jenny moved to the river's edge and knelt down. She dipped a hand into the water.

There was an immediate reaction. The water washing about her hand glittered and sparkled ever brighter. Her fingers shimmered and glowed.

She slowly lifted her hand out of the river. The water streamed off her hand and fingers. Jenny stood again, rubbed her fingertips together.

"Feels great, doesn't it?" asked Bill.

"Most curious." She curled her brow then and looked at Bill. "The cave goes dark?"

"Nah. There's enough that it's still day in here. Just loses some of the sparkle."

Mike continued to look out at the flowing water. "How much does the river go down?"

"Like I said, in a few days, it'll be a trickle." He looked up at the sparkling colors set into the walls, seemingly unconcerned. "The Old Man said the rocks in the walls react to something in the water. Minerals..." he shrugged. "Somethin'. Don't know if it's true. The Old Man got things wrong, and he had some weird superstitions."

"I expect in this he was right," said Mike. "Nine days?"

"Yep. Doesn't always start the same day each year, but always runs exactly nine days."

"How can you be so sure, Bill?" asked Jenny. "Without the sun?"

Bill grinned and brought out a pocket watch, held it up for the others to see. It was very old and very worn.

"Belonged to the Old Man," he stated with some satisfaction. "All these years, it still keeps good time."

"I see," Jenny cradled it a moment in her palm before handing it back.

"At least, I think it does." Bill put the watch away. "It could be completely wrong, I suppose. Couldn't it? How would I know for sure?"

They continued downriver then, came upon Daniel sitting on the bank. He had a bamboo rod in hand, a line in the water. He looked relaxed, content. He glanced up once at their approach, focused again on the river before him, the line in the water.

"How's the fishing, Daniel?" asked Jenny.

"Had a few nibbles."

"That rod's always done me right," said Bill.

"Appreciate the use, Bill." Daniel lifted it a few inches, let it settle gently back into position. "Comfortable feel. Good balance."

"That it does," said Bill.

Jenny looked further downstream, to where the river met the wall far in the distance. The trail they were on would take them to an opening in the wall to the left of where the river disappeared.

"Bill? Where does that go?"

"Ah! Yes. I'll show you. Let's get the others." Bill spoke again to Daniel. "Kid, do I have a fishing hole for you. Yes I do."

Bill led the way as the entire group followed the trail along the bank of the river. Daniel had the fishing rod resting on his shoulder.

They approached the wall. Beside them, the river churned noisily as it rushed against the wall and coursed through an unseen underground waterway.

Bill led them through a narrow opening. They stepped into a cavern that was quite a bit larger than the one they had just left, and onto the shore of a large lake. Away from the beach, the walls enclosing the lake rose up from the water to a domed ceiling several hundred feet above them.

"Holy cow," said Jack.

"Yes," Bill said proudly. "Holy cow."

The shore they were standing on stretched away in both directions for forty or fifty feet, bordered on either side by forests of colorless bamboo-like plants that stood twelve feet tall.

Mike took another step closer to the lake.

"This where you get your food?" he asked.

"Mostly."

Daniel's face lit up. "Trout?"

"Not trout, but not too bad. And there are plants in there that taste okay." Bill indicated a permanent campsite established off to their left, just inside the bamboo stand. He started toward it. "Here, look at this."

There was a fire pit, a handwoven chair and a small table. Toward the back were a number of woven bins. Bill stepped over to a large stack of four-inch thick logs made of dried, twisted paper-like material, the color of chocolate, each about a foot long.

"I make firewood from one of the plants that grows in the lake." He picked up one of the logs and handed it to Mike. "I cut the plants into strips, then twist a bunch of them together and dry 'em. They burn pretty good."

"Very nice," said Mike.

"The Old Man was makin' 'em long before I came along," Bill said with a shrug. He pointed to a different colored strip in the homemade log that Mike was holding. "This is my contribution. I put strands of this into the logs that I use to smoke the fish. It adds a real nice flavor."

Jenny admired the campsite. "It looks like you spend a lot of your time here, Bill. But then, you always did enjoy camping."

"Yeah, well, what with fishing, harvesting plants, smoking the fish, making logs, making clothes," he grinned then, "bathing..."

"You've done well for yourself, Bill," said Tom.

"Thanks. I do—"

A sudden tremor shook the ground beneath them. It set the surface of the lake to rippling. Several rocks came loose from the ceiling high above and splashed into the lake a ways off shore.

The earthquake slowly subsided.

"Wow," said Amanda.

"My words exactly," said Jack.

"Oh, my," said Olivia.

"Geez, Bill," said Jenny. "Do you get a lot of that?"

"Some," Bill said matter-of-factly. "More lately."

Mike nodded. "I used to see them in the caves now and then, but last time had to have been a year or more ago."

"Get 'em more often than that here. Especially the last couple a' years."

"Really? I never feel them at the house," said Jenny.

"Interesting," Mike said thoughtfully.

"Peculiar," said Tom.

"Yes."

"Why?" asked Olivia.

"You have to wonder where the quakes are coming from," Tom said, pondering.

"Here, I would think," said Olivia. "In the mountain."

"Mike hasn't felt a quake in the caves for a year."

It was becoming just a bit clearer to Jenny. "What makes you think the Christmas Cave is in the mountain, dear?" she asked.

"I would think that would be obvious, Mom."

"I'm sorry, but no, it isn't. Not really. Not anymore."

"The Old Man," said Amanda, realization dawning. She turned to her mom. "The Old Man didn't come here through the caves."

"Of course," said Olivia.

"Okay," Tom continued to sort it through. "But if the quakes originate in the Christmas Cave, and then radiate out through the gateway—"

"Perhaps through every gateway," Jenny stated.

"How many do you think there are, Grandma?" asked Amanda.

"There are at least two. But there can't be many." When the others looked curiously at her, she said casually, "Well, if there were, Bill would have had a lot more company."

The others then turned to Bill.

"Nope," he said. "Nobody since the Old Man."

Chapter Eight

Tom and Olivia sat near the fire pit in the center of Bill's permanent, lakeside campsite. They were each using several artificial logs as makeshift seats. Jack and Amanda were exploring the nearby stand of bamboo, and Mike and Bill were walking along the lake shore in the distance, coming toward the camp but still a ways off.

Jenny stepped up beside Daniel, sitting at the bank of the lake, fishing rod in hand.

"It's quite pleasant here," she said.

"Yes, ma'am. Real nice."

"Healthy for the soul, I'd say."

"I suppose I'd say the same," said Daniel.

Jenny maneuvered herself about and sat down. She brushed her pants and rested her arms on her knees.

"Good to see you have a bit of your color back," she said.

"I'm feeling pretty good."

"That's good to hear. Your parents were worried about you. Rather desperate to get your medicines to you."

Daniel reached into his shirt pocket. He opened his palm to Jenny, showed her three pills. He stuffed them back into his pocket. They were from a day several weeks earlier, the last time he'd skipped his meds. He kept them on hand, just in case.

"I see," said Jenny. "You may not think you need them, but you should take them nonetheless."

"I've never felt better."

"Doctor's orders."

"I mean, I really have never, ever felt better."

"Yes," Jenny said hesitantly. She grew thoughtful, finally gave a nod and a knowing smile. "I know what you mean. There is something about this place. Isn't there?"

"I'm sure of it, Mrs. Harper. There's somethin' here. This place does something."

Jenny looked out at the lake, at the ceiling overhead. She leaned near Daniel.

"My boy, I have been thinking on those very same lines myself." She looked thoughtfully around them. She looked out at the lake, at the ceiling overhead. "I haven't had a spell since we got here. Not a one."

Up at the campsite behind them, Tom and Olivia watched Jenny and the boy.

"Your mother looks better than she has in a long time," said Olivia.

"Finding her brother after all these years must have been a real shot in the arm."

Jenny and Daniel stood up as Bill and Mike approached. Jenny placed a hand on Bill's arm. They were animated, even playful.

"Look at 'em, Liv," said Tom. "What better medicine? Like a Christmas miracle."

"Maybe..." Olivia was doubtful. It had to be more than just finding Bill. There had to be something else.

Jack and Amanda relaxed in a small pool that was fed by a thin rivulet of water coming from the lake. The stand of bamboo separated them from the campsite.

Jack had his shirt off, Amanda was in her undershirt.

Jack leaned back, his elbows propped up behind him on the bank.

"A fella could get used to this. I may just move here for good."

"Mom may have something to say about that," said Amanda.

Jack laid his head back and closed his eyes. There was a slight smirk on his face. "Comes to Mom, it's all in how ya' bring up the issue."

He enjoyed the moment, which slowly stretched into an uncomfortable silence.

He heard his sister then...

"Hey, Jack?"

"Yeah?" He brought his head forward and opened his eyes.

A tall, long-legged bird stood on the bank opposite. It looked a lot like a flamingo, long neck and thin, spindly legs, but its feathers were solid white.

It looked curiously down at Jack and Amanda. It turned its head and let out a soft "*raaack*?"

"Uh, hello?" mumbled Jack.

The bird let out a second "*raaack.*"

"Is it talking to us?" asked Amanda.

The bird opened and closed it beak several times.

"Well..." Jack studied the bird. "It's either welcoming us to the neighborhood, or telling us to get out of its pool."

A second bird circled overhead, came in with wings spread wide. It glided down, flapped its wings several times and settled into the center of the small pool.

There was a slight splash as it adjusted its position on the pool's surface.

The bird looked from Amanda to Jack.

The first bird, standing on the bank, lifted itself into the air and dropped down into the pool beside its companion.

"Oh!" Amanda called out. "Look!"

A third bird appeared suddenly on the bank, and then another.

Within moments Jack and Amanda found themselves in the midst of a flock of six great white birds. One remained on the bank, but the others joined them in the pool.

They appeared to be friendly, and were not at all frightened by the two human strangers. They swam about the pool, relaxing, grooming, exchanging occasional beak touches with one another.

Jack relaxed.

"Like I said, I could get used to this."

"Yeah, me too," Amanda agreed. She leaned her head forward as one of the birds stretched its neck to get a better look at her.

The bird gave her another "*raaack!*"

Amanda laughed and Jack joined her.

Jenny walked up from the lake's edge to Tom and Olivia, leaving Daniel to his fishing, Mike and Bill beside the boy.

"Mike has a theory that we need to think on," she said.

"Is everything all right?" asked Olivia.

"Mike figures the access to the cave is only open for a few days each year."

"I don't understand."

"It has to do with the flow of the river. The same chemical reaction that generates the light show each year also creates the portal."

"So then, when the light show stops, the portal closes?" asked Tom.

"The —*whatever it is*— dissipates, and so the window dissipates."

"But this is good," said Olivia. "It means this isn't a one way trip. We can go back. We can go home."

"So long as the river is flowing, the power is turned on. So long as the power is turned on, the door is open."

"But Bill has been here for decades," Tom wondered. "Wouldn't he have figured it out?"

Bill and Mike came up beside them.

"I searched that cliff hundreds of times the first few months," said Bill. "There was no way back. I assumed there was no way back."

"Makes sense," said Olivia. "And so you finally quit looking."

Jenny took her brother's arm. "For all Bill knew, it was a one way door."

"Ah, but Mike knows something that Bill never knew." Tom looked at Mike. "You know that the way here had opened, then closed, and then opened again."

"And it only lasts a few days."

"And here, in the cave, the river only flows a few days."

While the river flows, the lights shine bright. When the river dies back, the lights dim.

"The river is flowing now," said Jenny.

At that moment, the earth began to tremble yet again, and there was a low, grumbling sound. The shaking slowly faded, the grumbling slowly faded.

Oh my, thought Olivia. *I could certainly do with a little less of that, if you please.*

She wondered aloud, "If this is true, how long do we have? How much longer is the door open?" She looked at Bill. "You said the river runs for nine days a year."

"We still have a few days," he said. "It usually runs full right up to the last, then slows to a trickle pretty quick."

"Good," said Jenny. "I think we could all do with a few hours sleep. It's been a very long day."

Olivia looked at Jenny with some concern. She looked okay. Very good, in fact. "Are you feeling okay, Mom?"

"Wonderful, dear. Never better. But it is awfully late, and it's a long way home."

"Mom's right," said Tom. He looked at his watch. It was the middle of the night. "It's long past my bedtime, and there's a maze of tunnels to get through once we get back into the caves. I know I can do with some rest. Best we start back fresh."

"If Mike is right," said Olivia, "and there is a way home..."

"Then we find the opening before it closes for another year," said Tom.

If we miss it, we're here for another year. Worse, if Mike is wrong, and there isn't an opening, we're here forever.

But she agreed, it was very late and despite her anxiety, she was very tired. They all were. After all, it was the middle of the night.

Bill started a fire in the fire pit, and after a light meal of dried fish everyone settled in for a few hours of rest. Most thought they were too excited after the day's events and too anxious about the possibility of finding a way out to get any sleep, but in a matter of minutes all were in a deep slumber.

Ninety minutes later, the fire little more than a warm glow, there came a slowly rising rumble. The ground began to shake. It was mild at first, but gradually grew in intensity. No one woke.

Small bits of rock fell from the ceiling, splashing harmlessly into the lake.

The rumbling sound grew louder. The ground shook more violently.

The sleepers began to wake, to sit up, to look about uncertainly.

There were several great splashes out in the middle of the lake as larger chunks of rock fell from the ceiling.

Fully awake now and realizing what was happening, Tom jumped to his feet. "Everybody up!"

Amanda was in a growing panic. "Dad?"

"Up! Up!" Tom circled the group. "Let's go!"

"Let's go, sweetie." Olivia grabbed Amanda's hand. She reached out for Jack, then, and the three of them started toward the opening to the inner cave. The others followed after them, several stumbling as the quake shook the ground violently beneath them. Rocks continued to rain down from above.

They were still thirty feet from the opening out of the lake cavern when it suddenly collapsed before them, billowing out dirt and stone dust.

Olivia didn't waste a moment. She pulled her children toward the wall, hovered over them, pulled them in close and pushed them down to their knees at the base of the wall.

The others in the group followed her lead, dropping down at the foot of the wall and covering their heads to protect themselves from the storm of falling rocks.

Chapter Nine

Tom was several feet up on the pile of rubble that blocked the way out of the lake cavern, pulling at rocks that when freed rolled down the pile, gradually forming a heap at the base.

Jenny and Olivia stood about a dozen yards away and were deep in their own discussion, while the kids were walking toward the campsite.

Tom pulled at another stone and let it fall away. He clambered up another few inches and poked his head into the small opening that he had managed to create.

"It's not that bad, really. I can see the other side." He pulled at another stone. This one wouldn't give. He leaned back and looked down at the upturned faces of Jenny and his mother.

"A bit of work, but—"

"How long ya' think, Tom?" asked Jenny.

"Hard to say, but not long."

"If Mike is right," said Olivia, "and the way out is going to close when the river stops, we have until tomorrow. At the latest. And it won't open again for a year."

Jenny frowned, dark and fretful. "And I had to talk us into a night's sleep."

"No, Mom," said Olivia. "You were right. Besides, we were only asleep for an hour and a half."

"At least we'd be on the other side of that pile of rocks."

Tom worked his way down and wiped rock dust from his hands. "We'll be fine. A bit of work, like I said, but we can do it. We only need an opening large enough to crawl through."

Jenny turned away, shook her head despairingly as she walked away. Tom watched her go, started to say something but finally decided against it. He instead called to Mike and Bill to come help clear away the heap of broken rock that he had been building up at the base of the blockage.

He looked once more at the retreating figure of his mother before turning again to the wall and climbed back up to within reach of the opening he had been creating.

Olivia told him she would be back and followed after Jenny. She came up beside her as the two stood at the shore of the lake.

"Mom? Are you feeling okay?"

"I'm fine," said Jenny. She couldn't look at Olivia. She kept her gaze out across the surface of the lake.

Olivia gently placed a hand on Jenny's arm. "Whatever happens, we're going to be all right."

"I suppose."

"This isn't your fault."

"If I hadn't insisted that we rest before heading back, we'd be in the other cave, maybe even in the tunnels by now."

"Don't you worry. They'll have the way clear in no time." She spoke with more confidence than she felt, more than she herself had expressed even before the wall collapse. She was afraid. The thought of being trapped here for a whole year was terrifying. But while she was concerned that her children might have to live primitive lives while they waited, she knew they could survive it if they had to.

Unless something bad happened; like collapsing ceilings due to earthquakes.

Or illness...

"Mom, how do you feel? Honestly?"

Jenny knew what Olivia was thinking. "I feel better than I have in years, dear."

"You're not just saying that?"

"No need to worry about me," she said.

"Jenny?"

Jenny looked about them, now with mixed emotions.

"There's something here, Olivia. Something in the air, the water, something in the rocks... something."

Jack and Amanda crossed the campsite and through the bamboo stand behind it. The surface of the pool was still. There was no sign of the birds.

"I'm sure they're okay, Jack," said Amanda.

"I'm sure you're right." Jack looked up to the dome of the cavern. He looked again at the pool, behind them at the bamboo wall. "We should get back."

The flow of the river winding along the floor was down to thin rivulets, the riverbed exposed in many locations. The walls and ceiling of this smaller cavern still had the glow, the colorful crystals in the riverbed, set into the rock walls and even wound into the rope of the Rainbow Bridge glittered and sparkled.

Nonetheless, the Christmas Cave was starting to dim. Dusk was coming.

Mike's head appeared in the small opening midway up the pile of rubble that blocked the way between the Christmas Cave and the Lake Cavern. He took a moment to take in the scene.

"I'm through!" he called back behind him. He pushed his shoulders through, scrambled out of the opening and worked his way down to the floor. He straightened, wiped his pants and shirt. "Come on across."

He wandered toward the river. He didn't like the look of it.

Tom's head appeared in the opening next. He looked about him, saw Mike kneeling in the distance.

"How's it look?" he asked.

Mike spoke absently over his shoulder. "We might want to pick up the pace."

Tom looked anxiously about him as he worked his way free and scrambled down. He turned about then and helped Jenny come through.

Meanwhile, Olivia, Bill and Amanda stood waiting near the opening on the lake cavern side of the opening. Amanda looked behind her, saw Jack standing a few yards away. He was looking in the direction of the lake.

"Jack," said Amanda, approaching. "We have to go."

Jack said nothing at first. He smiled then, nodded at something out above the lake.

"Look," he said.

He could see the silhouettes of half a dozen birds gliding smoothly above the water.

Mike stood at the river's edge. Jenny and Tom came up beside him.

"We haven't much time," said Mike.

"If we're not already too late," said Jenny.

Tom noted the colorful crystals that continued to sparkle through the cavern. No, it wasn't closed just yet.

Behind them, the Jack and Amanda helped Bill struggle through and scramble down to the floor.

"Looks like the river's going down, Bill," said Jack.

"It certainly does," said Bill, looking across the floor. "It certainly does."

"How long ya' figure, then?"

"Well," Bill sighed. "I expect the lights to start dimming any time now, history holds true. As for the portal outta here... since I never knew it was there, I'm afraid I couldn't tell ya'."

"Probably fades with the lights," said Amanda.

"Reasonable," said Bill.

"Then we better not waste any time," said Jack.

Olivia's head and shoulders appeared in the opening above them. "Little help here," she said.

All three rushed to help.

"Sorry, Mom," said Jack.

"Terribly sorry, Ma'am," said Bill.

Olivia was brought through, and finally Daniel. Once everyone was back into the Christmas Cave, they gathered at the river's edge and then started upriver. As they approached the Rainbow Bridge, Daniel was the first to note the stones woven into the rope, speaking mostly to Jack and Amanda.

"Do the crystals look like they're dimming to you?"

"Maybe," said Jack. "A little."

"Could be just less sparkle coming up from the river," said Amanda.

"Maybe," said Jack.

"We'll make it," said Amanda.

Tom stood at the bridge, waved for his mother to start across. She gave a quick nod and stepped up, started across. Tom then looked over at the kids, waved them over. He lined them up, held a hand on Daniel's shoulder and waited.

Jenny reached the other side and stepped off the bridge.

"Okay, Daniel," said Tom, and started him across.

Jack and Amanda stepped up and waited their turns.

"Daniel looks better, ya' think?" asked Amanda.

"Same as always," Jack shrugged.

"You don't think he looks better?"

"I always thought he looked fine."

Amanda gave him a reproachful look. "No you didn't."

Across the river, Jenny held out a hand and Daniel took it as he stepped off the bridge.

"How are you holdin' up there, Daniel?" asked Jenny.

Daniel gave a positive nod, turned and looked back behind him. Amanda was starting across. She was moving quickly and confidently.

Daniel was worried; not that they wouldn't reach the portal out of the cavern in time, but that they would.

What will happen to me when we leave the Christmas Cave, he wondered.

Jenny glanced down at the boy, saw that something was troubling him.

"Daniel?" she prompted.

"Nothing." Daniel struggled with his words. "I just... do you think we'll get sick again?"

"I honestly don't know."

Amanda finished her journey across. She immediately turned around and looked over at Jack. He started over.

Daniel is right, she thought. *The crystals are growing dimmer.*

Jack was midway across. The ground began to shake. A deep rumbling rolled through the cavern. The shaking intensified.

Jack struggled to maintain his balance, his feet on the single bottom rope, a hand holding tight to each of the handrail ropes.

Soccer ball sized rocks fell from above, splashed into the small pools of water and struck the rocks that made up the now mostly-exposed riverbed.

Jack's feet slipped from the foot rope of the bridge. He desperately hung onto the handrails.

Olivia cried out as Tom rushed out onto the bridge.

"Hang on there, Jack!" he called. "I got ya'!"

He reached him quickly, grasped the boy under the arm with one hand while holding onto the rope rail with the other.

The earthquake faded, the world stilled.

Tom pulled Jack up and the boy regained his footing.

"Jack!" Olivia called out. She was several steps out on the bridge. "Tom!"

"He's fine, Liv. Wait there," said Tom. He turned back to Jack. "Let's get across before your mother comes out here to rescue us both."

Jack just managed to get out, "Thanks, Dad."

"No problem, kiddo," said Dad. *Really... no problem at all.*

They worked their way the rest of the way across, quickly reached the other side. Jenny stretched out a hand and pulled Jack to her.

"Oh, you gave me a fright, boy!"

On the other side of the river, Olivia had already started over. Bill and Mike stood ready to follow her.

"Sorry, Grandma," Jack mumbled.

Jenny gave him a playful smack on the shoulder, then again pulled him to her. Olivia reached them within moments, and in another minute everyone was safely across the bridge.

The group continued to work their way across the floor of the cavern and then up the steep wall to the ledge where they had first come into the Christmas Cave. Once there, none knew exactly where the portal was, or should be, but they were all certain they were in the right place.

"It has to be here," said Mike, as he rubbed his hands across the rock.

"Maybe we're too late," said Jenny.

"I don't think so," said Olivia. She indicated the cavern behind them. "We still have the colors."

"Everyone look for it," said Tom. "Spread out. Look for it."

Mike continued to mumble, almost to himself, "It has to be here... it has to be here..."

Jack, Amanda and Daniel moved apart, sidestepping as they pressed hands against the stone of the cliff wall.

"I am so sorry," said Jenny. She stepped slowly back, held her hands to her face, over her mouth, fraught with grief. "I am so, so sorry."

"What are you talking about?" said Mike, brought out of his own distressing thoughts. "It's not your fault."

"If we had left the lake sooner."

"Mother, that's nonsense," said Tom.

"If it's anybody's fault, Jen, it's mine," said Bill. "You're here because of me."

"Oh, dear Bill." Jenny grew increasingly tearful. "Don't you ever—"

"If I had listened to you. If I hadn't run ahead..."

"Oh, Bill. An excited little boy runs toward magical Christmas lights. How can that possibly—"

"Here!" Amanda suddenly cried out. "Here!"

All looked to Amanda as she pulled her hand away from the cliff wall."

"Amanda?" Olivia asked.

"I found it." She moved her hand cautiously forward. Her fingers disappeared into the rock. A flickering of bright colors surrounded her hand, then her wrist. She pulled her hand back and smiled.

"Good job, Amanda," said Tom. He wrapped an arm about Amanda's shoulders, looked over at the others in the group. "All right, everyone. Let's go."

Jack stepped forward, looked about him with a wide grin.

"See ya' on the other side," he sighed spookily. He raised his hands up before him, moved forward, and disappeared through the rock.

Bill was awestruck. "I'll be."

"Most likely," said Mike.

A faint rumbling rolled through the cavern. The earth vibrated, again quieted.

Tom looked anxiously about, motioned quickly to Olivia.

"After you," he said.

"Okay," Olivia said softly, and she stepped forward. "Don't be long."

"Right behind you, hon," Tom said as Olivia stepped through the portal. He looked around at those who remained, focused finally on Daniel. "Waddya say, Daniel? Let's go."

Daniel took a step back, not forward.

"Daniel?" Tom asked curiously.

"I don't know," said Daniel.

"It's perfectly safe."

Jenny moved up and put an arm around Daniel. "It's not that, Tom," she said.

As Tom tried to sort out what the heck was going on with his mother and Daniel, Bill turned away and looked out across the Christmas Cave.

Mike stepped up beside him. "You're not thinking of staying, are you?"

"No. Of course not." Bill let out a deep sigh. "It has been home for a very, very long time. Good and bad."

"Of course." Mike rested a comforting hand on Bill's shoulder.

Bill took a final look out at the cavern. It was continuing to dim. He nodded to the portal behind them.

"Guess we need to be getting outta here, huh?"

"Yep."

They turned in tandem and approached the portal. Bill calmly stepped through and disappeared.

Mike pointed a sharp finger at Jenny. "Don't you be foolish," he said curtly, and followed Bill.

"Mother," said Tom.

Jenny still had an arm around Daniel.

"It's all right, Tom."

"I feel good," said Daniel, pleading. "I feel real good."

The cave continued to grow darker, less enchanting.

"You can't stay here, son," said Tom. He gave his mother a severe look. "You can't stay here."

The earth rumbled. The deep grumbling grew louder. The shaking grew increasingly intense.

The cave tunnels looked dark and confining after the openness of the Christmas Cave. They were short and narrow and the only light came from a single flashlight Jack was holding, and from the portal, a faint cloud of flickering color.

The earthquake continued to grow increasingly violent here on this side as well, making the tunnel all the more claustrophobic.

Everyone was looking to the portal, waiting anxiously for Tom, Jenny and Daniel.

Olivia whispered under her breath. "Come on, come on, come on."

Daniel appeared. There was an audible sigh of relief from everyone in the tunnel.

He stepped forward, was followed a few moments later by Jenny. She turned and took a step back.

The cloud of color continued to fade. The ground continued to shake and there was the constant low rumbling noise.

Tom stepped through. Olivia rushed up to him and hugged him.

Behind him, the portal closed.

The earthquake stopped suddenly, decisively, at that exact moment; at the very second the portal closed.

A heavy silence hung in the air.

"Well," Jenny said at last, breaking the silence. "That was rather sudden."

There were a few nervous chuckles.

"Is that possible?" asked Amanda. "The earthquake is there, but not here?"

"Amanda," Jack groaned. "We just passed through a portal that leads to some place called the Christmas Cave, and you wonder what's possible?"

"Right," said Amanda. "Good point."

Tom picked up the lantern that Jenny had left in the tunnel and Mike helped him get it lit. The other flashlights were turned on and the group made ready to get the heck out of there. The earthquake may have stopped, but the caves were still very unstable.

Mike led the way, confident of the path to the surface. Jack and Amanda brought up the rear.

"Do you think Mom was serious?" Jack asked his sister.

"What? Oh, yeah. We're grounded, all right."

"For six months? I mean... hey, we found Bill."

"Mike found Bill. We just happened to be with him at the time."

"S'pose you could look at it that way," said Jack, frowning. He suddenly grinned. "But the Christmas Cave. We found the Christmas Cave."

"Sure did."

"So cool... and you wanted to turn back."

"Sure did," she said again. "And I'm still grounded. Thanks for that."

As she finished those last words, they heard a low rumbling noise coming from the tunnel behind them.

"What is that?" she asked. "Another quake?"

"No. Not a quake. Oh, geez." Jack called out then to the rest of the group ahead of them. "Cave in! Cave in!"

The tunnel ceiling was beginning to collapse behind them. Dirt and dust billowed toward them. They ran. They all ran as fast as they could, but it didn't seem that it would be fast enough.

Leading the way, Mike saw thin streams of light far up ahead. He rushed toward it, everyone right behind him. The cloud of dirt and dust engulfed Jack and Amanda, still trailing the others.

The sun, enveloped in a glow of dark orange and red, was just coming up above the horizon. Golden rays streaked across the treetops and filled the clearing with the morning light.

A loud rolling rumble accompanied a great cloud of dirt and dust that swelled out of the cave entrance. Mike was little more than a silhouette in the cloud as he stumbled out. Jenny staggered out after him. Mike held out a supportive hand as she stepped past him. She dropped down to one knee, then both knees, leaned forward and began coughing.

Others came staggering out, dark shadows in the expanding cloud of billowing dirt. Last out were Jack and Amanda, hacking and choking. Olivia stumbled over to them, held them in her arms.

Tom placed a hand on Daniel, absently wrapped an arm around him.

The dust settled and the air slowly cleared. Jack turned and looked back toward the hillside. The cave entrance was gone.

"That's that," he said softly.

The world grew quiet. Bill took several steps toward the edge of the clearing. He looked outward, up at the sky... out toward the horizon.

Mike stepped up beside him. Jenny joined him.

The sun rose fully up from the horizon. Bright orange light splashed across the landscape.

"Welcome home, Bill," said Mike.

Chapter Ten

Jenny sat at one end of her dining room table, Christmas dinner spread out before her. Good company, good food, wonderful aromas. Olivia, Jack and Amanda sat to either side of her, Tom at the far end of the table. Two dirty plates sat in front of two now-empty chairs.

Tom leaned back in his chair, gave his belly a tender pat.

"Oh, Mother, Mother, Mother. I am absolutely stuffed."

"No room for cobbler, then?" she asked, teasingly.

"Oh boy," he grumbled, thumped his belly. "Five minutes. That'll give time for dinner to settle."

"Dad! That's disgusting," said Amanda.

Tom grabbed at his belly with both hands and gave it a good shake. "There we go. Fill in those empty spaces. Still plenty of room in there."

"Ah, geez," Amanda groaned.

"Tom!" cried Olivia.

Jack laughed cheerily with his dad.

Tom belched. "Oh! Excuse me!"

Jack laughed again.

The front door opened and Mike and Bill came back into the house.

"You've done a wonder with the place, Jen," said Bill.

"Get back over here and sit down, you two," said Jenny. "Time for dessert."

"Cobbler!" Tom cried out over his shoulder. "Finest in the western hemisphere."

"Never one to pass on cobbler," said Mike, and the two of them settled into the empty chairs.

"This has gotta be just about the best Christmas ever," said Bill.

Jenny leaned back to better take in the scene of her family around the dining table.

"It most certainly is."

§

A nice evening out; dusk, not yet dark. Tom and Olivia came out onto the porch, stood at the top step. They were dressed warm.

Laughter spilled out from inside the house. Jenny, Mike and Bill could be seen through the window, seated around the dining table.

"I don't imagine they'll be getting much sleep tonight," said Tom. "Me, I am dog tired."

"They have a lot of years to catch up on," said Olivia.

"A lifetime."

There was another round of laughter from inside. Despite that, a hint of sadness shadowed Olivia's face.

"Alone... all those years," she said quietly.

"Yeah. Once the Old Man passed on."

"And a way out, if he'd only known it was there."

A Christmas present, thought Tom. *Every year, just waiting to be unwrapped.*

It began to snow. It fell lightly at first, then the flakes grew larger, more numerous. The string of Christmas lights running along the rain gutter turned on, sending red and green and blue light out across the yard.

"A white Christmas after all," said Tom. He lifted an arm and Olivia slipped under it. They snuggled up close and watched the snowfall. The Christmas card setting was interrupted finally by the sound of an approaching vehicle. The Madsen vehicle came up into the yard and pulled up in front of the house.

Daniel and his parents climbed out of the car.

"Daniel, my boy," said Tom.

"Hey, Mr. Harper."

"Merry Christmas," said Olivia.

"Merry Christmas, you two," said Emma.

Tom took the steps down to the yard. "And a fine one it is, Emma, Carl."

Olivia followed him down from the porch and they all hugged and exchanged greetings all over again. Daniel's parents were happy and cheery. All the past worries and concerns had clearly washed away.

Tom started back up the steps, motioned the others to follow.

"Glad you could join us, Carl," he said. "Say... do you like cobbler? Of course you do. Silly question."

Jack came into Amanda's room, hopped onto her bed and slid back against the headboard. Amanda was sitting at her desk, the curtains of the window pulled aside. Outside, snow was falling.

Jack frowned at his smart phone, tossed it on the bed beside him.

Amanda glanced in his direction, smirked. "Why do you keep bothering with that?"

"No reason. It's just my only connection to the real world, is all."

"Real world?"

"Yeah. Real world."

"How can the real world possibly compete with what we've been through?"

"Can't," he said matter-of-factly. "Doesn't mean it isn't there. Doesn't mean we don't have to go back to it. It's where we live."

"Well, that's depressing."

Daniel came in through the open door. "Not necessarily," he said. He sat on the edge of the bed.

"Hey, dude," said Jack.

"Waddya mean, not necessarily?" asked Amanda.

"Yeah," said Jack. "I gotta agree with Amanda on this one. Gonna be tough competing with the Christmas Cave."

"I've been doing a little research." There was the hint of conspiracy in Daniel's voice. He pointed to Jack's phone. "Now me, I have a PC with a wired Internet connection."

"Ah... the web," Jack sighed. "Nice place, I hear."

Amanda pointedly ignored her brother. "Research?" she prompted.

"The Old Man. Bill's Old Man."

"How?" asked Jack.

"I looked up some of the words that Bill said the Old Man used. He was Norwegian."

"Yeah?"

"What does that give us?" asked Amanda.

"So then I looked up earthquakes in Norway over the last few weeks." He grinned then. "I think I found it. A few miles east of a town called Hamar."

"Okay, Daniel." Amanda was just a little bit impressed. "I'll bite. What are we going to do with that?"

"I'm going to go there."

"You're going to go there..."

Jack slid forward, gave a slow, knowing nod. "You're going to look for the portal the Old Man went through to reach the cave. You're going back."

"Our tunnels are done for," said Daniel. "There's no way we'll ever reach our own portal again. But the other, the Norwegian portal, might still be accessible. Each year at Christmas. "

"For nine days."

"How do you know it still exists?" asked Amanda. "We didn't see it in the cave."

"We never looked for it. We know it existed once. The Old Man is proof of that."

"And the earthquakes in Norway," Jack said, nodding.

"I think it was open. This week."

"You're going back in," said Jack. "That's cool."

"Yeah."

"And just how do you plan on getting to Norway to search for the way back in?" asked Amanda.

"Obviously I'm not going now," said Daniel. "I am twelve, after all. I doubt I'd make it home before dark. But I can plan for it now. And in six years, I'm taking a trip for Christmas."

"To Norway..."

"They got reindeer there, ya' know," Daniel grinned.

"I like it," said Jack. "Yes, I do. Very much. You mind a little company?"

"I thought you'd never ask."

Daniel and Jack both turned expectantly to Amanda.

Amanda frowned, sighed. "Reindeer, huh?" She hesitated, then grumbled through a soft smile. "I'm glad you're better."

And Daniel was feeling better. Off his meds, and so far, so good. Everyone was hopeful; for Daniel and for Jenny.

Olivia called out from the living room. "Jack! Amanda! Come on out here!"

Out in the living room, the Christmas tree was glowing bright with lights, everyone was gathered 'round it. Amanda went over to her mom, who reached out and pulled her in close.

Jack watched from the hall as they all started to sing Silent Night. His grandma Jenny pulled Bill near her on one side, and Mike in close on the other.

Daniel went to his parents and Emma wrapped an arm around him. Carl rested a hand on his shoulder.

Daniel turned and looked back at Jack. They smiled at one another.

They had plans for the future.

Norway.

And reindeer.

~ End

www.ingramcontent.com/pod-product-compliance
Lightning Source LLC
Chambersburg PA
CBHW021304250626
47155CB00002B/363